SILENCED
GIRLS

SILENCED GIRLS

ROGER STELLJES

Bookouture

Published by Bookouture in 2020

An imprint of Storyfire Ltd.
Carmelite House
50 Victoria Embankment
London EC4Y 0DZ

www.bookouture.com

Copyright © Roger Stelljes, 2019, 2020

Originally self-published by Roger Stelljes, 2019

Roger Stelljes has asserted his right to be identified
as the author of this work.

ISBN: 978-1-80019-050-4
eBook ISBN: 978-1-80019-049-8

To my family, for letting me pursue my dreams of becoming a mystery writer.

CHAPTER ONE

"There is no sign of a struggle…"

July 5, 1999, 4:14 a.m.

Manchester Bay, Minnesota

"Dispatch, I'm 10-8 leaving the Berglund place up on Little Birch," Sheriff's Deputy Ed Gregerson reported, noting his availability for service, having addressed the noise complaint. Once he was around the front of the cabin, he chuckled to himself. The two mid-twenties couples were still going strong with the bonfire blazing. The empty beer cans were plentiful on the ground, and the country rock music—along with their boisterous voices—was just a bit too loud for the cabins tucked in along Little Birch Lake.

Gregerson turned himself around and made his way back along North Little Birch Lake Road, stifling a late-night yawn as he approached and then turned left onto Highway 4, called the H-4 by locals of Shepard County. The highway was quiet with only one lonely set of headlights passing him in the northbound lane in the two miles before he approached County Road 48. He turned right, planning to work his way southwest to Manchester Bay for a short break. He reached for his now lukewarm coffee and took a drink as he eased around a gentle bend. Up ahead on the right shoulder he viewed a white car. Its lights were turned off, the hazard lights not flashing. He slowed and pulled behind it, a mid-nineties white Grand Am. He couldn't place his finger on it, but the car looked familiar to him for some reason.

"Dispatch, this is Gregerson. I'm 10-20 on County 48. Checking on a disabled vehicle."

Gregerson stepped out of his Bronco. With his left hand resting on his gun, he approached the car, scanning the interior with the beam of his flashlight. The car's doors were locked. As he peered inside, he didn't see any items to identify its owner. He walked around the front of the car to the passenger side and saw the problem. The right front tire was flat as a pancake, the mangled rubber mostly detached from and twisted around the rim like a pretzel. Gregerson slowly walked along, continuing to peer inside, moving the beam of the flashlight around, and then he stopped. Resting on the backseat he saw a balled-up hooded sweatshirt. He could make out the logo and some letters: Manchester Bay Girls Soccer.

"Huh. I better call this in," he muttered. He was now pretty sure who the car belonged to.

Gregerson climbed back into his Bronco and called dispatch: "I need a license check." A minute later he had his answer and his suspicion was confirmed.

"Dispatch. We need to 10-21 the sheriff. I found his girls' car abandoned out here on County 48."

*

Tori Hunter sat alone on the old green couch with her legs tucked tightly together. Her jean shorts were slightly soiled and her white scoop-neck tank top lacked its normal crispness, all a result of being in the same clothes for nearly twenty hours. A barely touched glass of water wrapped in a plain white napkin sat in front of her on the worn walnut coffee table. She could hear voices approaching in the hallway. "Nothing from the scent of that sweatshirt?" one voice asked.

"No. The dogs couldn't track it. There's a bulletin out for the girl, but…" the second voice replied before drifting out of earshot.

She languidly shifted her eyes to her left, to the aged, dusty-green microfiber of the couch and the faded, almost invisible, oblong brown stain. Unclasping her hands, she brushed slender fingers lightly over the blemish, a spot she'd been part of creating years ago when fighting over a can of soda. She must have sat, laid, slept, or jumped on the sofa a thousand times over the seventeen years of her life.

"Victoria? Victoria?"

She emerged from her trance and sluggishly glanced to her right to see a familiar face: Cal Lund, chief deputy sheriff for Shepard County. A proper and courteous man, he always called her by her given name.

"Can you come with me?"

Tori nodded before slowly standing up. She followed him out of the office and then trailed him down the long hallway toward a door with *Investigations* stenciled across the frosted glass. This was one part of the building she'd rarely been allowed to explore or experience.

Cal opened the door for her, and Tori walked timidly inside then followed him down a narrow, beige hallway and into a square room devoid of exterior windows. It contained only a sturdy, metal-legged table, four aged yet durable chairs with green padded seats, and a video camera mounted up in the corner. There was a one-way mirror on the left wall.

A black-haired man in a dark suit with a crisp white dress shirt and striped tie sat on the left side. Cal pulled a chair out for Tori on the right side of the table opposite the mirror. She seated herself and Cal slid her chair back toward the table before going around and taking the open seat on the other side.

"Have you heard from the sheriff?" Tori asked softly as Cal sat down. She always referred to her father as the sheriff, even at home.

Cal shook his head. "No, I haven't heard from him, at least not since he brought you in here. He's still out at the scene."

She suspiciously peered at the other man, who Cal introduced as Special Agent Johnson from the Minnesota Bureau of Criminal Apprehension. "They're assisting on the investigation."

"What am I doing in here?"

"Your dad wanted us to talk to you."

"But I told him everything I know."

"I'm sure you did," Cal replied matter-of-factly as he opened a spiral notebook. "But we need to go over it again. Do you understand?"

Tori nodded.

"Good," Cal replied as he took the cap off his pen. "Last night, let's start from the beginning…"

*

"The whole town must be here," Jessie exclaimed excitedly as she turned onto Lake Avenue. "This is going to be such a blast!"

"I hope so," Tori replied a bit nervously to her fun-loving twin sister Jessica, or just plain Jessie as everyone called her.

"What do you mean 'hope'?" Jessie replied with a grin, lightly punching her sister on the arm. "You're meeting up with Jason, right?"

"Yeah, so?" Tori replied, a small, self-conscious smile creasing her lips as she turned her face away.

"My serious and responsible twin sister has her *first boyfriend*!" Jessie teased happily. "I just love it, *love it* when my plans come together."

"Ha, ha," Tori mock-grumped in reply.

"Lighten up, sister, I set you up good. He's really nice and pretty darned cute, too."

They were identical twin sisters, each of them five foot five, lithe and athletic, with long auburn hair and soft, attractive features. They were both accomplished soccer players and students, but for identical twin sisters, their personalities couldn't have been more opposite.

Jessie Hunter, like their father, had a bigger than life personality that was fun-loving, easygoing, confident, and personable. On the soccer field she was the catalyst, scorer, vocal leader, and the one exhorting her teammates to work hard and hustle. Off the field, Jessie was always dressed to the nines with her hair fashionably styled and her makeup perfectly applied. It was that effervescence that made her the most popular girl in their class, the one all the boys swooned over.

Tori was often told that she was very much like her mother. She was the quieter, more reserved, and inwardly intense of the two. On the soccer field she was the tough-as-nails stoic defender who rarely said a word. She let her playing do the talking. While Jessie was the style maven, Tori preferred to dress more modestly. Whereas Jessie had flowing hair, Tori pulled hers back in a ponytail and often hid behind her glasses at school. It was that shy and reserved nature, not to mention her willingness to hide in her sister's shadow, that made her a little less approachable.

Yet as different as they might have been personally, they were inseparable—rarely, if ever, going anywhere without the other. They looked out for and protected each other. Mess with one, and you got the other. Perhaps the only time they were ever apart socially was when it came to boys, and for once it was Tori who would be the one to break away.

"So, what are your plans tonight?" Tori asked.

"I have no *specific* plans."

Tori detected the mischievous tone and knew her sister had something up her sleeve, some game she was playing. "No specific plans, huh? Does that mean we're perhaps trolling tonight?"

"Please, I don't troll. I don't chase. They come to me."

"Okay, so who will be coming to you this time? Tommy Josephs? Jeff Warner? I've seen that Greg Brodt hanging around more, Mike Webb maybe. Or, I know… Steak?"

Jessie laughed and then shook her head. "They're all friends but… I don't know, this will sound really shallow, but I'm kind of bored with all of them."

"Bored? You're *bored* with them?"

"Yeah, it's a little bit of been there, done that. I kissed Steak last week, but there was no… sizzle there."

"No sizzle," Tori laughed. "That's funny. What about Eddie?"

Jessie smiled widely. "He is cute and all, but—" she shook her head "—no. Now if his brother Kyle showed up…"

"He's twenty-three!" Tori protested.

Jessie smiled. "Six years more mature, twin sis. I think I kind of prefer the more mature guys at this point."

"But, but…"

"*Easy* there, sister. I'm not serious about Kyle. But there is this guy named Rance I met the other day over at the college. He plays on the football team, wide receiver. I'd like to run into him. And, to ease your worries, he's only two years older."

Tori shook her head in wonderment at Jessie's assessment and playing of the field. For Tori, lacking her sister's innate social confidence, there'd never been much of a field to play or assess.

It was the Fourth of July, and downtown Manchester Bay was filled with revelers. With a population of just under 19,000, the sleepy resort town sat on the southern shores of picturesque Northern Pine Lake in the middle of Minnesota lake country and two hours due north of the Twin Cities. Northern Pine Lake was the anchor for a chain of eight connected lakes to the north. The town's businesses and existence revolved around vacationers to the lakes and around the ever-expanding Central Minnesota State University, which rested up on the bluff a mile east of downtown.

Each year on the Fourth of July, Manchester Bay held a raucous party. The town center—from the intersection of Lake Drive and Interlachen Avenue, running several blocks north to South Shore Drive and the half-moon-shaped local beach on the bay—was blocked off. The streets were filled with partygoers, a mix of locals, vacationers, and cabin owners. For Jessie and Tori, it was a chance to gather with their large group of high school friends.

"Our last year together." As one of the ringleaders, Jessie was almost wistful about it. "It's going to be tough leaving and not seeing everyone all the time."

Tori, ever the practical one of the two, was far more sanguine. "By next summer, you'll be so excited to go off to Iowa State with me that you won't be sad at all."

"Ahh, here's a parking spot," Jessie said, pulling into a slot on Lake Drive. "Oh, and would you look who we're next to."

"Gee, *funny* how that worked out."

"What? You think I wasn't making plans all day while you were gone?" Jessie replied with a wickedly happy grin.

A group of their friends were awaiting their arrival, leaning against the back of Jason's rusted black Ford Explorer. Their joint best friend, Katy Anderson, was hanging with a bunch of girls on the sidewalk in front of the truck. "It took you two long enough," Katy needled boisterously once Jessie parked.

"Sorry, I was waiting for *someone* to get home from work," Jessie rejoined, throwing a thumb at her sister.

Tori made her way over to Jason. The two of them awkwardly said hello, trying to be sly about really liking each other, and in the process making it oh so obvious that they did. Jason was her first boyfriend, and she was his first, too. Their friends all thought they were cute together, trying to figure out the logistics of being boyfriend–girlfriend.

"Let's go," Jessie commanded with an arm wave to her friends.

Ahead was the entire town celebrating the Fourth of July. Lake Drive was filled with food stands, carnival rides, a mini midway, and multiple beer gardens. An eighties cover band was playing a passable version of A Flock of Seagulls' "I Ran" at the small stage a block ahead.

Before everyone walked away, Jake Williams, known as "Steak" since they were all young kids, called everyone over. "All of you go buy a big lemonade, the ones with the yellow covers and long green straws," he suggested, and then added under his breath, "then bring them back. We have vodka."

Everyone did as Steak suggested, making their way over to the stand.

"Can I buy you one?" Jason asked hopefully, extending his hand for Tori's.

"Yes, please," she replied as her fingers interlocked with his.

*

"You and your friends hung out at the carnival. Do we have all the names?" Cal asked, going through the ones Tori had provided name by name. There were over twenty.

"Those are the ones that I remember hanging around with us," Tori confirmed. "There were thousands of people downtown, but the names I gave you were in our group. It's the same people we always run around with."

"And did anyone cause you concern?" Agent Johnson asked with a furrowed brow.

"Of my friends? Gosh, no."

"I'm asking about anyone else, Ms. Hunter. You mentioned this guy your sister ran into over at the college, the football player. His name was Rance, right? Did he ever show up?"

"No, not that I noticed. She never said anything about that, and I never saw her with anyone I didn't know."

"And you two were together the whole night?" Cal asked for confirmation.

"Yes. I mean, I might have been talking to one group of people and she was talking to someone else. I might have been playing this midway game and she was playing another, but we weren't far apart. We almost never are."

"And you didn't notice anyone unusual hanging around?"

"What do you mean, 'unusual'?"

"Was there anyone who kept appearing that was new, that you didn't know or recognize? Was there anyone odd following you around? Was there someone that maybe creeped you out?" Agent Johnson asked, his pen hovering over his notebook.

"No," Tori answered, shaking her head.

"Come on, really?" Johnson pressed. "You saw no one? I just find that hard to believe."

"I didn't!"

"Do you think that's because you were with Jason?" Cal asked directly. "That was your focus, wasn't it?"

Tori nodded as she looked at her hands, a tear running slowly down her cheek.

"Tell me about your car," Agent Johnson inquired, flipping through some pages of notes. "Was it running okay?"

"Yes, why?"

"There weren't any problems with its operation?" Johnson persisted. "It wasn't running rough at all?"

"No."

"Any issues with the tires?"

"No. The car was just tuned up like a week ago."

"Tell me about the vodka," Agent Johnson said, changing course. "Who supplied it?"

Tori hesitated to answer.

"Victoria, the drinking isn't what matters right now," Cal counseled. "But we do need to know more about it. Who supplied it? Jason?"

"No, it was Steak."

"Steak?" Agent Johnson asked, looking up.

"Jake Williams," Cal answered. "A local boy."

"He had it," Tori stated. "We all poured from the bottle."

"And you had how much?" Johnson asked.

Tori looked to Johnson, then to Cal, and back to Johnson. "Jessie and I went back one more time, maybe an hour before the fireworks show. We poured just a little into our cups."

"Just a little?" Johnson asked skeptically. "Come on."

"Victoria, are you sure about that?" Cal added. "You have to be honest here."

"I am," Tori insisted and then looked at Cal, her eyes matching his. "The sheriff knows we drink sometimes. He once said to us both that he knew we'd start going to parties with our friends and there would be drinking. His instructions were to be careful and to call if we ever needed his help. No questions, no judgments, just call. We were having fun, but we were being careful, I swear."

"After you refilled your cups, what happened next?" Cal asked.

*

"The fireworks are going to start any minute," Jessie called out. She took one last sip from her lemonade before tossing it into an overflowing garbage can. "Let's get a spot to watch the show!"

Jessie led their ever-expanding group over to the east side of the beach and the playground. Tori held Jason's hand as they sat down on a bench off to the side to take in the show. Jessie was walking along with Katy, plus their soccer teammates Mickey Olson, Corinne Whitworth and Lizzy Cowger, and they all grabbed swings at the swing set. The boys in their friend group all grabbed spots on the jungle gym. Tori made eye contact with her sister, who beamed a smile back to her. Tori could tell her sister was almost giddy for her.

Manchester Bay always went big on the fireworks for the Fourth. Synchronized to music, they were launched from the end of the long fishing pier at the opposite end of the beach. A massive crowd gathered in lawn chairs or on blankets on the beach and in the park and then along South Shore Drive, which was barricaded for several blocks to allow for more seating. A flotilla of speedboats and pontoons were anchored in the placid waters of the bay, as well as in front of Mannion's on the Lake, a restaurant farther northwest up the shoreline.

As they settled into their seats on the bench, Jason casually put his right arm gently around Tori's shoulder. Self-conscious to a fault, she almost always held back her emotions and affection. Yet, in this moment, she was… content. For once, she stopped caring what anyone else thought or saw. Instead of keeping just a little distance between them, she snuggled closer to Jason and then turned her face to his. Rarely the initiator, she almost surprised herself as she leaned up and kissed him, first just a little peck on his lips and then a second, softer kiss that she held for an extra moment as the fireworks show began.

It was a long show, lasting nearly forty-five minutes before there was a rapid-fire launching up into the sky.

"I think this is the grand finale," Jason observed as one rocket after another shot up into the sky, exploding loudly into a kaleidoscope of colors over the waters of the bay. With his arm wrapped lightly around Tori's shoulder, he pulled her a little closer and then leaned down and kissed her again. "Do you want to get out of here? Just you and me?"

Tori froze. She knew what this question meant, to go off alone with him, and where it was leading. She'd talked about this with Jessie, who'd already taken the plunge. Tori had openly wondered whether she was ready. It had been a frequent discussion topic between the two of them.

"You are," Jessie had assured her. "You're ready."

"How do *you* know? How do *I* know?"

"Because you're asking the question. If you ask the question, this question, the *big* question, then you know—"

"—the answer," Tori finished the sentence. Her body was a jumble of nerves at the thought of… sex.

"Tori, he's a really nice guy. I'm pretty sure it'll be his first time, too. Enjoy it. It's one night and an experience you'll never forget."

She thought back to that conversation one more time as she pondered Jason's offer. She was ready. "Yes, let's go."

Tori caught her sister's eye, tilted her head ever so slightly toward Jason, and mouthed, *I'm leaving.*

Jessie smiled and winked back at her sister.

*

"And that's the last time you saw Jessie last night?" Cal asked.

"Yes," Tori replied, nodding with tears streaming down her face, clasping her hands and trembling.

"So, you and Jason went off by yourselves," Johnson accused.

"Yes."

"And what time was it you left your group of friends?"

"I think ten forty-five, around there. It was after the fireworks."

"And you two were off doing what?"

Tori looked to Johnson and then to Cal, panicked.

"Victoria, where were you and what were you doing?" Cal pressed.

She looked down, the tears cascading. "We were… parked, just Jason and me."

"Where?"

"Cal…" Tori pleaded.

"Answer the question, Victoria," Cal pushed. "Where were you?"

"At the college. There's that narrow road behind the visitor's stands for the football field that goes into the woods. We were back there."

"For how long?"

Tori wiped her cheeks with her hand. "A few hours. We were back there for a few hours."

"Just the two of you? Nobody else?"

"Just us."

"No other cars were back there?"

Tori shook her head.

"And you were doing what exactly?" Johnson questioned.

Cal cut in, "I think we have all we need on that for now." He looked back to Tori. "When did you get home?"

"I think two or maybe two fifteen. I snuck into the house through my window."

"And you went to check on your sister?"

"Yes," Tori replied, sniffling, wiping her puffy eyes.

"And she wasn't there. Your twin sister wasn't there and that didn't alarm you?" Johnson prodded.

Tori shook her head. "I figured she was just sleeping over at Katy's, Mickey's, Corinne's, or Lizzy's house like we always do." She looked to Cal, whose face remained stoic. "We do that all the time, Cal. All the time. So, I went to my room and to sleep."

"I see," Johnson answered, jotting down notes and shaking his head. "And the next thing you remember is what?"

"I guess the phone ringing," Tori answered. "But that happens in the middle of the night all the time, people calling the sheriff because something bad has happened. But then the sheriff came into my room and…" Tori started sobbing, now struggling to breathe, to speak. "Oh… my God…" she croaked.

The door burst open and Sheriff Big Jim Hunter stormed in. "That's enough!" the sheriff barked and then looked to his daughter. "I need some time with Tori."

"Yes, sir," Cal replied.

"Sure, Sheriff," Johnson added.

The two of them quickly packed up and left.

Through nearly swollen-shut eyes, Tori peered up to her father.

Big Jim Hunter was a force of nature. Tall and sturdy, he had a barrel chest and broad shoulders that supported a large, square head with salt-and-pepper hair cut high and tight. A menacing, bushy horseshoe mustache ran down to a bulbous chin, framing his rectangular jaw. He had a commanding voice and an imposing presence that demanded respect and instilled fear.

Yet in this moment Tori could see the giant bear of a man was a shell of himself. His face was ashen. His normally piercing eyes were panicked, and his typically booming voice faintly quivered. He took a chair next to Tori and slowly sat down. Even in this moment, with her own emotions roiling, she could sense that the man beside her had aged twenty years in a matter of hours. Her father bent over with his elbows on his thighs, looking despondently to the floor.

"Sheriff, what's going on? Where's Jessie?"

"I don't know, honey."

"What do you mean you don't know? What happened? Nobody has told me what happened."

The sheriff paused for a moment. "The car was found abandoned on County 48. We know that Jessie dropped off Katy at her house a little after one. We can only assume she was on her way home then because 48 is the shortest route back to our house. It appears she had to pull over to the side of the road because the right front tire went flat. One of my deputies found the car. It was locked and the hazard lights off. Your sister's purse and her keys are gone. The spare tire and jack are in the trunk, and it doesn't look like they've been touched. I have investigators at the scene but…"

"You can't find her."

"No," the sheriff replied, looking down once more.

"She was abducted, wasn't she?"

"We don't know for sure."

"Someone grabbed her off the side of the road, didn't they?"

"We don't know, honey. There is no sign of a struggle…"

"She's… gone. *Gone!*"

"Tori, we don't know that for sure."

"*Don't you dare lie to me, Sheriff!*" Tori wailed, the tears flowing again. "You've told me, *told us*, before that when girls go missing they don't come back!"

"I know I said—"

"You said that some crazy man gets them and… they don't come back. *Ever!*"

"That's not always the case. We have to believe…"

Tori knew. Deep down, she knew.

*

Twenty months later, Big Jim Hunter died. After her father's funeral, Tori Hunter left Manchester Bay for the last time and didn't return. Jessie Hunter was never found.

CHAPTER TWO

"What seems to be the problem?"

July 5, 2019

Manchester Bay, Minnesota

Nervously tapping his foot on the car floor, he glanced to his watch: 12:57 a.m. Thursday had turned to Friday. It was finally closing time for the Fourth of July revelers. Small groups as well as the occasional single were slowly trickling out the front door. They were making their way to the now small smattering of vehicles remaining in the long, narrow, banana-shaped parking lot. In a couple of cases, the partiers exercised the appropriate level of late-night caution, and a driver arrived to cart them safely away. He'd also seen another large group of people descend the length of steps to the marina dock and step onto the last remaining large pontoon, taking a moonlight cruise home.

Licking his dry lips in anxious anticipation, he once again reviewed his mental checklist. He reached for the right pocket of his light black nylon jacket to feel the thin rectangular bulge, assuring himself it was there. Flipping open the center console, he confirmed the two key items inside were ready to go for quick application. He peered to the sports car a hundred feet away across the street and could see the drop in tire pressure, the slightest listing of the vehicle to the right.

"Ahhh," he exhaled. "There you are," he murmured excitedly, his gloved hands tightly gripping the steering wheel, his muscles tensed, and his body coiled like a spring.

Genevieve boisterously exited the bar. She strode on her long, lustrous, tanned legs as she and her friend, arm in arm, noisily made their way to the end of the parking lot and her sporty little BMW convertible. The convertible roof was up now, although it had been down earlier in the evening. Threatening weather was predicted. It was a forecast soon to be realized as the night sky filled with a pulsating flash, and a husky gust of wind swirled the branches and leaves hanging above.

He glanced down to his cell phone. The weather radar displayed an ever-expanding amoeba of dark green, yellow, and red moving north-by-northeast. He estimated the storm's full arrival to be in fifteen or twenty minutes max. It would bring heavy rain and powerful winds, a good old-fashioned midsummer Minnesota thunderstorm. Long having planned to act on this night, the storm rolling in was serendipitous.

He'd methodically studied and tracked her for some time. Genevieve was attractive, with round yet firm breasts and a skinny waist with nicely swaying hips to go with deep brown eyes, luscious full lips, and a radiant smile. She was the type he'd normally be attracted to in his everyday, normal life—at least physically. As for her personality and treatment of others, that was less attractive. She came from money, not of her making but of Daddy's. The family money had given her an unearned sense of entitlement, a trait he loathed more than any other.

Genevieve started up the BMW, backed out, and then speedily pulled away. Knowing where she was going, he gave himself a ten-count before clicking on his lights and turning right onto South Shore Drive. This was where he had to trust things would proceed as he'd calculated. Given how Genevieve's car was swaying from side to side as she motored north on the H-4, he suspected she wouldn't notice her tire issue. As he observed her ahead, his only immediate fear was a state trooper lying in wait, hunting drunk drivers. Her erratic driving made her a solid pull-over candidate.

Ten minutes later she pulled into the driveway for her friend, another wealthy party-girl type in town visiting her parents at their expansive lake home on the northeast end of Northern Pine Lake. He turned left onto a side dirt road, quickly completed a U-turn, switched off his headlights, parked, and waited.

Five minutes later Genevieve came roaring back down the road. He could tell that the front of the car was riding lower as she zoomed by. She had nearly fifteen miles to go to Daddy's house. He gave her another ten-count before switching on his lights and continuing his pursuit.

Genevieve turned back onto the H-4 and motored north for three miles before her right turn signal blinked. Her car slowed, and she took a sharp right onto the narrow, winding, and tree-covered County Road 163.

Her parents' home was a vast compound on the west side of Big Spruce Lake, another twelve miles to the east. Strategically trailing her at a healthy distance, he sporadically lost sight of her taillights as she went around the tight bends and hairpin curves of the twisty, lightly used county road.

As he noted the odometer ticking away, his chest started to tighten. "Come on," he muttered nervously. "*Come on.*" She'd been able to drive farther than he'd calculated.

Then, as he came around a tight, ninety-degree corner, he spotted her a quarter-mile ahead, parked on what there was of the right shoulder, her hazard lights flashing. Genevieve was already out of the car, leaning over and examining her right front tire as large raindrops started intermittently pelting the windshield.

Flicking on his high beams, he gently slowed, pulled up alongside her car, and powered down his passenger side window. "Hey, I know you," he greeted. "It's Genevieve, right?"

"Yeah, hi. Hey, oh my gosh, how are you?"

"I'm fine, but I see your hazard lights flashing. What seems to be the problem?"

"My right front tire just blew out, if you can believe that." Genevieve looked up to the sky as the thunder boomed and the lightning flashed. The tree branches overhead swayed as the rain intensified. "Hey, my house is just a few miles down the road. Could you give me a lift?"

"Sure. Jump on in."

"Okay, let me just grab my purse," she replied, reaching for it and her phone before using the key fob to lock her car. "Thanks so much," she said as she slipped into his passenger seat.

CHAPTER THREE

"I know exactly what you're thinking."

Will Braddock, chief detective for the Shepard County Sheriff's Department, turned his Chevy Tahoe onto the long, circular driveway that curved in front of the looming Lash estate. He parked behind two other sheriff's department Explorers.

He opened his door and was immediately greeted by a blast of the post-noontime humidity of an eighty-eight-degree day. Braddock unfolded his lanky six-foot-four frame out onto the stone paver driveway. Jake Williams, simply known as "Steak" and his best detective, descended the steps of the front porch. The house itself was centered on a sprawling piece of well-manicured property along the thickly forested shores of Big Spruce Lake. As he got his bearings, Braddock noticed the leaves and branches scattered about the otherwise immaculately maintained grounds.

"Heck of a storm last night," Steak observed. "I have two sizable branches down in my yard. How about you?"

Braddock shook his head. "Just lots of leaves and twigs, although I had to retrieve two of my Adirondack chairs for the firepit out of the lake. So, what do we have here?" he asked as he removed his sunglasses and slipped on his sharp tan houndstooth sport coat.

Steak flipped open his notebook. "Genevieve Lash, the Lashes' twenty-seven-year-old daughter, has not returned home from last night's festivities."

Braddock nodded, reaching back into his Tahoe for his own notepad and cell phone, which he slipped into the inside pocket of his sport coat. He looked back to Steak. "Twenty-seven? Living here at her parents' place?"

Steak nodded and then pointed past Braddock to a two-story white clapboard house with emerald-green shutters, set among a grouping of Norway pines. "Miss Genevieve lives in that guesthouse that, I might add, is like twice the size of my own house. She isn't there and the guesthouse was still locked this morning. Her black BMW 435i convertible is not here either."

"Twenty-seven-year-old *rich* girl," Braddock mumbled, taking in the Lashes' expansive main home. "I take it that it's unusual she hasn't come home yet?"

"Not necessarily," Steak replied. "I don't know her well but know of her. Genevieve is a bit of a party girl, don't you know. Mom and Dad said the same thing inside."

"Again, so why are we here?"

"Because Genevieve isn't answering her phone."

"Again, so…"

"And Genevieve's girlfriend, Tessie Joyner, showed up ninety minutes ago. They were supposed to go boating, and Tessie was surprised she wasn't here since Genevieve dropped her off at home last night after they left Mannion's at closing time. Tessie went up to the house to talk to the Lashes, who then got worried and called it in as a missing person."

"And we're looking for the car?"

"Yes, I have a bulletin out for it, but nothing as of yet."

"What's your read on this?" Braddock asked Steak as they started walking toward the steps. "Is she really missing?"

"I don't know. I think it's just as likely she's shacking up somewhere. She's not unattractive and has been known to… sleep around a bit."

"I've seen the Lash name before around here. Big construction company, right?"

"Correct."

"How are they to deal with?"

"Worried," Steak answered. "And they're rich, so they expect answers and don't have a lot of patience."

"*Swell.*" Braddock sighed and then followed Steak up the steps and through the front door. The Lashes and Tessie Joyner were waiting in the sitting room in the back of the house. Braddock was introduced to everyone and went right to work, starting with Tessie.

"You last saw her when?"

"About one thirty this morning when she dropped me off at my parents' cabin."

"And what was she doing after that?"

"Going home. That's what she said she was doing. We were going to go out on the lake today and probably head over to the Wharf for drinks."

"She didn't have any plans after dropping you off?" Braddock asked with a pen in hand.

"Not that she told me about."

"You're sure?"

"She didn't say anything if she did."

Steak looked at his phone, which was buzzing, and stepped out of the room. Braddock continued, "Would that be unusual for her not to say anything to you?"

Tessie gave that question a moment's thought. "If she had plans later with a guy, I'd have known. She would have said something to me or I would've been able to tell."

"And?"

"I don't think she did, but even if she did…" Tessie looked to Genevieve's parents and hesitated.

"Tessie," Braddock pressed. "Even if she did…"

"Gen isn't the kind to stay and cuddle if she goes home with someone. She's generally the love 'em and leave 'em type." She looked to her friend's parents. "Sorry."

Braddock turned to the parents. "I'm sure you've tried to call your daughter?"

"Yes," Jerry Lash replied. "Several times. We still are. No answer, it just goes to voicemail."

"And no word of any kind from her? Neither of you has any messages—voice or text—from her?"

"No," Dorothy Lash replied. "Not a peep."

"Do you track her phone at all with a locator app?"

"No," her mother replied. "She is twenty-seven."

"And her cell number is?"

Dorothy recited it, giving Braddock the provider as well.

"So, Detective, what happens now? Are you searching for her?" Jerry pressed.

"Yes. We're looking for the car, for starters, and…" Braddock glanced out to the hallway, where Steak was urgently waving for him. "If you'll excuse me for a minute," Braddock said to the Lashes and Tessie, and he stepped out of the room.

"We found the car," Steak reported.

"Where?"

"A little under three miles away, parked along the south side of County Road 163 with a flat right front tire."

"And Genevieve?"

"Not there."

Braddock accelerated along County Road 163, which was tunnel-like under the dense canopy of trees lining the roadsides. It ran for a twisting and turning fifteen miles east from the H-4 to State Highway 6. It was one of many in the intersecting web of county roads, paved and gravel, used to reach the cabins on the scattered mass of small and mid-sized lakes northeast of Manchester Bay.

Approaching from the east, Braddock pulled past the BMW and the two sheriff's deputy SUVs parked behind it before completing a U-turn and then parking. Steak pulled the same maneuver, rolling in behind him.

Stepping out of his Tahoe, Braddock grabbed the BMW key fob the Lashes gave him out of his pocket and pressed the unlock button. The BMW's locks popped open. "That confirms it's hers."

Steak handed a pair of latex gloves to Braddock, who then did a quick walk-around inspection to the front of the vehicle and immediately observed the flat tire. It was a mangled-up jumble, almost detached yet still wrapped around the rim. He walked back to the driver's side door, and with his left index finger he slowly lifted the latch and gently pulled it open. He slipped off his sunglasses and leaned down with his hands on his knees, peering inside. There was no purse or cell phone or any other items visible beyond the empty water bottle in the center console cupholder and a white phone cord plugged into the charging port.

"It's pretty clean," Braddock reported as he stood up and once again walked around the front of the car and crouched down to reinspect the tire. The blown tire looked new, as did the car itself. There was more than enough tread. In fact, he realized as he took a quick look at all of the tires, they appeared to be the same vintage, with plenty of tread and still some of the bright sheen of newness. "The tire is a complete blowout, totally off the rim."

"Sure is," Steak agreed.

Braddock stepped back and examined the area around the car, including the narrow ribbon of gravel along the shoulder and the knee-high mix of wild grass, cattails, and buckthorn along the roadside. The grass was not matted down in a manner suggestive of any sort of a struggle, although the storm might have washed away any evidence of that.

At the back of the car, Steak popped the trunk and Braddock joined him to inspect it.

"It doesn't look like she tried to access the spare," Braddock remarked, seeing the tire, jack and tire iron secured under the trunk's fabric mat. He stepped back from the trunk, crossed his arms, and gazed upon the car, deep in thought.

"What do you think, boss?" Steak asked, looking at Braddock.

"I think she has a flat tire in the middle of the night and now she's unreachable. We had the storm last night. It hit around one thirty, maybe one forty-five, right?"

Steak nodded.

"Genevieve drops Tessie off. She's driving home along 163 here, which is a bit of an odd selection for late at night. I'd have taken County 22 to get home myself."

"But 163 is probably shorter."

"Yeah, maybe, but with all the winding and twisting, and the deer sometimes crossing the road, it's a far riskier one too. Especially because her tire goes flat and apparently rapidly. It doesn't appear she tried to change it. So where does she go?"

"There's not much around here," Steak observed.

"Nor," Braddock answered, "would there be much traffic at that time of night along here."

"It was the Fourth of July last night, though. People were out and about. Maybe someone picked her up."

"And took her where?"

Steak shook his head. "I don't know, boss."

With his hands on his hips, Braddock did a quick three-sixty look around, evaluating their location. There were no cabins or homes along this specific stretch of road. To either side were marshy wetlands surrounded by dense forest. There were perhaps two driveway entrances he could see. One was well to the west and another was two hundred yards to the east, marked by a barely visible mailbox.

As he silently evaluated the scene, a sense of dread percolated inside him. "She hasn't been seen in twelve hours. We're *way* behind." He called the two deputies over and directed them to start a canvass. "One of you go west, the other east. Check the places we can see from here and then work your way farther down."

He looked to Steak. "Get back to the Lashes'. Ask Tessie if there were any problems with this car last night. She didn't mention any earlier, but we didn't ask either."

"What do I tell the parents?"

"The truth. We found her car. It was abandoned and there is no sign of her. They're going to panic. It might be a good idea if they get some family and friends around them for support. I fear they're going to need it. Also, we need to have someone there in case the phone rings."

"Ransom?"

"Right now, that's the best-case scenario. The old man is loaded, so it's at least possible. That also gives the parents some hope."

"What are you doing?" Steak asked.

"I'm going to call the sheriff and loop him in. We need to get with the phone company to track her phone somehow, and I'm going to get a forensic team out here."

"Okay," Steak answered and started toward his truck, but then he stopped and looked back to Braddock, troubled. "You know, Will, we have an abandoned car along an isolated stretch of road. A flat right front tire. An attractive woman missing and it's…"

"July fifth," Braddock finished for him. "I know exactly what you're thinking."

CHAPTER FOUR

"This is an invitation."

July 6

New York City

Tori checked her watch and approved of her pace. It was just under seven minutes a mile, which would keep her morning run to around forty-five minutes. She'd run a good long loop south through Manhattan's Battery Park and now back along the Esplanade, with the Hudson River to her left. There were just a few blocks left on the way back to her condo building, the tip top of which was visible to her right. She turned right onto Albany Street, ran another half-block, and came to a stop, breathing heavily, checking her fitness tracker for her running time. Satisfied with the results, she reached for the bottle of water in her waist pack, and while taking a long drink she slowly walked the remaining hundred feet to the long, green awning marking the entrance to her building.

Her condo was a block off the Hudson. It was a mere ten minutes from the FBI field office and it was in Manhattan. Yet almost daily she questioned the wisdom of selling her old studio unit in Brooklyn for the hugely expensive upgrade. She was on the road so often she never really felt like she lived in it. The numerous unpacked boxes and the lack of any sort of personal touch or décor, save one thing, were evidence of that. She had a comfortable sofa, a stylish weathered trunk for a coffee table, a modest flat-screen television, a top-of-the-line and well-stocked wine refrigerator, three closets full of expensive clothes, and an old writer's desk straining under stacks of case documents. That was pretty much it. With her father's life insurance, monthly pension death benefit, proceeds from the sale of his house eighteen years ago, and her own salary, she was quite secure financially. Nevertheless, she cringed at the monthly mortgage payment for a condo she barely seemed to live in.

"It's an investment, dearie," her neighbor Ms. Mumford said to her one night when they were chatting in the hallway and she openly lamented the purchase. "Manhattan real estate only goes one direction, honey, and that's up. And these days, *way* up. Consider it a retirement annuity. You'll clean up when you sell."

As Tori walked in the front entryway, Arthur, the building doorman, greeted her. "Agent Hunter, you've been gone so much that your mailbox is stuffed full. We have the overflow for you in the office. Let me get it for you."

A moment later, Arthur came back with a small stack of mail. "It even has today's mail right on the top."

"Thank you, Arthur. I'll come back down and clean out my box."

"Yes, ma'am."

Tori took the elevator up to the eighth floor. With her mail pinned between her left arm and chin, she reached for the unit key in the tiny pocket in her running shorts, unlocked the deadbolt, and pushed the door open. She set the pile of mail on the edge of the counter, went to the refrigerator and took out a bottle of water and paced around her apartment, letting the sweat on her body dissipate. She stopped at her fireplace mantle and gazed proudly at her FBI Director's Award for Excellence, the one solitary personal memento she displayed. It was too good an accomplishment to sit in a box in a closet.

The FBI had not been her life's plan.

After graduating from Boston College with a government and political science degree, Tori went to work for the Massachusetts governor's office. Law school in a few years would have been the next logical step. In fact, she'd had three completed law school applications sitting on her kitchen counter with an LSAT score that was more than enough to get her into all three. Then life threw her yet another curveball.

Twelve months into her tenure with the governor's office, an eight-year-old girl named Libby Walton was brazenly abducted in Lowell, a suburb north of Boston, from a street corner on her way home from school. Her mother had been a mere hundred yards away, sitting on the front steps of their house, and witnessed it. The van had pulled up and a man had grabbed her daughter off the sidewalk and tossed her inside. Eight-year-old girls kidnapped in broad daylight off leafy street corners in safe suburbs draw instant attention and definitely not the good kind. The mother's frantic 911 call was played on the local news that night, and Libby's abduction quickly became a national news story. With that kind of profile, the investigation escalated, involving the resources of not only the Massachusetts State Police but also the FBI, including two special agents from the Bureau's vaunted Behavioral Analysis Unit—the BAU—flown in from Quantico.

Tori was assigned to the liaison team from the governor's office that worked directly with the investigators. Her staunch refusal to accept any form of commonwealth governmental bureaucratic red tape was welcomed by the FBI and state police professionals. Drawn to the case both intellectually and emotionally, Tori refused to leave it. Down to her core Tori could feel the mother's pain. Her sense of instant loss, the unbearable anguish, and the suffocating worry was made all the worse by Tori's father's warnings years ago that when girls went missing, they didn't come back.

Then Libby came home.

She was rescued a week after her abduction by the FBI from a cabin deep in the woods of northern Maine. Tori felt the relief and exultation the family felt when that little girl came through the front door and rushed into her mother's arms.

Tori had done everything she could to put her sister's disappearance and, later, her father's death in her own personal rearview mirror, but the Libby Walton case crowbarred open the locked mental file drawer of her past—though, for once, in a good way. Despite the return of those long-suppressed, gut-wrenchingly raw feelings, Libby's rescue spurred in Tori a sense of hope, for she'd seen someone who'd been thought lost come home alive.

It could happen. It could be done.

In the weeks following Libby's return, Tori couldn't stop thinking about the case and that moment Libby had come through that front door. She wanted to relive it. And more than that, she wanted to be the one responsible for making it happen. Tori saw a new path for herself, and in a sign of how she would operate her life going forward, she went about making sure things turned out exactly as she wanted—rules, regulations, and procedures be damned.

She reached out to the BAU agents she'd met, inquiring about a career with the FBI. She used connections through the governor's office to ensure a one-on-one meeting with the director of the BAU at the FBI Training Academy in Quantico, Virginia. To the director she stated she would join the FBI but *only* if she could have a career focused on child abductions.

"Well, Ms. Hunter, we don't necessarily let people choose like that," the director replied.

Tori was straight in her reply. "It's that or I don't come. And, Director, with all due respect, you want me here."

Such a blunt demand and statement would normally lead to an immediate deep-sixing of one's application. Yet two things made this situation different. First, not only did she have sterling credentials, but in the interview the director saw firsthand Tori's fearlessness, passion, and drive, not to mention her sharp analytical mind. Second, Tori assembled an impressive collection of endorsements, with telephone calls to the director from the governor of Massachusetts and one of its senators, along with a letter from the other. Then there was the grateful letter from the parents of Libby Walton. The BAU director decided Tori was right, that he indeed wanted her in the Bureau.

She had a new purpose, dedicating her life to preventing families from having to experience what she did. Tori had lost her family, but she was going to do everything she could to prevent it from happening to anyone else.

Tori proved she was worth the Bureau's investment and rose quickly. Despite only being in the Bureau for a short time, she was nevertheless part of the group of agents that advocated for and helped establish the FBI's Child Abduction Rapid Deployment team, CARD for short. Thereafter, her prolific success, including the recovery of children in two separate high-profile celebrity child disappearances, gave her a certain profile and cachet within the Bureau: She became the go-to on higher-profile child disappearances.

Tori had her career and dedicated her life to it. Beyond work, what little time she had left she used to train for triathlons and to enjoy fine wine and even finer clothes. While popular with and admired by her fellow agents, she had only a few truly close friends. She was attractive and athletic, with deep green eyes and shoulder-length auburn hair, and men were often interested yet rarely seemed to hang around for long. Perhaps it was because of Tori's workaholic nature, or perhaps because she was feisty on and off the job. It was the reason her work friends had recently given her a fitting T-shirt that read: *Honey Badger Don't Care.*

As she turned to gaze out the picture window there was a clatter back to her left. The massive stack of mail had collapsed and fallen to the floor.

"Naturally."

Exasperated, Tori walked over and dropped down to her knees. She started pulling all the pieces of mail together, finding miscellaneous bills, junk mail, a donation solicitation. for Boston College, her latest *Vanity Fair* and *Vogue* magazines, and then a yellow envelope that she flipped over to make sure it was addressed to her. There was no return address, but the postmark was for Manchester Bay.

Tori exhaled. She hadn't received a piece of mail from Minnesota, let alone Manchester Bay, in years. Pushing herself up from the floor, she went to her desk and reached for her letter opener. She sliced the top open, reached inside, and pulled out a single piece of paper.

"What the…?"

It was a photocopy of the front page of the *Manchester Bay Chronicle*, dated July 5, 1999, and the headline read: *Hunter Girl Missing*. In the lower left-hand corner, secured by a paper clip, was a typed note that read: *Check the Manchester Bay Chronicle. It will look familiar.*

She'd seen the clipping before, although it had been years. A copy of it was stored in a box in the closet. "It will look… familiar."

Tori went to her desk and powered up her laptop. She typed ManchesterBayChronicle.com into the search bar. On the home page the first headline was blunt: *Genevieve Lash Missing*. The subheadline read: *On Twentieth Anniversary of Jessica Hunter Disappearance*. As Tori scanned the article on the website, she learned that Genevieve Lash was last seen by a friend she dropped off at home early in the morning of July 5. In his press conference, Shepard County Sheriff Cal Lund reported that Lash's car was found abandoned and locked along the side of a county road with a flat right front tire.

"Cal…" Tori murmured.

Lund stated there were no signs of foul play at the scene. A search of the wetlands surrounding the area where the vehicle was discovered turned up nothing. "We have no evidence at this time indicating what happened to Genevieve Lash or where she is."

A separate link led to a map of the area and pictures of the location where the car was found. Given the date and details of the disappearance, the article writer wasted no time comparing Lash's disappearance with Jessie's.

The website included a link to a video of a comment from Shepard County Sheriff's Chief Detective Will Braddock, who was leading the investigation. Braddock acknowledged the parallels between the two cases but cautioned, "There are similarities and there are also differences. We are considering all possibilities in the search for Genevieve Lash." The Lash family was offering a hundred-thousand-dollar reward for any information leading to her return.

"Oh my God," Tori muttered as she dropped her face into her hands and sat in silence, just breathing with her eyes closed. She sat up, opened her eyes, and looked to the door of her spare closet.

In the twenty years since Jessie's disappearance, Tori had gone back through her sister's case just once, eight years ago, thinking that with her own FBI training and resources she might be able to discover a lead, see something that had been missed. She'd laid the entire case file out on her desk and taped it up on her apartment walls, living, eating, and breathing it.

However, other than searing every minute detail of the case back into her mind, she found nothing over an agonizing and fruitless twenty-seven days. With the frustration of failure building, and feeling herself beginning to mentally circle the drain, she made herself stop. She scanned all the documents onto a flash drive and then organized and re-boxed everything. She buried it all in the back of her spare closet, turning the box label against the wall and stacking other boxes around it so it wasn't visible. She'd seen the box just once since, when she moved from Brooklyn.

Nevertheless, her sister's disappearance, her father's death, and the guilt of all of it was a lingering presence in the back of her mind. She often viewed herself like a recovering alcoholic who had to fight for their sobriety every day. In her case, it was a daily struggle to carry it yet keep it all at bay.

She wasn't going to be able to do that now. The disappearance of Genevieve Lash, the article… it couldn't be ignored. She knew what she had to do and where she had to go.

Tori slowly pushed herself up out of her desk chair, found her FBI field backpack, and took out a pair of rubber gloves. Careful to lightly grasp the sheet of paper at the very top, she slipped it back into the envelope, which she then put into a large plastic bag. She closed her laptop and stuffed it into her backpack along with the plastic bag, and then went into her bedroom to quickly shower and dress. Her last task before leaving was to go to the spare closet. In the back-left corner was *the* box. She reached inside and took out the flash drive.

Three hours later she was in the FBI field office. Her friend Ruby Gaines, a lab tech, had come in and dusted the paper, typed note, and envelope for fingerprints.

"Negative, Tori, I'm sorry. There are no prints on the document other than your right thumb and index finger along the top," Ruby reported.

"What about the envelope?"

"We have all kinds of fingerprints there. I suspect from your doorman, the post office, the mailman, and anyone else in the postal service who touched it. I have run all of those prints, but nothing has pinged so far."

"I'm not surprised," Tori replied with a blank look on her face.

Ruby and another field office agent, Tracy Sheets, were two of the few people with whom Tori had ever discussed her past. Ruby knew the broad details of Tori's twin sister's disappearance. "It can't be a coincidence this happened on the twentieth anniversary."

"No, it can't," Tori agreed, shaking her head. "And look at the postmark. It was mailed on July 3rd, more than a full day before the abduction."

Ruby nodded in agreement. "What are you going to do, Tori?"

Tori held up the newspaper article. "This is an invitation. My sister's killer wants to play a game, so… game on."

CHAPTER FIVE

"She was dead by the time you found the car."

Braddock managed a couple of hours of sleep on the ancient, weathered, mustard-yellow leather sofa in his office. It was a couch so old and the cushions so flat that visitors often remarked that it looked like it had sprung a leak and needed to be re-inflated. At five his cell phone alarm blared. With a long, weary sigh, he unfurled his long body and set his size fourteens on the floor. After a minute of rubbing his eyes and face and collecting his thoughts, he made his way to the locker room, where he splashed cold water on his face and switched into some spare clean clothes from his locker. Dressed, he made the one-block walk from the government center to the diner while a thin ribbon of dark orange sunlight started to emerge over the trees in the distant eastern horizon.

The Wavy Café was quiet at 5:20 a.m. Just two tables were occupied. The rest were empty, awaiting the early-morning breakfast crowd, which typically started filtering in closer to six.

"Here you go, Will," Jan, the waitress, said as she slid a plate of two fried eggs, three pieces of bacon, and two pieces of wheat toast, and a side plate with four slices of melon, in front of him. She then quickly refilled his coffee cup.

"Thanks," he replied through a long yawn while he poured some half-and-half into the coffee and then slowly stirred it with his spoon.

"Any luck?" Jan asked.

Braddock shook his head as he spread a thick layer of strawberry jam on his toast.

"Everyone knows you're doing everything you can," she replied as she glanced to her right at the sound of the bell above the front door ringing, signifying new customers. Jan sauntered away to greet her newly arrived patrons, leaving him to his breakfast.

He'd cut his teeth as a detective with the NYPD and then later with the Joint Terrorism Task Force. He'd moved to Minnesota five years ago with his son after his wife's death to be close to her family, the only family the two of them had. Detective Jim Quinn, his mentor with the NYPD, had trained him to be a methodical, old-school detective. Quinn was a grinder and Braddock viewed himself as one too. Just keep grinding, digging and churning away at the case. You engage in the basics, including a good canvass and thorough witness interviews, and from that you should develop a solid lead thread. Once you have that, you relentlessly apply pressure and resources to the pulling of that thread, and the case will, in time, come together. Problem was, two days in he didn't have a good thread or *any* thread to pull. He had no momentum.

Genevieve Lash had simply vanished.

No ransom call had been received. Genevieve's cell phone had gone dormant and could not be traced. A review of her call and text history raised no red flags, although it provided a long list of people to talk to, and that would be happening today.

Thus far there was no indication that anything had happened during the Manchester Bay Fourth of July celebration or during her visit to Mannion's that raised alarm. And while the town had grown rapidly over the last several years, there was not yet a connected network of traffic and surveillance cameras that he could access to see if she had been tailed after her departure from Mannion's.

Braddock and his team evaluated Genevieve Lash's financial records. She worked part-time at a local clothing boutique but spent well beyond her means. While that would have normally been a red flag, the fact of the matter was that she was simply spending her parents' money. Jerry Lash had given his daughter an American Express card and she never left home without it.

Genevieve was a known party girl who dabbled in recreational drugs. Investigators in the sheriff's department narcotics unit were making the rounds to their informants. Thus far Lash's name was not on anyone's radar.

Her car was being examined by the state crime lab but he'd yet to receive a final report. A tip line had been activated but there'd been few calls despite the posted reward.

Braddock had just dug his fork into one of the fried eggs when Cal sat down next to him. "Get any sleep?"

"A couple hours on my office couch," Braddock replied after a drink of coffee. "You?"

Cal shrugged. "I tossed and turned and flopped for four or five hours and kept Lucy awake in the process. Who had Quinn?" Cal was referring to Braddock's eleven-year-old son.

"He stayed at his cousin's place. It's summer, so even money he'd be doing that regardless of what I'm doing."

Jan scurried over and already had Cal's usual ready to go, which was a bowl of oatmeal with a side of muskmelon. The two of them ate in silence for a few minutes.

"Did you dig out the old files?" Cal asked, dividing a piece of melon in half.

"Yesterday," Braddock answered before taking a bite of toast. "And?"

"It's not the first time I've reviewed *that* case, you know. Remember when I first moved here? You said if I was going to be the lead detective, I had to review the Hunter girl case, I had to know it."

"Right, but this is the first time you've gone through it when it could be… relevant."

"Cal, you know I thought the same thing you and Steak did when I saw the car and that flat tire. I see the similarities and noted the timing."

"As do many, *many* others, my friend," Lund replied, taking a bite of his oatmeal. "People are making the connection between the cases. You've seen what they're saying on TV. There's a reporter from the *Star Tribune* poking around, hounding our people, asking questions, and planning a big investigative exposé."

"I know," Braddock replied with a smirk. "I've been avoiding him."

"He's doing his job. He smells a story, a big story. Unfortunately, I do, too."

"It's been twenty years, Cal. *Twenty. Years.* That's a long time for a killer to be dormant and come back to life—*if* that's what's happened. Ask yourself, why now? And why Genevieve Lash? If we're going down this road, that's the question I keep asking. Why her? Why Lash?"

"Heck if I know," Cal replied with a sigh.

"Well, *that's* the question I think we need to be asking," Braddock answered while wiping the corner of his mouth with a napkin and then taking a sip of coffee. "There is something about the way Genevieve was taken. I don't think it's random, Cal. It doesn't feel random, and that gives me pause to just automatically say it's Jessie Hunter all over again."

Cal put his spoon down. "Look. I don't meddle, in part because I told you I wouldn't and in part because you're damn good at this."

"I sense a *but* coming."

"I need something."

Will sat up from his plate, nodding his head. "You're getting calls, aren't you?"

Cal nodded. "I get calls all the time. But on this one I'm getting pressure. Pressure from people vested in this town's growth and reputation. Those people have worked long and hard to develop this area into what it is now and to change how people perceive and think of Manchester Bay after the Jessie Hunter disappearance. So, whether you want to or not, if something doesn't pop and soon, you're going to get the opportunity to determine whether these cases *are* connected. We'll have no choice but to go all in on that and fold the Lash and Hunter cases into one investigation."

Braddock nodded as he rubbed his tired face. Politics was politics and business was business.

"Hey, I know you're doing everything you can, and actually so do the folks who are calling me. They all know, like, and respect you. But I think you need to know what this means to people and…"

"Since I wasn't born and raised here, I don't have the requisite appreciation for the history. I didn't live through it."

"I didn't say that."

"I get it, Cal. People don't want to relive the Hunter girl case all over again. I don't blame them."

"So, what's next?"

"It's still Genevieve Lash. That trail is not fully exhausted yet. I've got Lash's parents coming in along with a long list of her friends."

"Do you think you'll get anything you don't already have?"

"Sometimes sitting under the bright lights of a police interrogation room can motivate people to dig deeper into their memory banks. Someone knows or has seen something useful. We just have to keep digging."

*

Tori caught a seat on the first flight out of Newark and was on the ground at Minneapolis–Saint Paul International just after 8 a.m.

It was the first time she'd set foot in Minnesota since the day after her father's funeral.

That nineteen plus year absence left her a little unsure of how to drive the two hours north to Manchester Bay. She started up her rental car, punched a familiar address into the GPS, and let that guide her, first through the last vestiges of the Twin Cities' morning rush hour and then north out of the cities. An hour later she eventually found her way to the H-4.

After Jessie's disappearance, Tori had wanted to get far away from Minnesota. She chose Boston College, a large school in a major city where she could blend in and not see her sister around every corner. Where she could start over. And start over she did.

Growing up in Manchester Bay, she had been quiet and reserved, living in Jessie's shadow. But at BC Tori found herself cutting loose and morphing into a self-assured spitfire who was unafraid of speaking her mind to anyone.

"And to think I was just this shy, quiet little girl growing up," she said while drinking wine one night during her senior year with her roommate Chelsea.

"You were shy and quiet? *You?*" her roommate asked in shock. "Get out of town."

"Oh, yeah."

"I've known you four years. I've never heard this and I sure as heck have never seen it," Chelsea replied, still stunned, but then she asked a question, one Tori had avoided answering for nearly four years. "You know, you never talk about home, Minnesota, or family and friends. You never go back and visit. Heck, now that I think of it, I don't even know your hometown or what high school you went to. Why is that?"

Tori had always been a private person, never one to reveal much about herself, and that was *before* what happened to Jessie. As a result, at Boston College she didn't talk about home and what had happened in Manchester Bay, ever. There were no outward signs of home and no pictures of Jessie, her father, her mother, friends, or anything. All she ever said was that she was from Minnesota. Any more than that and it was too hard for Tori to talk about. She bottled it all up, making her past appear to be a blank slate to everyone she met.

Yet on that night, for some reason, she cut open a vein. "I'm going to tell you some things, but you have to promise you won't tell anyone else."

"About home?"

Tori nodded and let out a long sigh. "My actual story is… complicated and… well, you'll probably find it… pretty sad."

"Okay," Chelsea replied warily.

"Which is why you have to promise," Tori insisted. "I'm trusting you. I just don't want anyone else around here to know these things about me. I haven't talked about them since they… happened."

"I promise," Chelsea committed, crossing her legs in her soft chair and hugging a small throw pillow.

Tori told Chelsea everything, and by the time she'd finished an hour later, the tears were streaming down her face as she let it all out. Chelsea asked a question here and there but mostly listened patiently before eventually pushing herself up out of the chair, grabbing a box of tissues, and then coming back to sit down beside Tori on the couch.

"So, if I have everything, your mom died when you were five?"

"Yes."

"And you had a twin sister?"

"We were identical twins."

"She was abducted and never found?"

"Never found."

"And your dad died when you were a freshman?"

"Yeah, March of my freshman year, twenty months after Jessie disappeared. It was a heart attack."

"You know, we were living across the hall from each other back then. I remember you being gone for a week, maybe longer, and when you got back, you just said there were some things back in Minnesota you had to take care of. But… I had no idea it was… all this. You haven't told anyone about *any* of these things, ever?"

"No," Tori answered, shaking her head. "Only you," she added as she wiped away the tears before putting the tissue to her nose.

"That explains some things," Chelsea suggested. "Probably a lot of things."

"It's like all of that did something to me. It changed who I am."

"How could it not? Of course, *of course* all of that would impact you and change you," Chelsea assured her, wrapping an arm around Tori's shoulder. "You say growing up and in high school you were quiet, shy, and self-conscious?"

"Yeah," Tori answered and then dabbed at her eyes. "I came here, and I turned into this fierce, confrontational, opinionated chatterbox. It's like a switch went off or something. Why did *that* happen?"

Chelsea, a psychology major, took a sip of the cheap Zinfandel in her dime store wine glass and thought for a moment. "Well, the obvious answer could be that you grew out of it. New environment, new people, and no preconceived notions of you. You came to BC and felt free to be someone different. That's one answer." She took a slow, deliberate drink of her wine. "There is, I suppose, another possible answer."

"Which is?"

"You were joined at the hip with your twin sister. Inseparable. You were the left hand, she was the right. Never apart, always together, living each other's lives. It was as if you were one and the same, right?"

"Yeah, pretty much."

"That's not uncommon with twin sisters," Chelsea replied analytically. "Together, you were kind of one person, but you each had roles. She took some traits and you took others. But now I think what you're doing is you are living two lives... yours *and* Jessie's. You didn't consciously decide to do it. You didn't declare one day, 'I'm going to be like Jessie, too.' But subconsciously you took the best traits of your sister—her confidence, her assuredness, her bigger-than-life personality—and made them all part of you. In that way, Jessie's spirit lives on inside you. And you know what? That's a good thing."

"Maybe," Tori answered. "Except Jessie was popular, loved, and really happy. I'm combative, argumentative, and not always what you would call cheery."

"Well, you're putting your own personal spin on it," Chelsea quipped with a smile.

Tori sniffled and laughed, shaking her head in amusement. "I suppose."

"And for the record, you're not *always* combative and argumentative. Just when you think you're right, which… on second thought is most of the time."

"Thanks a lot," Tori replied with a light laugh, dabbing at her eyes again with the tissue.

"I'm your best friend around here, so this I know. You are a blast to hang with, especially after you've had a few at a party and you let that flirty side show. I wish you'd do that more often, let your guard down and just cut loose. And you've got more friends and more people that care about you than you know." Her roommate held up her wine glass for a toast. "And as for your sister, let me say this. Jessie would have loved who you've become. She'd be happy you're living your life and that she's a big part of it."

"I'll drink to that."

The two of them clinked their glasses and took long drinks of their wine before each pouring another full glass.

"You know," Chelsea stated after a moment, swirling her glass, "it might not hurt you to talk to someone about all of this."

"Therapy?"

"Yes."

"With someone like you?"

"I'm not that person yet, but in a few years I will be. In the meantime, I could help you find someone to work with now if you wanted."

"I'll think about it."

"When you're ready, you let me know."

Now, Tori thought back to Chelsea's offer and wished she'd taken advantage of it as she approached Manchester Bay. With the miles to town rapidly ticking down, the nervous fidgeting started. Her sweaty grip squeezed the steering wheel. There was the nervous tapping of her left foot. Her eyes darted pensively around the horizon. Her heart was beating faster, the anxiousness building at the thought of coming home and of actually investigating her sister's disappearance where it happened. Then the first signs of Manchester Bay started appearing, far sooner than she'd expected.

When Manchester Bay was home, the H-4 was a slender, two-lane highway that went through the center of town as it meandered its way farther north into the dense, forested depths of Minnesota lake country. Now there was a sign for the "Old H-4 Cutoff," which was the old highway route into town. Instead, the highway veered more northeast. *This is new.*

The H-4 was a true highway now, a wide, four-lane, flowing highway via a bypass that swung well to the east between the outskirts of the town proper and the Central Minnesota State University campus. The university's soaring spired clock tower was visible in the distance, perched high upon the bluff overlooking the town.

"My gosh, this all looks so different," she murmured, seeing two suburban-like housing developments springing up in what were once densely wooded areas southeast of town. She got her first real shocker as the Manchester Bay city limits sign appeared on the right. *Population 44,234.*

"That many? Holy cow!"

And it wasn't only the population that had grown; commerce had multiplied with it. Big-box retailers and open-air strip malls flanking the H-4 greeted her as she approached the exit for Lake Drive.

At the bottom of the exit ramp she turned left and cruised ahead into town, looking about in wonder as she passed big brand retail stores and then a string of chain restaurants and fast food drive-thru joints.

However, once she was past those staples of suburbia and drove deeper into the downtown area, she became thoroughly amazed by the modern transformation of Manchester Bay's once dated downtown core, now a quaint yet bustling business and entertainment district. Amid the historic, two-story, brown-and-red-brick storefronts housing Bloom Drug, Babe the Blue Ox Ice Cream Shop, Martha's Place, the Wavy Café, and the Ace Hardware store was an impressive collection of new boutique clothing shops, antique stores, art galleries, a coffee house, and a wine bar interspersed with a mixture of small ethnic restaurants and at least two craft beer taprooms. Kitty-corner from each other at the intersection of Lake Drive and Interlachen Avenue, in the center of downtown, were two impressive, identical, five-story square office buildings with exteriors comprising a mixture of dark-tinted glass and Kasota stone. With the noon hour approaching, the streets were teeming with shoppers and casual walkers, and there was a lively vibe along the town's main street.

Is this really Manchester Bay? My Manchester Bay?

A block short of South Shore Drive and the bustling beach on the shores of Northern Pine Lake, Tori found the imposing and historic Shepard County Government Center, financed by the thirty-plus mining companies that once operated in the Cuyuna Range, when iron ore mines ruled this part of the state.

As a child she had always thought the building dwarfed the rest of the town. Three stories high with four tall, round, ribbed pillars across the front, the building was a sturdy and handsome mass of granite, marble, and concrete, an edifice the sheriff once said was so indestructible it could easily withstand a nuclear attack. "Everything else would be flattened, but this sucker would still be standing, and not a stone, block, or panel would have moved," Big Jim Hunter once said to his girls.

She pulled into a visitor parking space, sat back, and took the old building in. It was the only thing in town that hadn't seemed to really change. The years of her youth had been spent running its halls with Jessie. Yet the last time she'd walked out of it had been a solemn occasion, leaving with her father's personal effects from his office following his death. She hadn't been back—until now.

Now that she was here, she wanted to make an impression, even on a Sunday. Dressed in one of her best black power suits, she added three-inch black stilettos and dark-rimmed glasses, and her shoulder-length hair was up tight in the back. Taking in and then exhaling a long, deep breath, she got out of the car and grabbed her black shoulder bag. She made her way up the wide front sidewalk and drew in the fresh Minnesota air; the sun was bright and warm, and a gentle breeze ruffled the deep green leaves of the mature maple, elm, and oak trees.

She stepped inside the building and observed that while the exterior looked the same, the interior had undergone a modernizing renovation, particularly the sheriff's office, which was straight ahead. She went right to the receptionist and, without preamble, flashed her identification. "I need to see Sheriff Lund."

Tori didn't recognize the receptionist, but given how the receptionist's eyes bulged when she reviewed her identification and then looked up, it was clear she recognized the name on the ID.

The receptionist turned in her chair and pointed behind her. "His office is at the end of the hall. That's where you'll find him. Would you like me to let him know you're here?"

"No, that's okay."

Tori walked quickly down the hall and saw Cal sitting at his desk. He had far less hair now, and what hair he did have was nearly white, but otherwise he looked much the same. He was reviewing a sheet of paper with another old friend standing to his side, peering over his shoulder. She reached the small entryway, leaned against the doorjamb, and observed the two of them.

"We've interviewed these ten so far and nothing," Steak said, pointing to the top of the sheet of paper.

"And Jerry Lash?"

"Soon."

Tori allowed herself a smile. "I swear, nothing has changed around here. Not a *single* thing."

Steak looked up, did a double take, and then—once there was recognition—his mouth practically hit the floor in shock. "You have got to be kidding me!"

"Hey, Steak," Tori greeted him warmly, moving into the office to give her astonished friend a big hug.

"I'm blown away," he bellowed in wonder, still stunned at the sight of her.

"Victoria, my word," Cal Lund said, coming around the desk and embracing her. After a moment he also wisely noted, "This is an awfully interesting time for you to finally pay us a visit."

"There's a good reason for it," Tori quickly answered, reaching into her shoulder bag. "I received this in the mail yesterday in New York City," she explained, taking out the copy of the old news clipping along with the typewritten note, both now encased in a large clear plastic evidence bag. "I've been invited to the 'party' you've got going on around here."

"Well, now, this is interesting, isn't it?" Cal mused before handing it to Steak for a quick look.

"Cal, I want in."

"Hmm, I imagine you do," Cal replied, taking the bag back from Steak. "And this ought to get you in the door. But it's not me you have to convince."

"Then who?"

Cal waved for Tori to follow him, walked out of his office and into the hallway, then pointed to the left. "See that tall drink of water down the hall, in that office with all the people hanging around?"

"Do you mean the guy with the stubble, dressed in the blue jeans and off-white cotton shirt?"

"Uh-huh."

"I presume that's your chief detective that I read about?"

"Will Braddock. *He's* running the investigation. Will is a former NYPD detective I hired five years ago to lead my investigative unit. He's Steak's direct boss. You want in on the investigation in a meaningful way, you'll have to convince him."

"Why do I have to convince him? Aren't you *his* boss?"

"Because when I hired him from New York, I said I wouldn't micromanage his cases, and that includes who he uses or who he assigns work to. Right now, he's got plenty of help. He has everyone in this department, and the Minnesota Bureau of Criminal Apprehension is angling in on this, not to mention your employer sniffing around and offering their expertise. In other words, he's up to his eyeballs in assistance and *advice*."

"I see."

"And Tori," Steak added, having joined them, "you'll find that Will is not exactly the kind of guy who likes people telling him what to do or how to run his case."

"What are you saying, Steak?" Tori asked with a mischievous smile.

"I see you're all confident and self-assured, back in what you now probably view as your simple little hometown full of dumbass rubes."

"That's a little harsh."

"No," Steak replied plainly, shaking his head with a wicked grin. "It might be close to twenty years since I last saw you, so I might be a little rusty, but I can still read you. I know your expressions and body language, and so I know, *I know* that's exactly what you're thinking."

Tori grinned back at her friend.

"I'm just warning you, if you come off like that to him—" he pointed to Braddock and laughed, a deep warning laugh "—well, he will show you the door right quick."

"Talk with Will *nicely*, then come back and talk to me," Cal counseled. "We need to catch up."

"Cal, I mean no disrespect, but I'm not really here to catch up."

"Victoria," Cal replied with a warm smile but a gentle sternness in his tone, "humor an old man and an old friend who, despite the unfortunate circumstances that have brought you home, is delighted to see you."

"Okay, Cal," Tori relented, patting him on the arm.

Cal and Steak stepped back into the sheriff's office. Tori stood for a moment in the hallway with her arms folded, leaning her shoulder against the wall, and sized up Braddock.

There was certainly no burgeoning stomach roll like the prodigious one Cal displayed and the one Steak was showing signs of developing. Braddock was tall, at least six four, lanky yet with wide shoulders and what she could tell were long, strong arms. He was sporting wavy black hair with some small flecks of gray mixed in. While she initially thought the stubble made him a bit of a poser, she noticed his weary eyes and imagined he'd simply been working around the clock and hadn't shaved. He appeared to interact with the people around him firmly but also with a comfortable ease. After assessing him for a few minutes, she thought two things. First, he had a certain rugged handsomeness about him. Second, watching him she could see the NYPD in him. There was a certain air about him, a gravitas she didn't often find in smaller towns.

Tori pushed herself away from the wall and walked straight toward Braddock's office as the chief detective picked up the ringing phone on his desk. She lingered in his doorway while he conversed with the person on the other end of the line. When he hung up, he looked to her and asked, "Can I help you?"

"Detective Braddock, Cal Lund sent me to see you. I'm Special Agent Tori Hunter with the FBI."

Braddock didn't visibly react, except for the almost impercep-tible widening of his eyes at the utterance of her name. He made a show of deliberately examining her identification. "And you're *the* Tori Hunter…"

"Yes."

"I see. Your arrival here can't just be coincidental, can it?"

"No." Tori once again pulled out the plastic bag and handed it over to Braddock. "I just showed this to Cal, and he sent me your way. I received this in the mail yesterday in New York City. It seems someone wanted me to know what was happening back here in my hometown."

Braddock reviewed the article and the typed note. He'd seen the article before, but the note was certainly new. "I assume you've had this evaluated forensically?"

"Yes. I took it to my field office in New York. No prints other than mine are on the article."

"And the envelope?"

"There were five different sets on the envelope besides mine. None registered in the system. We theorized the prints were from my building's doorman and people handling the envelope as it went through the postal service. It seems highly unlikely that whoever sent it would be careful enough not to touch the article but leave prints on the envelope. Nevertheless, the prints are in the system now, so if we get a match, we'd have that."

Braddock went back around his desk, sat down, and studied the article, not saying a word for a few minutes.

Tori could handle the silence for only so long. "I don't know why, but that sure looks like the killer is reaching out to me."

"That's what it looks like," Braddock replied, a slight hint of skepticism in his voice, a hint that didn't escape Tori's notice.

"Come on, Detective, really?" Tori asked, slightly exasperated. "You can't think Lash's case and my sister's case aren't connected. Look at the commonalities. Abandoned car in a remote area, flat right front tire, happening on the Fourth of July. You do see the pattern, don't you?" she pressed, with more than a trace of condescension in her voice.

Braddock looked up from the paper and locked his eyes on Tori, who was standing at the front edge of his desk, her arms folded across her chest.

"I mean, come on, it's the twentieth anniversary!"

"It is, and there are similarities, but there are also some interesting differences."

"Enlighten me."

"Jessie Hunter was seventeen; Genevieve Lash is twenty-seven. Jessie's car was found outside of Manchester Bay whereas Lash's was found well east of here. Your sister was the effervescent daughter of the sheriff, an ambitious high school student with plans to attend Iowa State with her more serious and straight-laced but equally determined twin sister. Conversely, Genevieve Lash is a quintessentially rich, party-going, twenty-seven-year-old, no-talent, Kardashian-like wild child with a history of drug use living on her family's fortune. To say the victims are different would be an understatement."

Tori wasn't buying it. "Yet here I sit with this in my mailbox."

"Is this the first time the killer has reached out to you?"

"What do you mean?"

"Ever get a little reminder like this before?"

"No."

"So, no previous taunting, no mail, no phone calls out of the blue, no contact whatsoever for twenty years, right?"

"That's right."

"And you haven't been back here in what? Eighteen or nineteen years?"

"Yup."

"So, you've been gone all these years, yet now after all this time, someone drops this note in your mailbox and that means everything is all connected?"

"What's your point?"

"Yes, this could be connected. In fact, everyone seems to think it is."

"Sounds like everyone but you," Tori asserted.

"I didn't say that," Braddock replied calmly, not taking the bait. "But think about this: What better way to get everyone's attention than getting hometown girl and FBI agent Tori Hunter back home to investigate her sister's disappearance? What a story. It's about the Hunter girl. The media will eat it up. Of course, then as a matter of self-preservation we'll have to jump on it. But what if that's *not* what this is all about? Now, could it be connected? You bet. I knew exactly what day it was when Lash went missing, and when I saw that flat right front tire, I knew what it could possibly mean. But I can't foreclose the possibility that someone could be using that anniversary for some other reason."

"Like what?"

"For starters, Lash's father is wealthy. He owns the biggest construction company around here, and I'm sure it hasn't escaped your notice that the town is a wee bit different from your days matriculating at Manchester Bay High."

"And Lash's father is what?"

"A cutthroat businessman who has put people out of business—a lot of people. Maybe someone is striking back. Or maybe it's Genevieve herself. She runs with the party crowd. She has a history of drug use, has been known to hang around with some people who like the high-end blow. What if she had something on someone and they abducted or killed her to protect it, and bringing you here is a sideshow to deflect from what I ought to be looking at?"

"Or maybe, rather than all that bullshit you just rattled off, you're afraid it *is* connected and what *that* means."

That got Braddock up out of his chair and nose-to-nose with her. But he didn't yell as she'd anticipated. "Fear is not my issue,

Agent Hunter," he growled quietly and then went for her Achilles, "but objectivity is *clearly* yours."

"Now, wait a minute—"

"No, you wait," he countered coolly, his eyes boring into hers. "There's a lot that says Genevieve Lash and Jessie Hunter are and are not connected," the detective noted, towering over Tori even though he was on the other side of the desk. "So, despite you flying a thousand miles, I can't just drop everything on *your* say-so and go down only that rabbit hole. I'm investigating *all* possibilities."

"Rabbit hole? Rabbit hole! How dare you," Tori barked back. "This is my sister's killer we're talking about here."

"Maybe!" Braddock replied. "Maybe." He took a breath. "This is personal for you and your history here, and that of your family; that buys you some accommodation, I'm sure, from Cal. From me too. And getting something like that in the mail…" His voice trailed away. "Well, I can only imagine that ripped open some old wounds. Right?"

Tori nodded.

"But let's get something straight right here, right now. If this is how you're going to conduct yourself, you might want to take your very nice Theory open-blazer pantsuit, Jimmy Choo stiletto heels, Movado watch, and Versace eyewear—that whole Miranda Priestly power ensemble meant to overwhelm me and everyone else here in your little wayward hometown—and march it all right out of my office and onto the first flight back to America's favorite airport, LaGuardia."

Tori did a double take. He knew the brands she was wearing, the watch and even the shoes. She'd underestimated him, despite Cal's and Steak's warnings, not to mention her own initial assessment.

He had her back on her heels, muted, unsure of what to say, but he skillfully filled the silence.

"Look, Agent Hunter," Braddock started, sitting back down and relaxing in his chair, trying to ease the tension now that his territory and authority were established. "I think the two cases are most likely related, and that is…" Braddock slowly shook his head and exhaled, "not a comforting thought at all. And while this might sound harsh to you, the fact of the matter is your sister has been gone twenty years. Genevieve Lash has been gone two days. Which trail is warm right now?"

Tori was irate with herself. The no-nonsense, laser-focused investigator was all emotion and fury, and the guy applying cool logic was kicking her ass. *Way to go, Tori. Brilliant. Piss off the guy you need to not piss off,* she thought.

It was time to start digging out of the hole she'd dug for herself. "Look, on that point, you're right," she conceded.

"I'm sorry I had to say that. I didn't like doing it," Braddock stated, extending an olive branch.

"Oh, I think you liked it a little bit. I mean, the Miranda Priestly shot was kind of harsh."

Braddock chuckled and shrugged. "Maybe."

"However, when you're as direct as I am, you ought to expect it back on occasion," Tori offered knowingly, extending an olive branch of her own. "And you're also right, it is personal to me and that perhaps affects my objectivity. But at the same time, I still think I can help. I want to help. I'm dying to help."

"Are you sure you can handle it?"

"Yes," Tori replied. "I am sure."

"And is this the New York Field Office of the FBI offering up assistance or are you here of your own accord?"

"Own accord. I took some… personal time. I'm not here as an agent per se."

"Do your superiors know what you're up to?"

"Kind of."

Braddock chuckled. She was going a little rogue. "And I assume that if I don't accept your desperate offer of assistance, you'll just end up providing it anyway, right?"

Tori shrugged. "Yeah."

"That's what I figured," the investigator replied with a wry smile. He made an offer. "It's my case, I run it. We're agreed?" he asked, extending his hand.

"Yes," she replied, taking Braddock's hand, holding it for an extra second. "Thank you."

"Welcome aboard."

With the turf battle over, Braddock gestured for Tori to take a guest chair, which she did. "Now, at this point I think this thing is now a homicide, *not* a missing person case."

"She was dead by the time you found the car."

"That's become my thinking as well." Braddock tipped his head toward the hall behind Tori. "Those folks are Lash's parents. Steak and his partner, Sheryl Eggleston, are—"

"Steak and… Eggleston?" Tori asked.

"Yeah," Braddock smiled, "I know, Steak and Eggs. In any event, they're reinterviewing Lash's friends and I'm going to take another run at her parents. You can watch if you like. What evidence we have—which to be honest isn't much, I'm sorry to say—you are free to look at." Braddock walked out from behind his desk and bellowed, "SHEILA!" out the door.

A moment later a woman that Tori recognized as Sheila Cassidy, who had graduated three years ahead of her in high school, walked into the office.

"Tori, I heard you were in the building."

"Hi, Sheila."

"Good, you two know each other," Braddock observed. "Sheila will get you set up, it'll probably take her a few minutes. In the meantime, I'm going to sit down with Jerry Lash."

"Come on, Tori," Sheila said. "Let's get started."

CHAPTER SIX

"This town is haunted by the memory of that case."

While Sheila went to work on setting her up on a computer, Tori kept her promise and went back to see Cal.

Shepard County Sheriff Cal Lund had been her father's best friend and second in command, and he took over when Big Jim died. Tori's parents were both only children, so when her father died, she had no other family to lean on. All she had was Cal and his wife Lucy.

Cal helped Tori bury her father, sell the house, and collect the life insurance, and he even drove her down to the airport in the Twin Cities when she flew back to Boston after her father's funeral. She doubted Cal had thought that the last time she left town would have been the last time he'd see her until now.

He spent some time catching her up. Cal's three children were now grown and had moved on, all living elsewhere. "It's just me and Lucy these days," he said. "I was re-elected two years ago and I think this is my last term. Then it'll be Tucson in the winter and up here on the lake in the summer."

"Sounds like the good life, Cal."

Cal said he'd followed her career from afar with interest. "Although, it's funny, nobody around here seemed to know you'd gone into law enforcement. I had to stumble across your name in the headlines once to learn that." It was a gentle gibe.

"I haven't kept in contact with *anyone* from here, Cal."

"Nobody?"

She shook her head. "I should have kept in contact with you and Lucy, though. I'm so sorry I didn't. It's just that…" Her voice trailed off and she looked to the floor.

"I understand."

"I don't know if I never planned to come back, and initially I just couldn't bring myself to do it. After a few years it was just easier not to; the thought of it just kind of drifted away. At least until yesterday."

Cal simply nodded, knowing that there was little in Manchester Bay for her but pain. "The sheriff would be proud, Victoria, he really would. I hope you know that. And," he added with a whimsical smile, "I imagine he'd be amused, *highly amused*, that his serious and studious daughter who always asked a million questions is an FBI agent."

The two of them chatted for a few more minutes and Tori promised she would come over for dinner if there was a good time. She finally turned to leave the office, eager to get into the investigation, when Cal offered a final warning. "You may have broken off contact with everyone here, but someone kept track of you. Watch your back."

Tori walked out of Cal's office and was greeted by Sheila, who'd had a visitor's badge made for her. "Will's in interrogation room one. You can observe from the booth," Sheila pointed out while opening the door to a narrow room containing a cabinet with a computer monitor and recording equipment. Tori clipped the badge onto the pocket of her blazer while stepping into the small room to stand behind the one-way mirror. Braddock and another detective were interviewing Lash's parents. Or was it the other way around?

"Dammit, Braddock, where's my daughter?"

"We're doing everything we can, sir…"

"It sounds like you're questioning me… us. Some crazy man out there took my daughter. And some crazy man took the Hunter girl on that same day twenty years ago. Isn't that what you should be concentrating on?"

"We are strongly considering that connection, and I have someone very well-versed in that case who has joined our investigation. I also think it's possible that there isn't a connection between the two cases, and I need to be able to eliminate other possibilities, ones that would be fresher than a connection to a twenty-year-old cold case. So, the reason I'm pursuing this line of questioning is that, yes, we might just have a repeat killer out there, or that crazy someone could have some sort of beef with you."

"What does that mean?"

"It means," Braddock replied calmly, "that you probably didn't get to where you are without making a few enemies along the way. We're looking at whether Genevieve's disappearance is connected to that of Jessie Hunter. But we're also looking at whether what happened to Genevieve could have something to do with you, your business, or whatever she might have been mixed up in. We're looking at it all."

"You think this has something to do with my business?" Jerry Lash barked defensively. "What kind of question is that? Don't you think, Detective, that you should be spending your time finding my daughter rather than putting us through some sort of inquisition?"

"Jerry, I think the detective is just doing his job," Dorothy Lash interjected calmly, reaching for her husband's arm. "He's trying to help."

"Sounds like the son of a bitch is coming after me! Coming after us!"

Braddock put down his pen and leaned forward with his elbows on the table and his hands lightly clasped, eyeing up Jerry, and said,

"Mr. Lash, I'm not coming after you or blaming you. This is not your fault. I want to find your daughter and I'm just exhausting every possibility, but… let me be honest with both of you. Genevieve was last seen sixty-two hours ago. Her car was found abandoned in an isolated area, and by the time we found it, she'd been missing eleven to twelve hours. We're investigating every possible lead we get, but to be honest, there are few promising leads right now."

I can think of one, Tori thought as she watched from the observation room.

"My daughter isn't coming back, is she?" Jerry asked directly of Braddock.

Tori winced, thinking, *No, she's not*.

"We have to keep up hope," Braddock replied evasively. "You want answers and so do I, and I'm not going to stop until I get them. That's why I'm doing what I'm doing. So again, tell me, is there anyone you've done business with that I should be looking at?"

"You can look at my business, my finances, my deals, and anything you want. My books and records are open to you, no restrictions. Send your people over, but…" The father slowly shook his head, coming to the realization his daughter was gone. "I play hardball in business, Detective. I always have. It ain't beanbag, it's construction. Shit gets broken, you know what I mean?"

"Yes, sir."

"And I have no doubt that some of those people would absolutely rip *my* head off if given the chance, but to go after my daughter in retaliation? I just don't see it."

"And in my experience, when people lose a lot of money to someone, when they are put out of business, when they're bank-rupted, when they think they were robbed or scammed, they want nothing more than payback," Braddock cautioned. "And often they want to see people suffer in the process and be as mentally and emotionally destroyed as they were. And what way can you make a parent suffer more than by going after their children?"

"You really think this has anything to do with something I've done?"

"I don't know yet. There's only one way to find out."

Sheila stuck her head into the observation room. "Tori, I have your desk ready." She led Tori to a cubicle set back in a corner. "This spot should give you some privacy. This sheet explains how you access the computer and create a password, and this file is where you can find the case evidence, notes, reports, and whatnot."

"And physical evidence?"

"There really isn't any right now other than the car, which is at the BCA forensic lab in Bemidji."

"Has there been a forensic report on the car yet?"

"No," Sheila answered. "Will expects the report any time now."

Tori sat down at the cubicle, logged on to the computer, and began reviewing the case file. Her first move was to examine the photos of the car. As she did, she couldn't help but think back to Jessie and their car, with the flat right front tire out on County Road 48. Lash's car looked eerily similar, listing to the right on the shoulder but otherwise undamaged. The case notes revealed Lash did not try to access the spare tire. Neither had Jessie. Lash's car was empty; no purse or other personal items were left inside. It was the same with Jessie.

The note she'd received was hauntingly correct: *It will look familiar.* It all was.

One thing that was different was the existence of a cell phone. In 1999, neither Jessie nor Tori had had one. In fact, Tori didn't buy a cell phone until her junior year of college. However, Lash had a cell phone, so it was interesting to Tori that she had not made a phone call. Her phone still hadn't been found, and the phone company records listed her last location as County Road 163. The last message activity was an innocuous text from a friend named Kelly Orville asking where Genevieve was. There was a one-word text reply: *Mannion's.*

Mannion's on the Lake.

Back in the day, it had been one of the few restaurants around. From what she'd seen driving into town, there now existed a great deal of competition.

Tori clicked on the file for Mannion's surveillance camera footage. It took her some time to orient herself to the black-and-white surveillance video. Mannion's was clearly the place to be. It was jam-packed with hardly any room for people to move.

There were four surveillance cameras. Two were in corners of the restaurant and the other two were in the bar area proper. After a minute or so she found Lash on the feed, mixed in with a group of people at the far corner of the bar.

A small smile came across Tori's face a moment later when she identified an old friend. "Eddie."

Eddie Mannion was sitting near the same far corner with another man, and after a few minutes of observation, Tori thought she recognized him as another high school acquaintance named Gunther Brule. Also walking by at one point was Kyle Mannion, who chatted for a moment, and then there was Jeff Warner, who stood for a few minutes with Eddie and Gunther before strolling away.

"It's old home week," Tori murmured. She watched the footage for a while longer before tiring of it.

Tori remembered that Lash's friends were being questioned again. She left her cubicle and stepped into a different observation booth to watch Steak and his partner, Detective Sheryl Eggleston, conduct the interviews.

She observed for a few hours as a parade of people came through to be interviewed. While Steak and Eggs were able interrogators, there was an unsatisfying pattern to it all. Most people had been at the party in downtown Manchester Bay just like she and her sister had been twenty years ago. Lash and her small pack of friends eventually made their way over to Mannion's. Everyone had a lot to drink. Most left by 12 or 12:30 a.m., and Genevieve and Tessie Joyner were still there when they left. Nobody noticed anyone that caused any sort of alarm or concern. As one person said, "It's our usual hangout. Everyone knows everyone. It was the typical crowd at Mannion's on the weekend or a holiday."

The last two to come into the interview room were Genevieve's friends Tessie Joyner and Sarah Mueller. Steak and Eggleston ran through the drill with them again, and the answers all seemed rote now. They hadn't seen anything or anyone that caused them any concern. They had been partying and having a good time. Everything had been normal.

"Just like always," Tessie stated. "There was nothing unusual. Gen took me to my parents' cabin, we made plans for the next day, said goodnight, and that was that. Same as always. It was normal."

"No, it wasn't!" Steak barked in frustration as he sat back hard into his chair. "It wasn't normal. It wasn't the same, Tessie."

"She's gone. Genevieve is gone. *Gone!*" Eggleston railed, equally aggravated. "You two were with her all night and you've got nothing for us?"

"Come on," Steak pressed, slamming his hand down on the table. "There wasn't something that surprised you? There wasn't something out of the ordinary? There wasn't one thing that was maybe weird or unusual? There wasn't someone hanging around that you didn't recognize or that gave you pause? No incidents, nothing? You're telling me there wasn't a guy or two who made their way over and tried to make some time with her?"

"I'm telling you there was nothing, absolutely nothing, out of the ordinary," Tessie answered emphatically. "I want to help, but—"

"Well, there was that one thing," Sarah mentioned, looking over to Tessie. "That guy who pinched Gen on the ass."

"Pfft. That happens all the time," Tessie responded with a dismissive wave.

"Who was that?" Eggleston asked.

"It was the guy sitting with Eddie Mannion. What was his name?" Tessie said, trying to think of it.

"Gunther Brule," Tori muttered and gave a gentle knock on the one-way mirror.

Steak turned around, surprised, not knowing anyone was watching. He exited the room to find Tori in the hallway.

"Sorry, I was watching surveillance footage earlier," Tori explained. "Eddie was sitting next to Gunther Brule."

"Hmpf," Steak snorted. "I'll try that out with them."

Steak walked back into the interview room. "Gunther Brule."

"Yes!" Sarah replied, pointing to Steak. "That was his name."

"And what happened after that? After he pinched Genevieve on the ass?"

"Nothing," Tessie answered. "I mean, Gen turned around, sternly looked at him, and acted kind of offended, but Eddie Mannion stepped in. Kyle did, too. Before anything else happened, Kyle and Eddie walked Gunther whatever away and that was that. It was over in like less than a minute. It was nothing, the guy was sloppy drunk."

"And when did that happen?" Eggleston asked.

"I don't know, maybe ten thirty or eleven, somewhere in there. We were there for a long time after it happened. It really wasn't that big of a deal."

Steak and Eggleston finished with Tessie and Sarah and let them go. They met with Tori in the hallway after the two women had left. Steak looked to his partner, unsatisfied, wiping his tired face with his hand. "We spent all day in there, and the best we got was a drunk Gunther Brule pinching Lash on the ass. Awesome, fucking awesome. What are we supposed to do with that?"

The three of them walked down the hallway to Braddock's office, where they found him sitting at his desk reading a report. He listened to the summary of the interviews from his detectives. He shared their aggravation and disappointment, not to mention their exhaustion. "Look, you two, you've barely been home since Friday," he said to Steak and Eggleston. "It's a reasonable hour. Go home, see your families, have dinner, and we'll dig back in first thing in the morning."

Tori had no such place to go so she lingered, taking a seat in the chair in front of Braddock's desk. "Have you checked all the boxes now? Have you completed the checklist?" she asked while rhythmically tapping her fingernails on the arm of her guest chair.

Braddock didn't appreciate the tone and peered at her with narrowed eyes over the papers he was holding. Yet, at the same time, he understood he was sitting across from a victim, someone who'd been suffering for twenty years. Tori Hunter was someone who was looking to help, and she brought a certain expertise, not to mention motivation. From that perspective, he thought to himself, *If I were in her shoes, I'd be really fucking impatient, too.* So instead he looked down to his right desk drawer and asked, "Agent Hunter, I could really use a bump, how about you?"

"Uh… yeah, sure."

"Bourbon okay?"

"Yes, absolutely." Next to wine, bourbon was usually one of her go-to drinks. It was familial; the sheriff was a bourbon drinker.

"Do me a favor. Grab two coffee cups off the rack out there by the coffee pot and then close the door. There's been a *Star Tribune* reporter snooping around, and the last thing I need is him snapping a photo of me boozing in my office."

Tori came back to find that Braddock had pulled a bottle of Knob Creek out of his desk drawer.

As they each drank from their coffee cups, Braddock leaned back in his chair, exhaled, and closed his eyes.

Tori, someone who viewed all silence as uncomfortable, started with, "So?"

"Agent Hunter, I'm—"

"Call me Tori."

"Okay, Tori, call me Will. I'm ready to expand my investigation to include a *full* dive back into your sister's case, but not necessarily because of you or your little verbal digs."

"Then why?"

"Because this afternoon yielded next to nothing, and because of this," Braddock answered, sitting up in his chair and reaching for the report he'd been reading. "I have here the BCA forensic report on Lash's car."

"What does it say?"

"Genevieve Lash's tire suffered a blowout and was tampered with, specifically a fresh puncture hole near the rim of the right front tire, on the inside."

"On the inside?"

"Yeah. Whoever did it would have had to lie down on the ground, get under the car, and puncture the inside of that tire. The hole was smooth, not a rough puncture wound. It was intentional, probably done with a knife—a damn strong knife."

Braddock reached for another, more worn, file on his desk. He opened it and flipped up some pages. "Now, the puncture wound on your sister's car was on the right front tire, but on the outside—as were, by the way, five other puncture wounds to tires that night in Manchester Bay. All six cars were in downtown that night. It was assumed at the time to be something of a prank."

"You know the case, then."

"Not like you," Braddock answered, taking a drink of bourbon. "But I do know you haven't been here in a long time. This town is haunted by the memory of *that* case. You know, Manchester Bay, the home of the Hunter girl disappearance. No matter what success they've had here, and no matter how positive the news is, that case is never far from anyone's memory. Manchester Bay and that case are inextricably linked, and now the town is going to have to go through that again."

"They're not the only ones."

"No, they're not, but it's time to go back there. I've been on this job here five years, and I've been through that case file a few times, including the last couple of nights, seeing if I might find or see something someone else didn't, or if there was some piece of evidence that didn't seem relevant at the time but does now. One piece is the confirmation of the tire tampering. In my mind, *that* really ties the cases together—that and the newspaper clipping you showed me. It tells me they're connected, but I'm still wondering about the 'why.'"

"Why now? Why Lash? Why contact me?"

"Yeah, all of that, but Lash in particular. She was not random. Her car was sabotaged. She was targeted. Why? There's a reason. That's what's eating at me right now."

"When do we start?"

"First thing in the morning," Braddock answered. "I haven't seen my son in three days. I'm feeling the need to go home and give him a big hug."

CHAPTER SEVEN

"I will make time."

Tori checked into the Radisson on the edge of downtown. After she'd settled in and had a quick room service salad, she sat cross-legged on the bed and opened her laptop and the file for her sister's case. As she read through one of Cal Lund's written reports, there was a light knock on the door. Tori, mindful of Cal's warning, reached for her gun, carefully approached the door, and peered out the peephole. Her jaw dropped. "No way." She opened the door to find three people waiting.

"Oh my God, it *is* you!" Lizzy exclaimed, jumping forward, embracing a stunned Tori before she could even react. Corinne quickly joined them in an embrace while Jeff Warner simply stood back, grinning with his arms folded.

"We heard you were in town!" Corinne cried happily.

"Word travels fast," Tori replied, regaining her composure. "I assume Steak let everyone know."

"A discreet text might have gone out," Jeff replied cagily with a sly smile. "It's good to see you, Tor."

"It's good to see you too, all of you."

"We figure you're here because of—"

"The Lash disappearance. Yeah, I'm here to work and—"

"Tori," Jeff said, holding up his hand, "on the first Sunday night of each month, those of us still left here from our graduating class—and there are actually quite a few of us—meet at the Steamboat Bay Tap Room just down the street. A whole bunch of us are there now. Come and join us."

"Oh, I don't know," Tori replied reluctantly, looking back to the laptop on her bed. Her purpose in coming home wasn't to reconnect with anyone, but, upon quick thought, she realized that wasn't realistic. She'd already seen Cal and Steak. Her return would not go unnoticed. And these people standing right in front of her were her friends, her good friends, for as long back as she could remember. She was happy to see them but somewhat shocked by the warm welcome. Would everyone feel that way? "I haven't been back in so long. People probably feel like I abandoned them."

"I think everyone understands why you left, Tori," Lizzy said.

"We all know you're not here for a reunion, or for anything like that," Corinne added and then reached for Tori's arm. "But you're here and we haven't seen you in so, so long."

"And it's just really good to see you," Lizzy exclaimed, wrapping her arms around Tori's other arm. "Come see everyone, even for just a little bit, just to say hi."

"Do they all know I'm here?"

Jeff shook his head. "Steak only texted Lizzy and Corinne, and they wrangled me into coming along, so it'll be a surprise, a big one, and those are *always* fun. What do you say?"

Tori sighed. She couldn't really say no, not to these people. "Okay. I'll come for one."

It was a four-block walk to the tap room. Much to her surprise, it took only a block for old warm feelings to seep into her consciousness. She started asking questions about their old group of friends, and Lizzy and Corinne eagerly filled in all the details of who married who, who was divorced, who had kids, and who did what and where.

"Here we are," Jeff announced, reaching for the door handle, looking to Tori. "You ready?"

"I don't know."

"Too late," Jeff replied, opening the door.

The four of them went inside. Tori immediately saw familiar faces. After a moment she drew some looks, people wondering who the fourth person with Corinne, Lizzy, and Jeff was. Then one of them, another old close friend, took a longer look; her eyes went wide in recognition and a huge smile spread across her face.

"Tori? *Tori!*" Mickey Olson screamed, running up to her. "*Oh. My. God.* It's you, it's really you!" Mickey exclaimed with a huge smile, wrapping Tori in a big, warm embrace, which after a hesitant moment Tori happily returned.

"Mickey Olson, how are ya, girl?"

"I'm great, but it's Webb now."

"You didn't marry Mike?" Tori said with a huge smile.

"Yeah," Mickey sighed with a smile, looking to her husband, "I sure did."

The warm greetings happened again and again for the next ten minutes as she made her way through her old friends and classmates, all happy to see her, welcoming her home.

It amazed her how so many of their old crew were still hanging out together. She stayed for three hours and even managed to sample a couple local microbrews as she reconnected with old friends. She expressed her astonishment to everyone at how the town had grown.

"That's the Mannions and Jeff over there," Mickey explained.

"Really? I mean, don't the Mannions just have the restaurant?"

Mickey laughed. "Oh my goodness, you have been gone a *long* time. Kyle Mannion has built this big drone business out on the edge of town and owns a bunch of businesses around here that support, supply, or distribute for it. He's a big benefactor of Central Minnesota State University, and he has funded an engineering program over there so then graduates are funneled into his businesses. Plus, he is venture-funding business ideas of kids studying in that program. So not only are we growing but the growth is young, so it will be long-lasting. The company went public, and at this point the Mannions are billionaires."

"What about Eddie? I didn't see him here tonight."

"And he usually is but I suspect he's out of town on business. He'll be sorry he missed it. Eddie runs the Mannion restaurant businesses. It isn't just Mannion's on the Lake here. There are Mannion's restaurants all over the Midwest and Eddie runs all of that. I think they have catering and supply businesses too, and there's a hospitality management program that they've developed at the university."

"And Jeff? What's his story? I didn't ask him on the way over."

"He's the lawyer for Kyle and Eddie and all their companies. He has a law firm in town that he merged with some national law firm, must be three or four years ago. Just like with Kyle, if you have a business in town, you would most likely work with his firm to get things done."

"They're all so… young to have such success."

"That they are but they've really led the charge around here. I used to have to go down to the Twin Cities or even St. Cloud for real shopping options. Now, I can just go down the street. It's great."

As the party started winding down and people started departing, Tori realized there were a couple of people she'd have liked to have seen that weren't there. She decided to have one more small beer with Corinne and Lizzy.

"Where is Jason Rushton these days?"

"I wondered how long it would take for you to ask about him," Lizzy replied with a smile. "He lives in Denver. He's married, two kids. I think he's a banker, a vice president of some kind, living a good life."

"And where's Katy? What's up with her, does she still live here?"

Both Lizzy's and Corinne's smiles evaporated.

"What?" Tori asked warily. "What happened to Katy?"

"You really don't know anything about the town, do you?" Corinne asked.

Tori shook her head. "Tell me about Katy."

"She still lives here," Lizzy answered, "but we never see her."

"Why not?"

Corinne and Lizzy shared an uncomfortable look.

"What's the deal, girls? What is it with Katy?"

"Tell her," Corinne said, looking to Lizzy. "She should know this."

"Tell me what? I should know what?"

"Katy is still here. She lives with her mom in the same house out in the country, northeast of the lake. But she is a… shut-in."

"A shut-in?"

"She almost never leaves the house," Lizzy explained. "She hasn't for years."

"Why?"

"I think… well, I think it all goes back to when Jessie disappeared. It just impacted her bit by bit over time. She became withdrawn from everyone, then afraid of going out, then of leaving the house, and then afraid of pretty much everything."

"It's not that we haven't tried to get her out," Corinne added. "I have her cell number and send her texts from time to time, but she never replies."

"I tried going out there for years to see if she'd come out, but she just won't leave," Lizzy added. "She's really just a shell of her former self, and… God I hate to say it…"

"Say what?" Tori pressed.

"I think she's gone crazy."

"You should go see her," Corinne stated. "If you have time."

"I will make time."

*

Tori Hunter was back.

Sitting low in his car seat, he observed Tori and her two friends exiting the tap room, laughing, smiling, and appearing happy.

"*Well, well, well.* After all these years you fell right into old times with your friends, didn't you?" he murmured excitedly. "*Interesting.*"

He watched casually with his right hand draped over the steering wheel as Tori Hunter exchanged hugs one last time and then waved to her two friends. She stood guard as they finished the walk to their cars, got inside, and pulled safely away. Only then did she turn and start walking in the opposite direction. He watched as she moved briskly on the sidewalk along the north side of Lake Drive.

When she was a block from the Radisson he started his car and pulled out along Lake Drive. Rolling east, he closed the gap on her, taking in her movements: the purposeful strides and the erect posture with her ponytail bouncing along. Most would see a petite, attractive woman strolling along, but he knew better. Inside that small body was a coiled weapon.

As he pulled through an intersection, she glanced back as if to check if anyone was behind her. He was far enough away that she didn't register him as a threat, but she had an obvious wariness about her. She knew someone out there wanted her back in Manchester Bay, and she was exercising caution.

"You should be on guard," he muttered. "You're not in New York City anymore, Tori."

Now that she was here, he hoped there would be a time and a place for them to meet, to come face to face, for Tori Hunter to be able to look into the eyes of her sister's killer. Tonight was not that night. The timing wasn't right.

There was so much yet to be done.

CHAPTER EIGHT

"Not only that, they *trusted* him."

Tori woke early and quickly scanned the local trail maps on her computer, identifying one that followed the east side of the H-4 north out of town. With the sun rising, she went for a brisk six-mile run to get her blood going and purge her body of the toxins from her unexpected night of beer-drinking.

After the run, she showered and then dressed more casually in a light blue blazer and blouse paired with dark gray slacks. She arrived at the government center just after 7 a.m. with two dark roast coffees and two breakfast sandwiches from Starbucks. Braddock was already in and at his desk with three open bankers boxes from the original Jessie Hunter investigation.

She held up the coffee carrier and food bag. "Man, I wish I could wear jeans on the job."

"I'm not stopping you," Braddock replied, eyeing the food she was holding. "Is one of those for me?"

Tori nodded, took a cup out of the carrier, and handed it to Braddock.

He took a sip and gestured his appreciation. "Thanks. Our coffee… well, it's only a caffeine delivery mechanism."

"What time did you get in?"

"Half an hour ago," Braddock replied. "I got up early, took a swim, and then rolled in here to get a start."

"Swim? Where?"

"I'm on Northern Pine Lake. I have a place over on the southwest side."

"No kidding. I grew up on the lake, just northeast of town," Tori replied and then held up the white bag. "I brought us some breakfast as well," she added, grabbing an open chair at the small conference table.

Braddock readily accepted and opened the sandwich wrapper. "I heard you got re-acquainted with some old friends last night."

"How do you…?"

"Don't let the growth around here fool you. Manchester Bay still behaves very much like the small town you grew up in. News travels fast, very fast."

"I guess," Tori replied. "Steak told you?"

"He might have sent a text."

Tori changed topics as she opened a file folder containing original photos of the car she shared with Jessie twenty years ago. She glanced around the office, taking in the stacks of folders and papers from the case spread out. "You've been busy."

Braddock nodded, finishing a sip of his coffee. "Just absorbing this file so I can attempt to converse on it at your level."

Tori nodded then looked through another file that contained witness statements. There was her own statement and those of many of her friends, some of whom were at the bar last night. As Braddock crumpled up the sandwich wrapper and tossed it into the garbage can, Tori asked, "What's the plan?"

"Steak and Eggs are going to stay on the Lash angles," he answered, wiping the edge of his mouth with a napkin. "They're digging further into her and her family's background and going over to Lash Construction to look through records there as well. If they get names of interest, they'll investigate those and cross-check them against the master list from your sister's case." Braddock held up a document stapled in the upper-left-hand corner. "This is everyone whose name came up twenty years ago. I imagine you recall every name on the list."

"We probably need a database to cross-reference this."

Braddock nodded. "That's in progress," he replied as he reached for his light gray and navy patterned sport coat from behind his office door.

"And you and me?"

"We are going to reinvestigate your sister's case through the lens of Genevieve Lash. Let's go."

Braddock's first stop was to take Tori to where Lash's car had been found abandoned along County Road 163. He pulled to a stop and turned on his hazard lights.

The morning was humid yet cool with a thick blanket of fog hovering over the wetlands to the north and south of the thin stretch of county road. The fog would burn away as soon as the sun got above the treeline. Tori took it all in and found the eerie quiet a little unnerving.

Braddock handed her a red folder that contained investigative notes and photos of Lash's BMW convertible. "Her car was parked thirty feet ahead, on what there is of the right shoulder, and was leaning to the right into the tall grass because of the blown tire."

Tori nodded and opened the folder, which contained photos, Braddock's handwritten investigative notes, and the forensic report on Lash's car. She started walking away from Braddock's Tahoe, flipping through the photos.

Having been over the scene multiple times himself, Braddock leaned against the front grille of his car and sipped his coffee. He wanted to give Tori the chance to walk the scene and form her own impression.

Tori slowly strolled along the pavement, her eyes darting between the road, the shoulder, and the photos. As she read through the notes, one item caught her attention. Lash's car was found locked.

"How'd you open up the car?"

"Her parents had an extra key fob."

Interior photos of the car didn't reveal a phone, purse, or any other personal belongings beyond an empty water bottle in the cupholder and a phone charging cord. The glove box contained the car's manual and a flashlight.

Tori walked the area slowly, taking in the surroundings, gazing in every direction before scanning back through Braddock's investigative notes and then flipping to the forensic report. She was particularly interested in the evaluation of and conclusions for the flat tire. There was a one-inch penetrating wound on the inside of the right front tire, two inches from the rim. Based on the size of the puncture wound, the report made a certain number of assumptions followed by conclusions based on the assumed facts.

The first assumption was that—considering the condition of the other three tires, their age, and their proper level of inflation—the right front tire had been properly inflated to begin with. Second, it was assumed that the tire had been tampered with sometime on the night of the Fourth of July. Based on information provided by Tessie Joyner, Lash picked her up at 7 p.m. and they drove into downtown for the Fourth of July carnival. They parked on a side city street and remained in Manchester Bay until 9:30 p.m., when they then drove two miles to Mannion's on the Lake. They remained at Mannion's until approximately the 1 a.m. closing time.

Given the above parameters, the actual size of the puncture wound, and the distance driven after having left Mannion's—considering the likely speeds driven and general road conditions, and calculating the rate that air would have escaped the tire both while parked and being driven, —it was the forensic conclusion that the tire had been tampered with while parked at Mannion's. It was further determined, based on the puncture size and the distance driven, that the tire would have started to deflate rapidly once Genevieve Lash had started driving and stressing the tire, leading to the blowout, particularly given the many sharp turns, some nearly ninety degrees, found on County Road 163. The report also noted that the low tire warning light was illuminated on her dashboard.

"It was only a matter of time before it blew," Tori muttered to herself.

She flipped to Braddock's notes on Tessie Joyner. He'd specifically asked about the operation of the vehicle and the tires. Tessie did not recall Genevieve having said anything about her tire going flat. Tessie didn't notice if the warning light was on or if Genevieve was having any difficulty with her car.

Tessie indicated that Mannion's parking lot was packed and that Genevieve was forced to park her BMW in the last slot at the far end of the parking lot that backed up to a thick grouping of trees.

"I remember the parking lot at Mannion's where she parked the car," Tori remarked. "That's a long way out."

"Yes, it is," Braddock answered. "It's a poorly lit area. On the passenger side there were trees and a four-foot high hedge framing the end of the lot. Our guy would have had easy access to puncture that tire, and with the trees and hedge, nobody would have seen a thing unless they were standing right on top of him."

Tori closed the folder and made a slow 360-degree turn, taking in the entirety of the area. "Could he have possibly found a better place for her tire to blow out? We've been out here awhile and only one vehicle has driven by."

Braddock agreed. "This is about as desolate as you can get around here."

"What do you think happened with her car?"

"The report says it's likely her tire would have deflated rapidly before it blew. The tire was losing pressure and the warning light came on. Now, when I see that warning light appear, that tells me I need to put air in my tire relatively soon. Most people would see that warning light and think the same thing. They certainly wouldn't think a blowout is imminent. I'm guessing Lash was like most people. She didn't have far to go. She figured she could make it home and deal with it later."

"But she didn't."

"No. Her tire was severely compromised, but she didn't know that. I think she got on this road with its winding turns, some of them tight, with rapid, albeit short, elevation changes and definitely some rugged humps and bumps. All that turning puts added strain on a tire that's rapidly losing inflation." Braddock shook his head in disgust. "She almost made it home. Her parents' house is only another couple of miles down the road."

Tori nodded. "The tire blows. She has to pull over to the side."

"No choice at that point."

"What jumps out at me is she didn't call anyone." Tori reopened the file and flipped some pages. "And she had a cell phone, a new one. Plus, there was a charging cord so even if the battery was dead, she could have plugged it in and made a call."

Braddock nodded. That was on his mind as well. "So why not call?"

"Because… someone is Johnny on the spot to offer a ride. After all, he punctured the tire. He was following her and had a good idea of how long it would last. When it blew, there he was to help a damsel in distress."

"Like you said, she doesn't call anyone, so he wasn't but a minute behind."

Tori nodded. "At most. I mean, she didn't use the flashlight in the glove box. She didn't make a phone call. There's no evidence that she tried to access the spare tire." She looked to Braddock. "But isn't she wary? I mean, I would be. All women *should* be."

"Yes, they should be, but then there was the X factor: the weather," Braddock replied, pointing to the file folder. "You saw the weather report. I'm thinking she was in this spot around one thirty. That's right when the storm was rolling in here, and it was a bad one, big wind and heavy rain. It produced a small tornado that touched down just east of Crosslake."

"She needed to get to shelter."

"That's right. She has a flat tire with severe weather bearing down on her, so someone comes along and offers her a ride."

"And she takes it."

"Now she's gone," Braddock replied.

Tori folded her arms over her chest. "Did our guy really calculate that her tire would blow here, or at least along this road? Is he that… precise?"

She had just voiced something he'd been troubled by for the past day. "If that's the case, we really have our hands full."

"That takes some—" she shook her head "—serious planning and calculation."

"Or he really knows tires."

"Our killer doesn't strike me as the National Tire and Battery kind of a guy."

"No, he doesn't," Braddock agreed before giving a follow motion with his arm, "but it does suggest to me that she was far from a random selection. He studied her thoroughly, knew her patterns, anticipated what she'd be doing on the Fourth, where she might be driving, and he was ready."

"He stalked her."

"Not so much that anyone noticed, but yeah, I think he did." Braddock waved his arm again. "Let's go."

"Where?"

"You know where."

As Braddock cruised south on the H-4, Tori rode quietly, inhaling long breaths through her nose, steeling herself. At the junction for County Road 48, Braddock turned right and drove southwest. He eased around a gentle curve and then slowed to a stop just short of the site where Jessie's car had been found abandoned twenty years ago. It wasn't hard to identify the location. There was a sturdy, four-foot-high, bright white cross pounded into the ditch just to the right of the shoulder. The horizontal arm of the cross simply read: *Jessie Hunter, 7/5/99.*

Braddock killed the engine and glanced to his right. Tori silently stared straight ahead.

"How long has it been?" he quietly asked.

"March 7, 2001, the day I buried my father," Tori replied softly. "Who placed the cross here?"

"I imagine one of the friends you ran into last night," Braddock answered. "Cal says it's been there for a long time, but given its crisp white condition, I'd say someone clearly tends to it."

Tori reached for the door handle and stepped down out of the Tahoe. Braddock did the same and then opened the rear passenger door and took out another file folder. He walked around to the front and handed it to Tori. "This is what I was working on this morning," he said. "I knew we were going to do this, so I put it together." It was a summary folder of Jessie's disappearance, containing photos, investigative notes from that time—mostly from Cal Lund—and other pertinent information.

Tori opened the file, quickly flipping through the contents. All this information was seared indelibly on her memory. Yet it was one thing to look at it in the privacy of her home, or to lie down on her bed or couch with her eyes closed to think about it. It was quite another thing to be in the very spot once again.

"Do you need a minute?" Braddock asked.

Tori shook her head. "No, walk it with me," she answered, handing the file back to Braddock, who opened it and scanned the first page.

Jessie Hunter's white Pontiac Grand Am was found by Sheriff's Deputy Ed Gregerson at 4:14 a.m. on July 5, 1999. Deputy Gregerson identified the car as belonging to the sheriff's daughters.

He radioed it in and then a call was routed to Sheriff Hunter's house. Jessie was not home and there had been no phone calls from his daughter about trouble with the car. Early-morning calls were made to Jessie's friends' homes, but she was nowhere to be found.

As for the right front tire, a one-inch, slice-like puncture was found along the outside of the tire close to the edge of the rim. The crime scene investigators' conclusion was that the tire had been intentionally tampered with that night, that the hole and air pressure loss was steady, eventually causing the tire to blow under the stress of being driven. It was likely that Jessie Hunter would have heard a loud pop and then the lower right front of the vehicle would have immediately dropped, forcing her swiftly to the side of the road.

"Both tires were tampered with," Braddock stated, getting the discussion started.

"Yes," Tori replied with a nod. "Jessie's was on the outside of the tire, Lash's on the inside, but a similar method nonetheless—a one-inch slice."

Tori stepped down into the ditch and crouched in front of the cross, bowing her head and then murmuring, "Hey, sis."

After a moment, she opened her eyes, cleared away some debris, and then stepped down hard on the dirt around the base, firming up the ground and slightly straightening the cross.

She stepped back up onto the road and took a good long look around. "Both locations are awfully isolated," Tori noted. "I'm kind of surprised that highway bypass for the H-4 didn't cut right through this area instead of going out so wide to the east."

"That was the original plan," Braddock answered. "However, politics being politics, Kyle Mannion and other local leaders argued that the bypass had to run farther to the east. There were two homes on the state historic register that could potentially be harmed, and some anthropology professors from the college argued there were Native American burial grounds out here somewhere."

"Are there?"

Braddock snorted. "Who knows? The objectors were mostly the college professors and the members of the Manchester Bay Historical Society. They had surprising clout, though, and hired Jeff Warner as their lawyer. With Warner and—I suspect—Kyle Mannion's financial help, they had the resources to lobby for a change. A year after the H-4 bypass route was originally announced, a re-route was approved by the State Department of Transportation. Then, lo and behold, three months later Kyle Mannion announces he's building his corporate campus where? Along the east side of the H-4 bypass re-route, where, as luck would have it, he owned a prime hundred-acre plot of land."

"A billionaire's kind of luck."

"Exactly."

Tori shook her head, bemused. "Kyle was behind the re-route."

"Yeah, he downplayed that, said he had nothing to do with it and claimed he was just fortunate that it worked out that way, but everybody knows otherwise. But hey, it's Kyle Mannion. He owns the biggest employer in what is now a company town."

"It's the way of the world."

"Indeed, it is. The bypass has been fully open for three summers now. It's been fine."

Tori walked over to Braddock. "Open the file for me. I want to see the photos again."

"Okay."

The two of them examined photos of the car, the flattened tire, and the surrounding area, which itself was largely unchanged other than now there was an asphalt shoulder whereas twenty years prior there was only gravel.

"You've walked both scenes now. Thoughts?" Braddock asked.

"No sign of a struggle at either location, but particularly at Jessie's, where you might have seen some in the gravel of the shoulder. The only definite foot impressions are from Jessie and her size fives."

"Not only that, but both cars were found locked. Keys gone, purses gone, lights turned off, no hazard lights flashing," Braddock added.

Tori nodded. "They both locked their cars and were leaving them for later when they came back and picked them up because there was…"

"No struggle," Braddock finished the thought as he leaned against the right front fender of his Tahoe with the folder opened on his hood. "What's that tell you?"

"They both got into another car easily. They got in because—" Tori's eyes flashed "—they knew their abductor. They *knew* him."

"Not only that, they *trusted* him. Especially Lash. She's just three miles from home with a cell phone, yet despite all of that, she gets into the car with him."

"Could he have had a gun on her?" Tori asked.

Braddock contemplated that idea for a moment before shaking his head. "What would Jessie have done if someone pulled a gun on her?"

"She'd have run like hell for the woods, made the guy chase her, take a shot at her. That's what my dad told us to do. Run, yell, scream, and whatever you do, don't…"

"Get in the car," Braddock finished. "I've told my son the same thing. I don't see any evidence of that taking place here. I think our first thought is right. They knew him. They trusted him."

Tori nodded. "Yeah, I think you're right." She shook her head at the thought. "So why now? Why now, after all these years? Is it just that it's the twentieth anniversary? Is that the reason to kill again, to bring me home because of some number on a calendar?"

Braddock shrugged. "I've been asking a similar question in a different way, which is why Genevieve Lash? What made *her* so special? She was selected. What made her worthy of all of this preparation and calculation?" He sighed. "Please don't take offense to what I'm about to say, but your sister's case always had an air of randomness to it. Some deranged guy on the Fourth of July slipped by unnoticed, punctured several tires, and just so happened to get lucky with Jessie."

"No offense taken, I've long thought that possible myself."

"But now I'm not so sure about that."

"Because of Lash."

"She is not a… vulnerable person. Genevieve is not apt to expose herself to the risk of abduction. Kidnapping? It's possible, but we've had no call and there is no sign that's what's going on here. She has some history of drug use, is a party girl, sleeps around some, but she's also street-smart and is not someone to necessarily let her guard down."

"She's not an easy mark is what you're saying."

"Right. So why pick *her*? That's why I've focused on that— because obviously more people know her and what her life is all about at this point than would remember your sister."

Tori looked to Braddock. "I can understand why you had reservations about the two cases being connected."

"Yeah, but then you showed up with that article and note," he replied. "We either have a situation where they are connected, and your sister's disappearance was not random, or someone is using the disappearance of your sister to deflect and hide some other agenda."

Braddock drove them into the town of Holmestrand, where there was a small, out-of-the-way deli, so they could grab some lunch in relative privacy. They each ordered a sandwich and a soda and then grabbed a picnic bench covered with an umbrella out back. Under the shade they dug into lunch and talked.

"Let's eliminate a couple of other things," Tori stated. "I assume you've looked at all sexual offenders?"

"The BCA has been making the rounds of registered sex offenders in the area. So far, nothing, and since your arrival, I'm really skeptical that will net anything."

"Why?"

Braddock finished a bite of his sandwich. "Twenty years between cases narrows the possible suspects; and, really, how many of these guys would have had the ability to keep track of *you* over twenty years? I mean, think about that for a second. Is your address public, like in the White Pages? Is it findable on the Internet?"

"No. I've done everything I can to prevent that, given what I do."

"Right, I mean you live in a city of eight-point-five million people. So, whoever reached out to you has either kept close track of you somehow or tracked you down. You'd know better than me, but most sexual predators don't profile to have that ability, and to be honest… this just doesn't have the feel of a sexual offender case. It's too well-planned, too well-executed, especially with Lash."

Tori thought about that for a moment while she chewed on a potato chip. "Sexual offenders often give off a whiff of perversion. Genevieve Lash, for all of her partying and whatnot, would have sensed that and would not have gotten into a car with one."

"I agree. It's not impossible, but it is extremely unlikely. Like we said, it appears Jessie and Genevieve trusted the person they got into a vehicle with."

"Was it the same person?" Tori asked. "I'm betting it was."

"We can't know for sure but… for now, I'm operating as if it was." Braddock took a bite of his sandwich, looking away, deep in thought before he turned back to Tori. "Have you kept in contact with anyone from here?"

"No."

"Nobody?"

Tori shook her head. "I didn't keep in contact with anyone, not even Cal."

"You left and…"

"I basically never looked back."

"Hmpf," Braddock grunted. "Were you surprised by the warm reception last night?"

"Yeah, I kinda was," she replied. "I'm not sure I deserved it. I cut off all contact."

"Well, despite your efforts, someone appears to have kept track of you."

"Cal said that, too. He said I need to watch my back."

"He's right about that," Braddock agreed. "And, like it or not, there is something we have to do."

"Which is?"

"Reinterview your friends from twenty years ago who are still living here."

"You think one of them had something to do with Jessie?"

Braddock shrugged. "Maybe. *If* these cases are connected, odds say it's someone living or working around here."

"I just find it hard to believe any of my friends would hurt Jessie."

"I'm looking with a wider lens than that," Will answered. "If there is a connection, your friends who still live here might be able to help bridge the twenty-year timeline between your sister and Lash. When you start thinking about twenty years and the growth and expansion of this town and area, maybe there is some obscure connection that we haven't recognized or found that could spring from talking to *your* friends. That's the job a lot of the time: you keep going around and talking to people. That's what I'm thinking, anyway. That is, unless you have a better idea. I'm all ears if you do. The suggestion box is *wide* open."

Tori shook her head. "No, it has to be done. And if it must, well…" she sighed, "I'd like to do it with you."

CHAPTER NINE

"I'm not some sort of Harvey Weinstein sympathizer."

The main reason Tori had stayed away from Manchester Bay was that everything there was a reminder. Despite the never-ending support of all her friends, who had made sure she was rarely alone, Tori felt suffocated by the darkness of her senior year. It was a long, joyless, torturous slog to graduation and her eventual escape. Then, after seven months away at college, she received the fateful call from Cal. Her father had died. She had seen it at Christmas when she came home from Boston, the drastic change in the sheriff, his gloomy mood and deteriorating health. She'd begged him to go to the doctor, to get himself checked out, but he'd refused. "I'm fine."

She knew better. He'd lost a wife to breast cancer and now a daughter on his watch as sheriff. It was all too much for him. The doctor said he died of a massive heart attack, but Tori knew better. Her father died of a broken heart.

Tori spent years finding distractions and inventing ways to suppress the memories of it all to varying degrees of success, but she couldn't avoid them now. She was fully reliving it again. And now that she was back, she was going to have to make her friends relive it, too. The good news, if there was any, was that at least she had Braddock along to go through it with her. He wasn't burdened by all of it.

They started with Lizzy Cowger, whose married name was now White. She first made sure to introduce Tori to her husband and three children before the three of them sat around the kitchen table to talk. Lizzy remembered the night clearly. "We were all down at the beach watching the fireworks. After that we went over to Tommy Peterson's house on the lake and sat around the bonfire pit for a while."

"Who was there?" Braddock asked, his spiral notebook open, pen at the ready.

"Corinne, Mickey, Katy, Eddie, Jeff, Steak, the Mouse and the House."

"The Mouse and the House?" Braddock asked with eyebrows raised, looking up from his notepad.

"Casey Schmidt and Terry Bird," Tori replied with a wry smile at the mention of them. "Those two," she shook her head, "they were tight, always together." She looked to Braddock. "Casey was the little guy, shorter than me, who somehow played defensive back, and Terry was the big guy, tall as you but girthier, played tackle. Hence the Mouse and the House. Who else, Lizzy?"

"My gosh, there were lots of people. Those that still live around here? Jamie Sedor, Jill Gregg, Michelle Fritz, and Jenna Berneck were all there. Jeff Herrmann and Adam Smith were around, too. Adam moved west to Alexandria and owns a resort on Lake Darling, but he still comes over this way every so often."

"I know Jeff," Braddock nodded, jotting down the name. "He has a son who plays hockey with my son Quinn. He lives on the east side of Northern Pine but owns a machine shop up in Holmestrand."

"It was just a normal, fun night, like we always had," Lizzy said, staring away before she looked back to Tori and Braddock. "I don't think about it as often as I used to, at least until the last few days when I've thought about it a lot again. But what has always gotten me about that night is it wasn't any different than anything we'd done before."

"Do you know Genevieve Lash?" Braddock asked.

Lizzy shook her head. "I recognize Lash Construction, everyone does, but I don't know her."

They visited Corinne next and her recollections were pretty much the same. "I remember Leanne Carlson and Sue Tomczik being there as well, so you could talk to them. They still live here."

"Lots of the girls still living here, it seems," Braddock commented, taking notes.

"A lot of the guys we hung with back in the day, including Goth, Korton, Joey, Odie, Hall, and Kly, were there that night, but they've all moved down to the Twin Cities except for Kly. He lives somewhere outside of Chicago, I think."

"But all of these guys were our friends," Tori added. "We hung out together as a pack, all the time. Heck, and don't take this wrong, Corinne, but you, me, we could be recalling someone just because we all were always together—*always*."

"True statement," Corinne agreed.

"Did you see Jessie Hunter leave the party?" Braddock asked.

Corinne nodded. "Sure, I can remember it clear as day. There was the hug goodnight like always. She and Katy got into the car and away they went."

"Did everyone leave at the same time?" Braddock asked.

Corinne thought for a minute. "I think so, although…" She closed her eyes for a moment. "I think most of us were there to the end. I suppose some people filtered off earlier. I just remember Tommy's dad coming down to the firepit and saying it was almost one o'clock and time for everyone to go home. It was no big deal, he wasn't mad or anything, he just said that was it for the night."

She looked to Tori. "I go out to that cross along the road a couple of times a year. God, I wish I could remember anything from that night that seemed wrong, but I just… can't. I mean, you probably don't want to hear this, but we all talk about it at the class reunions, we toast Jessie, and…" Her voice trailed off as she reached for Tori's hand, her eyes getting watery. "She's never far from our thoughts… nor are you."

Tori nodded, her lip trembling. "I know Jessie would love that you all still think of her. That would have been important to her. It's important to me."

Mickey Webb told the same story. "Mike was there," she added, referring to the man who became her husband. She looked to Braddock. "I was Mickey Olson back then. Mike was there that night with Gunther Brule."

Tori and Braddock shared a quick look at the mention of Brule.

"What?" Mickey said. "Gunther?"

"He is one connection between your group and Genevieve Lash," Braddock explained. "Gunther was at Mannion's on the night of the Fourth and he had a brief little issue with Lash at the bar. He pinched her on the butt."

"Really?" Mickey shook her head in disbelief. "He must have been drinking then."

"Do you still see Gunther much?" Braddock asked.

Mickey shook her head. "Not really other than maybe around town. He and Mike were friends then, but not so much now."

"They have a falling out, Mick?" Tori asked.

"No. They're not… not friends. It's just that Mike teaches at the high school like me. He coaches hockey and baseball, plays golf, and runs the kids all over to their activities. Gunther, on the other hand, works at the explosives plant out west of town. He is divorced, has no kids, and hunts and fishes, so they don't have that much in common anymore. Gunther still hangs around with Eddie Mannion, though. They're tight, I guess. They both were in the service, went to Iraq, and I think they bonded over that."

"And were Mike and Gunther there at the end of the night?"

Mickey nodded. "Yeah. I mean, Mike and I were kind of dating at that point. So he hung around as long as I did and then left with Gunther in Gunther's truck, I think. They did that and then I…" Mickey's eyes began to tear up, and this time Tori was the one to provide comfort, reaching for her friend's hand. "I remember, vividly, *vividly* saying goodbye to Jessie that night. You know, a big hug like we always did. I mean, we made a silly thing about that. The guys would all mock us. Don't you remember the *big* hug?"

"I do."

"It was so stupidly obnoxious." A tear ran down Mickey's cheek. "But I'm always thankful we did that back then. You know, I got to hug her one last time, I got to do that."

Mickey's husband Mike arrived home with their son, and they ran through it all with him again.

"Gunther dropped me off at home and then he went home," Mike explained. "That's what I remember about that night. Gunther lived a mile from my house, so he'd have been home less than five minutes after he dropped me off. As for the other night, what you mentioned happened at Mannion's, Gunther had to have been drinking—*had* to be. Otherwise he wouldn't have the balls to speak to a hot woman, much less pinch her on the ass."

"Somehow I don't think you'd be so afraid, Mike," Tori needled.

"To talk to a hot woman? Come on, Tori, you know they all talk to me."

"Oh God, don't encourage him," Mickey moaned.

"But pinching a woman on the bum?" Mike glanced warily to his wife. "Those days are long over, sweetie."

"They better be, buster."

None of Tori's closest girlfriends knew Genevieve Lash personally, although they'd all heard of the Lash family due to the construction company and then her disappearance. Genevieve was a decade younger and lived the party life. All of Tori's friends were now in their late thirties with families and busy lives. A big night out was a Sunday at the Steamboat Bay Tap Room.

In all, they made eight stops throughout the evening, finishing after 11 p.m. "That had to be tough to do," Braddock offered quietly, looking straight ahead as he drove. "Going through that night over and over again with your friends."

Tori simply nodded, looking off in the distance. "The good news is all the friends I saw tonight are all doing well. They're married, have kids, and seem perfectly happy and healthy. I'm grateful that's the case."

As Braddock pulled to a stop in front of the Radisson, Tori reached for the door handle and then looked back at him. "You know what the hardest part of tonight was?"

"The fact you weren't at the bonfire."

"Yeah," Tori answered. "You know where I was and what I was doing?"

He nodded.

"She'd be alive if I'd been there."

Braddock shook his head. "I know this is of little solace to you, but it wasn't your fault."

"I should have been there," she insisted.

"No," Braddock answered, shaking his head. "No. You were doing something completely… normal, something I'm pretty sure your sister probably encouraged you to do, didn't she?"

Tori looked down and nodded.

"That's what I thought," Braddock answered, looking over to her. "What happened to your sister was tragic. What it wasn't was *your* fault."

Braddock picked Tori up at six thirty the next morning.

"Did you get any sleep?" he asked.

"Not much, a bit here and there. I finally got up at four forty-five and went for a run. You?"

"I got some, although I was tossing and turning, too," he replied. "I took a long swim in the lake about the same time you took your run."

Braddock took her to an early breakfast at the Wavy Café and then they kept going, finding her old friends at home or at work. By midday they made their way over to Mannion Companies to find Eddie in his office. "Tori!" he greeted her, with a big smile and a warm hug. "Jeff told me you were at the tap room the other night. I'm sorry I missed it."

"It's good to see ya, Eddie."

They spent a few minutes reminiscing before Eddie exclaimed, "I just can't believe you're actually here!"

"Well, I am. And I'm sorry to do this, but we need to ask questions about the night Jessie went missing."

"I kind of figured you might."

"What do you remember about that night?" Braddock asked.

"Man, Will, it's been twenty years. My recollections are that it was a regular old night for us, other than it was the Fourth of July. We were downtown, watched the fireworks, and went to the bonfire at Peterson's. I mean, back in those days, with our group in the summer, that's what we did. Lather, rinse, and repeat, day after day."

"Who were you there with that night?"

"Steak, for sure. Jeff, of course. The Mouse and the House. Mike Webb, I think Gunther was around. I remember Goth and…" Eddie rattled off many of the same names and no new ones. "I know you and Jason were around for some of the night but, well… sorry… never mind. I didn't mean to go there."

"It's okay, Eddie," Tori replied. "Do you remember leaving Tommy's that night?"

"Yeah," he nodded. "I remember leaving and I dropped Jeff off at his dad's house."

"And then after you dropped him off, *you* had to go home," Tori suggested solemnly.

"That's right," Eddie sighed, looking away.

Braddock briefly glanced to Tori, wondering what the hidden meaning was with Eddie going home. He didn't press it and instead asked about Gunther Brule. "I have witnesses who say he pinched Genevieve Lash on the ass at your bar on the Fourth and it caused an incident."

Eddie tipped his head back in laughter. "I shouldn't laugh, given what happened to Genevieve and the times we live in. I'm not some sort of Harvey Weinstein sympathizer. I support the MeToo movement. And for the record, all of that with Gunther and Genevieve was probably my fault as much as Gunther's."

"How so?" Tori asked.

"Because I own the place and Gunther was a little too well-served, and I let him be too well-served. And then Genevieve... well, she was a *looker*."

Tori rolled her eyes at him.

"What?"

"Blame the victim much?"

"Sorry, but you're asking what happened."

"You say she was a looker," Braddock prodded. "You say that like you... have a history with her?"

Eddie smirked. "We had a night or two once a few years ago."

"Still like the chase, do you?" Tori asked.

"Maybe," Eddie replied coyly. "In any event, Genevieve was at the corner of the bar being kind of loud and obnoxious, and she was wearing a bright pink thong and the top was visible just above the waistline of her white Daisy Dukes. I noticed it and clearly Gunther did too. I think he was looking at that for an hour. I mean, she was from me to you, less than five feet away from him, so…" Eddie shook his head and grinned slyly, "the dummy pinched her on the ass. Hell, I watched him do it. He wasn't what I'd call sly about it, either."

"And then what?"

"His timing wasn't great. She was talking to a couple of big guys when he did it. She reacted, although it wasn't over the top. I mean, Genevieve was someone who might invite the pinch."

"Eddie!" Tori scolded.

Braddock didn't approve either but asked, "Would she have invited it, for example, if you did it?"

"Yeah, sure. But when she turned around and saw *who* it was, she wasn't that happy. I jumped off my stool and got between them. Her guy friends stepped in between them as well. A few salty words were exchanged. But then Kyle was there. He stepped in and… well, it's like that old E.F. Hutton commercial from when we were kids. If Kyle talks, people—"

"Listen," Braddock finished for him, nodding.

"Right. So, with his presence it was over like that." Eddie snapped his fingers. "It was really no big deal. To be safe we called a car service and had Gunther driven home. Kyle bitched me out for setting a real fine example with a drunk-ass friend and then that was the end of it."

They spoke with Eddie another ten minutes and then departed.

"Eddie hasn't… matured much," Tori mused, shaking her head.

"No, I don't think he has, not like your other friends. What was the deal with him going home when you were kids? Why was that a problem?" Braddock asked.

"I sometimes forget you're not from here," Tori answered, admonishing herself. "Eddie's old man Irv, who owned the res-taurant on the lake, was a big, drunken, miserable, and abusive beast of a man. Bar none, the biggest asshole I've ever seen in my life. He'd knock his wife around and he'd beat Eddie and Kyle if they tried to step in. Or he'd whip up on those two, and especially Eddie, who was smaller, for some other reason, or sometimes for no reason at all."

"That's rough."

"Yeah, it was. My dad went out there a bunch of times and arrested Irv. A few times Big Jim got Irv back to the jail and worked him over, giving the bastard some of his own medicine, back when you could kind of get away with that stuff. Problem was Mrs. Mannion would never press charges."

"That must have been rough for Eddie," Braddock suggested.

"Yeah. I think he enlisted in the Marines after high school just to get away from Irv. He must be long gone now. Good riddance."

Jeff Warner was their next stop at the law offices of Wilson Day, which had seventeen offices across the United States. Tori thought it was an odd juxtaposition to see a law firm with offices in places such as New York, Washington, Chicago, Los Angeles, and Dallas also have one in Manchester Bay, Minnesota, but Warner explained that he'd merged with Wilson Day four years ago. "Mannion Companies was getting so big that we needed more and more big law firm resources. Kyle, to his credit, was loyal and wanted my firm to remain as counsel to the company since I'd been there since day one. Heck, I went to work for him doing restaurant stuff when I was still in law school. Anyway, we'd worked with Wilson Day and they understood what Kyle wanted and proposed a merger, so we'd have their resources and they would have a client who was about to take off into the stratosphere. It's a public company now, hell of a thing here in little old Manchester Bay. But enough about all that, let's talk about why you're here. July 4, 1999, and Genevieve Lash, I presume?"

"Good guess," Tori replied.

"It seemed logical."

"So, what do you remember?" Braddock asked.

Warner recounted what everyone else had also recalled. "I remember the bonfire at Tommy's. I remember being a little angry that I had to go home earlier that night."

"Why was that?" Braddock asked.

"My dad was out of town and my grandma was watching me and my sister. Grandma, God rest her soul, was firm and you did not cross her. She said be home by twelve. I complied. Eddie dropped me off and then, of course, he had to go home."

"Yeah, Irv."

"Fucking Irv," Warner replied, shaking his head disgustedly. "What a worthless prick. I'm not sure how Eddie made it through all that. I'm not sure how anyone could."

"We just saw Eddie. He seems okay now," Tori remarked.

"Yeah, Kyle looks after him, and Eddie has done well for himself with the restaurant business. That's booming, too. They're opening a new joint every six months or so, it seems."

"We have another woman who's gone missing," Braddock said. "Anyone you know tie in between Jessie Hunter and Genevieve Lash?"

Warner thought for a moment before slowly shaking his head. "You know, until this whole Lash business, more than anything else I just always figured that what happened to Jessie was really bad luck." He looked to Braddock. "If I recall, there were a bunch of people who reported their tires being damaged that night, correct?"

"That's right."

"So, when I've gone back to that night and thought about what happened, I've always kind of believed that Jessie's car was one of the cars that got hit. Her tire blew out on 48 and she had the misfortune of being in the wrong place at the wrong time. Some guy came along and something bad happened. That's the lawyer in me thinking it through."

"I noticed you were at Mannion's on the night Lash went missing," Tori stated.

"How'd you know that?" Warner asked and then realized. "Surveillance video, right?"

Tori nodded.

"Yeah, I was there for a while having drinks and an appetizer with a lawyer from my firm and his wife after the big fireworks show. I saw Eddie and Gunther sitting at the bar. I went over to say hello as I was leaving."

"Did you see Genevieve Lash standing there?"

Warner shook his head. "I know Jerry Lash. His company was the general contractor on the Mannion corporate campus. I've worked with him often and I knew he had a daughter, but until all this happened, I didn't know who Genevieve was. I wouldn't have been able to pick her out of a lineup. Now Eddie claims he had a little fling…"

"He mentioned that," Tori said. "As for Genevieve, I take it you didn't see Gunther's dust-up with her later in the evening."

"What dust-up?"

Braddock explained.

"He must have been drunk."

Their next to last stop was to finally track down Gunther Brule at his house back in the woods, west of Manchester Bay.

"I heard you were in town," Gunther bellowed from his porch as Tori and Braddock approached. He was sitting in a lawn chair, a Miller High Life in one hand and a lit cigarette in the other. "I suppose you're wondering why I pinched Genevieve Lash's butt. The honest answer is, so am I."

"Well, she did go missing later that night."

Gunther offered a dismissive wave. "Hell, I was in bed. After I did that thing at the bar, Kyle shoved me into a car and I was home in ten minutes." He gestured to his garage, where a new Dodge Ram pickup truck was parked, along with a white van parked around the side. "The pickup stayed there in the parking lot overnight. I picked it up in the morning."

"And why did you pinch her on the buttocks?" Braddock asked.

Gunther laughed lightheartedly. "Probably because she had a really nice ass. Not any more to it than that."

Tori pushed him back in time. "What do you remember about the night Jessie went missing?"

"Not that much, to be honest," Gunther replied. "I didn't hang around you guys all that often back then, although I would have liked to. You guys were all the *cool* kids. Eddie Mannion is a friend now, a good friend, but back then that was one of the first times I was with that big group of people. I went over to Tommy Peterson's place with Webb, I think, which is where all of you guys were hanging out. He was all hot for Mickey so we kind of followed you all around that night. That's what I remember, but like I said, I wasn't really part of the group."

It was late in the day, the sun starting to work its way lower in the clear western sky, when they left Gunther. As Braddock reached the end of the long driveway, he said, "That's pretty much everyone."

"No, there's one more," Tori said. "We need to go see Katy."

"Anderson? You really think she can give us anything?"

"She was the last person to see Jessie alive."

"And, I don't want to sound insensitive, but she hasn't left the house in fifteen years, so what possible connection could she have to Lash?"

"I can do this myself if you want."

"No, no, no, I'll go," Braddock replied before whimsically adding, "This should be interesting."

"Don't be an asshole."

"Sorry."

Twenty years ago, Tori and Jessie's best friend—other than each other—had been Katy Anderson. The three of them had sat at the same small table in preschool, and after Tori and Jessie's mom died, it was Katy's mom who would often watch all the girls after school. Katy's mom ran an in-home daycare, and her dad ran a truck repair business out of a large pole barn at the back of the property. Back then there were signs for both businesses out front along the road, a busy and lively place.

Tori could tell that was no longer the case. The house was the same, but the signs were gone. A conspicuous amount of disrepair had overtaken the property. The raggedy yard needed mowing, the unkempt bushes needed trimming, the driveway looked as if it hadn't been sealed in twenty years. The pole barn at the back of the property was closed and probably hadn't been accessed in eons.

"Maybe hang back on this one for a few minutes," Tori suggested. "I have no idea how this will go."

"Copy that."

Braddock waited by the Tahoe as Tori deliberately made her way up the front steps. At the top, Tori closed her eyes and took a breath before she lightly knocked on the front door. After a few seconds she heard rustling sounds and then the door creaked open and Katy looked out, squinting into the late-day sun at the person on the porch. After a moment her eyes went wide in recognition and her hands went to her mouth in shock.

"Hey, Katy," Tori greeted quietly.

"Tori?" Katy gasped, frozen in shock.

"Yeah," Tori replied, trying to keep her own expression together.

When they were all kids, Katy was a lively and pretty girl. She played soccer with them, was rail-thin, attractive, and outgoing. The Katy now standing behind the front door was a shell of her former self. She was far heavier now, wearing baggy sweats, and her black hair was graying prematurely and pulled back in a loose ponytail. Her eyes were hidden behind dated, gold-rimmed glasses.

After a moment, Katy's mom, Gail Anderson, appeared behind her daughter to see who was at the door and was equally astonished to see Tori. She opened the door and stepped onto the porch to embrace Tori while Katy looked on, still too stunned to move.

"Why are you here?" Katy finally asked.

"The Genevieve Lash case," Tori answered. "There are some things about it that brought me home, the similarities between it and Jessie's disappearance. I wanted to come out and see you. And… well… I'm sorry, but—" she gestured over to Braddock standing by the Tahoe "—Detective Braddock and I need to ask some questions about the night Jessie went missing."

Braddock joined them on the porch, let Tori introduce him, and then followed them all inside. Tori sat down with Katy on the couch. It took some time to get Katy talking after the initial surprise of Tori's presence. But Katy didn't want to talk about twenty years ago. It was challenging to keep her on topic and difficult for Katy to talk about Jessie's disappearance. She was more interested in Tori, New York City, her job and life.

Slowly, over the course of an hour, they fitfully worked through the details of that fateful night. Yet, despite those efforts, Katy didn't remember anything new, or anything beyond what others had reported.

"When she dropped me off it was like always," Katy said. "I stood right out on the porch and I waved to her before I went inside. Jessie waved back and then pulled away and…" Fresh tears welled in her eyes. "I never saw her again."

Katy knew of the Lash disappearance and that it had occurred on the anniversary of Jessie's disappearance, but she didn't see the connection. "I don't know anything about her, Tori. I don't get out too much."

"I saw Corinne and Lizzy. They say they've tried to call you to invite you out."

"They have but I… can't go out." Katy looked down to her hands, which she nervously rubbed together while rocking slightly. She was starting to shut down.

Tori slid closer, sliding an arm around her. "It's okay. It's okay."

"I'm sorry."

"No, it's okay," Tori replied softly, tenderly massaging Katy on the back. "It's okay."

That ended the interview.

Gail walked a rattled Tori along with Braddock out to the driveway.

Tori asked, "How long has she been…?"

Gail shook her head. "After Jessie disappeared, she tried to move on like everyone else but that whole thing just… impacted her in such a drastic way. She had…" she put her hand to her mouth and closed her eyes. "She had a breakdown, Tori, a really bad one."

"When?"

"A few years after you'd left for college. She was in a mental hospital for a year, and when she came out, she just wasn't the same. At first, she just stayed home more but would leave and go out and try to work and go to college, but over time she couldn't handle it. These days she doesn't hardly leave the house."

"Not at all?" Tori asked, flabbergasted.

"No. For a time she'd go places with me, shopping or out to eat, but after a while," Gail sighed, "I couldn't get her to do even that. I'd say she's been this way for nearly ten years, maybe a little more. She has a driver's license, but the last time she left the house was probably three months ago to drive me to a doctor's appointment." Gail sighed. "She just can't seem to handle the world out there."

"Does she work?"

"A bit. She does some remote data entry work. She reads lots of books, watches movies, and for a while she tended to the bushes and the gardens, but now she barely even leaves the *inside* of the house. It's like her world just keeps shrinking and shrinking. I fear one day she won't even leave her room. If something happens to me…" Gail just shook her head.

Tori looked to Braddock. "You were right." She then turned to Gail, saying apologetically, "We shouldn't have come out here."

"No. I'm so glad you did. You'll find this hard to believe after what you just saw, but that's the most vibrant I've seen Katy in quite some time. That was really hard for her to talk about, and I don't think she'd have done it for anyone else but you. Seeing you, Tori… *that* was good for her."

Tori and Braddock left Katy's and drove back into town and to the government center in silence. Once they reached Braddock's office, he dropped down into his chair, exhausted. Tori sat in one of the guest chairs, looking blankly away.

For once it was Braddock who broke the silence. "You thought you'd come to town and just break this thing wide open, didn't you?"

Tori snorted her reply, nodding lightly.

"There is a reason your sister's case was never solved. There is a reason that after five days we're nowhere on the Genevieve Lash case, absolutely nowhere. Sometimes things happen, and we just can't find the answers."

"People don't just vanish."

"Yeah, sometimes they do," Braddock answered plainly. "Be honest. You don't solve every child kidnapping with the child returning home, do you?"

After a moment Tori shook her head.

"In this job there's nothing better than saving a life. The problem is that the flip side is usually more the case, and there's nothing worse than having to tell someone their loved one is gone, and it's doubly worse when you can't answer the question *why*. To me, delivering *that* message is the toughest part of being on the job. Because without the why, loved ones can't get closure."

"You think we're there? That we won't find the answers?"

"I don't know."

"Someone sent me that newspaper article. They want me here. We're missing or not seeing something."

"Or he's just jerking you around and he's not even here," Braddock answered. "All I know is that right now we're going nowhere fast. We're striking out and—" he held up a message slip "—Steak and Eggs are striking out, too. They've got nothing new from Lash's friends, and at least initially, they've found nothing in the records at Lash Construction."

Tori simply shook her head, looking away, not wanting to agree with anything Braddock had just said but at the same time knowing he could possibly be right.

"Or maybe we have everything we need to crack it, but we just don't know it yet," Braddock added as he sat up in his chair, checked his watch, and said, "I'm calling it a night."

"What? What about the case? How can you just leave?" Tori asked exasperatedly, unaccustomed to just going home if a case wasn't solved. You worked until it was one way or another, personal life be damned.

"It's almost eight. It's been a fourteen-hour day. I'm going to try and catch the end of my son's baseball game."

"What about his mom?"

"She died six years ago," Braddock answered quickly. "I've hardly seen Quinn in days, and he's going out of town with his grandparents for several weeks soon. And besides, I don't obsess over work. It's not healthy. I work hard and then I leave it *at work*."

"No work at home?" Tori asked in surprise. She always worked at home.

"No. The case will be here in the morning and so will I."

CHAPTER TEN

"Apparently, I'm not the only crazy one here."

Braddock dropped Tori off at her hotel and then sped away to catch the rest of his son's Little League game. She went up to her hotel room, stripped out of her clothes, and stepped into the shower, trying to forget about the day, the failure, but what she couldn't shake was the state of Katy.

She simply hadn't appreciated Lizzy and Corinne's warning about the depths of Katy's mental state. And what was more, she was ashamed she hadn't known any of this had happened and felt a certain amount of responsibility that it had. She dried herself, wrapped up in a towel, sat down on the bed, and turned on the television. But try as she might she couldn't get Katy out of her mind.

Her other friends had figured out a way forward the past twenty years, acknowledging a tragedy, thinking of Jessie often, but moving past it to live good, fulfilling lives. But not Katy. She hadn't been able to get past it and make a life. She was stuck and afraid of the world.

Yet something Katy's mother had said also stayed with her. She'd said that Katy seeing Tori was good for her. Gail used the word vibrant, as if there were signs of life in there.

Tori wasn't in the mood to be cooped up in her hotel room. She jumped off the bed, quickly dressed, and slipped on her running shoes. Ten minutes later she was back on Katy's front porch, knocking on the door.

Gail smiled and let Tori back inside. "She's in her room."

Tori lightly knocked and then cracked open the door, and Katy's eyes brightened. "Hey, it's a beautiful night. Can we sit out on the porch?"

The two of them talked for three hours, and slowly Katy emerged from her shell. Tori saw flashes of the smart-aleck friend who was whip-smart and always smiling. *That* Katy was still in there, fighting to emerge. Tori poked and prodded her to talk about it all, including the mental hospital, what she felt when she left the house, and how she had basically stopped experiencing the outside world. Katy became more and more animated as they talked. She was fully aware of her phobia, of her fears, and that she just couldn't overcome them. "Enough about me and all my screwed-up issues. Can we talk about something else?"

"Anything you want. Let's just keep talking."

"I know you went to Boston College but then I lost track of you. How did the FBI happen?"

"It's a long story…" And Tori proceeded to tell it. "I'm based in New York City now, but I travel all over on cases."

"Are you married?"

Tori shook her head.

"Boyfriend?"

"No, I'm notoriously single."

"I find that hard to believe."

"Why?"

"Look at you, Tori. You're successful. One look at your clothes, your watch, your hair… heck, your skin tells me you have money. And my goodness, you just look so gorgeous."

"Now stop that, I do not."

"You do. You're pretty and you clearly spend some money on yourself."

"I must confess that I have a terrible, *terrible* online shopping habit. I have like four pieces of furniture in my whole condo but three closets stuffed full of clothes. I could never wear them all. I also work *a lot*. I travel all the time and live half of my life out of suitcases and in hotels. While you're not seeing it here, I tend to—at times—have a prickly demeanor that I'm quite sure, based on several years' data, puts men off after a while."

"You never did suffer fools gladly," Katy remarked knowingly. "Even when we were kids."

Tori eyed her friend. All this talking was therapeutic. Katy seemed to sense it, too. Three hours ago, she had been curled up in a nervous ball. Now she was sitting comfortably with her body relaxed, twisting her hair in her fingers, laughing, smiling, and even needling her a little bit.

"How long will you be here?" Katy asked.

"I don't know. I came home looking for answers. I'm not finding any. The job could call at any minute and I'm on a plane to somewhere else."

"Just like that?"

"That's my gig. Pick up and go at a moment's notice."

"No wonder you don't have a beau."

"Just go in for the kill, why don't you?"

"I'm just saying," Katy replied, serious. "Nobody's going to commit if you're not around. It's a two-way street."

"Well," Tori sighed, "that is true. In my defense, I've yet to meet anyone who really made me want to do that."

"I see," Katy replied. "Well, while you are in town, will you keep coming out here?"

"Yes," Tori replied, grinning. "But I want you to do something for me."

"What?"

"Go out with me—to dinner or for a drink. Will you do that for me?"

Katy hesitated.

"Come on, just with me."

"Just with you?"

"Yeah."

"O-o-okay. I'll do it with you."

Tori smiled and then reached for Katy's hand, pulling it close to her, holding it in both of hers, squeezing it gently. "It is inexcusable I didn't know you were going through all of this. I'm so sorry."

"It's okay."

"No." Tori shook her head. "No, it's not. I should have been here for you and I wasn't. I wasn't here for anyone. I just bailed on… everyone and everything."

"For good reason," Katy replied understandingly. "Maybe I should have done the same."

Tori snorted. "I'm here now, though. And even when I'm back in New York, you and I are not going to stop talking to each other now. On that I promise."

"I'd like that."

"And I'll tell you something else. You're young. You're only thirty-seven years old, and sitting here with you, I can see your old self is in there."

"Tori, I'm not the person that can—"

"Katy, you can do this. *We're* going to do this." Tori suddenly had an inspiration, an idea.

"Do this? What do you mean? Do what?"

Tori smiled, making a declaration. "Six months from now, after you have time to get ready, you and I are taking a trip somewhere. You said you should have left. We're going to get you out of here."

"A trip? I can't get myself to leave the damn house. Apparently, I'm not the only crazy one here."

"We can do this. You and me," Tori insisted. "You and an elite, armed special agent with the FBI. What could possibly be safer than that?"

"Where?"

"Anywhere *you* want. It'll be the dead of winter so let's go somewhere warm, maybe the Caribbean. We can sit on the beach, watch the waves, have drinks with umbrellas in them, and get all tan."

"I can't afford that."

"You don't have to. I have money. I'm buying, and we're going first class *everything*. We're going to spend six months talking, texting, planning, and buying clothes for it. Then we're going to do it. What do you say?"

Katy was suddenly nervous, curling back up in a ball, paralyzed by the thought of it all. This wasn't idle talk. She could see that Tori was serious and determined to do this. "Just you and me?"

"Yeah, just you and me. What do you say?"

"I'll promise to try."

*

Katy watched from the porch as Tori pulled away, giving one last wave and a smile.

"That sounded really good," Katy's mom said, grinning at her daughter as she came back into the house. "A trip."

"You were listening?"

"How could I not, you two carrying on and cackling out there."

"Cackling?"

"Uh-huh. I can't begin to tell you how much I *loved* listening in. Tori was serious about that trip, you know."

Katy sat down in a chair and sighed. "I know."

"What are you going to do?"

"I think I want to… try to do it."

"Yeah!" Katy's mom replied brightly.

"Yeah," Katy echoed, surprised with herself. "I hope Tori knows what she's in for."

"Tori Hunter is one tough cookie, always was. She can handle anything anyone could throw at her, including you." Gail Anderson pushed herself up out of her chair and came over and kissed her daughter on the forehead. "I'm going to bed. I love you."

"Love you too, Mom."

Katy stayed up, making herself a cup of tea in the kitchen. Then she went back out and sat on the porch for a while, listened to the crickets, and watched the occasional car or truck cruise by while thinking about taking a trip. The thought of it thrilled and terrified her all at the same time. One thing she knew for certain was that if she was going to do this, she didn't want to make Tori miserable dealing with all of her issues. No, a trip like that she couldn't go on cold turkey. If she was going to do that, she had to start venturing out, at least a little.

"No time like the present," Katy muttered as she went back inside the house and took the keys for her mom's Camry off the hook in the kitchen. She pulled on a light hoodie and a Twins baseball hat and went out to the garage.

Her mother didn't know it, but a few times a year Katy would summon up the courage to take a late-night drive. She didn't want crowds or traffic, but late at night, especially on a weeknight in the early spring or late fall, the roads would be quiet. The resort visitors and cabin owners were long gone for the season, and the remaining locals were all tucked in bed. She could drive through Manchester Bay and look in wonder at all the new development and growth by herself while the streets were empty and the town was asleep. Then each time, on her way back home, she would finish the drive by stopping by the cross she'd erected for Jessie on County Road 48.

Tonight, she skipped the trip into town and instead drove straight to the cross. She pulled onto the shoulder and parked, leaving the car running, and leaned against the front fender, looking at the cross. This was why she would occasionally get up the gumption to leave the house, to make sure the cross remained in good condition and lay flowers. Given the spur-of-the-moment decision to go out, she didn't have flowers this time, but she nevertheless walked down into the ditch and knelt in front of the cross. She noticed that the ground around it had been tended to recently: the cross was perfectly erect and no weeds were around the base. She surmised that Tori had probably stopped by.

She walked back up the ditch as a car approached and slowed, the two people inside eyeing her questioningly.

Katy gave them a little wave and thumbs up. "I'm fine," she hollered.

After a moment's hesitation, the car pulled away.

She gave the cross one last look. When she turned to walk back to the driver's side door, a gust of wind kicked up and blew her hat off her head. It swiftly tumbled down the road behind the car.

Katy gave chase, trying to catch up to it as it bounded along, getting farther and farther out of her reach. Out of shape and therefore out of breath, she stopped and bent over with her hands on her knees and watched as a big wind gust blew the hat well down the road. As the hat was just about out of sight, the wind jolted it left and down into the ditch, then halfway up the hill before it stopped moving, caught up in some taller grass.

She looked back to her car, perhaps seventy yards behind her, and then ahead to the hat that was now caught up on the hill. Still breathing heavily, she walked back to the car, got in, made a quick U-turn, and then drove back east over 200 yards before pulling to a stop. She walked across the road and then climbed up the hill to recover her hat, which was still hung up in some tall grass guarding the opening of a deep, ragged gouge in the bluff. As she brushed dirt and leaves off the hat, she caught a flash of light and movement to her right. She looked up into the woods and a jagged rocky indentation that led up a steep hill and saw a bright light and then the silhouette of a body moving through it.

"What's that?" she quietly muttered to herself as she didn't recall there being any development in the area. Suddenly curious, she walked toward the light, just wanting to get a peek. The incline was steep but just gradual enough that she was able, with some effort, to climb up the twenty or so feet, only having to steady herself twice with her hands. As she reached the top, she could see a portable camping lantern sitting on the ground to the left of a pile of dirt. There was also something wrapped in plastic near the lantern, and that's when she saw it: a foot… a human foot… sticking out of the plastic.

"What the hell?" she said out loud, without thinking.

Then behind the pile she saw a man move, digging down with a shovel and then turning toward the pile to toss the dirt. He was wearing a stocking cap. She couldn't see his face.

She took a step to her left, but her foot gave way and hit a branch.

CRACK!

*

He spun around at the sound and saw her.

*

Oh my God! Oh my God! Oh my God!

He started pushing himself up out of the hole.

Katy pivoted as quickly as she could to get down the hill. She took a step forward but misjudged the slope. Her body got too far out over her feet and she flipped over forward, tumbling and rolling down the hill, pinballing off exposed rocks and downed trees. At the bottom she landed hard, back first against a large, exposed rock.

"*Ahh! Ahh! Ahh!*" she groaned as searing pain coursed through her body. She fluttered her eyes open. Through the dark fuzziness she could make out a moving blur coming down the hill.

She knew she needed to move, to stand, but her legs wouldn't respond. Katy slowly rolled onto her stomach and tried to push up with her arms. She could hear him approaching, his steps getting closer.

*

He deftly shuffled his way down the steep hill, using the shovel for balance, eyeing her as she slowly rolled her body over.

At the bottom, he set his feet and walked forward as she struggled to push herself up on all fours. She wasn't going anywhere fast.

*

Katy pushed up onto her knees as the pain that felt like she was being stabbed with a thousand knives radiated through her body. She struggled to move her left leg under her to push up.

She could hear him, feel him approaching, and looked back.

*

It was Katy Anderson.

"Doing a little detective work, are we?" he growled as he raised the shovel over his head.

"No! No! No! No!"

He brought the shovel down with all his might.

The metal hit the back of her head with a sickening thud. Katy Anderson's body collapsed. Yet she wasn't done.

She reached forward with her left hand, and pulled her right leg underneath her, trying to activate her body.

He swung again, this time a golf swing, hitting the side of her head.

Katy's body completely crumpled, spasming violently.

He took another step forward, adopted a solid stance, and raised the shovel high over his head once more.

This time to finish the job.

CHAPTER ELEVEN

"Is she lost in the house?"

Tori's alarm roused her at 6 a.m. She rolled out of bed, quickly pulled on a pair of running shorts, a sports bra, and tank, and then slipped on her running shoes. With her water bottle stuffed in her waist pack and her ear buds in place, she walked out the front of the hotel and started jogging, making her way to the path that ran along the H-4.

Her daily runs, while vital for training, also served as mental therapy. A chance to clear her head and meditate on the task at hand. This morning she had two conflicting thoughts occupying her mind: Katy and the case.

She wasn't sure what she was getting into with the whole trip idea. It had been a spur-of-the-moment inspiration.

Was it born of guilt? Without question, but guilt wasn't always the worst motivator. It often lent a certain urgency to a call to action, to make amends, and when it came to Katy, Tori felt some serious amends were in order.

Tori shook her head slightly. It might not end up the most relaxing endeavor. A trip with someone who'd been a recluse for the past ten to fifteen years, barely leaving home, afraid of the outside world, would pose certain unique... challenges. But she was up for it. *I can be pretty damn stubborn, too*, Tori thought. She would not be easily deterred by Katy's anxieties. Her friend was an only child who'd often been babied and spoiled. Tori thought Gail may still be babying her daughter, and if Katy were pushed, she might be capable of more. Tori just so happened to be someone comfortable with pushing.

Her watch beeped at the three-mile mark. She stopped, reached into her waist pack for her water bottle, and took a long squirt of water before turning south to run back to town.

As she started the three-mile leg back to town, her second thought was of the case. She reviewed in her mind everything they'd done, which was a by-the-book investigation. Get the forensics, evaluate the crime scene, and interview witnesses and acquaintances. There just didn't seem to be a connection between Lash's case and her sister's. Yet, she was home because of the article—someone wanted her here for a reason.

That someone had gone undetected for twenty years; finding him from forensics, from witnesses, from going over the old and new crime scenes was unlikely to bear fruit, and the last five days were proof of that. The one thing they thought they knew for certain was a man had come along and offered the victims a ride. It was someone Jessie and Lash likely knew, or if they didn't know him, for some reason they certainly trusted him enough to get in his car or truck.

So, who would fit a profile that the two women would trust?

"That's what we need to work on," Tori exhaled out loud as she jogged over the pedestrian bridge stretching the width of the H-4, the hotel in sight.

*

Six a.m., ten feet out from his dock, Braddock floated in the warm waters of the lake, his eyes closed and his breathing light. The tranquility of the early morning was calming. Tall and lanky, he'd played basketball through high school and had had opportunities to play regularly at the division two and three levels of college. But dreams of division one basketball danced in his head. He'd walked on at Long Island University in Brooklyn, twenty minutes from home, believing he could work his way to consistent playing time and a scholarship.

Division one basketball was a massive time commitment, even for a walk-on. You were up at 6 a.m. for lifting and conditioning. There were long, grueling practices. You ran all the laps and then you were required to attend all film sessions and go to every study hall. All of which left little time for the actual fun of being in college. After two years he'd experienced many long bus rides and played a grand total of ninety-two minutes for a middle-of-the-road team with little chance of making the Big Dance and getting its one shining moment. He loved basketball, but on a cost–benefit basis, the time commitment just wasn't worth it. After his sophomore year he hung up his high tops. He needed a new athletic release.

Two non-basketball-playing friends introduced him to the swimming pool. It was a great full-body workout that kept him lean and the beer belly at bay. Even after he joined the NYPD, he managed to find the pool two or three times per week to supplement his other workouts. Now that he lived on a lake, for at least five months of the year he was able to get in a good swimming workout daily if he wanted.

As he lay in the water looking up at the wispy clouds, he thought about the case and an issue that was nagging at him. He had been struck, in interviewing Tori's friends, by how they'd all said that the night Jessie disappeared was just a normal night. Lash's friends had said the same thing. The nights were normal, just like any other.

That meant something.

As that issue teased him, he heard his phone ring. He rolled over and swam to the dock, climbed the ladder, and found his phone on the bench under his towel. It was Cal.

"Katy Anderson's mother just called. Katy is missing."

"What?" Braddock replied, gobsmacked. "Is she lost in the house?"

"No. Katy's gone and so is the car, a ten-year-old, aqua-blue Toyota Camry. You better get over there."

Twenty minutes later, Braddock pulled up to the Anderson house. He'd not yet called Tori, wanting to get a feel for the situation first.

Gail Anderson explained that usually in the morning when she brewed some coffee and started making breakfast, Katy would get up and join her. However, when Katy hadn't stirred, Gail had gone to her daughter's room and found her bed empty. Then she'd looked out to the garage and seen that the Camry was gone.

"I left yesterday with the impression that your daughter never left the house unless it was with you."

"That's mostly true."

"Mostly?"

"Yeah, it is, but every so often she sneaks out for a drive in the middle of the night."

"I see."

"And then last night Tori came back out here."

"Tori was here?"

"Yes, she came back out to talk to Katy. She stayed, it must have been for three hours. The two of them talked about going on a trip in six months. Tori was going to take her somewhere warm this winter. So, I don't know if that motivated her to take one of those late-night trips or what, but she's… gone. She's never been gone this long."

"Does she have a cell phone?"

"Yes."

"Did she take it with her?"

"I think so."

"I assume you've tried to call?"

"Yes. I've tried again and again. No answer."

Braddock took down the details on the Camry and Katy's cell phone number, and told Ms. Anderson to stick by her phone. He called in to Cal to put out a bulletin for the car and Katy Anderson.

Then he went to find Tori.

*

Tori turned off the main running path and ran along the east side of the hotel, rounded the corner, stopped, and then walked toward the front entrance when she noticed Braddock parked under the canopy waiting for her. He was early.

"I've been thinking about the case. I think we should be looking at this another way. Who is our guy?" Tori said as she approached him. "What characteristics does he have?"

"Tori…"

"What's his profile?"

"Tor—"

"How is it Jessie and Genevieve would know or trust him?"

"Tori, hang on," Braddock replied, holding up his hand. "That all sounds good. But we have another more immediate problem."

"What's that?"

"Care to tell me what you did last night?" Braddock asked, a hint of accusation in his tone.

"What does that mean?"

"About going out to see Katy again."

"I went out to see an old friend."

"Why?"

"Because I was trying to understand what happened to her, how she ended up a recluse. I was trying to help her maybe not be a recluse."

"Well, whatever you said must have worked. Because she and the car are gone, and nobody knows where she is."

Tori's shoulders slumped as she croaked out a guttural, "Oh God."

CHAPTER TWELVE

"But how does she go from being here to being gone?"

Braddock and Tori went back out to the Anderson house and put Gail through the paces. Why, in the middle of the night, did someone who almost never left the house sneak out with the car? How often did she go for these late-night drives? Did she ever leave for days at a time? Was there anyone she regularly talked to? Was it possible Katy led a secret life that Gail didn't know about? Was Katy the recluse just an act?

Gail said, "No, but… but then again, I don't know what she might have been doing online."

Braddock called for a crime scene investigator to go through Katy's computer. The investigator found little. "Will, her computer is really old and she's no latent computer genius. Her email is filled mostly with spam, and I don't think she ever downloaded virus protection. Emails from people of any recent vintage, which I'd define as the last three to four years, are limited to those for the remote data entry work she does for a couple of different companies."

"What about Internet history?" Tori asked.

"Katy Anderson likes to shop online, although she doesn't buy much, which is reflective of her meager assets. Her reading interests appear to be entertainment, pop culture, and baseball related. She reads pretty much anything about the Twins. She binge-watches a lot of television shows, working her way through the Netflix library. For what it's worth, she likes watching and re-watching *Breaking Bad* and *The West Wing*. But contact with others?" The tech shook her head. "I see no evidence of that. She doesn't have a Facebook page. She isn't on Twitter or Snapchat. I see no entry into chat rooms, either on her computer or her cell phone, both of which are older models."

"In other words, her computer and cell history fit with that of someone who is a recluse," Braddock remarked dejectedly.

"Correct. She reads about—and I think *is* interested in—the outside world, but she has had little actual engagement with it."

Braddock and Tori walked down the front steps and out to his Tahoe. He took one look at her, the anxious twitchy mannerisms, the demoralized eyes, and he sensed Tori was teetering on the edge.

He stepped away from her, created some space for himself, and called in to Cal. There had been no sightings or even signs of Katy Anderson or the missing aqua-blue Camry. Bulletins had been issued throughout the state and all nearby jurisdictions were on alert and on the lookout.

"Did she just run off?" Cal asked. "Was Tori returning and all that is going on, the memories, too much for Katy? Did she just run away from it all? It wouldn't surprise anyone if she did."

"I don't know," Braddock replied quietly, feeling suddenly defeated in his own right. "Let's test that theory. Check with the bus company, see if maybe she jumped on one to get out of town. I suppose airlines, too. Now," he shook his head and sighed, "Cal, that just doesn't compute with what Tori and Gail Anderson have told me about Katy's mood last night, but... who knows?"

"I'll see to it."

Braddock hung up and turned to find a pensive Tori eyeing him. He shook his head as he strolled back over to her.

"Where do we even start?" Tori muttered, almost panicked. "Tell me, where do we even start looking for her?"

Braddock simply stated, "I don't know."

For the second time in a week he was faced with a woman's disappearance, and this time he had even less to go on. "What the hell is going on around here?"

*

Sleep wouldn't come. After a kill, he always slept. The exhilaration, the expended energy of it, the sexual release always leading to a long, exhausted, restful sleep.

Not this time.

Every time he seemed to be drifting off, Katy Anderson popped back into his mind.

He'd tried reading but couldn't focus on the words in the book or on the stack of papers for work. A long, late-night walk had done nothing to ease his whirring mind. Three stiff drinks had failed to take the edge off. The memory of Katy Anderson, the thought of her, kept coming back over and over and over again.

He'd had no choice. She'd come out of nowhere.

Katy Anderson was not the type he pursued. Katy was benign, someone he would have hardly given a second thought to if he'd seen her on the street—heck, if she was *ever* seen on the street. She was the single last person he'd have ever expected to see anywhere, let alone fifty feet away in the middle of the night while he was digging a hole. Yet there she'd been on the edge of the ridge, staring right up at him as he'd thrown a shovelful of dirt, Genevieve Lash's plastic-wrapped body to the side.

Letting Katy go had not been an option.

After he'd hit her on the head with the shovel the third time, her body had stopped moving, other than the light, twitchy spasms as the last bit of life drained from her.

That's when he asked himself the question: *Where had she come from?*

He quickly shuffled his way down the hill to the edge of the treeline and saw her car parked down on the far shoulder of the road. It was still running. He couldn't leave it there. Taking a careful look both directions for oncoming vehicles, he ran down the hill and across the road. He got into the car, circled his way around and didn't pass any other vehicles as he drove the car back to the hole he was digging for Lash, parking it next to his own SUV. He then went back down the hill, picked up Katy Anderson's dead body, heaved her over his shoulder and hauled her back up the hill.

Back at the hole, he pushed Genevieve's wrapped body into the pit and begun refilling it, sweating profusely as he frantically shoveled the dirt. By the time he'd finished, it was 3:40 a.m.

He looked at Anderson's body and then her car. Given all that had happened recently, the search for her would be intense. He needed to dispose of the body and the car.

Driving back to his house with his own SUV, he retrieved his ten-speed racing bike and riding clothes and then drove back to the gravesite. He rolled Katy's body up in plastic and stuffed it in the trunk of the Camry and then jammed the bike into the backseat. The drive was an hour north to an isolated piece of property east of Leech Lake. He drove the car down a tight winding road into the woods and reached the spot he was looking for at the end of the narrow path. He backed the car into a tight space deep in the thick woods. At this time of year, with the thick foliage, the car wouldn't be visible from the air. It could only be found if someone drove all the way back in along the road and to the car, it was tucked in so deep. It would be safe for now.

He pedaled his bike the fifty-six-mile trek back down to Manchester Bay, cycling into town just after the morning rush. He'd arrived at work an hour later than normal. Nobody had been the wiser.

*

The following morning, Tori couldn't bring herself to go for her run. Just showering and then dressing for the day was proving to be a chore as she lay on her bed, staring at the ceiling, wrapped in her wet towel.

Her cell phone buzzed. It was Braddock. "I'm on my way in now. Get over to the government center. We might have a break."

"Did we find Katy? Her car? What?"

"It's nothing *that* good, but it might be a start."

A local man and his girlfriend had come forward. They'd seen Katy Anderson around 1 a.m., a few hours after Tori had left Katy's house, along the side of County Road 48, just a few miles north of town.

"That's the general location of where Jessie Hunter's car was found," Braddock remarked.

"That's the place," the man, whose name was Doug, confirmed. "That's where she was, right by that white cross."

"And what was she doing?"

"I don't know. She was walking back up from the ditch where the cross is, so I can only assume she was paying her respects."

"And you didn't stop and see if she needed help or ask if she was okay?" Tori asked, dumbfounded.

"We slowed down, gave her a chance to wave us down."

"Well gee, I'd hope so," Tori snapped. "A woman *alone* on the side of the road in the middle of the night. Slowing down seems like the most minimal of things you could possibly do."

"Hey, hold on," he replied defensively. "We slowed down. We wondered if she was in trouble. But her car was running. I saw the exhaust from the tailpipe, the lights were on, she gave us a little friendly wave, a thumbs up, and yelled, 'I'm fine,' as we slowed down. She was not in any distress. What are we supposed to do?"

"Plus, she's kind of crazy," the other witness, Donna said.

"Hold on a second… " Tori started, her voice and anger rising.

Braddock jumped in, "So you two know she's probably a vulnerable person, and still you don't stop and roll down the window to at least check on her?"

"I feel like we did," Doug said. "She looked just fine. She smiled at us."

"But you didn't stop. I mean, I just can't believe you didn't stop and talk to her?" Tori growled, now on the edge of her chair. "What's the matter with you?"

Braddock sensed his partner was about ready to blow. He'd seen it coming for a day, the stress, the anguish and now the guilt. He turned in his chair and tilted his head for her to leave the interview room. Tori didn't move. "It's okay," he whispered, patting her on the arm and the looking her in the eye. "I got this one."

After a moment Tori let out a defeated sigh and reluctantly left the room.

"Geez, what's her problem?" Donna griped.

Braddock snapped his gaze back to the woman. "Agent Hunter's problem is that twenty years ago her sister was abducted at the same spot on that road."

"You mean she's…" Doug started.

"Yeah," Braddock replied curtly. "Add to that a vulnerable woman, who is also her good friend, was left alone out on that road in the middle of the night and you didn't even stop to speak to her?" Braddock growled, his voice also rising before he caught himself, stopping for a moment to corral his composure. "I think all Agent Hunter was asking of her fellow man was for you to have made sure her friend got into her car and was able to pull away. Particularly given the history of that location. Especially given that Genevieve Lash disappeared from a dark country road just like that less than a week ago. Right now, people need to be looking out for each other and… you know, you two could have done more here."

The two of them sat in their chairs, navel-gazing, fully chastised. "You're right, I guess we should have," Doug whispered after a minute. "But, Detective, it was shocking to see her out. It took me a few seconds to recognize her. You know, Crazy Katy."

"How do you even know her?"

"I was three years behind her in school. Donna, too. So, we don't know her, but we know *of* her, kind of like all the locals around here because…"

"She's Crazy Katy."

"Yeah. I thought it was weird she was out at that time of night. But, Detective, I know you're looking at me, at us, like we're these awful people, but I swear to you she seemed totally okay."

"And you didn't see anyone else there?" Braddock asked.

"No," Doug and Donna replied in unison. Doug added, "She was totally alone."

Braddock excused Doug and Donna, and as he watched them walk down the hall, he looked to Steak and murmured, "Look into them."

"Will, they came forward voluntarily," Steak replied.

"I know, but a day later. Did they need twenty-four hours to get their story straight?" He shook his head. "We can't afford to overlook anything. See if there is any reason to question their word."

Braddock walked back into his office to find Tori looking out the window with a vacant stare.

"Sorry," she offered.

"I understand how you feel. I'm getting really, really, tired of searching for missing women," Braddock remarked with an exhale. "I know this is tearing you up inside, but you have to keep your shit together here. If you can't, you can't work it and you know that, right?"

Tori simply nodded.

"Let's go."

"Where?" Tori asked.

"Back out to County Road 48."

They met a forensic team at the cross, but after four hours of poking around the potential crime scene, investigators found no evidence of anything having happened there.

"It's been at least thirty hours, Will," the lead crime scene investigator stated. "And we had a lengthy thunderstorm roll through last night. Even if there was something here, that storm would have washed it away."

"She was seen here," Braddock muttered, "but that's it."

"She was visiting the cross," Tori speculated. "But how does she go from being here to being gone?"

*

He watched as Hunter and Braddock walked around the cross and the shoulder of the road again. Interestingly, they weren't examining the area of the road where he'd found Katy's car, which was another two hundred yards to the east. He dropped the binoculars from his eyes, hiding back in the trees.

How did they even know to search this area? He'd seen nobody when he'd driven the car away. Perhaps it was related to why Katy Anderson had climbed the crevice in the first place.

Katy Anderson, killing her, the disposal of her body and car, made him think long and hard about Tori Hunter. He'd drawn her home to play the game, but that didn't account for Katy. Had she known something? Was that why she'd been there, staring up at him? And if she had known something, did she tell Tori?

He didn't know the answers to any of those questions. What he did know was that Katy had once been Tori's best friend. Her disappearance would only serve to motivate Tori Hunter more.

It changed the calculus.

The investigation would require close monitoring. He had some out-of-town business to attend to, but when he returned, some decisions would need to be made.

CHAPTER THIRTEEN

"I've applied my detecting skills and have observed that it's written all over your face."

"It's been three days," Tori muttered late on Friday afternoon, taking a sip from a lukewarm Diet Coke, sitting on the weathered couch in Cal Lund's office.

Braddock sat in a guest chair, perched forward with his elbows on his knees, while Steak and Eggleston both leaned against the wall behind him.

"What did I do, going out to see her that night?" Tori whispered, despondently. "What did I do?"

"You just went over and saw a friend," Cal counseled softly. "And tried to help her."

"How is what I did helpful? If I hadn't gone over there, she wouldn't have left that house. She'd be alive."

"Was she really alive, living like she was?" Braddock asked evenly, leaning back in his chair. "As a shut-in, never going out, and having everyone think you're nuts. Is that being alive? Is that living?"

"What are you saying?" Tori's eyes narrowed. "What are you trying to say?"

"Only that maybe seeing you, talking to you, observing what you're doing with your life, and hearing you talk about taking a trip brought her to life. She went out to live. She wanted to be able to take that trip."

"Then where the hell is she?" Tori replied angrily, not accepting that anything she'd done was at all helpful or worthwhile. "Where is her car? Where is she? What happened to her?"

Nobody had any answers.

"No. No, no, no." She shook her head angrily. "I went over and stirred up all those bad memories, such that she went out to that damn cross, and just like my sister, now she's gone, too."

"Not *entirely* like Jessie," Cal noted.

"This time the car is missing, too," Braddock added. "Is that an important fact? Who knows? It might be."

"What's important is that there's someone out there making women disappear," Tori declared.

"The question is," Braddock stated, "does he live here or is he just passing through?"

"He's here," Tori assured. "Why else send me the news clipping? Why else take Lash on the twentieth anniversary? Why make Katy disappear?"

"Is Katy's disappearance related to it? It could be unrelated."

Tori looked at Braddock severely. "You can't *possibly* think they're unrelated," she stated derisively.

Braddock shot a look back at her and had a ready retort, but then quickly thought better of it. She was torn up inside and was lashing out, spoiling for a fight, ready for one if given even the slightest opportunity.

"I hope he's passing through," Cal muttered under his breath after an awkward silence.

"He's a local," Tori answered quickly, daring anyone in the suddenly quiet office to challenge her.

"You're probably right," Cal answered calmly after a moment, having picked up on Braddock's wise lack of reaction and not taking the bait.

Braddock was in no mood nor did he any longer possess the energy to continue to discuss, let alone argue, the point. Between Lash's disappearance and now Katy's, he'd been going nearly nonstop for a week. As had Steak and Eggleston, who were both looking weary, and to boot, he thought it was a seventy–thirty chance Tori was right. All the disappearances—Jessie, Genevieve, and Katy—were connected, and he thought it was ninety–ten that the killer was in their midst. "Let's just say, Special Agent Hunter, that I agree with most of what you're saying," he said, and then exhaled while closing his eyes. "But at the moment we're kind of stuck."

"It's not kind of; it's *we are* stuck. We have to get unstuck," she pressed.

Braddock snorted. "Yeah, we do, but it isn't going to happen right this minute. We need to take a break."

"Excuse me?"

"I think what Will is saying is that it's time for a barbecue," Cal suggested.

"A barb-a-what?" Tori asked, incredulous. "You can't be serious."

"For our sanity, we need a night away from the case," Braddock declared. "I'm firing up the grill and cooking up some steaks. It's going to be a beautiful night. Bring your spouses, something easy to share, and your swimsuits. If we have time, maybe we can take the boat out."

"Take the boat out? Steaks? Barbecue? How can you have a party at a time like this?" Tori exclaimed, flabbergasted. "How can you just… walk away from this?"

"One, nobody is walking away from anything. Two, it's not a party, it's a mental break with a good meal," Braddock answered, grabbing his Tahoe keys and then writing his address on a slip of paper. "And three, you said it yourself, we're stuck. We don't have a good lead to pursue right now, so grinding away another night isn't going to do any good. The case isn't going anywhere. It will be here in the morning."

"But, but…"

Will handed her the slip of paper. "Here's my address. Come or don't come. It's entirely up to you, but we're—" Braddock waved to the others "—going to get out of here for a night."

On his way home Braddock stopped at the local meat market and bought thick ribeye steaks. An hour later, he and his son Quinn talked and relaxed on the deck, letting the grill heat up. Braddock lamented the fact that a case like this took him away from his ever-growing and maturing eleven-year-old son. Quinn would be tall like his father yet had the soft facial features and light wavy brown hair of his mother. Thankfully, the boy's grandparents lived a half-mile down the road, and five cousins, two of whom were his exact same age and grade, lived not much farther away than that. The three of them were inseparable, whether it was hanging out, going to school, or playing baseball or hockey. Braddock felt blessed that the grandparents, the aunts and uncles, the cousins all looked after his son at times like this.

Steak and his wife Grace arrived first, followed shortly by Cal and his wife Lucy, and then Sheryl Eggleston and her husband Bruce. They all unwound and drank a few beers on Braddock's deck overlooking the calm waters of the bay. While Braddock worked the grill, they asked Quinn about his baseball season and his upcoming trip to Michigan with his grandparents.

"How long will you be gone?" Bruce Eggleston asked.

Quinn looked to his dad. "It's three weeks, right, Dad?"

"That's right," Braddock replied as he turned over one of the steaks to inspect the char, and then explained, "It's the one time of the year he gets to see his other set of cousins. It'll be nonstop time in the lake, fishing, tubing, surfing, and go-karting. He'll miss me for all of five minutes."

"Maybe ten," Quinn replied with an impish grin, and then looked past his father and nodded his head.

Braddock turned around just as Tori was climbing the deck steps.

"You said steaks, right?" she asked, stepping onto the deck, holding up two bottles of wine and handing one to Braddock. "I brought red."

"And *good* red," Braddock assessed with an approving nod. "I'm glad you came."

"Thank you for the invitation."

Tori brought the wine inside and put it on the kitchen's center island. She took a quick look around Braddock's lake home. It was a warmly furnished, two-story log A-frame with a lofted second level and a walkout basement that sat on a picturesque, treed lot on the southwest side of the lake, overlooking what she recalled was Murphy Bay. "It's… beautiful out here," she remarked as she stepped back out onto the deck. "This is really nice, Detective Braddock."

"Thank you," he replied. "We'll save the wine for dinner. In the meantime, can I offer you a cold beer?"

"Yes, please."

A half-hour later the steaks were prepared, and everyone made up a plate, sat around the long deck table under the expansive umbrella, and dined. The case was not mentioned once as everyone relaxed and loosened up, even Tori, who sat next to Lucy Lund, and they started going down memory lane. After the plates were cleared and everyone had a fresh beer or glass of wine and a seat on the deck, Steak gazed out to the lake and remarked, "The water *is* absolute glass, not a ripple."

Braddock took the hint. "Who's up for a ski?"

Steak, Eggleston, and their spouses instantly agreed. The Lunds were eager to get in the boat and watch.

"Tori, do you want to ski?" Braddock asked. He could see the hesitation in her eyes. "Come on," he goaded. "You don't see nights like this in New York City, *I know*."

"I haven't waterskied in twenty years. I doubt I can even get up."

"One, you're an athlete, you'll get up. Two, use two skis," Braddock answered. "*Come on*, Tori, live a little," he goaded good-naturedly before lowering his voice. "And trust me, you need to live a little."

"But… I didn't bring a swimsuit," she replied, this time looking curiously out to the placid water.

Braddock grinned broadly. He'd won. "Come with me," he replied, waving for Tori to follow him. He led her down into the basement, where a closet next to the guest bathroom held two shelves full of men's and women's swimsuits. "I guarantee you there's a one-piece in there that will fit you."

Forty minutes later, Tori looked nervously out to the lake as a soaking-wet Braddock lifted himself up onto the back of the boat and unbuckled his lifejacket, having just finished his ski run. Everyone else had taken their turn.

"Only one person left," he noted as he dried himself off before sitting down behind the wheel. He took a sip of his beer and looked over to a pensive Tori with a teasing grin. "It's the moment of truth, Special Agent Hunter. Let's see what you've got."

"This could be ugly," Tori replied as she stood up, tugging on the bottom of the slightly loose-fitting, white, one-piece suit she was wearing. She pulled on a dry life jacket, stepped onto the back deck of the boat, and jumped feet first into the lake.

The splash, the smell, and the feel of the warm water transported her back in time. She'd forgotten how refreshing midsummer-lake water could feel. Braddock expertly tossed her the two waterskis. Quickly, she slipped her feet into the boots before grabbing the ski rope handle floating next to her. She leaned back in the water with her ski tips straight up and the rope strung between them. Braddock straightened the boat out, easing the rope tight and dragging her lightly, waiting for her to call out.

You did this for years as a kid, and you were good at it, Tori told herself. "Here goes nothing," she muttered before yelling, "Hit it!"

Braddock gunned the in-board engine and she popped right up. He took her on a long, straight run paralleling the south shoreline of the bay. He looked back and circled his arm in the air, the signal he was going to turn around. Surprising even herself, before he started the turn, Tori pulled her foot out of the left ski and slipped it into the back boot of the right ski. She could hear the whistles and cheers.

She took a long slalom run while everyone in the boat clapped and yelled encouragement. As the boat sliced through the flat surface, she became more and more aggressive with her turns, leaning harder and digging in more each time, even sneaking a peek back to see the rooster tail she was shooting out of the water.

And then it happened.

She cut across and jumped the far wake. But as she landed, her weight shifted too far forward. The ski's front tip suddenly submerged, propelling her body forward, yanking her feet out of the boots. With the rope handle flying away, she violently cartwheeled twice along the surface before slamming face down into the water.

"*Ohh*," she groaned as she rolled onto her back, "wipeout." She smiled and floated a while, letting the wonderful stinging feeling of a colossal yard-sale wipeout slowly recede from her body while Braddock drove back to retrieve the skis.

After docking the boat, Braddock started a fire in the pit down by the lake while everyone else took turns going inside to dry off and change. Tori was the last to go inside, taking a lengthy shower in the spare bathroom to wash the lake water off. Once changed, she came back out to find only Braddock at the roaring fire, sipping from a glass of wine.

"Where did everyone go?"

"Home," Braddock answered, looking up from the chair. "They were all tired."

"I see."

"You know, you brought a very nice bottle of wine," he complimented. "Can I pour you one and help soothe the sting of that wipeout?"

"Sure," Tori replied, sitting down in the big green Adirondack chair next to Braddock while he poured her a glass. "And by the way, that wipeout felt so awesome."

"You skied well there, too. Those were some pretty deep cuts."

"I grew up on this lake; I waterskied all the time. I guess it was like riding a bike," she replied, taking a drink of her wine before turning to him. "I still can't believe you had a swimsuit that fit me. And it was a Hayes Limited—a *really* nice swimsuit."

"It was Meghan's."

"Who's Meghan?"

"My late wife."

"Oh, I'm so sorry, I didn't…"

"It's okay, Tori," Braddock replied softly. "It's okay. She died six years ago. Brain tumor, glioblastoma. That was one of her swimsuits—she actually designed it."

Tori did a double take. "Wait, wait a minute. Meghan. Meghan Hayes? Meghan Hayes was your wife?"

"You knew Meghan?" Braddock asked, eyebrows raised.

"Not really. She was four years older than me, but I sure knew who she was and followed her career. In case you haven't noticed, I kind of like clothes. Nice clothes."

"That has not escaped my attention."

"And now I understand how you recognize the brands. I loved her designs and not just because she was from Manchester Bay. She did pretty well for herself."

"She was really starting to when she died."

"How'd you end up back here?"

"I didn't have any family, really—my parents were long gone. I'm an only child, and raising a five-year-old son as a single parent in New York City as a police detective, with the hours and all that… It wasn't an easy thing."

"I don't imagine it was."

"Meghan's family—her parents, her brother, and one of her sisters—is here. Quinn's cousins are here, and I'd always loved Manchester Bay, and especially the lake, when we'd visit in the summer. Roger, Meghan's dad, said he was good friends with Cal. I think Roger was pretty motivated to have Quinn come live here."

"And you, too."

"Well, we're a package deal," Braddock answered with a wry smile. "Anyway, Cal called a week later. We talked for a couple of hours. Two days later he offered me a job. The rest, as they say, is history."

"How did you meet Meghan?"

"Oh, that's a great story."

"Let's hear it," Tori urged as she sipped her wine.

"Well, there was this party in Manhattan on the Upper East Side. A college buddy of mine, who could talk his way into or out of anything, got us into a shindig in this swanky high-rise. It was hilarious—the minute we walked in, everyone's eyes in there said, 'Who let the riff-raff in?'"

Tori laughed.

"We were working-class college kids from Long Island, and at this party there were a lot of pretentious, moneyed, trust fund types hanging around."

"So, what did you do?"

"What I *always* did. I found the beer—or, in this case, the bar. There was a keg, a little to my surprise, and to my even greater astonishment nobody was charging."

"I don't imagine on the Upper East Side someone's collecting five bucks for a glass."

"Uh no," Braddock replied with a grin. "Anyway, I hung out there because sooner or later everyone comes for a beer and that's how you meet people at a party."

"You mean girls."

"Is there any other reason to go to a party?" Braddock answered, toasting Tori's glass. "And sure enough, this pretty little brunette with big beautiful brown eyes strolled up, smiled, and asked for a refill on her beer."

"Meghan."

Braddock nodded. "Meghan. I filled her glass and we just started talking. Here I was, this tall, goofball ex-basketball player at LIU, essentially majoring in beer drinking, and she was this pretty, stylish fashionista studying at the Parsons School of Design. Two more opposite people you could not find."

"Yet you connected."

"I don't know what it was, but we talked on and off for like two or three hours. So, as the end of the night approached, I started calculating my odds with her."

"Men fear rejection."

"*Everyone* fears rejection. But yeah, that runs through your head. And it wasn't like we were at some LIU party where, if I had doubts, I knew I'd see the girl on campus and could let it play out. There, in that moment, I had to ask or I'd never see her again. I said to myself, what was the worst thing that could happen? So, I asked her out."

"And she said yes."

Braddock smiled. "Yup, she said yes."

"Opposites attract."

"We sure proved that theory. We got married three years later, the New York City cop and the fashion designer. It could have been a sitcom. It often was. We laughed a lot. We didn't have a long run, but man," Braddock wistfully shook his head, "we sure had a good one, and we had ourselves a boy. I couldn't have asked for more."

Tori smiled. "Meghan Hayes. That was a good catch, Will, a very good catch."

"She sure was," Braddock agreed as he took a sip of his wine. "How about you, ever married?"

"No. Not even close."

"Boyfriend?"

"No," she answered with a quick headshake.

"Sorry," Braddock said sheepishly, "it's really none of my business."

"Oh, it's okay. Maybe I just haven't met my fashion designer at a keg party yet."

"Hah!" Braddock laughed out loud. Then, on a dime, he turned serious. "Now, look, I know you stayed because you want to discuss the case."

"I never said that."

"*Please*, I'm a detective. I've applied my detecting skills and have observed that it's written all over your face. So, let's just dispense with the bullshit and talk a little shop. Who is our killer?"

Finally, Tori thought, they were going to go in a direction *she* wanted to go. "We need a profile," Tori answered. "But I think at a minimum we're talking about…"

They talked for an hour. After a while, Braddock typed notes of their discussion into his phone. They assumed they were dealing with a male and, given the demographics of this part of the state, most likely Caucasian. If it was the same man, in a twenty-year period he must have been someone who both Jessie Hunter and Genevieve Lash would have known and at least trusted enough to perhaps get into a car with. "It has to be someone who's lived here for longer than twenty years," Tori suggested. "Someone at least forty—or maybe a few years younger—and sixty to sixty-five."

"We can assemble a list of people but there's one very problematic thing to think about."

"Summer."

"Exactly. This is another reason why I'd hoped to get onto our guy by investigating Lash and her background. Manchester Bay is smack dab in the middle of vacation land. Think about it, when you grew up here the town was less than half the size it is now. Plus, both disappearances happened in the summer when, as you know, the population up here swells exponentially with cabin dwellers and vacationers. And we're not just talking Manchester Bay. The other towns in the county, like Holmestrand, Crosslake, Pequot Lakes, Pine River, Crosby, Deerwood, and so on, have all grown, although not necessarily to the same degree. The lakes are now all fully developed with cabins, if not homes. Plus, I'm just talking Shepard County. We should think about Cass, Aitkin, Hubbard, Morrison, Itasca, and Lake Counties at a minimum if we're thinking our killer is in some way local."

Tori nodded. "I see the issue, especially if we're thinking male, most likely white, age late thirties to perhaps sixty to sixty-five years of age. That could describe about eighty percent of the men in northern Minnesota."

"That's right. The suspect pool is massive. We'll need to find a way to whittle that down."

"That's why we need another potential data point."

"Such as?" Braddock asked.

"Other victims."

Braddock sighed and closed his eyes. "I was really afraid you were going to say that."

"I don't think our guy took Jessie and then waited another twenty years to take Genevieve Lash," Tori added. "I think there is a good chance he was operating in between."

"I don't think it was here if he was," Braddock replied.

"No," Tori answered in agreement. "I think it would be beyond here, perhaps way beyond here."

"So, we're looking for more victims. *Great*," Braddock groaned.

"I just think it's possible. And I have someone who can help us with that search."

"FBI?"

"I don't have a lot of close friends, Will. But the ones I do have are Bureau and loyal. I have someone in mind. I can have her do some research on other potential victims to see if there are any similar ones. Jessie and Lash give us a workable victim profile. Attractive, younger women, an age range of seventeen to twenty-seven, and abducted or missing over the past twenty years. At least for now we limit the search to the Midwest and see what turns up."

"You know, he could have started before the disappearance of your sister."

"I doubt it," Tori answered.

"Why?"

"That newspaper article. That's what I keep coming back to. Why make the point of delivering that to me after all these years?" Tori asked rhetorically. "Because he was making a point. It all started with my sister."

"And it ends with you?" Braddock finished ominously. "I sure don't like the sound of that."

"I'm touched," Tori replied lightly, looking over to Braddock.

Braddock turned in his chair to face her. "Don't be flippant. If the goal was to draw you close, well, here you are. And if he's good enough to have gotten your sister, Lash, Katy, and maybe a few others… then he can get the drop on you."

"I'm not like the others. I carry a gun."

"Maybe," Braddock replied. "But he has one very big advantage on you."

"What's that?"

"He knows you, but you don't know him. You may not see him coming," Braddock warned.

Tori peered over to Braddock and thought, *Sometimes people surprise you.*

Braddock must have caught the expression on her face. "What?"

"I kind of thought you might be throwing in the towel today."

"Oh, hell no," Braddock answered quickly, dismissively shaking his head. "No way. I just needed a night off to relax and get away from it. I try not to get obsessed by a case at work. It's a job. To be good at it requires a certain… detachment. I leave it at the office and I don't bring it home to Quinn. That's my rule."

"I'm not wired the same. I can't let it go, and especially…"

"This one. You need closure, that I understand."

Tori closed her eyes for a moment. "I'm afraid of what happens if I don't get closure," she answered darkly. "For twenty years, I've used every trick in the book to distract my mind from reliving what happened to Jessie, from thinking about the disappearance and what it did to my father. I've suppressed it with work, with exercise, with shopping, the distractions of New York City, and anything else to not think about it. But now? I get that article, so now I'm here. If we don't solve this thing, I worry if I'll ever be able to let it go, to ever be at peace."

"It defines you."

Tori nodded. "Not only that, it drives me, it compels me to do whatever I can to prevent other families from having to experience what I did. And here I am, back in Manchester Bay, chasing it. I'm actually investigating it, here where it all happened and—" her voice went soft "—flailing away at it."

Braddock sat back in his chair for a quiet moment. "When it came to the light bulb, Thomas Edison said, 'I haven't failed. I've just found ten thousand ways that won't work.'"

"Meaning?"

"You may think you're flailing, but you're not. We've just found the ways that don't work. But we're not done trying yet. Just now we've come up with a couple of more ways to dig into this."

"My God, you sound almost optimistic," Tori stated approvingly.

"This case is *far* from over," Braddock answered, and then his mood darkened. "And someone sent you that newspaper article like they're playing some game. Well, I'm one competitive motherfucker and I don't like to lose."

"Me neither."

"Then the guy is in for one hell of a fight, Tori."

"Yeah, he is."

Tori's phone rang. She looked down at the screen. "Excuse me, I need to take this." She stood up and walked away from Braddock, down the shoreline for some privacy, and answered the call from Special Agent in Charge Richard Graff. "Hello, sir."

"I need you in Des Moines as soon as possible."

"Sir? Des Moines?"

"A two-year-old was kidnapped right out of her home in West Des Moines. The Omaha office is on the scene. A call was made for an agent from the CARD team and you're already out there."

"But, sir, my case here…"

"Tori, you have no case there. You were never assigned to that case, and from my discussions with Sheriff Lund a half-hour ago, my understanding is the case is pretty much dead in the water."

"Sir, it's not dead. In fact, we—"

"Special Agent Hunter, this isn't a topic that is up for debate. I've just assigned you to a case. There is a missing two-year-old girl and the clock is ticking. You will proceed with great haste to West Des Moines. I expect you there first thing in the morning. Do I make myself clear?"

Tori sighed. "Yes, sir."

*

Joanie had stirred the hunger in him as he observed her these past weeks.

She was educated but adventurous and flirty. Joanie was shorter, just a shade over five feet tall, with rosy pale cheeks and a body full of inviting curves. She walked with a snappy sway of her hips and featured round breasts that she displayed in her clothing choices, albeit in an understated, South Dakotan kind of way. There wasn't a lot of cleavage, but her tight tops left little to the imagination. The skirts weren't short, but they hugged her hips quite nicely. All of that raised that urge inside of him, that hunger and need.

The parking lot was empty, and his car was parked next to hers.

*

"Oh my God! Are you kidding me?" Joanie Wells exclaimed angrily. Her new Jetta sported a deep and long gashing scratch running the entire driver's side of her car.

"What happened?" he asked, approaching quickly. "Is everything okay?"

Joanie turned. "Oh, hey. Would you look at what someone did to my car," she replied, and turned her back to him. "Someone keyed—"

*

He jabbed the stun gun into her left side and she immediately went down to the ground.

He pulled a leather sap out of his pocket and struck her twice at the base of her skull, further disabling her.

With his key fob, he popped open the trunk of his car then quickly picked her up and stuffed her inside. Joanie stirred and moaned. He jabbed her with the stun gun again, holding it for an extra second or two. Next, he bound first her wrists and then her ankles with white plastic handcuffs, cinching them both tight. Finally, he ripped off a piece of gray duct tape and put it over her mouth.

The whole takedown took less than a minute before he drove away.

He hauled her over his shoulder and down the steps into the bunker, then dropped her onto the stool, letting her sit facing him.

He ripped the tape away from her mouth.

"What are you doing to me—"

He slapped her with the back of his hand, stunning her, before he reached for the collar on her blouse and yanked it down, ripping it open. Next, he reached for a long knife. He stepped to her, slipped the tip of the knife between her two breasts, and cut open her bra.

"Oh my God!" she wailed. "Someone help me! Somebody please help me!"

He turned her around and pushed her down onto the desk. Leaning down, he loosened the nylon cuffs around her ankles just a bit, allowing her legs to separate, before he ripped down her skirt and underwear and cut them away.

"No! Please no!"

He finished dressing, zipping up his jeans and then pulling on his T-shirt.

Joanie was sitting on the stool, mostly naked, only her ripped blouse still hanging in tatters on her body. Her skirt, underwear, and bra all lay on the floor in front of her. Her hands were still bound behind her, and her ankles were re-cinched tight now that he'd finished ravaging her.

As if the past few hours hadn't been bad enough, Joanie now clearly deduced what her immediate future held. Yet that didn't stop the pleading. "Please, just please let me go," she begged. "You got what you wanted. I won't say a word to anyone, I promise."

"Come now, Joanie, you must certainly understand what comes next," he said, eyeing her intently, taking a step toward her.

"Why are you doing this to me?" Joanie wailed. "Someone help me! Please, somebody help me!"

He laughed wickedly before taking the long and jagged knife back out of its sheath, which he then tossed casually away. "Joanie, nobody can hear you here. *Nobody.*"

"Stay away from me! Stay away! No! No! *Nooooooo!*"

CHAPTER FOURTEEN

"Tragedy rarely is."

Tori's last words to Braddock were, "Whatever you do, don't stop. I will be back." She thought back to those words as she peered out the plane window, sailing over the vast, green-hued checkerboard of northern Iowa's farm fields. With a heavy sigh she turned her gaze back to her laptop. It was time to focus on the task at hand.

Two-year-old Ava Taylor had been kidnapped out of her West Des Moines home yesterday afternoon. Ava's mom, Erica, had put Ava down for a nap around 2 p.m. in her Pack 'n Play crib and then lain down herself for a nap in the upstairs master bedroom. When Erica had awoken at four, she'd gone down into the living room and found Eva was gone. Erica had reported she hadn't heard a thing while napping. The father, Jake Taylor, had been out of town on a business trip.

In the file, there were pictures of the house, an upscale, executive, beige stucco, two-story home, on a heavily treed lot in a neighborhood of similar-sized houses. Interior photos were included, centered on the living room and the portable crib. There were no signs of forced entry, yet the mother indicated that the doors *had* been locked. An initial canvass of the other homes in the neighborhood failed to turn up anything useful, as most homes contained two-income families, including the house directly to the south. To the north, a neighbor had been home, but he'd been working in his home office on the opposite side of the house and hadn't seen or heard anything.

The early theory of the investigators on scene was that the abductor or abductors approached the house from the rear, making their way through the dense woods behind the house. A brief call from the kidnappers stating they had Ava and that they would be in touch had triggered FBI involvement, and ultimately the call for Tori. That follow-up call had not yet been received.

The West Des Moines Police and Iowa Department of Public Safety were on the scene and conducting the investigation on the ground. Agents from the Omaha field office of the FBI were also on scene, and that was who Tori was to liaise with.

After landing, she walked briskly through the concourse toward baggage claim. As she did, she placed a call to her good friend Tracy Sheets, a research genius in the New York field office.

"How's Des Moines?" Tracy asked cheerily. Tracy was one of those people who was always upbeat, something Tori often wasn't but deep down inside really wished she could be.

"I'm about to find out. How's your workload?"

"The usual," Tracy answered, knowing that question always led to a put-whatever-you're-doing-aside request. "What do you need?"

"It's not going to be about Des Moines," Tori answered with a grunt as she lifted her travel bag from the luggage carousel.

"Ah, I see. Would this have anything at all to do with my jurisdiction here in the New York field office?"

"Umm, probably not," Tori answered as she started weaving her way through the crowd to the sliding doors out of the terminal. "This falls more in the seriously solid favor for a friend category."

She could almost hear Tracy smile on the other end. "Intriguing. What do you need?"

Tori stopped walking and explained what she was looking for as it related to her sister's case.

"And how wide do you want this search to be?"

"At a minimum, Minnesota and the surrounding states, but use your discretion," Tori advised as she reached for the door handle of the waiting FBI car. "I'll be in touch."

*

Braddock took his morning swim extra early so that he could let his mother-in-law into the house to look after Quinn. Even though it was Saturday, he was in the office by 6 a.m. with a purpose.

After Tori had abruptly left, he'd gone to bed, but sleep had proved difficult to come by. Instead, as he'd watched the ceiling fan spin, he'd thought about the profile of their killer that he and Tori had discussed. Investigating that profile required a list of people and an easy way to search and cross-reference. Solving this problem quickly necessitated the assistance of one highly effective staffer and a state agency.

That was still on his mind when he heard rustling outside his office. "Sheila?"

"You rang?" his assistant replied pleasantly, coming into his office with two cups of coffee, one for him.

Sheila was already working in the sheriff's office when he'd arrived five years ago. When he'd first met her, she gave off an air of being a Chatty Kathy, perfectly content to answer calls, take messages, run a little interference, order office supplies, fetch coffee, and do it pleasantly and efficiently while engaging in idle small-town gossip about the office. She did all those things quite effectively, but as was often the case, looks were deceiving. Sheila possessed a paralegal degree from Central Minnesota State, and Braddock quickly learned that she was resourceful, technically proficient, and an excellent researcher with an eye for detail who, despite her gabby persona, also knew how to be discreet and keep a secret.

"What can I do for you?"

"Research. You'll need to coordinate with the BCA to corral the data, and here is the agent to call to get that started." He handed her a business card. "And, most importantly, I need you to keep this very quiet. Don't discuss it with anyone, not even Cal. If for some reason he asks what you're doing, tell him to come see me and I'll explain it, okay?"

"Got it," Sheila replied without hesitation. "I assume this is about the Lash and Hunter cases?"

"Correct. I want you to put together a list of males…" he provided her with the profile he was looking for. "Narrow it for now to men fitting the profile who reside in Shepard County as well as the surrounding counties."

"That's a really wide range, Will."

"It's a start. We're going to be looking to whittle it down. To the extent you can, it includes men within those parameters whose addresses are in fact local, such as Manchester Bay, Holmestrand, Crosslake, you get the idea. But I also want weekenders with a cabin or lake home up here who aren't necessarily year-rounders."

"Because both abductions took place in the summer."

"Exactly. I want all the vitals, addresses, residential history, vehicles, marital status, dependents, employment history, military service, criminal record, tax history, wage, education—anything we can get. The more data points the better. Whoever our guy is, he knows the local scene, so that could be locals or a man who spends half the year up here."

"Anyone, broadly speaking, you're particularly interested in?"

"I'm not sure how this would pop, but anyone who has a connection of some kind to Genevieve Lash, Jessie Hunter, Katy Anderson, or their families. The tie could be employment, education, residence, who knows."

"We do have that report the BCA provided already," Sheila noted.

"That was for sex offenders only. It didn't cover spousal battery, for example," Braddock countered. "It didn't necessarily cover your garden variety sexual assault or rape."

"Anything else?"

"One red flag that might interest me would be if you found anyone who lived here in July 1999 and then moved back here recently. I'm predominantly interested in anyone with a criminal history, particularly for domestic abuse or sexual assault, anything evidencing a bent to violence, especially against women."

"And what do you want me to do with this list?"

"You're going to coordinate with the BCA on the compilation of data and then make a searchable database."

"Okay, I'm on it."

Sheila left to start her project, and Braddock thought about the second question that had kept him up last night, the one that Tori said she'd have her friend at the FBI dig into. However, with Tori gone, would that happen? He decided he would spend some time looking into that problem himself. If there were others, that would be another data point to run against the list Sheila was compiling.

*

Tori arrived at the Taylor house and was immediately debriefed by two local FBI agents, Newsom and Fry. They were joined by two investigators with the Iowa Department of Public Safety.

"Let me get this straight. In broad daylight, someone breaks into this house and abducts a two-year-old little girl, and nobody sees or hears a thing. Nobody?"

One of the Iowa DPS agents simply nodded and then shrugged his shoulders. "So far, Agent Hunter, that's what we have."

Inside the front door she immediately noticed, in what was a spacious office, two FBI agents sitting with recording and tracking equipment, awaiting the ransom call.

Before proceeding further, Tori stood in the grand entry, where she was able to view much of the main level. The Taylors lived in a tastefully furnished executive home with all the bells and whistles of suburban success: There were expensive cars in the driveway. The rooms of the house all looked to have been decorated by a high-end interior designer. There were large, top-of-the-line electronics and appliances throughout. On the oversized desk in the office, Tori could see specs for a swimming pool.

She walked ahead into the family room. Erica and Jake Taylor, an attractive couple in their mid-thirties, were sitting on opposite ends of the sectional couch. Jake looked pensive yet composed; Erica was a teary wreck.

Newsom introduced Tori. "Agent Hunter is a child kidnapping specialist out of our New York City office."

"Are you here to help with the ransom call?" Erica asked.

"If it comes to that, yes," Tori answered. "But, as Agent Newsom said, I specialize in missing children cases," she added as she pulled a chair closer to the couch. "I have some questions. First, tell me about yourselves."

Jake was a chief information officer for Internal Medical Solutions, a local medical device company. He traveled occasionally to his company's other facilities across the country, particularly over the last six months as they installed program upgrades into their system.

"Can you think of any reason someone would want to harm you or your family?" Tori asked. "Does anyone come to mind?"

Jake shook his head. "I make decent money, but I don't have any enemies to speak of. I can't think of anyone who I'd have made so mad as to do something like this. I'm in IT—how many enemies could I make?"

Erica was once in medical device sales; it was how she'd met Jake as they worked at the same company. But since the birth of Ava she'd been a stay-at-home mom. "I do a little consulting from home, but for the most part I'm here with Ava. That's my life."

"You were out of town on travel?" Tori asked Jake.

"Kansas City. We have a production facility down there, and for the last several months I've been going there on Tuesday mornings and coming back on either Thursday or Friday night as part of our system upgrade."

"And this has been your standard schedule for how long?"

"The last three months or so. Why do you ask?"

"Someone came into your house and abducted your daughter in the middle of the day in an upscale suburban neighborhood. That is only done if the kidnapper has a good idea of your schedules and patterns—yours and your wife's."

Tori flipped through her notes and looked over to Erica. "Now yesterday, you put Ava down at two o'clock for a nap, is that right?"

"Yes, that's correct."

"And was that the usual time she went down?"

"Yes."

"And she would typically nap for how long?"

"An hour and a half, sometimes two hours."

"And you laid her down where?"

"Right here in the family room in her portable crib. Then I went upstairs to take a nap of my own. Ava isn't a great sleeper at night. She usually wakes up a couple of times, and I get up with her."

"Does Ava have a bedroom upstairs?"

"Yes," Erica replied.

"Is there any particular reason you have her nap down here and not up in her room?"

"Ava just seems to nap better in the portable crib, so I've taken to having her nap down here."

"And how long has that been the case?"

"Two, maybe three months."

The house phone rang.

The Taylors bolted to the home office, with Tori and Newsom right behind them.

"We want proof of life," Newsom counseled as Jake Taylor picked up the phone.

Tori held an earphone to her right ear to listen in on the call. "Keep them talking, string it out."

"Hello?"

"We have your daughter," a disguised voice stated.

"I want to speak to her."

"No. Yancy Road, northeast of Adel between Quinlan and R Avenues," the voice instructed. "There's a mailbox: 17645. You'll find a package inside."

Click.

Tori looked to the agents monitoring the phone. They both shook their heads. "Too short," one announced.

"Adel is twenty minutes away," Jake declared.

Tori jumped into a car with Newsom and Fry. A DPS unit was right behind. "What's the story on the Taylors?" Tori asked as they sped along I-80 west of Des Moines.

"Married six years. First marriage for both," Newsom answered while Fry drove.

"Are they native Iowans?"

"He is, born and raised in Des Moines. Went to Iowa State University. She's actually from Oklahoma, went to Tulsa for college and moved here eight years ago for a sales job."

"What about family?"

"She's an only child. Her father is still alive, although he's in his seventies and lives down south of Tucson, Arizona. Jake Taylor's parents are both deceased, but he has an older sister named Cindy."

"I take it she doesn't live here?"

"No, she does," Fry replied, glancing back.

"Why isn't she at the house?"

"Cindy and Jake had a falling out a few months back," Newsom replied. "Apparently they haven't spoken since."

Even with lights and sirens, it still took nearly twenty minutes to reach the mailbox. The gray, dented rusted mailbox was at the end of a gravel driveway for what appeared to be a long-abandoned, dilapidated farmhouse. There was another farmhouse visible, perhaps a half-mile down the road.

Inside the mailbox was an unmarked plain yellow envelope, which the forensic tech extracted and carefully opened. Inside was a flash drive, which was immediately plugged into a laptop. There were two files on the drive. The first was a video. The tech clicked on the icon, summoning footage of a dark room that showed Ava Taylor alive, resting in a small crib with a blanket, doll, and juice cup. The time display in the upper right corner read 5:02 a.m. The footage lasted for one minute.

The second file contained ransom instructions. It was straight-forward.

- $1,000,000 cash in a mix of non-sequential $100 and $20 bill denominations.
- Have ready by 10:00 p.m. Tuesday night.
- Drop instructions to follow.

Newsom, Fry, and Tori sped back to the Taylors. Tori replayed the video and then opened the ransom note for them to see. "Do you have that much money?"

Jake and Erica Taylor looked to one another with raised eyebrows, both doing the mental math.

"Just barely, I *think*," Jake finally answered. "We'll have to liquidate our investments. My 401k through work is around $550,000. Erica's retirement account from her old job, the last time I looked, was $225,000 or so. We have that, plus we have a few stray mutual funds." He looked to his wife. "There *is* your inheritance."

Erica nodded and looked to Tori. "I received some money when my mom died a few months ago. It's a little over $200,000. We've been trying to decide what to do with it."

"And we have around $30,000 in our checking account," Jake noted. "So, I think we can make it. It's close, anyway."

Tori turned to Agent Fry. "Let's get our people involved. You can't liquidate a 401k if the person hasn't terminated employment, but we have exigent circumstances. We'll need to facilitate the withdrawal and coordinate with the IRS so no tax penalties are imposed on the Taylors or the employer's retirement plan for permitting the immediate withdrawal. And they've left us a tight timeline to convert all of their funds to cash so we have to move fast."

"I'm on it," Fry answered, reaching for his cell phone.

The timeline left them two days to figure out what had happened to Ava Taylor. Tori pulled Newsom aside. "This is all over a million dollars?" she asked skeptically.

"A million is a million."

"But… one million dollars? That isn't *that* much these days. It's not an amount worth life in prison."

"What are you saying?"

"And these guys seem to know *exactly* how much the Taylors can pull together."

"They did their research. They got in and out of the house, after all."

"Maybe," Tori replied, lightly shaking her head. "Maybe."

*

Braddock had spent the morning buried in his office, researching on his computer and making phone calls to jurisdictions with open missing women investigations that fit their victim profile. His first two calls to investigators in Springfield, Missouri, and Decatur, Illinois, proved to be dead ends, the characteristics seeming too dissimilar to the Jessie Hunter and Genevieve Lash cases.

Just after lunch, he found a possible match when he spoke with the police chief in Oshkosh, Wisconsin, about a nine-year-old case that had similarities to the Lash and Hunter disappearances. Now he was finishing up with the police chief and lead investigator with the Bismarck, North Dakota, police department on a similar case.

"I appreciate it, Chief. I'll keep an eye on my inbox," Braddock said. "And I'll forward you what I have as well. Let's stay in touch."

Braddock moved the mouse to his inbox just as the file from Oshkosh arrived. Right as he was going to click it open, there was a knock on his door. It was Cal. "Can you come down to my office?"

"Sure."

Braddock followed Cal back to his office to find a large group awaiting his arrival: Kyle Mannion; Mayor Miller; Skip Sauer, the president of Northern Pine Bank; Walter Johnson, president of Central Minnesota State; Jeff Warner; Shepard County Attorney George Backstrom; and a few others. Huddled in Cal's office were all the business, political, and educational leaders of Manchester Bay.

"I know what this meeting is," Braddock remarked guardedly as he leaned back against a wall with his arms folded, able to eye up everyone in the room. "Surprised I wasn't summoned to the country club."

Cal took a seat behind his desk.

The powers that be looked around to each other to see who would speak first.

The mayor finally shrugged and broke the ice. "Will, a couple of hours ago I got off the phone with an investigative reporter from the *Star Tribune* down in Minneapolis."

"That guy has been pestering me, too."

"But you haven't spoken to him?" the mayor asked.

"No, he hasn't," Cal replied, folding his right leg over his left. "But I have."

"You have?" Will asked.

"Yeah, to keep him from you. You've got enough to worry about," Cal answered. "But apparently he's got a big article for the

Sunday paper tomorrow about the case, about the Jessie Hunter disappearance, about Katy Anderson, and about how women seem to disappear from Manchester Bay."

"I see, and I imagine that makes everyone in this room nervous."

"It should make you nervous, too," Skip Sauer popped off.

"Will," Kyle Mannion started, "we're just... well, we're all worried about the case, the investigation, the—"

"Media attention?" Braddock asked, his arms folded.

"Damn right," Sauer snarled again from his seat on the couch. "It's abated some, but still, we're on the news a lot here lately, and the coverage is hardly positive."

"Tragedy rarely is."

"This isn't about us questioning you," Mayor Miller stated.

"Oh, well, that's great to know," Braddock replied sarcastically.

"I know it probably feels like it, but it's not. *It's not.*"

"Will, it's not," Kyle Mannion echoed. "I know... We know you're doing everything you can."

"It's just that," Jeff Warner started. "We've worked so hard the last ten to fifteen years to build the town, to get past the Hunter girl abduction and the reputation it gave us. And now..."

"It's all back again," Walter Johnson chimed in.

"Now, Will," Cal said, leaning back in his chair, "I've been explaining to these fine folks that we're doing everything we can to figure out what happened to Genevieve Lash."

"We are. Katy Anderson, too."

"Do you have any idea, any inkling of an idea, who is doing this to our town?" Kyle Mannion asked.

"I'm trying to figure that out, Kyle," Braddock answered. "It's the only thing on my plate these days. It's all I'm working on."

"*You're* trying?" Sauer inquired, gesturing to Braddock, clearly the one person in the room not inclined to grant him any slack. "I was under the impression Tori Hunter is assisting you."

"Victoria *was* assisting," Cal responded.

"But now she's not?" Warner asked, eyebrows raised.

Braddock shook his head. "She was called away to Des Moines last night by the FBI to work a child kidnapping, which is, after all, her specific area of expertise. She wasn't assigned here by the FBI; she was here of her own accord."

"With Tori Hunter gone, do you have the resources you need?" Mayor Miller asked.

Braddock nodded. "Yes, Mayor. I know you don't see the BCA swarming around like they were, but that changes with a phone call. The FBI office down in the Cities checks in with me every day. But, to be honest, right now we have no solid leads, so we don't have anywhere to deploy those resources here."

"Then what are you working on?" Sauer asked pointedly. "I mean, if there are no leads."

"Working on finding one."

"By doing what?"

"Investigating," Braddock replied opaquely but testily. Sauer was clearly there to grind his gears.

"Investigating *what*?"

"Well, *Skip*, unless you've been elevated to sheriff, county attorney, or mayor, I don't answer to you."

"Huh, I see," Sauer replied just as curtly. "Maybe you shouldn't answer to anyone around here."

"Fuck off."

"Hold on, hold on," Kyle Mannion interjected calmly, stepping into the middle of the room and giving Sauer a stern glare, backing the banker down before Braddock put him through the wall.

"Skip, I think it would be a good idea if you and I stepped into the hallway," Warner suggested, having stood up, a wry smile on his face. "Come on."

Sauer glared harshly at Braddock before he pulled on his shirt cuffs and followed Warner out of the room.

After the door closed, Kyle shook his head. "Sorry about that, Will."

"Yeah, well…"

"He had it coming. However, Skip and I are on the phone daily with Jerry Lash. Jerry is going through hell right now, as any parent would."

"I understand. I wish I had more to report."

Kyle nodded in understanding. "Will, we're here to convey the message and let you know that *all* of us in this room would provide any assistance we could, *anything*. I don't know what that would be. Speaking for myself, if there is something my company or I can do, if there are any resources that I have at my disposal or that I could get for you that would be helpful, I hope you won't hesitate to call me. Manchester Bay is your home and it's my home, too. You and I, all of us, want it safe for our families, and to be perfectly honest, we want it safe for our businesses, too. So again, if there is anything you need."

"Kyle, I appreciate that, I really do, and I'm not shy about asking for things. Just ask Cal."

"He's not," Cal nodded in agreement.

"But I won't waste them either, even in this case," Braddock added. "We are working hard. We're doing everything we can."

"Good, then we all understand each other," Kyle Mannion replied, satisfied, handing Braddock his business card. "My cell is on the back. You can call me at any time, no matter the hour, and I'll get you whatever you need, just ask." Kyle shook Braddock's hand then looked back to the rest of the room. "Come on, gentlemen. We've taken the sheriff and detective away from their work for long enough. Let's go see if Jeff simmered Skippy down."

After everyone left, Braddock looked over to Cal. "How many phone calls have you been getting from these guys?"

Cal waved it off. "Plenty, but it's my job to handle that. I've noticed you holed up in your office all day. What gives?"

"I've got something going but I want to keep it quiet. I can tell you about it now, but then you wouldn't have honest deniability."

"Honest deniability?"

"Yeah, if something came up that made some folks around here—for example, the ones who just left—uncomfortable."

"What are you up to?" Cal asked warily.

"Collecting a lot of information and putting it in a database that I can search if and when I come up with some evidence."

"And a lot of people might be upset if they found themselves in this database, or that you felt the need to create one?"

"Maybe," Braddock answered. "Now if you give me another day or two, then I can let you know if I have anything worth discussing."

"Okay," Cal replied. "Do what you gotta do."

Braddock went to the door to leave.

"Do you want a word of advice?"

Braddock turned around, a little grin on his face. "Kyle Mannion."

Cal nodded. "Skip Sauer is a banker. He wets his pants every time the market takes a shit, so don't worry about him. As for the others… well, Mayor Miller is important, Warner has some juice, the county attorney is important, *I'm* important, but the real power around here is Kyle Mannion. Keep him an ally."

CHAPTER FIFTEEN

"Are you up for some wild yet educated speculation?"

Braddock grabbed the suitcase and carried it out the back door to the Suburban belonging to Quinn's grandparents, Roger and Mary Hayes. Quinn had already loaded his backpack into the backseat, where he would ride along with two of his cousins. In the backseat there would be movies and much gaming on the lengthy drive to northern Michigan's Crystal Lake.

Quinn was just as excited for the trip with his two best buddies and their grandparents as he'd been the last two summers. Yet it was always hard for Dad to say goodbye for three weeks.

"Behave yourself."

"I will, Dad."

"And, of course, have fun, right?"

"For sure."

"And don't be afraid to send me a text or two with that new cell phone of yours. Pictures, too."

"I will," Quinn replied, holding up the new phone. "I promise, Dad."

"Alright," Braddock replied, tousling his son's mop of light brown hair. "I love you, buddy."

"I love you too, Dad," his son replied sincerely, hugging his father hard, holding the embrace for an extra second or two before climbing up into the backseat and buckling himself in. After Braddock exchanged a brief word with Roger and Mary, the Suburban roared to life. He watched as they pulled out of the driveway and drove down the road, finally disappearing from view. He would have loved nothing more than to have climbed into that Suburban and gone to Michigan with them.

It was a breezy morning, creating a wavy chop on the lake. Given the conditions, he eschewed his typical morning swim. Instead he showered quickly and was in the office just before 7 a.m. Turning on his computer, he settled in to begin working. However, before he could get too engrossed, there was a light knock on his office door. Sheila was standing with Gail Anderson in the doorway.

Braddock greeted her, closed his door, and then guided her to one of the guest chairs in front of his desk. He took the guest chair opposite, turning it to face her.

"I'm sorry to bother you, Detective Braddock," Katy's mother started meekly.

"It's not a bother, not at all," he answered, leaning forward in the chair with his elbows on his thighs and hands lightly clasped together.

"I know you're busy and all," she continued, her eyes already lightly moistened.

He could tell that she wasn't sleeping well, and it looked as if she'd aged years in a matter of days. The wrinkles on her forehead had multiplied, and dark, puffy bags had developed under her eyes. She now looked frail, and her clothes were exceedingly baggy, hanging on her withering body. He wondered if she'd been eating.

"Is there anything new?"

Braddock looked down for a moment before slowly shaking his head. "We are still investigating, still looking, but I don't have anything new for you. I'm sorry."

"Is Tori still helping? I didn't see her around here."

"Agent Hunter has been ordered by the FBI to investigate another case down in Des Moines."

"Is she coming back?"

"I honestly don't know," Braddock answered. "She wants to but there is no way of knowing how long the case she's assigned to could take."

"I see." She reached for a tissue from the box on Braddock's desk and wiped her nose while sniffling. "Do I give up?"

"You never give up until there is… certainty," Braddock replied softly, looking to the floor before looking directly up into Gail's eyes. "But I also think we need to be realistic."

"No false hope, right?"

"Right," Braddock agreed. "But I'm not giving up, not until I get some answers. I promise you that."

Gail Anderson stayed for another fifteen minutes before leaving. Braddock watched as she slowly shuffled out of his office and down the narrow hall. He sat back down in his desk chair, leaned back, and closed his eyes. "Shit," he muttered angrily before sitting up and looking to his computer and the results of his search for similar cases.

In the search, he'd focused on missing women ages seventeen to twenty-seven where the disappearance involved an abandoned car. So far, through his research and working the phones, he thought he'd found three that had some commonalities to the disappearances of Jessie Hunter and Genevieve Lash.

The first case was from 2004. Carrie Blaine, age twenty-four, with long blonde hair and blue eyes, disappeared after leaving work as a waitress at the Grey Wolfe Bar in Bismarck, North Dakota. Her car was found in the parking lot behind the bar, the keys on the ground underneath it. She was never seen again.

The second case was from 2009. Ginger Zeller's car was found abandoned in an alley behind her apartment building in Oshkosh,

Wisconsin. Age twenty-two, she was a senior at the University of Wisconsin-Oshkosh and was last seen leaving a party at 2:30 a.m.

The third case he came across was from 2011 in Cedar Falls, Iowa. Leanne Benson, a twenty-six-year-old graduate student seeking a master's degree in biology, was last seen leaving a night class at the University of Northern Iowa and walking toward the Panther parking lot, an overflow lot on the southeast edge of campus. In the morning, her car was still in the parking lot, found with the driver's side door open and a small streak of fresh blood on the edge of the driver's seat. It was theorized that she was attacked with her car door open. Although it was a university parking lot, there were no surveillance cameras in operation in that lot at that time.

In all three instances the women had disappeared and were never heard from again. Their bodies were not found. All three women had cell phones, but the phones were not found nor were they able to be traced. There were no witnesses of any kind. The women were all presumed dead and had been declared as such. In each of the three cases, the killer had been uncanny in his ability to seemingly attack, subdue, and get away without anyone seeing anything. "It's like you get right up close and personal, their guard is down, and then, *wham*," he said quietly to himself.

"Will?" Sheila asked, sticking her head in his office. "I have a call on line two that I think you need to take. It's from a detective in Brookings, South Dakota."

"Okay," he replied and picked up the phone. "Will Braddock."

"Detective Braddock, I'm Jeff Bruening. I'm a detective in Brookings, South Dakota. I'm calling because I have a case that I've been investigating the last two days, and there might be some similarities to your Genevieve Lash case. I was wondering if you had some time to talk a little shop."

*

Tori tried sleeping in an easy chair in the office of the Taylors' home. With the number of times she'd done this in various houses, buildings, and offices over the years while working a kidnapping, she ought to have trained her mind and body to be able to sleep anywhere and on anything, no matter its size or level of comfort. Yet every time it was a struggle. And now, while loath to admit it, especially with a two-year-old child kidnapped, her mind was elsewhere.

No matter the lengths she went to bury it, the memory of her sister and her disappearance was always there, lurking in the back of her mind. Thoughts of Jessie were ready to be triggered by the littlest thing from 1999, like if she heard "Scar Tissue" or "Californication" by the Red Hot Chili Peppers. Or if she happened to stumble across a *Friends* episode, something she and Jessie always watched. If *Austin Powers: The Spy Who Shagged Me* was on, the last movie they'd gone to before she disappeared, it would all come flooding back. They'd spent three weeks saying: *Oh be-have* and *Not if I can help it* or *Felicity Shagwell. Shagwell by name. Shag- very-well by reputation.* It was the little moments and memories like that which, in a flash, brought her sister's case out of the dark corners of her mind.

That memory was no longer the lurking, occasionally painful distraction that would appear and then fade. Now it was once again all-consuming. She had the taste of reopening her sister's case—of Manchester Bay, of walking the stretch of highway where Jessie was abducted, cruising the streets of their old hometown knowing, *knowing* that somewhere nearby the killer was skulking, maybe even watching, and even possibly hunting her. More than anything, that was why she was wide awake in the pitch-black of the night.

Instinctually she reached for her phone and checked her text messages and emails. There was an email from Tracy Sheets from late last night indicating she was working on the project and thought she'd have something to share later tomorrow, which was now today. Later in the day—how much later? How long would she have to wait? And if Tracy had something, what did she have? And even if Tracy did have something, Tori wondered what she could then turn around and do with it.

She'd considered calling Braddock but then thought better of it. They were on good terms now and she didn't want to do anything to distract or, knowing herself, annoy him before she heard from Tracy. Besides, she had no idea when she'd be able to get back to Manchester Bay.

Trying to sleep in the chair was worthless. As if her own insomnia wasn't enough, it was a cloudless night with a full moon, and the light filtered in through the six tall and lightly curtained windows of the office. Turning on a light was not required for her to inspect the many pictures on the shelves of the long, built-in bookcase. There were family pictures, several of the Taylors with Ava over her two years. A high shelf contained a set of photos of Jake Taylor with what appeared to be college friends, and on another lower shelf was pictures of Erica Taylor and what looked to be several of her friends. A shelf in the middle of the bookcase contained pictures that were perhaps ten years old, of Jake with three people, who Tori presumed to be his sister Cindy and their parents. There were also several pictures of just Jake and Cindy.

She quietly made her way down the wide corridor dividing the main level of the house. To the left she glanced into the living room to see Jake, his back turned, sleeping on the couch. In the kitchen she could see a red light illuminated on the coffee maker. There was half a pot of warm coffee left. If she was going to be awake, she might as well do it with coffee. She took a ceramic coffee cup out of the sink's drying rack and filled it halfway.

Blowing to cool the coffee, she stepped to her right to look out the side window of the kitchen into the neighbor's backyard. As she raised the cup to her mouth, she caught a flash of light and then looked up to the second floor of the neighbor's house.

In a narrow window, she saw a man who she recognized as the neighbor. She'd seen him in the driveway putting the garbage out earlier. He was holding his cell phone and appeared to be typing a message. After a moment, he looked up and to the Taylors' house, waving the phone. Tori leaned forward over the sink, trying to peer out the kitchen window to look up to her right but she had no angle to see up to the second floor. She was aware of only one person being up there.

Tori set her cup softly on the counter and walked back to the front of the house, quietly opened the front door, slipped out onto the front stoop, and then pulled the door gently closed. She turned to her right, stepped over some bushes and flowers that were planted along the sidewalk and front step, and then made her way around the south side of the house and into the backyard. Jutting out from the northwest corner of the house was an expansive deck. Crouching down low, using the spindled deck railing as cover, she picked her way along to the corner of the deck and then peered around it and up to the second floor of the Taylor house. As she'd expected, she saw Erica in the window with her phone, looking over to her neighbor.

Tori watched the two of them for five minutes, texting and waving to each other before Erica stepped back from the window. Staying crouched low, Tori made her way back around to the south side of the house, stopped, and placed a call to Newsom, who groggily answered on the third ring.

"Agent Hunter… uh, what's up?" Newsom greeted her drowsily.

"Pick me up in ten minutes two houses down from the Taylors' house."

"Can I ask why?"

"I'll explain when you get here but bring along your investigative file. I think I might have us a lead."

"At this time of night?"

"Best time to find them."

Newsom arrived fifteen minutes later and drove the two of them to the parking lot of a Kum & Go convenience store a few blocks away. They quickly went inside to get coffees and then convened in the parking lot.

"What's up?" Newsom asked, taking a sip of his coffee.

"I'm pretty sure there is something going on between Erica Taylor and her neighbor to the north."

"Ooookay," Newsom answered hesitantly after a moment, surprised. "And what makes you think this?"

Tori described what she'd seen. "So, what do we know about the neighbor?"

Newsom opened a file folder. "His name is David Hutchinson. He's lived next door for five months."

"Own or rent?"

"Rent with an option to buy. He's been out of work. The company he worked for was purchased and he received a sizable severance package, so he said he's enjoying the summer at home before starting up his job search in the fall."

Tori snorted with a smile. "Are you up for some wild yet educated speculation?"

"Isn't that why an FBI special agent ends up in the Kum & Go parking lot at four forty-five in the morning?"

"Here's what might have happened to Ava. Erica Taylor puts Ava down for her nap. Interestingly, she doesn't put her in her crib in her bedroom upstairs, but instead downstairs in the family room. Once Ava is down and sleeping, a few minutes later, David Hutchinson slyly makes his way over and those two go upstairs for an activity nap."

"Activity nap, that's a new one. Back in the day, my wife and I always called that an afternoon delight."

"Like that song, what was the name of that group?"

"Starland Vocal Band, their one and only hit," Newsom answered drolly. He was tracking with Tori. "So, while those two are upstairs doing their thing, someone swoops into the house and scoops up Ava."

"And does it quietly and without Ava putting up a fuss or making any noise, at least according to Mrs. Taylor."

"Well, if you're right, she's upstairs in the height of passion. She might not have heard anything anyway—not that she'll be willing to admit that's what was going on if it was. Like you said, wild speculation."

"Based on what I just saw, it's not *that* wild. Those two looked like lovers longing for one another."

The two of them took drinks from their gas station coffees as the sun started peeking over the flat eastern horizon of Iowa.

"So, let's just say the kidnapper knew those two were having an affair; where does that get us?" Newsom asked.

"Probably nowhere, unless…" Tori's eyes brightened. "Jake Taylor knows his wife is having an affair?"

"Again, if they are."

"Let's just assume, at least for the moment, that they are, with the added twist that Jake Taylor *knows* it," Tori added. "Does it make him angry?"

"What are you saying?"

"What if he knows? A guy like that. He works hard with regular travel and long hours. You've been inside the house. Everything is designer. They have splashy cars. A swimming pool on the drawing board. And while he's out on the road grinding away to pay for all of that—"

"His wife is at home banging the out-of-work neighbor," Newsom finished. "Man, it sure as hell would piss *me* off."

"Enough to want a divorce?"

"Hell yes."

"And what happens to the familial assets should you get divorced? The majority of which you've worked so hard to accumulate."

"They get… split in half," Newsom answered haltingly, suddenly understanding where Tori was going. "You don't think?"

"It's bothered me that the kidnappers know what the Taylors have for assets. And to only ask for a million dollars for ransom? Who risks life in prison for a million dollars? You don't. A million isn't going to get you very far these days."

"You think a father could do this?"

"This is nothing," Tori replied dismissively. "I think it is entirely possible that Jake Taylor had his daughter kidnapped. Think about it for a second, because I think he has. The ransom is a million dollars, which is pretty much all their assets, give or take $50,000. The ransom gets paid and Ava comes home safe and sound. Once that happens, phase two of his plan kicks into action. He knows, and therefore will convincingly allege, that his wife is having an affair with the neighbor. So, what does he do? He files for divorce and moves for full custody of Ava—and who knows, he might get it. At worst, he gets joint custody, and if I'm right, he does it with a million dollars in his pocket. Hidden, of course, but he has the money, nonetheless, socked away somewhere to be accessed ten or fifteen years down the road."

"You think a father, any father, would stage a kidnapping of his daughter just to get all the money? Really?"

"Come on," Tori replied with some exasperation. "When it comes to money, people do irrational, stupid, mendacious things all the time. I've seen parents use their children as pawns in all kinds of ways to get at one another. This isn't *that* much of a stretch, even here in supposedly genteel Iowa."

After a moment, Newsom exhaled. "Man, when you speculate, you speculate."

"I prefer to view it as speculation worthy of exploration. Let's ask the question a different way to show it makes logical sense. Examine the kidnapping. The Taylors live on a quiet street in an upper-class neighborhood. In the middle of the afternoon, someone kidnaps a two-year-old girl out of the family room. How do they get in the house?" Tori knew the answer to the next question but asked it anyway. "Any signs of forced entry?"

"Nope," Newsom replied, shaking his head.

"So, the door is either unlocked or they had a key. You can't sit there for a minute or two and pick a lock in broad daylight in a suburban neighborhood, even if it's on the back deck. Too risky, too much exposure. And besides, would your average kidnapper really know that the Taylors have a million dollars in assets?"

Newsom shrugged. "It's a nice neighborhood, really nice."

"Yeah," Tori replied with a dismissive wave, "but it's not *that* extraordinary. If you're a pro looking to pull off something like this, you do it for more, a lot more than a million dollars. But if you're Jake Taylor, a million dollars sounds pretty good, and if he had his daughter kidnapped, he knows she's safe. Heck, if he did it, is it even really a kidnapping?"

"That would be one for the lawyers," Newsom replied and then, after a moment, offered, "Let's say hypothetically that Jake arranged this. He was in Kansas City when it happened, so he didn't do it."

"You checked that?"

Newsom nodded. "He was in a meeting starting at one thirty in the afternoon and didn't get out of it until Erica Taylor called him. Five witnesses. So, if he put all this together, who did he have kidnap Ava?"

Tori turned and leaned against the sedan, mentally going back through everything. Thinking about what she'd seen Erica doing, how she'd awoken in the chair, made her way to the kitchen… and then she stopped and thought back to the bookcase with the family photos. "You know, the kidnapper might do it for free if they were family," Tori replied. "Where's Jake Taylor's sister?"

CHAPTER SIXTEEN

"In college towns."

"Will? Will? *Will*, wake up," Sheila said as she tapped his shoulder. "*Wake up!*"

"What? What?" Braddock sprang awake, jumping up quickly off his office couch, papers flying off his body onto the floor. Sheila was standing in front of him with her hands on her hips and a severe look of disapproval etched across her face.

"Will Braddock, did you sleep here last night?"

"I guess I did," Braddock replied slowly, wiping his face with his hands and then rubbing his eyes before sitting back down on the couch. It was 7 a.m. or just shortly after that because Sheila was standing in front of him, and she was punctual. He leaned forward and picked the papers up off the floor before looking up. "Would you be willing to make me a—"

"Cup of coffee?" Sheila guessed correctly, stepping back to his desk and reaching for a cup, which she handed to him.

"Thanks."

"Since when do you sleep on the office couch?"

"Quinn is gone for three weeks, so I was here late. I got tired of sitting at my desk so I came over here to lie down and read and must have dozed off."

"What time?"

"Good question," he replied, taking a drink of coffee. "Last time I remember looking at my watch was a little before three, I think."

"I see."

"Sorry, Mom," Will said sheepishly, looking up to his assistant. "How's *your* project coming?"

"Go clean up and I'll run through it."

He went to the locker room, changed clothes, washed his face, brushed his teeth, and straightened out his hair. He was back in his office ten minutes later, by which time Sheila had a laptop set up on his desk and was sitting in a guest chair waiting for him.

He sat down and took a long drink of coffee. "Show me."

"This database has every male within your profile range. The population of Shepard County and the five surrounding counties is a little over 263,000, as official residents. You add in cabin folks, and we get to just north of 408,000."

"Huh. I would have thought it was more."

"That's based on ownership records, Will," she responded. "If we need to get into family members of these people, that might require more horsepower than I can provide."

"Understood. Keep going."

Sheila moved the cursor to the top of the screen and hit a tab. "Out of a little over 400,000 there are 189,000 males. Whittled down, there are just over 67,000 males who fit our criteria. If you want to break it down on race, you can. You just need to set some filters, although up here it's going to be predominantly Caucasian."

"Okay, I'm following so far."

"If you screen it by criminal records, we get down to a little over 11,200."

"That many have criminal records?" Will asked, mildly surprised. He then thought to a statistic he'd seen from the FBI recently that one in three adults had some sort of criminal record, especially if you included arrests. "I presume that number includes arrests?"

"Yes," Sheila answered. "If it's narrowed to just convictions, the number is considerably lower. From this point you can filter out drug charges and convictions, weapons charges and convictions, robberies, and so on. If I pull records with either a domestic assault or a sex crime, we get down a little lower to 1,325, at least in Shepard and the surrounding counties. This also has vehicle, residential, employment, tax, education, and other miscellaneous records as well."

"And that's based on property ownership records. There could be people leasing property or family members we can't account for."

"Correct, but it's easy enough to include more data if you tell me what to add or where I can access it. Now, you said something about data points that could help narrow this down. Where are you on that?"

"Five *possible* connections," Braddock answered as he sat back in his office chair.

"Five now? It's a serial?"

"That's why I was up late. I think I have two more. One in Lincoln, Nebraska, and then maybe one from Brookings, South Dakota, from that call you transferred to me yesterday.

"In the Lincoln case, the victim's car was found with a flat tire. In Brookings, a young woman named Joanie Wells' car was found keyed on the entire length of the driver's side of her VW Jetta.

"In the other cases, cars again were tampered with. In one case, the woman's car was found with a huge pool of antifreeze under it, having leaked from a big puncture wound to the radiator. There was one where the driver's side window was smashed, the glass all found inside the car on and around the driver's seat. In still another, the car wasn't damaged but it was found with the door open and a small smear of blood belonging to the victim.

"Take Jessie Hunter and Genevieve Lash—the tires were tampered with. We have a pattern developing. Put the vehicle in distress and then attack."

"In college towns," Sheila noted quickly.

"I noted that as well," Braddock answered. "And the women often fit the profile of college or post-graduate students, or they worked in a college town or near one. So if these are all connected, our guy travels to those kinds of towns. If we get some more information, we may eventually shave this list down more, finding some sort of connection between here, these towns, and someone on the list you've built," he noted. "Good job."

"Thanks. Now find this guy, would ya?"

*

Tori returned to the Taylor house to find everyone awake and Special Agent Fry on a conference call, coordinating the completion of the liquidation of the Taylors' assets. Jake Taylor and two other agents were gathered around the desk in the office.

Erica Taylor was sitting by herself at the kitchen table, drinking a cup of tea. She was the picture of a distraught mother. Her beautiful little two-year-old daughter was missing, abducted while she was upstairs. For all anyone knew, she'd simply been taking a nap. But given her completely devastated appearance, Tori was convinced Erica felt an even heavier burden of guilt because of what she'd been doing when her daughter had been taken.

"If we get to the point where we have to pay the ransom, do you think we'll get Ava back?" Erica asked Tori, staring into her cup of tea.

"We'll do everything we can."

"Have you ever been involved in a case where ransom was paid?"

"Once," Tori answered.

"And did you get the child back?"

Tori nodded. "The good problem with a ransom is the kidnappers have to try and get it. That works in *our* favor."

Erica was an emotional wreck. Jake, while clearly worried, remained calm, almost stoic. Tori couldn't get a read on whether he felt any guilt. Instead, he was acting like the executive that he was, all business, on task and laser-focused on the liquidation of assets. In the three hours she observed him, he never made a move toward or spoke with his wife.

By the close of business for the day, the liquidation was complete. The assets would be converted to cash and would be delivered to the house in the morning.

One thing gnawing at Tori, though, was why the long wait on the next step? Had Jake miscalculated how long the liquidation would take? Maybe that was it, that he thought it might take longer. However, as she observed him, he was now more pensive and fidgety, as if now that the money was addressed, he just had to wait twenty-eight hours until 10 p.m. tomorrow night. He was looking anxiously out the window when his cell phone rang. He took it out of his pocket and stared at the name for several seconds before tapping the screen with his thumb and answering. "Cindy? Yeah… I'm okay, hanging in there. The sound of your voice is garbled. Where are you?"

That piqued Tori's attention as her own phone buzzed. It was Newsom.

"I'll pick you up in ten minutes."

Like clockwork, Newsom pulled up to the Taylor house and Tori jumped in. "What's up?" she asked as he pulled away.

"Let's get away from the house first," Newsom answered, driving them back to the Kum & Go. Once there, they grabbed some waters and leaned against the side of the car.

"So?" Tori asked.

"David Hutchinson is most likely having an affair with Erica Taylor, *but* I'm not so sure about the second part of your theory," Newsom stated. "I don't think Jake Taylor is behind this."

"I think his sister just called him."

"I'm not surprised," Newsom replied. "We tracked her down. They *are* currently estranged. However, she and her husband are on a Mediterranean cruise. We reached her on the ship. Cindy Taylor McCaffrey was stunned to hear the news of Ava's abduction. I suspect she called her brother right after we were done with her."

"It could still be—"

"Jake Taylor?" Newsom finished for her and then shook his head in disagreement. "We've been looking into him and we still are, but I think your discovery of Erica and David may have triggered us to find something else to look at."

"What?"

"David Hutchinson. He has an interesting history starting with his name, which is *not* David Hutchinson."

"Excuse me?"

"We think it's Thomas Martens and he has a *fascinating* backstory. Mr. Martens previously worked for a company called Spinal Intelligence. They make certain devices used in back surgeries, like fusions. He left their employ eighteen months ago. Spinal Intelligence is a direct competitor of Jake's company, Internal Medical Solutions."

"Okay," Tori replied, "he worked at a competitor. Is Spinal Intelligence based here in Des Moines?"

Newsom shook his head. "Cleveland. They have nothing here. *Nothing.* And Martens is not from Des Moines. He has no known history here. So, the idea he's spending his summer looking for a job here is looking spurious."

"What about his wife?"

"He's not married."

"There's a plot twist. Who is the woman listed in the case file then?"

"We don't know yet. He introduced her when we were interviewing neighbors as Avery Bronson, his wife, but there is no record of her that we found. We're working on an identification of her now."

"But this Avery… Bronson left in the morning. I wonder who she's working for?"

"Perhaps Spinal Intelligence as well."

Tori knew where Newsom was headed. "Spinal Intelligence plants this guy next door to the chief information officer of a rival. What are they after?"

"I don't know yet."

"Let's go ask Mr. Hutchinson, or this Mr. Martens."

Newsom grimaced. "Yeah, about that."

"What?"

"Martens seems to have gone missing. He and the woman left in a car together this morning. You and I had talked about the affair, but we didn't know about his fake name or his employment history with Spinal Intelligence at that point, so we didn't think anything of it. However, now knowing what we know, it obviously would have been prudent to pay him a little more attention."

"Then we need to go to Erica and Jake Taylor. Let's put it to them, all of it, and see what we come up with."

CHAPTER SEVENTEEN

"You look like you've just seen a ghost."

Tori and Newsom drove back to the Taylor house. As they walked up the front steps, they could hear shouting inside. Newsom opened the front door and it became clear the shouting was coming from upstairs: Jake and Erica Taylor were arguing.

"How long have they been doing this?" Tori asked Fry in the front entryway.

"About ten minutes," the FBI agent replied. "But it's been escalating."

"What started it?" Newsom asked.

"The two of them were in the kitchen. She was trying to engage with him, but he didn't really respond and kind of ignored her. Then she said—"

"'You blame me for this,'" Tori anticipated.

"Exactly," Fry answered. "And Mr. Taylor exploded with, 'You're damn right I do.'"

"Oh boy," Newsom chimed in.

"Then the donnybrook started as he chased her upstairs. They've been barking at each other nonstop ever since."

Tori and Newsom made their way up the steps to the second level. Tori could hear Erica crying and Jake berating her. She couldn't help but think theirs was a marriage not long for the world as she knocked on the door. "This is Agent Hunter."

"*What?*" Jake growled.

"Agent Newsom and I need to speak with both of you—*now.*"

Jake yanked open the door. "We're having an argument. It's none of your business."

"That's not why we're up here," Tori insisted, pushing her way into the room to find Erica crying and standing in the doorway to the master bathroom on the far side of the bed. Tori took a position on the far wall with her hands on her hips, pushing back her blazer, exposing her service weapon on her right hip. She often found just the exposure of the gun had a calming effect when people were heated. Newsom remained by the bedroom door to the hallway, leaning against the doorjamb. Fry and two Iowa BCA agents were positioned halfway down the stairway to the main level, listening and ready to jump in, just in case.

Tori looked to Jake severely. "For the next few minutes, you're going to need to be calm." She then looked to Erica. "And for the next few minutes, you need to be honest."

"What's that supposed to mean?" Erica asked, offended.

"Have you been having an affair with David Hutchinson?" Tori asked coldly.

"Oh God," Erica moaned, turning away with her face in her hands. It was true.

"*What?*" Jake barked, starting to charge across the room after his wife.

"I don't think so," Newsom said as he quickly stepped in front of Jake, stopping him in his tracks and then walking him back to the wall. "*Stand. Listen.*"

"How long?" Tori asked evenly, her arms folded.

Erica shamefully looked down to the carpeted floor. "A couple of months."

"And what do you know about him?"

"He moved in with his wife some months ago. He's unhappy in his marriage. Obviously, I'm not terribly happy in mine."

"Oh, really?" Jake growled.

"Oh, like you are!" his wife shot back.

"We'll be doing something about that!"

"Hey! Hey! Hey! How about we get your daughter back first?" Tori snapped at the Taylors. "How about we do that?"

She looked to Erica. "Let me tell you a few things about the neighbor. For starters, he's not married. Second, we think his real name is Thomas Martens, *not* David Hutchinson. And third," she turned to look at Jake, "Martens' last known employer, up until eighteen months ago, was Spinal Intelligence in Cleveland."

"They are a competitor of your company, are they not?" Newsom asked.

"Yes," Jake answered, nodding along.

"Who is his wife then?" Erica asked. "Or the woman he says is his wife? I know her name is Avery."

"We don't know," Newsom replied. "We just know the man is named Thomas Martens, or at least that's what we've found out here in the last hour or so."

"Are you saying he kidnapped my daughter?" Jake asked.

"Him?" Tori replied before shaking her head. "Probably not. He was running interference up here in this room with your wife, right?" she asked Erica, who nodded while looking away again. "While Erica and Martens are up here, someone else slips very quietly into the house, perhaps the woman we know as Avery, or maybe someone else, and takes Ava."

"Why aren't you questioning him?" Jake asked. "Why aren't you over there right now?"

"Because Martens and the woman aren't there," Newsom replied and looked over to Erica. "Do you know why?"

"Uhh… he said last night that they had planned to leave for a few days," Erica offered meekly, now dabbing at her eyes with tissue. "He said he wouldn't be back until Wednesday."

"We need his cell phone number. I know you have it. I saw you and Martens texting each other in the middle of the night last night," Tori stated before recapping what she saw. "We need that number. Get it now."

Erica sheepishly left the bedroom in search of her phone.

Tori looked to Jake. "If, and this is a big if… but if this is Spinal Intelligence doing this, the question is why? Why target you?"

"I don't…" Jake started to answer and then stopped for a moment. "Because I'm the chief information officer."

"That strikes me as a management position," Newsom stated.

"In most companies, that's true," Jake answered. "But I'm not only a manager of people, I know all the systems backward and forward. I've designed the security protocols and implemented them all."

"Could you take down the security if you had to?" Newsom asked.

Jake nodded. "Yeah, easily. It would only take a minute or two, really."

"From where?"

"From pretty much anywhere if I wanted to with my laptop. I just need Internet access."

"Here's the number," Erica said, coming back in the room and handing a slip of paper to Tori. "That's the number I was texting."

Tori called in Agent Fry and handed him the note. "Run the number, see what we get."

Jake asked, "If this is Spinal Intelligence behind this, why are they asking for a ransom for Ava?"

Tori thought it through for a moment. "It's a head fake. This is supposed to look like a straightforward kidnapping for ransom.

If you're getting a ransom call, we're not asking why they would target *you*, beyond the fact people want money for your daughter. They don't want us to think it has anything to do with you being the CIO for your company, but Martens—or the people he works for—wasn't careful enough in burying his history. Now that we know what we know, maybe we can start turning the tables."

*

Under orders from both Cal and Sheila not to spend another night sleeping in his office, Braddock instead returned home and immediately felt its emptiness. With Quinn gone, the house had little of its usual pulse and life. It made for a lonely existence. At least Quinn had been true to his word, as he'd used his new phone to make two calls and send three texts and five pictures.

One other thing that inevitably happened when Quinn left for this annual vacation was that Braddock's diet took a three-week turn for the worse. Tonight's example of gluttony was the double butter burger basket and large fries. He took the greasy bag of goodness, grabbed a non-lite beer out of the fridge, and headed upstairs to his home office while reminding himself to make sure the swim went a little longer in the morning.

His nonstop research and continuous phone calls and networking over the past two days had him up to six women who'd gone missing with some similarity to the Genevieve Lash and Jessie Hunter cases.

His latest case was from Iowa City, continuing the noticeable college town theme. Dani Baxter, a twenty-six-year-old literature professor in her first year of teaching at the University of Iowa, was last seen leaving a play at the university's Hancher Auditorium before she disappeared. She'd told the friends she attended the play with that she was skipping a post-play glass of wine and going home. The next morning her car was found abandoned behind a service garage on the western edge of the city. She was never seen again.

There were distinct commonalities between all the disappearances: They always happened at night. With the lone exception of Jessie Hunter, who was seventeen, the women were all in their twenties, falling between the ages of twenty-two and twenty-seven thus far. Jessie Hunter went missing in July 1999 and Lash was twenty years later. His six other cases were in a window of 2005 to 2019, with Lash, and then, if connected, Joanie Wells just three days ago in Brookings, South Dakota.

If all of these cases *were* connected, they spanned twenty years and left him with an uncomfortable thought: there was a decent chance there might be more victims.

This guy is a predator. He hunts and sets them up.

That thought in and of itself made him think of Tori. Surprised he hadn't heard from her, he wondered what she would think of the connections he'd found. Of course, being the pro that she was, he had no doubt she was engrossed in her own case. *And,* he chortled, *being a big thorn in someone else's side for a few days.*

Her last words were "don't stop," and he hadn't. He reminded himself of that as he took a drink of his beer and started removing files from his brown expandable folder.

The victims were pretty women, attractive, in all cases single with no boyfriends or steady men in their lives at the time of their disappearances. All of them were in their twenties, with the exception of Jessie, and all were intelligent, educated, and social. "Not loners, or shy, or withdrawn," he murmured.

All of which brought him back to the lack of witnesses. It reflected planning and discipline. *Because if he sees a witness or has any worries, he simply backs off and tries later or moves on,* Braddock mused as he looked at the files spread across his office desk.

Interestingly, in all of the cases, the women, their purses, and cell phones disappeared. *What does he do with them?* he contemplated as he took a bite of the large burger and then a sip of beer. *Where are the bodies? Probably buried in unmarked graves somewhere around Iowa City, Oshkosh, or Brookings,* he thought.

He stuffed a French fry into his mouth and unfurled a large map of the Upper Midwest on the desk, marking the cities where the disappearances had taken place. "How am I going to nail this down?" he wondered out loud. "How?"

And how could he confirm the cases were in fact connected?

His gut told him they were; they felt connected. Elements of the methods of abduction, the common traits of the women, the college towns all at least suggested there was a connection or a pattern, but could he prove it? And as he evaluated what was in front of him, he couldn't help but wonder whether he was the one who should even try to prove it.

*

As the clock slipped past 9 p.m., Tori stood in the Taylors' home office. With her arms folded she was peering through the blind slats out the picture window, frequently glancing left to the house next door with the faintest of hope that Thomas Martens would return.

She suddenly heard footsteps running to the front of the house. "We have a location on the phone. We need to get moving," Newsom called out as he opened the front door.

"Where?" Tori asked, following him outside.

"I'm surprised, but the Hyatt in downtown Des Moines. We weren't getting a trace there at all, but he must have turned on his phone, and that's where he is."

"He's actually there?"

"Working on confirmation now."

Ten minutes later, as they sped toward downtown Des Moines, Newsom got his answer. "Two Des Moines PD detectives confirmed with two employees at the front desk. Interestingly, he's registered as Thomas Martens," he added as he depressed the accelerator, pushing eighty miles per hour on I-80, with his flashing light moving traffic. "What I can't figure out is why he's still in town."

"To play out the long con," Tori supposed, having thought through the setup since they'd confronted the Taylors hours earlier. "Let's game this out. Say there is a ransom drop, the kidnappers make Jake Taylor take down the network security at his company, they get what they want, and Ava is returned. Don't you think it looks odd if Martens never returns home as David Hutchinson? If he didn't come back, wouldn't people start asking questions?"

Newsom nodded. "Right. He comes back, at least for some time. He and his fake wife."

"Right, because nobody knows their real story. They play it out for, say, a month or maybe two," Tori continued. "Maybe he even keeps the affair going, at least for a bit, before one day saying his wife found out about it. He wants to save his marriage, and to do that they have to move away. With Ava home, or even if Ava doesn't make it back, nobody ever hears of David Hutchinson or Avery Bronson ever again. They disappear and nobody's the wiser."

"I could buy into that."

Newsom pulled into the parking ramp for the Hyatt, and a minute later they were walking briskly into the lobby to find the two local detectives.

"He's in the lobby bar right now," a detective named Grimes reported. "We have two men inside monitoring him and I have two more on the way. This Martens fellow is staying in room 607."

"Any sign of the woman?"

"We showed the photos we have of her, as distant as they are, to the bellman, the front desk, security, and some other hotel staff, and they all said no," Grimes answered. "We've made a walk around the main and upper level here and we haven't seen her."

"What do you think?" Newsom asked Tori.

"Get a keycard for 607," and then Tori looked to Grimes. "Here's what I want you and your men to do."

Five minutes later, Tori was sitting in the swivel chair for the desk and Newsom was leaning against a wall in the entryway of room 607. They heard the release of the door lock and Grimes, with three other detectives behind him, guided an ashen-faced Thomas Martens into the room.

"You're in a lot of trouble, Mr. Martens," Newsom stated flatly, leading Martens by the arm to a soft chair in the corner of the room and forcefully sitting him down. Newsom stood over him.

"Where is she?" Tori asked while turning in the chair to face him.

"I don't know," Martens answered, knowing he was cornered. "I don't know!"

"Where is your lady friend? And does she know?"

"Look, I—"

"Answer Agent Hunter's question," Newsom ordered, reaching down for some extra menace in his voice. "Now!"

"She's not here in this hotel. I'm supposed to turn my phone on every four hours. She calls to check in."

"Show me the number," Newsom demanded.

Martens took out his cell phone, powered it on, and then called up the phone directory. The number was attached to the name Chloe.

"What's her full name?"

"Chloe Moore, if that's really her name. I honestly don't know if it is."

"And what is she to you?"

"She's here to make sure I do what I'm supposed to do."

Newsom took out his own cell phone and made a call. "I've got another number for you to trace," he stated as he stepped out into the hallway.

Martens slumped in the chair.

"Spinal Intelligence, right?" Tori asked.

Martens shook his head. "It's not the company. It's an investor or would-be investor who bought a bunch of stock in the company when the price was way down. He wants something that Internal Medical Solutions has that could give his investment a boost and give him a big windfall."

"Why? Why did you do this?"

"Debts. I have gambling debts. I got in too deep in a regular poker game. Those debts were owed to associates of this investor, apparently. I think he's Romanian. My betting debts in Cleveland were to some Romanians. Anyway, Chloe, on his behalf, says he'll solve my money problem, but I have to do something for him."

"And the something was this? Kidnapping a two-year-old girl?"

"*No. No. No*," Martens answered, shaking his head vigorously. "I'm not a monster. I was just supposed to find some way to compromise Jake Taylor, to blackmail him to drop the security system for his company. There is something this investor is after; I don't know what it is. I was trying to get to know Erica to get to her husband. I could tell she wasn't all that happy in her marriage. I dropped some similar hints, playing the sympathetic neighbor so we have something in common angle. So, day after day I'd stop over to see Erica and we'd talk. One afternoon after about six weeks, she put Ava down for a nap in the family room. We were having a glass of lemonade in the kitchen, talking quietly and standing close, when all of a sudden she leaned in and kissed me—I mean *really* kissed me. And then she asked me if I wanted to go upstairs."

"Just like that?"

"Basically, yeah," Martens replied. "And I went up. Why wouldn't I? But that's when things changed. At first, I was able to get a key, and Chloe and I went into the house when the Taylors were gone, looking for something, but we couldn't find anything for leverage. Jake Taylor is on the straight and narrow. The guy works his ass off and is honest as the day is long. Then I guess the people who put us out here wanted faster action. I didn't even know they were going to do it, but while I was upstairs with Erica, Chloe slipped into the house and took Ava."

"And you just let them do it?"

"I didn't know they were going to kidnap the kid."

"Oh, come on!" Tori protested indignantly.

"I didn't know!" Martens insisted. "I didn't know they were going to do that. I have a six-year-old girl back in Cleveland. I told Chloe I didn't sign up for this but then she stuck a gun in my face and showed me pictures of my parents, my brother, and then my…"

"Daughter."

"Yeah," Martens replied nervously. "If I didn't go along, I wasn't the only one who would pay the price."

"And the million-dollar ransom?"

"They said that would be my payment," Martens replied, slowly shaking his head and sighing. "But it dawned on me while I was sitting at the bar downstairs that it will not happen. I'm too big of a liability now. They're just going to put a bullet in my head when this is over. I deserve it."

"You're going to live, Mr. Martens," Tori stated after a minute. "But you're going to pay a pretty high price for life."

Newsom burst into the room. "Let's go."

They left two Des Moines detectives behind to sit with Martens. As they walked down the hall to the waiting elevator, Tori's phone rang. It was Tracy Sheets. "Hey, Tracy, things are really moving here and I'm stepping into an elevator."

"Okay, call me in the morning. But let me leave you with one number."

"What's that?"

"Twenty-three, and yes, that number means what you think it means." The line went dead.

Tori just stared at her phone.

"You look like you've just seen a ghost," Newsom remarked.

"Yeah, maybe… twenty-three of them," Tori replied, snapping out of it. "So where are we going?"

A half-hour later they were parked along the side of a street in an industrial area in southeast Des Moines. Situated between a salvage yard to the east and a meat-packing plant to the west sat a dirty, one-story cinder block building with two cars and two minivans parked in front of it. Though the windows were covered, around the edges they could see a thin glimmer of light. The signal for Chloe Moore's phone was beeping from that location.

On their way over, Newsom had asked the question, "Is Ava where Chloe Moore is?"

Tori thought it was likely. "From what Martens says, I think she's the brains behind the operation, at least here in Des Moines."

Two plainclothes officers for Des Moines were in the process of slowly approaching the building to try and peer inside. While they made their approach, Tori was once again evaluating the proof-of-life video snippet the kidnappers had left with the ransom demand. The footage of Ava had been filmed in a darker room, but beneath the crib a grimy cement floor was visible. Looking up, Tori could envision such a floor in the cinderblock building.

The radio buzzed to life, with a whisper of a voice reporting, "We can't see inside the windows. They're either painted black or boarded over."

"What do they have for SWAT here?" Tori asked.

"Des Moines has their Metro STAR team: special tactics and response," Newsom answered.

"They probably have some thermal imaging gear. Let's get them down here."

A STAR team was onsite an hour later. Within fifteen minutes they had their answer. There were five human heat signatures inside the building: four in the front and one small one near the floor in the back.

"It's late. They put her down to sleep," Tori reported into the radio. "And they may be going to sleep soon as well."

"Probably in shifts. Someone will be up."

They pulled back nine blocks to a staging area in a parking ramp. There was an eight-man STAR team, four Des Moines detectives led by Grimes with additional patrol units nearby, and then Tori and Newsom. A map of the immediate area was laid out on the hood of a car. Continued thermal imaging of the building revealed the same number of people inside. "There is little movement," an officer reported. "It's very quiet right now."

A plan came into focus. Five STAR men would hit the front with three more taking the back, supported by Tori and Newsom.

"Let's gear up."

Twenty minutes later, with everyone in position, the five-man team parked their truck along the street in front of the salvage yard; using the tall fence as cover, they approached from the east. The three-man team with Tori and Newsom following approached the rear, having worked their way around the perimeter fencing for the meat-packing plant to the west. There was an old, heavy wood door with a deadbolt along the back southwest corner of the building.

A STAR officer named Cowens carefully approached the door, crouched down, and applied a vertical strip of plastic explosive and then a detonator just to the left of the deadbolt. A second officer named Reller had his hand up to his ear. Tori heard him whisper, "Copy," and then, "They're making the approach to the front."

After another thirty seconds, Reller replied, "Copy," again and then nodded to Cowens and the third officer, Brooks, who both gave a thumbs up. Reller then looked back to Tori and Newsom, who'd taken a cover position behind a dumpster ten feet from the back door. They nodded that they were ready.

Reller held up three fingers for several seconds, then two, then one, then pointed at Cowens.

Cowens detonated the explosive. It blew a hole in the door to the left of the lock, but the door remained intact. Reller stepped forward and kicked the door but it didn't give. "Shit!"

At the same time, in her earpiece, Tori heard the STAR officers in front had had the same issue. She shared a quick, wary glance with Newsom.

Not good.

"Kick it again!" Cowens yelled.

Reller did as ordered, and this time it gave in.

Brooks peered into the open doorway. The first shot hit him in the shoulder, sending him down. "Ah fuck! Fuck!"

From the cover of the dumpster, Tori shuffled quickly left, peering inside. She could see down a narrow hallway and spotted a man crouched down, peeking around the corner with his gun up.

Tori slid left another step, set her feet, and had her gun up.

The man peeked around the corner again, this time too far.

Tori fired three times.

The man fell backward, away from view.

"Go! Go! Go!" Tori yelled.

Cowens peered around the corner. With his rifle up, he took a step forward and fired one burst and then another. Tori took another step left and another man, now down farther inside, came into view. Reller fell in behind Cowens and they both moved quickly inside.

Tori looked to Newsom. "I got you."

Newsom leapt around to the front of the dumpster, grabbed Brooks under the armpits, and pulled him back from the line of fire.

"We have an officer down back here! We have an officer down!" Tori reported and then looked inside the building again.

"Police! Police! Down! Down! Down! On the floor now! Now!" voices commanded inside.

Then all went quiet.

Tori left Newsom and stepped inside. The man she'd hit twice in the upper left shoulder was lying on the floor, bleeding, with a STAR officer standing over him.

A second man, the one shot by Cowens, was lying face down in a pool of blood. He was dead.

The STAR officers had two more people now face down on the floor, one of them a woman. Tori quickly recognized her as Chloe Moore.

Then Tori heard it. A whimpering sound.

She looked back to her right and spotted a padlocked door. A STAR officer turned the butt of his gun around and beat down on the padlock. On the third strike, the lock broke apart enough for Tori to yank it out of the clasp. She slowly turned the knob and eased the door open while the STAR officer's flashlight beam illuminated the room. Standing in a crib in footie pajamas with tears running down her cheeks, frightened at all the noise, was little Ava Taylor.

Tori found a light switch and flipped it up, turning the overhead light on before she slowly approached the girl. She picked Ava up out of the crib. "Ooohhh, sweetie, hi," she greeted as sweetly as she could. "Oh, you're okay now, you're okay. Ava, you're okay. *Shhhh.*"

A half-hour later, Newsom and Tori, following a police escort with lights and sirens, pulled into the Taylors' driveway. Erica and Jake came running out the front door and raced to Tori, taking and embracing their daughter. For at least a moment in time, the three of them were reunited as a family.

"Does watching that ever get old?" Newsom asked as the Taylors happily went back inside their house.

Tori shook her head. "No."

CHAPTER EIGHTEEN

*"Does pissing people off come naturally
or do you actually try to do it?"*

Tori was finally able to break away from the scene at the Taylors'
a little before 4 a.m. Newsom wanted her to appear for the 7 a.m.
press conference but she declined.

"We couldn't have brought her home without you."

"I just happened to see something is all. Just remember to speak
slowly and clearly in front of the cameras. People tend to speak
really fast when the bright lights turn on."

After she left the Taylors' she completed her after-action
interview and then went to her hotel and collapsed face down
on the bed in her business suit. She awoke to the buzzing of her
phone at 9:12 a.m. "Yeah," she answered sleepily, not even looking
at the screen.

"Tori?" Tracy exclaimed. "You're still sleeping?"

"Hey, Trace," she answered groggily, slowly flipping onto her
back. "It was a long, long night. It's been a really long few days,
in fact."

"I assume because of that case in Des Moines that's all over the
news this morning?"

"Hang on," Tori replied as she rolled onto her side, finding the
remote and turning on the television, selecting the local station

WHO, where they were replaying the press conference. Newsom was front and center, along with the police chiefs of Des Moines and West Des Moines and the commissioner for the Iowa DPS, speaking about Ava Taylor's return. Tori knew the story and muted the television, then thought back to Tracy's call from the night before. "Twenty-three. Tell me."

"You'll find my documentation for all of it in your email inbox, which includes factual summaries of the circumstances and evidence of each case, a profile of each victim, and contact information for the investigator in charge. As you've surmised, I found twenty-three cases since 1999 that I think fit the profile of your sister and the Lash woman who disappeared a couple weeks ago. That includes one case that's like four days old from Brookings, South Dakota."

"Four days!"

"Yes."

"Are they all in Minnesota, Iowa, Wisconsin, and the Dakotas?" Tori asked in astonishment.

"No. If these are all connected, they're spread out over a far broader area than that. Think the next ring of states around those five and that's the area this involves. The scope of this goes as far west as Bozeman, Montana, to as far east as Grand Rapids, Michigan, to as far south as Manhattan, Kansas. The one thing that seems to ring true about the cases is the women who go missing are either from or live very near college towns; these disappearances are not from major cities. That's one noticeable trend. Another trend is it usually involves a vehicle in some way. In most cases, the women are never found. However, I included four cases where the women were found in the trunks of their cars, bound and strangled. I included them simply because the other factors seemed to fit based on age, use of a vehicle, and college-type town. They might not be a part of all this. In fact, I think that's likely the case."

"What else?"

"With the exception of your sister, the victims' age range is twenty-two to thirty. The other thing, and you'll see this, they gradually get older over time. The last six women are in an age range of twenty-seven—Lash in Minnesota—to thirty."

"Meaning at the beginning, they were closer to twenty-two and now we're closer to thirty," Tori answered.

"Right, they get older as—"

"The killer gets older," Tori finished the thought. "There has to be something to that. How about physical evidence?"

"Little to none, even in the four cases where the women were found bound and strangled," Tracy replied with a sigh. "No eyewitnesses to anything. No surveillance footage of any kind. Forensic evidence is nonexistent for your killer—not even a hair or a print, not anything. The women were last seen leaving work, an event, or a party of some kind, and always at night and well after dark. The next day, except for the four that were found strangled, the women are discovered missing and their cars are still parked at the event, at work, a party site, or somewhere else that has no relationship to anything in the victim's life."

"As if he drove their car to a place where he had another vehicle waiting."

"That's a distinct possibility," Tracy answered.

"And the victims? Besides age range, what do you have?"

"They're educated and have college degrees with a few exceptions. They're all attractive, thin, and smaller in stature, with the tallest being Lash at five seven. There is a mix of blondes and brunettes and one redhead. There is no rhyme, reason, or pattern to the months or the gaps between disappearances. Although there are usually several months between them, with the notable exception of Lash and this case in Brookings, which is the smallest gap by far between abductions."

"That is odd," Tori answered. "If Brookings is connected, I wonder why he'd move so quickly."

"Ask him when you catch him," Tracy replied.

"And we have no forensic evidence, nothing on our killer? Twenty-three women and zip? Even with the four women who were found?"

"No, other than one thing that might clinch the deal: the four women who were found strangled are connected. They all had marks, two dots on their lower backs, an inch or two apart."

"Which could be from what?"

"One medical examiner theorized they could be markings from a stun gun."

"Interesting," Tori replied. "Have you discerned any other patterns to the women and their disappearances?"

"No," Tracy answered. "Not beyond what I've told you, and to be honest, I've put about as much as I can into this without being *too* noticeable, although the boss has figured out that I've been digging into something."

"Graff?"

"Yeah. Hell, he's staring at me right now. It's only a matter of time before he asks."

"You've done more than enough, Trace," Tori replied. "Do me one last favor. I need you to email this to a detective named Will Braddock. Send it in twenty minutes, I want to call him first." She recited Braddock's email address, double-checked it, and then thanked her and hung up. Her next call was to Braddock.

"I thought I might hear from you," Braddock said as he answered his phone. "I saw the news about Des Moines, congratulations."

"Thanks, heck of a case."

"You'll have to tell me all about it later. I've been doing some research since you left. I think I've found six other cases that might match your sister and Lash. We have a serial."

"You're not the only one still working the case," Tori answered eagerly, explaining what she'd had Tracy Sheets doing. "Tracy pegs the number at twenty-three missing women who fit the profile of our victims and who have gone missing since my sister did. I'm not sure the number is that high. She included four women who were found bound and strangled in the trunks of their cars, but they fit our victim profile. That, and interestingly, all four have a similar marking on them which might be from a stun gun…"

She stopped talking for a moment.

There was silence on the other end of the line.

"Braddock? Will? Are you still there?"

"Uhh… did you say… twenty-three?"

"If you include those four, yeah. Plus, you add in Jessie and Lash, you get to twenty-five. Katy doesn't fit the profile, but she figures into this somehow, so that gets this up to as many as twenty-six."

"Cripes." He sighed. "Are you coming back up here?"

"I just woke up. The flights to the Twin Cities are full so I'll be in my rental car in twenty minutes. I should be there later this afternoon."

"And the FBI is good with that?"

"They will be. I have a lot of unused leave time."

"Color me shocked at that," Braddock replied dryly. "I'll keep an eye out for the email. Lord have mercy, twenty-three."

Tori hung up from the call with Braddock and jumped in the shower. As she got out, her phone rang. It was Graff.

Graff was far from on board with Tori going back to Minnesota. "Agent Hunter, I have work for you here."

"I'm not done with this yet."

"Tori, you know as well as I do that this is not how it works. Agents don't get to fulfill their own personal agendas on cases. And given your relationship to that case in Minnesota, you shouldn't be within a hundred miles of it."

"I'm going back to Manchester Bay," Tori replied simply.

"Tori, if you don't come back, I can't guarantee you'll have a job when you do return. I have people to answer to as well."

"Because of my dedication to the job, I have months and months and *months* of unused paid time off, Rick. The Bureau owes me, not the other way around. Apply my unused paid time off or grant me an unpaid leave of absence."

"On what basis?" Graff asked, stunned by the pushback he was receiving from his subordinate, even if it was Tori.

"I don't know, make one up," Tori replied brusquely. "Or fire me."

"Tori…"

"You know what, I'm fine with any of the three options. You choose, but I'm not coming back right now."

Click.

"I can't believe I just did that," she muttered, admonishing herself. She was self-aware enough to understand her combative nature to be what it was. Nevertheless, even she was surprised at how short she'd been with Graff, a demanding but exceedingly fair boss. She would have to call him back and smooth things over, if for no other reason because of the respect she had for him. Her brusqueness, however, was a sign of something she needed to remedy soon. "Tori, you need more sleep," she told herself, already dreading the lengthy drive back to Manchester Bay.

She wasn't the only one who lacked rest. Seven hours later, she found Braddock in his office. Will Braddock, the detective who said he didn't bring work home, that he didn't let it eat away at him, was the picture of something entirely different. He was unshaven, rumpled, and visibly weary.

"When's the last time *you* slept?" Tori asked with just a slight hint of concern in her voice.

"I should probably ask you the same question," Braddock answered. "But for the record, I haven't really been sleeping." Then quietly, with his voice low, he gestured to his computer screen and a map of the Upper Midwest. "Nobody else around here knows about this… yet. At least not about *twenty-three*."

"What do you think?" Tori asked as she walked around behind Braddock's desk and leaned in close, looking over his shoulder. The two of them examined the map on his computer screen and quickly scanned the mass of information they now had on each of the cases. In total there were twenty-three dots on the map. The FBI's list included the six that Braddock had found on his own.

"These nineteen cases *feel* connected," Braddock answered. "There are so many consistencies with the age of the women, their look and background. And then you have the circumstances of their disappearances, the involvement of a vehicle, college-type towns, and so on. It definitely feels like *something* is there."

"What about those other four?"

"They *were* found. The other nineteen weren't, so they don't fit our guy's pattern. But these nineteen? I think they're the same guy."

"It's amazing that nobody picked up on it before now," Tori remarked.

"Yeah, but they're all so spread out," Braddock reasoned. "Over such a wide area, over a long period of time, and there is just enough of a difference in the cases that unless someone was really motivated to go hunting for the connections, they wouldn't make it."

Tori nodded. "But we are really motivated."

"Yeah, but Tori, these findings again bring up an important question."

"Which is?"

"Is the killer really based here? Given the breadth of area covered, he could be living anywhere in the Upper Midwest. Why wouldn't we present this to the Bureau, the BAU? This is their thing. I mean, if this is the work of one man, he's operating in at least twelve states by my count. I'm just a little ol' sheriff's detective in north-central Minnesota."

"I know he's here."

"How? How can we know that?"

"Katy Anderson."

"Other than timing, how could you possibly know that's even connected to this?"

"How can you think it's not?" Tori demanded, her voice rising. "I show up here. We start investigating these cases. We go to see Katy and then suddenly she's gone—*vanished*!"

"Why?"

"Maybe she knew something? Maybe she saw something?"

"What could she know, Tori? What could she have seen?" Braddock asked sharply in reply, his voice rising to meet Tori's. "We interviewed her. The detectives on Jessie's case interviewed her years ago. She didn't know anything. So again, how do we know it's connected?"

"But the timing of it?"

"Is the only thing that might tie it in, *might*. I know she's your friend, I *know* that. And I know you feel responsible, but she doesn't fit the victim profile in the least. She's seven years older than the oldest of our possible victims. She doesn't fit the physical or educational profile. Katy's the answer to which one of these doesn't belong with the others. Other than timing and that you're here, what says her case is related? What piece of evidence says that? There's nothing. Katy Anderson does not mean the killer is here!"

"Then what about the article I got?" Tori fired back hotly. "What about that? The only logical conclusion to be drawn from that is the killer wanted me back here, in Manchester Bay. Why? Because that's where *he* is. Genevieve Lash was taken on the twentieth anniversary of Jessie's disappearance. Explain *that*, Detective!"

Braddock stood up. "He's taunting you. He's in your head, right where he wants to be. He has you chasing this thing but that doesn't mean he's here. He could be hundreds of miles away for all we know."

Tori wasn't having it. "It's staring you right in the face, Will! You have a serial killer here, right here in Manchester Bay. He killed Lash, Katy—he killed my sister, and you're too damn afraid to admit it or to go after it. You just want to pass the buck to someone else and wash your hands of it so you can go back to barbecuing and waterskiing."

"Oh, is that right?" Braddock replied bitterly. "I've been working this case morning, noon, and night because I want to give it away? Go to hell, Tori. What I want is it solved."

"Me too."

"No!" Braddock barked, pointing at Tori. "You want to solve it. *You.* I don't care if I close it as long as it gets closed, as long as the killing stops."

"This is not about me!" Tori shouted.

"Ohhh, it's *all* about you," Braddock accused, hitting at her weak spot. "You know, I checked on you with people I know in the FBI. As an agent they called you a brilliant investigator—cool, calculating, logical, methodical, and dogged. They respect the hell out of you, every one of them."

"Then what's the problem?"

"All of them also said you could be a complete and total pain in the ass. Ever since you've been here, I've seen *little* brilliance but *plenty* of pain."

"Oh, is that so?"

"You're not objective, you're not being methodical or calculating. You have tunnel vision on this. You're going in just one direction, forgoing all others."

"It's about goddamned time someone did!" Tori yelled, losing control. "You're not!"

Braddock snorted, shook his head, paused, and then started grabbing his keys and a folder full of papers. "Tell you what, Special Agent Hunter, how about you get the hell out of my office and out of *my* investigation? I think I've had enough of what you call help."

"Your investigation?"

"Yeah, remember our agreement? It's my case, I run it. Let me ask you, did the Bureau assign you here?"

Tori didn't respond. She couldn't respond.

"That's right, they didn't. You have no jurisdiction here, *none*. You weren't invited to this. I didn't call and ask for *your* assistance. I don't need your help, and even if I do, I can get it from someone who isn't constantly in my face, second-guessing everything I think and do."

"Don't do this," Tori pleaded.

"Hell, this isn't even your area of expertise. I don't have a missing child or a missing teen. I'm not dealing with a kidnapping. And if I were, it would be for an adult, not a child. For that, I've got a very capable, professional, non-pain-in-the-ass Twin Cities FBI office I can liaise with."

"You can't do this!"

Braddock pushed past her to reach for his suit coat hanging behind his office door. "It's been a *real* pleasure working with you," he added as he walked out the door.

Tori, angry and steamed with her body trembling in rage, could only watch as Braddock stormed out. Everyone in the hallway had heard the argument and was staring back at her, including a visibly perturbed Cal Lund, who was leaning against the wall with his arms folded just outside his office door. Tori spotted him and walked directly toward him.

"Victoria…"

"He can't do that! You can't let him do that!"

"In my office," Cal replied calmly as she marched inside. He closed the door behind them.

"Cal, he can't—"

"Victoria, please sit down."

"Cal!"

"Sit down and shut up, *now!*"

Tori froze, stunned. In the entirety of her life, she'd never heard Cal raise his voice like that to anyone. Sheepishly, she did as she was told, slowly taking a seat and lowering her face into her hands. "Cal, he can't do that to me."

"Yes, he can," Cal replied, now sitting down behind his desk. "That is, unless I were able to convince him otherwise."

"Then convince him otherwise," Tori demanded, looking up. "He needs me on this. He can't possibly solve this thing on his own. Hell, I don't think he really cares to."

"Dammit, that's enough," Cal ordered, glaring angrily at her. After a moment, he calmed a bit and added, "You need to get control of yourself because you're on about everyone's last nerve around here."

Tori simply nodded, looking to the floor.

Cal sighed, shook his head, and then checked his watch. It was after five. He took his service weapon and dropped it into his desk drawer, locked it, and then loosened his tie. He pulled open a lower drawer and took out a bottle of Wild Turkey and two white ceramic coffee cups, pouring a small amount in each and sliding a cup across his desk for Tori.

Tori looked at the cup for a bit before she reached for it. She took a slow drink while still leaning forward, her elbows resting on her thighs. It wasn't often she found herself in the principal's office.

"Now, young lady, Will Braddock has done nothing but work this case since Genevieve Lash went missing. Day after day. I had to send him home last night for Christ's sake because he slept in his office two nights ago. The man is obviously totally spent, yet you get all up in his face anyway."

"Cal…"

"I'd have told you to go to hell, too. And let me tell you something else: he thinks I don't know about all these other women who have gone missing, but I do. I know what he's up to. If you count your sister and Lash, there are eight women—"

"Actually," Tori interjected, but quietly, "it's maybe twenty-three, and if you include Jessie and Lash, it's twenty-five."

That set Cal back. "Excuse me? Twenty-three? Twenty-five? Where the hell are you getting this?"

Tori explained what Tracy Sheets had found researching out of the FBI field office in New York City. "The file was sent to Braddock earlier today. Twelve-state area. It all starts with Jessie in 1999 until now."

"And you think the killer lives around here?"

"I do. Braddock questions that."

"Whether the killer is here or not, I think Will is probably right… maybe somebody else should be working this besides just us. More resources need to be applied to this."

Tori sat back in her chair, exhaled, and closed her eyes for a moment. She wanted to choose her next words carefully, something she hadn't done in the last hour.

"Cal, I see why you and Will might think that. I…" Tori exhaled a sigh. "I see the sense in that… I do. But let me say this first. I haven't been able to really review all twenty-three cases yet to see how strongly they fit together. These are twenty-three cases that might be tied together, or they might not. There are four that may not be part of this at all because the victims were found strangled in the trunks of their cars, so those don't fit the overall pattern. But that still leaves nineteen. I'd like a chance to work it, and work it with Braddock first to see if we can figure that part out. If we do, then we have something to go to the Bureau and the other states with, and maybe we can get some sort of joint investigation or task force put together on it. But I don't think we're there yet."

"Well, that brings us back to Will then. He is *not* happy with you."

"I can tell he's been working it hard," Tori replied earnestly. "One look at him and you can see it. But with all due respect, he needs me—you need me. I'm sure he is a fine investigator and all, but—"

"Fine investigator? That's all you can muster for him?" Cal chuckled in reply, shaking his head in dismay. "Let me ask you something, hotshot, what do you really know about him? We know *all* about you and your background. But have you even bothered to consider his? He called around on you. Have you called around on him? Maybe completed a rudimentary Google search?"

Tori shook her head. "No," she replied, but she could tell Cal was leading somewhere.

"Then you have no idea who you're dealing with. Do you think you're the only one who's had to deal with tragedy? Will Braddock is right there with you."

"I know he's from New York, was a detective with the NYPD, and was married to Meghan Hayes and moved here after she died of cancer. What else is there to know?"

"There's a lot more to him than that," Cal replied as he took a long drink from his cup. "In New York, Will had his detective's shield for about two years and was working the First Precinct. You know where that is, right?"

"South Manhattan."

"He was on duty on 9/11. He and his partner were standing on the street drinking coffee when the first jet flew right over them and went into the North Tower. They jumped in the car and drove to the World Trade Center, helping with building evac. They were both in the South Tower when the second plane hit. Will barely escaped when the tower went down but his partner, his mentor—a veteran detective named Jim Quinn—was still inside and died."

"Quinn is his son's name," Tori remarked.

"That's right, Quinn James," Cal answered. "A couple of months later Will Braddock joined the Joint Terrorism Task Force. If you have any Bureau friends who worked in New York with that unit, ask them about Will. I'll guarantee you they know who he is. He's something of a legend."

"Legend?"

"He was involved in a number of cases where terrorist attacks were stopped. The biggest occurred six months after Meghan died. Will was shot multiple times by a terrorist while thwarting an attack in Times Square. Case ring any bells?"

Tori nodded. She remembered her phone pinging with text message after text message about first the search for the terrorist and then later the shooting in Times Square.

"Will almost left Quinn without a parent. It was maybe four months later, after he'd recovered from his wounds, that I got a call from Meghan's dad, Roger Hayes, asking if I needed any investigative assistance or knew of anybody in our neck of the woods here who'd be interested in hiring an NYPD detective with Will's background. He was looking to move here to raise his son and be closer to the only family they had." Cal refreshed his drink. "I jumped at the chance to hire him, so much so that I basically created his position. He's a damn good man who is fully, *fully* invested in your sister's case, and all you're doing is pissing him off."

"I'm sorry…"

"Does pissing people off actually try to do it?"

"I think a little of both," Tori replied, sitting back in her chair, tipping her head to stare at the ceiling.

"Maybe you ought to think about sitting down with someone and figuring out that little character quirk of yours. I imagine there may be a number of issues you've deferred work on."

"You're probably right, but…" She sat forward and sighed. "I'm sorry, Cal. I'm really sorry," Tori said softly, feeling fully admonished and only more embarrassed. "It's just that this case… Jessie… Katy."

"You should walk away from it."

"No. I can't quit it, not now. I just can't."

"No," Cal replied with an exhale, "I don't imagine you can."

"What do I do? I'll do whatever you think I need to do."

"Well, tomorrow is a new day," Cal reasoned. "Give Will a night to clear his head and get some sleep. I'm going to call him in a bit and make sure that's what he does because Lord knows he needs it, as do you. You look totally fried, young lady. I imagine all that ruckus down in Des Moines has left you a bit sleep-deprived, am I right?"

Tori nodded.

"But you got the girl back?"

"Yeah," Tori said with a nod. "Yeah, we did."

"Good, you see, the day is not a total loss then. Come back in tomorrow and mend the fence—and I mean really mend it. If you don't, then you've got a problem because if it comes down to a choice between you and him—" Cal shook his head "—I'll have his back."

"I'd be supremely disappointed in you if you didn't."

Twenty minutes later, Tori checked back into the Radisson. After a long shower and room service dinner, she jumped underneath the covers, turned on her computer, and typed in an Internet search for Will Braddock.

*

"So, you're back in town," the man mused, sitting behind the steering wheel of his car after watching Tori Hunter transport her bags into the entrance of the hotel. "We begin again."

He'd known when he took Lash and sent Tori the newspaper clipping that there was a good chance he would finally draw her back home and into the little drama he was creating.

That's what he wanted. He wanted to tease and torment and ultimately terrify her, and—if the opportunity presented itself with the right circumstances—reunite Tori with her sister.

That was a part, a juicy byproduct, of his overall plan. And it had been proceeding as he'd hoped.

Then Katy Anderson showed up that night and now he was exposed.

Braddock and Hunter had at least some information, if not evidence, that if they pieced together just right could lead to him.

Tori, as evidenced by her return, would never give up now that he'd drawn her here and she'd had a real taste of it. She would be relentless and would never stop coming, not now.

And Braddock surprised him. He'd viewed him as a more than competent cop, but that assessment was short of the mark. Braddock was far better than he thought. The detective was onto the other missing women that he'd killed. More urgent than that, his own level of investment in and growing obsession with the case was unexpected. He hadn't properly anticipated the effect Tori's presence would have on Braddock. She was dragging Braddock into the vortex, her pull irresistible.

He sensed danger in the two of them reuniting.

The good news was, the two of them were very predictable in one specific way.

CHAPTER NINETEEN

"A mercury switch?"

Tori awoke at 6:20 a.m. She inhaled and felt… rested. The last time she remembered looking at her watch was just after 8:30 p.m. So assuming she'd fallen asleep around that time, she'd managed to get a solid nine plus hours of sleep, something she'd needed for weeks. What she did remember before falling asleep was what she'd read about Braddock.

Of all the things Cal had said to her, the one that really stung was that she didn't know anything about Braddock. The chagrin got worse when it took her less than a minute to find article after article about the shooting in Times Square.

*

Detectives and agents with The Joint Terrorism Task Force closed in on Mahmoud Abidi, a suspected terrorist.

Abidi traveled to Pakistan twice in the two years before his name appeared on the task force's radar. In his travels he became radicalized, as further evidenced by his associates in Pakistan, his online activity, and intelligence chatter. The task force began closely monitoring Abidi and determined there was a high risk he was going to act.

The suspected terrorist lived in an apartment building in the Bronx. A task force entry team moved in to make the arrest. However, despite Abidi being under constant surveillance, and having been seen entering the apartment building a half-hour before the team moved in, Abidi was not in his apartment.

NYPD Detective Will Braddock was onsite out of interest as Abidi was operating in the same circle with another target that Braddock's particular team was investigating. He wasn't in full tactical gear and was part of a loose perimeter around the building. When Abidi wasn't found in his apartment, all officers fanned out to search the area surrounding the building. It was Detective Braddock who spotted a man in a long black coat, matching Abidi's description, hurriedly taking the steps up to the platform for the number 2 subway line a block outside the perimeter.

Detective Braddock pursued the man and managed to get onto the last car of the train just as the doors closed. The problem was, Detective Braddock had left his hand radio in his car, and his cell phone wasn't working once they descended into the subway tunnels.

As the train progressed south into Manhattan, Detective Braddock worked his way forward and was able to identify that the man was in fact Abidi.

Unfortunately, Abidi also spotted Detective Braddock and the two of them stared one another down.

Abidi jumped off the train at Times Square at the last second as the doors were closing. Detective Braddock didn't beat the doors but still managed to get off the train by kicking out a window and jumping out as the train was beginning to pull away. Abidi was climbing the steps up to the street and Detective Braddock gave chase.

As he neared the street level, Abidi peered back and saw Braddock coming up from behind. Abidi sprinted up the last steps to street level and into Times Square. It was five o'clock on a business day, and the streets were full of people at the height of rush hour.

As he reached street level, Detective Braddock saw Abidi pulling back his long trench coat. The terrorist had an assault rifle and—as was found out later—two pipe bombs, several grenades, and two other handguns. Detective Braddock ran into the middle of Broadway to get away from the crowded sidewalks, yelling for people to get down while drawing Abidi's attention.

The terrorist pivoted to the detective and fired. Braddock, without Kevlar, stood his ground and returned fire high. He managed to kill Abidi, hitting him in the head, thwarting the deaths of possibly hundreds. But he was wounded three times himself in the process, twice in the right chest and once in his right thigh.

*

Tori had sat back after reading the story, silently admonishing herself for not knowing any of this.

All of that was once again ruminating in Tori's mind as she changed into her running gear and then filled her water bottle. She wanted a good, long run to get herself going, clear her head, and think about how she was going to apologize and put herself back in Braddock's good graces.

Tori exited the front of the hotel and was immediately enveloped in thick and humid air. People often thought of Minnesota as some sort of frozen northern tundra, and in January and February it was. But the summers were warm, frequently hot and full of humidity, even up in lakes country. Today was going to be a classic Minnesota steamer—hazy, moist, thick air and a blazing sun.

She took a few minutes to fully stretch out her legs before taking a drink from her water bottle, which she then re-tucked into the back sling of her waist pack. She then secured her Oakley shades tightly, slipped in some earbuds, selected one of her music mixes, and then started her run over to the path that ran along the east side of the H-4. It took her a quarter-mile before the sweat started seeping out of her pores and she realized a headband would have been in order.

*

He preyed on the predictability of human nature.

Tori left in the same direction as she had the week before. She was taking the running path up the east side of the H-4.

It took him less than ten minutes to drive north, park, and pick his way through the woods to his nest. Cloaked under a dense canopy of pine and spruce trees, he raised the binoculars to his eyes. Seven minutes later Tori came into view, jogging around a gentle bend in the path southeast of his position. She was perhaps three-quarters of a mile away.

He was perched up high on the hill, crouched down just inside the treeline, peering down to the path running along the far side of the highway. Dressed fully in camouflage, he mixed in with the dense coverage of mature, thick buckthorn fronting the woods and the low-hanging, droopy branches.

With one last look through the binoculars, he could clearly make out that it was her coming along in her tight black and pink running attire, maintaining a brisk, steady pace. He put the binoculars down and raised his rifle. Through the scope he tracked her, turning his body gently left along with her, allowing her to come into a more comfortable range, keeping her steady in the crosshairs.

*

She glanced to her Fitbit, nearly three miles into her run, her whole body now fully engulfed in a heavy sweat. The air was like a humidity blanket wrapping around her body, and it wasn't even 7 a.m. yet.

Needing to hydrate, she reached for her water bottle. She took three more strides before stopping. She took out her earbuds for a moment, holding them in her right hand while popping open the bottle's cap with her left. She raised the bottle to her mouth and squeezed.

The bottle exploded, splashing her face with water.

"Ow! What the hell?"

Her left hand seared in pain and oozed blood.

She tossed the water bottle and bolted to her right as another shot rang out, whistling by her head to her left.

Tori desperately searched for cover as she ran through the uneven ground of the high grass, but straight ahead there was a wide, steep, treeless rise. She'd be a sitting duck if she tried to climb it.

Another shot rang out and zoomed by on the left again.

Tori veered hard right, spotting a grove of smaller trees. She sprinted over the undulating ground, pumping her arms and legs, diving into the grouping of trees as another shot rang out, passing right over her and spraying bark from a birch tree that hit the left side of her face. She rolled headfirst into the trees, awkwardly somersaulting and landing with her back against a small tree with a thinnish trunk.

Another shot pelted the tree's trunk.

Frantically she searched around for denser cover. She scrambled on all fours behind the base of a thicker tree, ten feet deeper into the grove, as another shot sailed by, hitting the trunk of a tree to her left. Now behind the thicker trunk, she pulled her arms and legs in, making herself as small as possible, her back tight to the base of the tree. Two more shots rang out. Both hit the front of her tree at her head height, and the bark and pulp showered down.

Gasping heavily and shaking, she held position. She unzipped the phone compartment in her waist pack, pulled out her phone and dialed 911.

*

"I can't have you burning out on me," Cal had ordered. "Eat a healthy meal and go to bed."

Braddock allowed himself an extra half-hour of sleep, until six thirty, before he slowly rolled his long body out of bed, heeding Cal's demand that he get a long night's rest.

He felt better. And he needed the energy, because he knew he'd be dealing with Tori again. That absolutely required that he be refreshed and *patient*. She wasn't going to just go away and, being honest with himself, he didn't want her to. Agitator that she could be, the reality was he needed her. Although, he thought devilishly, for payback he was going to make her grovel a little before he let her back in.

He made his way down to the basement and pulled on swim trunks, grabbed a pair of goggles and a bright yellow rubber swim cap, and made his way down to the dock. A sultry yet calm morning, there was barely a ripple in the dark blue water. He made his customary long flat dive off the dock and began his swim in the refreshing lake. With long, smooth, freestyle strokes, he glided through the calm water thirty feet out from all the cabin docks jutting from the shoreline. As was his custom, he swam as far as his in-laws' house.

Once there, he climbed up the dock and ran up to Roger and Mary's house to quickly check on it. All seemed secure. Back along the dock, he briefly inspected the covers for the pontoon and the wave runner; both were still tightly cinched.

Already he could feel the humidity enveloping him as he stood for a moment on the end of the dock. The lake would be busy later today, he thought as he dove into the water and made his way back north. Swimming freestyle, he made long, languid strokes. Sensing he was approaching home, he quickly glanced up, looking for his dock now a hundred yards away, and saw Steak running full speed down the hill from his house.

That can't be good, he thought as he hastened his pace.

"Holy cow, thank God you're alright!" Steak exclaimed with relief as Braddock stepped up the ladder and onto the dock.

"What the hell is going on?" Braddock asked as he reached for his towel and then his phone. One look at the screen and he realized he'd missed a mass of texts and calls.

"Someone just took a bunch of shots at Tori," Steak answered.

"Shots? Gunshots?" Will asked, his mouth agape.

"Yeah."

"Is she okay?"

"Yeah. Someone tried to sniper her while she was jogging along the running path on the H-4, a couple of miles north of town. She managed to get away, but just barely, man. Grazing wound to her left hand and a couple of scratches on the face," Steak reported and then asked, "What are you two on to?"

Braddock snorted. "Hell if I know, buddy. I feel like all we've done is spin our wheels on the ice and argue with each other."

"Maybe not."

"Maybe not is right. We need to get into town," Braddock stated as they both made their way up the small hill to the cabin. "I have to dry off and get into clothes."

"Do you want to ride with me?"

"Nah, I'll need the Tahoe at some point," he said as he ran upstairs. He took a one-minute rinsing shower, eschewed a shave, rapidly dressed, and hustled back down to the kitchen to find Steak starting coffee.

"We need to get going!" Braddock exclaimed.

"We can wait for coffee," Steak answered calmly. "She's alive and okay. Tori's fine. I bolted out here because you weren't responding to my calls and texts. I hoped you were taking that swim and something else bad hadn't happened. The coffee will be ready here in a minute. You might want to remote start the truck though, it's parked right in the sun. It's hotter than blazes out there. Get your air conditioner cooling that bad boy down."

"Good idea," Braddock answered. He fished his keys out of his pocket and hit lock then the remote start button. "Huh."

"What?"

"Didn't start," he replied as he opened the back door and stepped out onto the stoop. He hit lock and then the remote start button again.

BOOM!

Braddock was blown back through the door and crashed with his back into the angled corner of the kitchen island while glass from the blown-out windows rained down on him and Steak. Braddock rolled onto his left side and looked out the back door to the towering ball of flames engulfing his Tahoe.

"What the fuck, Will!" Steak yelled, dropping to his knees. "You okay?"

"Yeah," Braddock replied as he pushed himself up and stumbled forward out the door, shielding his face from the inferno of the fireball in the driveway. "We need to get those hoses!" he shouted to Steak as he jumped off the stoop and grabbed the hose gathered up in the landscape rocks next to the back of the house. He quickly twisted on a spray nozzle and turned on the spigot. The Tahoe was toast, but he needed to keep the fire contained and away from the house and garage.

"I called 911!" Steak bellowed before disappearing around to the front of the house. Seconds later, he was hauling up a second garden hose. Braddock's neighbor was doing the same, rushing over with his own hose. The neighbor and Steak watered down the grass and trees while Braddock applied water to the area between the front of the Tahoe and the house and detached garage. Fifteen minutes later, with the SUV still ablaze, a fire department pumper truck pulled up, and familiar local faces started disembarking from the big rig and hooking up a firehose.

"Will, we got this," a volunteer fireman named Jersey yelled.

The two detectives and neighbor stepped back inside the house to assess the interior damage. The back windows of the house were blown out; glass was everywhere. Braddock ran upstairs and found the windows for his office, bathroom, and bedroom were blown out as well. "Cripes, what a mess."

He descended the steps back to the kitchen, where he found Steak out on the stoop, watching Jersey and another man douse the fire with a powerful stream of water. A larger group of neighbors had gathered as well, including one that Braddock sought out, Sam Edwards, a home builder. "Sam, can you help me out here?"

"You bet, Will." Edwards got on the phone. "I'll get a couple of my guys out here. We'll get you patched up."

"Thanks, Sam," Braddock replied, shaking Edwards' hand. He walked back over to Steak, shaking his head. "Buddy, what the hell was that?"

"I don't know, but you need to get the bomb squad out here. That wasn't some short in the transmission wires or something. That explosion was intentional, boss. Someone tried to barbecue you." Then he looked to Braddock. "Seriously, what is it you and Tori found?"

"Honest to God, Steak, only more missing women but no clue who's responsible," Braddock insisted and then grabbed Steak by the shoulder. "By the way, damn good thing you told me to start the car from the house."

"*Fuuuuck*," Steak blurted in reply, his tanned face suddenly going pale, remembering the suggestion. "Holy mackerel, that's right. Oh, man."

Two hours later, early morning was turning to late morning. With the fire long extinguished, a forensic team from the BCA crime lab out of Bemidji arrived along with the bomb squad, closely followed by Cal and Tori. Her left hand was freshly bandaged, and she had a butterfly wound closure on her upper left cheek.

"I'm really glad to see you're okay," Braddock greeted quietly.

"Ditto," Tori replied, taking a long look at the Tahoe.

"You're going to need a new vehicle," Cal noted. "You can use your own pickup truck if you want, or there are two department Ford Explorers not in regular use. You can use those until we replace the Tahoe here."

"I'll take one of the Explorers," Braddock said.

It didn't take long for a bomb squad officer to figure out what had caused the explosion. After the tech took photos, with gloved hands the bomb squad officer pulled a small object from underneath the frame of the truck, just under the driver's seat. He slipped it into a plastic bag and then walked over.

"Detective Braddock, it's a good thing you started the Tahoe from your house," he said as he held up the bag.

"What's that?"

"Looks to be a mercury switch."

"A mercury switch?" Braddock asked, taking hold of the bag. "And how does it work?"

"There was likely a glass tube that was part of this that had mercury in it," the officer explained. "Any small movement or vibration, such as starting the vehicle, would trigger the mercury in the glass tube to move, which would close the circuit. That triggers the explosion."

"I see," Braddock replied, twisting the bag in his hand and inspecting the contents.

"The device was placed on the bottom of the chassis, right under the driver's seat. Whoever placed that there was expecting you to be in the seat starting the truck, not using your remote starter. Why, if I may ask, did you use the remote starter?"

"Steak suggested it, thank God. It's hot and the Tahoe was parked in the sun. The truck would have been boiling hot and I wanted it cooled down when I came out to leave."

"Is there any way to trace these pieces?" Cal queried.

The officer grimaced. "We'll work with the crime scene folks and see what we can do, but one, these pieces are really charred so getting anything off them forensically will be really difficult. Two, the reality is you can make one of these switches in your garage at home. It's not rocket science."

"But it does require mercury, liquid mercury, right?" Tori asked.

"Yes, yes, it does," the bomb squad officer affirmed.

She looked to Braddock, Cal, and Steak. "Where around here can you get mercury?"

"My guess is you could order it on Amazon," Braddock answered, to which the officer and Cal nodded.

"There is the explosives plant," Steak suggested with a shoulder shrug. "I bet they have mercury out there."

"Someone takes a shot at *me* and then they try to blow *you* up. Someone doesn't like what we're doing," Tori stated, clearly determined to keep going.

"All I know is we better find out who that is before both of us end up *dead*," Braddock answered darkly, now visibly angry. He looked to Tori. "We've seen what happened here. Let's go evaluate what happened with you."

Tori, Braddock, Steak, and Cal drove back to the site of the shooting along the H-4. Eggleston was on scene. The crime lab was getting a workout this morning, with two techs working the area. Tori showed Braddock where she'd been when the first shot had come. The exploded water bottle was in the ankle-high grass to the right of the path, denoted with a yellow numbered marker. Fifty yards to the east, two investigators were now examining a tree, taking photos and measurements; it looked as if a bullet was embedded in it. One tech was holding up a thin red stick, assessing the trajectory of the bullet lodged five feet high in the tree trunk. The trajectory looked to be from a higher angle.

"You'll probably find three or four embedded in trees," Tori remarked to the tech.

Braddock turned and looked to the bluff towering high on the west side of the highway. "Have you found the sniper's nest yet?"

"No," an investigator answered, "that is next."

"We'll get that started," Braddock ordered. He, along with Tori, Steak, Eggleston, and Cal, all pulled on rubber gloves before they worked their way up the steep hill, moving fifty or sixty feet high to the edge of the treeline that was a mix of spruce, pine, elm, and white birch. Based on where Tori said she was when the water bottle had exploded and where the second shot had hit the tree, they spread out about the length of a football field.

Steak found the spot five minutes later. "Over here!"

"What do you have?" Tori asked, reaching him first.

"Shell casings."

"He didn't clean up the brass?"

"I guess he panicked and ran," Steak speculated, looking over his shoulder, deeper into the woods. "But he sat here and waited for you," he conjectured, turning back to her and then pointing to the right another three feet. "See that?" He pointed to two cigarette butts.

Braddock arrived, and when he saw the casings and cigarette butts, he immediately ordered everyone to keep back while Eggs called across to the techs on the other side of the road. Braddock, Tori, and Cal then moved twenty feet farther south along the treeline. "So, tell me again what happened," Braddock asked Tori.

"I was taking my run along the path over there. It's hot, obviously, so I slowed and reached around for my water bottle and stopped. As I was starting to take a drink, the water bottle exploded." She held up her left hand. "My hand was burning. It was dripping blood."

"And then?"

"I took off into the high grass and then made for those trees." Tori pointed to the small grouping of trees across the highway. "He just kept shooting and shooting."

Braddock nodded. "How many times have you run this path?"

"At least five times before this morning, but all prior to leaving for Des Moines."

"I see," Braddock answered. "This is a good spot: it has height and an unobstructed view of the H-4. The highway is in the valley here so what little wind we have is blocked by these trees behind us and the bluff. Pretty optimal shooting conditions. You're lucky."

Tori simply nodded, staring across the highway.

"Will? Tori?" Steak yelled from deeper in the woods, waving to them. "This way!"

Steak tracked deeper into the woods. He found fresh indentations in some tall grass on the rear edge of the treeline that looked to be the width of tire tracks. The tracks led onto an old dirt road, and because it had rained recently, there was some soft mud on the edge of the road where the two tracks emerged from the woods and knee-high grass.

"This is why I deer hunt with you, man," Braddock remarked with a grin.

"We need photos and molds of those tracks," Steak suggested.

Braddock looked back to Eggleston, who was already calling it in.

"So where does this road lead?" Tori asked Steak.

Steak peered around the area. He'd lived in Manchester Bay his whole life, but even he had never been in this particular area. "The impressions are angled such that the vehicle went north. I think if we go that direction, it eventually leads out to County Road 96."

Braddock had his phone out, using Google Maps, and showed Steak the screen.

"Hmmm. This road isn't even on the map, but…" He took the phone from Braddock and tweezed the screen with his fingers, zooming in on the satellite image. "That's Fran Larson's house on that corner there, and that's a mile, maybe a little more, away. Might be worth visiting her."

Cal called for crime scene at their location and another vehicle. "You all need to keep on this."

Fifteen minutes later, Braddock, Steak, and Tori were motoring along the dirt road and discovered Steak had called it right. It led to County Road 96, and on the corner was Fran Larson's place.

The two-story plain white clapboard house with red shutters was situated south of the intersection, set back from County

Road 96 by perhaps fifty yards, with a long, well-manicured lawn gently sloping out to the road. They found Fran Larson sitting on her front porch, a pitcher of lemonade and several newspapers and magazines strewn haphazardly on a small rectangular wicker table in front of her chair. Her two black labs popped up and came galloping down the steps and out to greet them, their tails eagerly wagging.

Fran immediately recognized Steak as the three of them walked up, calling him by his given name. "Jake, good morning, or—" she looked to her wrist "—I guess it's good afternoon now. What brings you out here this warm day? I mean, my goodness, you look like you've been through the wringer already. You all do."

"If she only knew," Tori quipped under her breath, which drew a wry chuckle from Braddock.

"We just need a few minutes, Fran," Steak started while staring at the pitcher of lemonade. "You know, I would never impose, but my gosh, the lemonade looks fantastic."

Fran smiled. "Well, of course, three more glasses coming up then," she answered, clearly happy to have a little company as she scurried back into her house. Fran was back a moment later with a fresh pitcher of lemonade, three more glasses, and a plate of gingersnap cookies. With Steak's help, the lemonade and cookies were quickly served and greatly appreciated.

Steak took a chair opposite Fran while Tori and Braddock leaned back against the porch railing. "Fran, we've been busy this morning and we're wondering if you can help us." He provided some background as to why they were all on her front porch drenched in sweat.

"Heavens to Betsy, you two went through all that yet you're still working?" Fran asked Braddock and Tori.

"We have to, ma'am," Tori answered. "While the trail is hot."

"I do suppose that's the case."

Steak looked over to Tori. "What time were you running?"

"At that point it was probably six fifty, give or take a few minutes," Tori replied. "The first time I remember looking at my watch after everything happened, it was six fifty-eight, but that was after I called 911."

"Well, I was out here reading," Fran Larson answered, nodding. "I'm up at five thirty each morning. I let the boys here out to do their business while I grab my newspapers and magazines. I sit here on the porch, have my coffee, some toast, and catch up on the world's events. There's much to read about, don't you know."

"So, between six forty-five and seven fifteen, you were out here then?" Braddock confirmed.

"Sure, you betcha."

"Do you recall seeing anything that caught your attention around that time?" Steak asked.

Fran shrugged. "What would I have been looking for?"

"Did you see a car or maybe a truck come racing down that dirt road over yonder? At any point in that time window we just discussed?"

Fran thought for a moment, sitting in her rocking chair and looking out to the road. "Now that you mention it, I remember seeing a white van come down the road and turn hard onto the county road out there, squealing the tires. It didn't hardly stop at all. Blew right through the sign, turned hard, and kept flying away."

"Is that unusual?"

Fran nodded. "That dirt road doesn't get much use these days now that 96 is all finished. It used to be part of the road people drove to get back this way before they paved 96 all nice and straight-like."

"Can you describe the van?" Tori asked.

"Sure. White panel van. Had racks on top for ladders and other stuff."

"It wasn't Panel Van Dan, was it?" Steak asked, referring to a well-known local handyman.

"Oh no, no, no. I know Dan's truck, he's done some work for me. There was no writing on the van I saw. But I can see why you'd reference Dan. The van I saw was plain white and had a rack, ya know, and…" She paused for a moment. "It had a black bumper, the back bumper was black. I remember that, too."

Tori looked to Braddock, who was already reaching for his phone and had stepped off the front porch. "Sheila, yeah… I'm fine, we both are… Yes, thankfully. I need you to look something up for me."

Ten minutes later Tori and Steak stepped down off the porch and walked back to find Braddock finishing up a call. Before Tori could ask him about it, Braddock blurted, "I'm hungry. Let's get lunch. Judy's Counter isn't far from here. Let's go."

They grabbed a quiet table in the back of the small restaurant, awaiting their order of greasy sandwiches.

Once they'd sat down, Tori looked to Braddock. "What gives?"

"I had Sheila run a quick search of our database of men in the area ages thirty-seven to sixty-five, you remember that list?"

"I do."

"You have a list?" Steak asked quizzically.

"I'll explain later," Braddock answered and then looked to Tori. "She did a vehicle search, and there is someone on that list that we all know who has a van like that."

"Who?" Steak asked.

"Gunther Brule, and he works at Sidwell Explosives, too."

"You don't say," Tori remarked.

Their sandwiches were delivered. Everyone grabbed napkins and, in Tori's case, silverware.

"That's a sandwich, you know," Braddock noted, gesturing to Tori, who had a fork and knife in her hand.

"I'm not holding that. Look at all that grease and cheese, it's a mess."

"You mean oozing goodness," Steak stated gleefully, putting his big mitts around his sandwich and delivering it to his mouth. "That's heaven right there," he mumbled while he chewed a gigantic bite.

"I suppose you use a fork and knife on pizza, too?" Braddock asked as he picked up his sandwich.

"Sometimes," Tori replied.

"Seriously? You don't fold a long slice in your hand?"

"No."

"Pfft. Some New Yorker you are."

"Oh fine, *whatever*," Tori replied, dramatically dropping the plastic utensils and picking up and squeezing the sandwich. The cheese, mustard, and mayo oozed out the sides as she dove face first into it, taking a huge bite and then slowly chewing as a greasy, cheesy smile spread across her face. "God, that's so good."

Braddock approved. "That's what I'm talking about."

Steak got them back to business. "You know, Will, I do recall Gunther having a white panel van, and he has a pickup truck, too."

"And he was at least around the night Jessie went missing," Braddock remarked. "We know that."

"He said he was; others also said he was," Tori confirmed. "I don't honestly really remember if he was or wasn't. He wasn't lying when we interviewed him: he didn't necessarily run in our crowd back in that day."

"But he said he wanted to."

"I'd have to agree with that," Steak added. "Gunther was something of a friend back then. For what it's worth, I'm still friendly with him now."

"How friendly?" Braddock asked.

"To say hi and spend five minutes chatting if I run into him somewhere, but he's not a social friend, if you know what I mean. He's just someone I know from back in the day."

"Did Jessie have any sort of relationship with him?" Braddock asked.

"Jessie certainly didn't date him, if that's what you mean," Tori answered.

"She probably led him on, though," Steak remarked.

"Steak!" Tori protested.

"Tori, she was a tease."

Tori shot him a dirty look, but Steak didn't back down. "We're talking relevance here. Jessie was a flat-out dick tease. She led guys on, a total flirt, and she'd leave them hanging all the time. She did it to a lot of guys, whether it was me, Eddie, or someone like Gunther. She would have taken perverse pleasure in giving someone like Gunther a glimmer of hope by even just saying hi to him in the hallway."

"Come on, that's not fair."

Steak was undeterred. "Your sister was my good friend, but don't you ever think of denying it."

Tori's defensive look receded. She sighed and reluctantly admitted the truth of the statement. "My sister had a way with the boys, always did. She had them calling and asking her out. If we had texting back then, I can only imagine what that would have been like. A date for Homecoming was never an issue for Jessie. The question was simply which one. It was like *The Dating Game*."

"Dates probably weren't a problem for you, either," Braddock offered.

Tori snorted a little laugh. "To the contrary. We were identical twins, but Jessie was always the prettier one, the more social and outgoing of the two of us. Her friends were my friends—if we double-dated it was because Jessie set it up. I was the more… serious, intense one."

"That I can believe," Braddock replied with a snort of his own.

"What?"

"The serious, intense part."

"And you haven't changed," Steak added, drawing another defensive look from Tori. "What? *What*, Tori? You haven't. The only difference now is you're not afraid to speak your mind too."

"What are you saying, Steak? That I'm feisty? Difficult? A pain in the you know what?"

"Well… yeah, maybe a little of each of those."

"So I've been told," Tori replied with a knowing headshake. "I guess I really need to start working on that," she added, looking apologetically to Braddock. "And I will."

"Fire is good," Braddock offered agreeably, "when channeled properly. So, you want to start channeling it on Gunther Brule?"

"Does a bear shit in the woods?"

"Ahh," Steak laughed. "There's your Minnesotan showing through."

*

He pulled his truck to a quick stop in front of the small house. Grabbing the rifle from behind his seat, he fast-walked to the shed and opened the lock. Inside the door, he pulled back the rectangular floor rug, reached down, pushed in the small blank, and heard the click. A door-sized segment of the floor popped up. He hit the light switch on the wall, and he walked down the steep steps into the basement underneath and to the gun cabinet, where he placed the rifle inside. Taking a quick look in the mirror, he noted how sweaty he was and the small scratch near his eyebrow, undoubtedly from running through the woods to the van.

With the gun put away, he went back up the steps, locked everything up, and then jumped into the truck and drove back up to the main house. Inside the quiet, musty house, he took a quick shower, waiting some time for the water heater to kick in before washing away the sweat and dirt. Out of the shower, he examined the cut on his brow and became a little less concerned. With the blood cleaned away there were two small scratches, both of which could easily be concealed with some makeup in a day or two.

Having fully dried his hair, he went to the closet in one of the bedrooms and took out a spare white T-shirt and pair of khaki shorts, clothes that would be good enough to get him home.

His phone buzzed with an incoming text from a friend:

Did you hear? Someone tried to kill Tori Hunter and Will Braddock this morning.

He typed back in response:

Tried? Are they okay?

Yes. They both lived, although there was an explosion at Will's house.

How was there an explosion yet Braddock wasn't dead? How had Braddock avoided that?

CHAPTER TWENTY

"Everything tells you something."

Tori, Braddock, and Steak made their way back to the sheriff's department late in the afternoon and they reassessed where they were at. It would take some time, hours or more likely days, for ballistics to come back from the crime lab, and they would have value only if they could find a gun to match it with.

"Forget it," Steak mused. "That gun is at the bottom of a pond somewhere. It's too hot to keep."

The cigarette butts had been collected, but DNA results would take time. "I might be able to help expedite that," Tori offered, and Braddock said he just might take her up on it.

The crime lab had also collected pieces of the mercury tilt switch and would evaluate them, but just as the bomb squad officer had done, the tech from the crime lab tempered their expectations. "We'll do everything we can, but given the charred state of the pieces of the device, I doubt there will be much for us to find forensically."

Then there was the matter of Gunther Brule.

Tori was giving him serious thought and looked to Steak. "You know, back when we were in high school, Gunther was nice enough. He was a pretty good-looking guy who liked a party, but he was a little on the quirky, awkward side too. Which is maybe why he didn't necessarily… fit in with the group."

"You guys were the cool kids?" Braddock asked.

"Pretty much," Tori replied, "and as Steak noted earlier, Jessie was the queen cool kid."

Steak agreed. "That's how it was. As for Gunther, I'd agree with the quirky comment, and over time he got even more so. He served early in the second Gulf War as an infantryman and I think he experienced some serious shit over there. He came back to Manchester Bay and the quirkiness was gone. When I saw him after he got back, Gunther seemed…" Steak struggled for the words. "He just wasn't the same guy. You could see it in his expression, in his eyes. He seemed damaged; there was more of a darkness to him. A lot of guys came home from the war that way."

Gunther was a hunter; he liked guns and owned them. And he was a smoker now, so the cigarettes they'd found by the shell casings could be tested. "But tested to what?" Braddock asked. "I checked and there isn't an on-record DNA sample, at least not in CODIS, of Gunther Brule to compare them to."

"Not yet, anyway," Tori answered. "One thing at a time." She paused for a moment, pacing in front of Braddock's desk, a disconcerted look on her face.

"What are you thinking?" Will asked.

"We kind of eliminated Gunther a couple of weeks ago."

"Eliminated is a strong word," Braddock countered, nonplussed, leaning back in his desk chair with his hands locked behind his head. "I'd prefer to say he was downgraded as a suspect. We're allowed to miss on occasion, but I also think it's a little early yet to conclude we were wrong."

"You're saying you don't think it's him?"

"No. What I am saying is we don't want to get ahead of ourselves. We have a *maybe* identification of his van in the area of your shooting from an elderly widow sitting a good distance away."

"I don't know, she seemed pretty on it to me."

"I agree, but we still need another way to tie him to that area."

"Then let's go get some."

"How?"

"Would he be home?"

They all drove over to Brule's house. While Steak waited in his vehicle, Tori and Braddock walked around the house, but Brule was not home.

"It's a weeknight, where else would he be?"

Braddock closed his eyes and thought for a moment. "It's a weeknight, there is one place he could be, the VFW."

"Well," Tori mused, "if he's there, I also have an idea of how we could get a DNA sample."

Roger Hayes, Braddock's father-in-law, was a Navy veteran who liked to go to the VFW and would invite Will to join him on occasion for beers. Brule was often there, especially on weeknights. As Braddock and Tori pulled up to the front entrance, they had immediate verification Brule was inside. His white panel van was parked on the street in front of the bar.

"Ballsy, driving that thing out in public tonight," Tori remarked.

"Everything tells you something."

Braddock and Tori went inside while Steak, who had followed along in his own truck, remained outside. He took photos of the van, getting some close-ups of the tires and their tread, along with photos of the front, sides, and back to show to Fran Larson.

As Steak took photos, Tori stopped and said, "Wait."

"Okay. Why?"

"I need to do something first." Tori looked in the truck's side mirror then reopened the door, reached into her purse, took out some light red lipstick and applied it. Next, she took off the butterfly bandage and then applied some makeup to the scratch.

"The hair needs work," she murmured as she undid her hair from her ponytail. She let it fall to her shoulders, tossing and re-tossing it with her fingers, giving it some life, letting it fall along the sides of her face for a sultry look. She'd let her red blouse hang loose, but now she tucked it tight into her pants so that it hugged her body, and then she undid an extra button, revealing just a hint of cleavage. She turned to him. "What do you think?"

Braddock stammered, "Uh… wow!"

"Down, boy," Tori replied lightly with a bright smile, a little surprised by both his visible appreciation of her new look and that she felt a tingle of excitement that he did.

"Well, you'll get his attention, that's for sure. My question is what's your play here?"

"If he's a killer of women, let's see how he reacts to me and *this* look, especially since looking like this is about as close as I could ever get to looking like Jessie," Tori said, taking another look in the mirror.

"Make him think he's looking at a ghost."

"A little something like that," she replied, still tossing her hair, using it to help cover the scratch on her cheek. "If I had more time, I could do a little more with all this," she noted with a light laugh before turning back to Braddock. "Let's go."

"You lead, I'll follow," Braddock replied agreeably as he followed Tori and let his eyes just briefly gaze upon her as she walked. With her hair down and walking with a little extra sassy hip sway, she was strikingly attractive. *Down, boy* was right.

Inside, Braddock and Tori found Brule sitting at a table with another man. Tori led them over, striding purposefully.

"Gunther, we need to ask you some questions," Tori said matter-of-factly, and a little loudly, as she pulled out the chair next to him to sit down. Braddock looked over to the other man at the table and tilted his head toward the bar. The man took the hint, picked up his beer, and hastily walked away.

"I'll catch up with you," Brule said to his friend before taking in Tori, who was leaning forward in her chair smiling, her eyes warm and friendly. If her plan was to get Brule to look her over, to appreciate her physical beauty, to leer, it had worked. His mouth was agape. It was clear he wasn't sure what to make of her approach.

After a moment, Braddock intentionally snapped Brule out of his stare by slamming his chair down and turning it around backward before sitting, resting his arms over the chair's back, and facing him.

Brule glanced over to Braddock, who was relaxed and casual. He eagerly turned his attention back to Tori, who'd gone from a pleasant smile to a suddenly intense glare that instantly made Brule visibly uncomfortable.

"I heard someone took a shot at you today," Brule said flippantly to Tori. As an overall conversation starter, it was a mistake.

Tori held up her left hand. "Yeah, about that," she replied, her glare boring into him and her voice rising. "You got anything you want to tell me? Perhaps some grudge against me or Jessie that you're trying to avenge? Tell me, *Gunther*, did my sister, my gorgeous identical twin sister, turn you down twenty years ago? Did Jessie not welcome your advances or the look? And you know what look I'm talking about, it's the hungry look you just gave me. Jessie didn't like that look, she wasn't interested in you, so you *killed her!*"

"*Whoa*," Gunther replied, stunned at the hostility and suddenly realizing where the topic was going. He glanced around the VFW. People were peering in their direction with interest at the disturbance and the raised voices. "Let's take this outside."

"Oh, let's."

A minute later as they gathered on the sidewalk, Gunther lit up a cigarette.

"Are you going to answer my question?" Tori pressed angrily with her arms folded across her chest. Braddock just let her go.

"Why? Why would I know anything about that?" Brule replied.

"Where were you at six forty-five this morning?"

"At home sleeping. I've been taking the week off of work."

"Can anyone verify that?"

Brule looked at her with a blank expression before slowly shaking his head. "No, I don't suppose anyone can. I live alone—the old lady bailed on me six years ago. I guess I had a lot to drink last night. I didn't wake up until, I don't know… it was like noon, I think."

"I see," Tori replied, unconvinced.

"Why are you asking me about this?"

"I'm asking the questions," Tori shot back. "Tell us about last night."

Brule explained that he'd had a lot to drink at Eddie Mannion's house. "We went out on the pontoon for a bit and then sat around drinking into the night."

"You said we. Who else was there?" Braddock asked.

"Eddie, Jeff Warner was there. Kyle stopped by. They'll all verify I was there."

"Well, it's not last night that's the problem, Brule," Braddock noted, his notebook now out, but he nodded to Tori to go ahead.

"Tell me, do you still work at the explosives plant?"

"Yeah."

"And what do you do there?" Tori queried.

"I'm an operations manager."

"So, you run the place?"

"I'm one of the people who does."

"You guys have mercury out there?"

"Sure. So?"

Tori turned to look at the panel van. "I assume that's yours."

Brule acknowledged that the white van was indeed his.

"Gunther, what kind of guns do you own?"

Brule's eyes widened and he sensed danger. "My guns are none of your business."

"You really think that's the play here?" Tori asked, leaning in.

"You have a warrant, Tori? I have rights."

"Do you think I'm going to have a problem getting one?" she replied with amusement. "What do you think, Will?"

"A lot of interest in the Lash case and your sister's disappearance, plus we shouldn't forget that Katy Anderson has gone missing and Gunther here certainly was a denizen of our fine town when all of these unfortunate events occurred. I'm sure one of our honorable judges would share our noble interest in the pursuit of justice."

"Now, wait a minute—"

"No, you wait," Tori cut him off, raising her voice. "You like guns. You like to hunt. You were in the army, a soldier, an infantryman. You served in Iraq on the front line."

"So?"

"What's the farthest distance you've ever shot someone from, a hundred yards? Two hundred yards?"

"I'm not responding to that."

"Why not, you got something to hide?" She looked over to Braddock. "I think he's got something to hide."

"Could be," Braddock replied more casually, pivoting slightly left and gesturing toward the white panel van. "Your van there, Gunther. You're sure, you're absolutely sure you weren't out driving that rig on County Road 96 this morning?"

"No. Again for the tenth time. I. Was. Sleeping."

"Which nobody can verify," Tori asserted hotly but she was in control. Braddock could tell she was trying to provoke Brule.

"Why would somebody have to verify it? Why are you asking me all these questions?"

Tori and Braddock responded with silence, being patient, waiting for it.

Suspects being interrogated couldn't stand silence. It made them nervous, so they asked questions or made statements that provided more information. And then, there it was.

"What? You think I took a shot at you this morning?" Brule laughed. "Good luck with that, Tor," he said as he flicked his finished cigarette aside and exhaled smoke. "I can tell you this: if I took a shot at you, you wouldn't be standing here now."

"Hmm. Really? The shot at me this morning was from a good distance, 150 yards or so with a moving target. It was a tough shot. It would require someone with experience to even attempt it, let alone execute it. How many folks around here have that? How many people have that experience and a history with Jessie, me, Katy Anderson, and Genevieve Lash? I bet pinching her ass that night wasn't all you did."

"Now, Gunther," Braddock started, stepping in while Tori backed away. "Right now, we're just asking questions," he stated calmly, evenly, and without emotion while closing his notebook and stuffing the pen through the spirals. "But someone tried to blow me up with a mercury tilt switch underneath my truck. Now where around here might someone get mercury?"

"I could take a wild guess," Tori snarked.

Braddock chuckled and then nodded to his partner. "Someone tried to shoot Tori, and in looking at who that could be, your name came up. Like Special Agent Hunter here said, you knew Jessie Hunter, you were a classmate of Katy Anderson, and you had an incident with Genevieve Lash the night she went missing."

"And someone drove me home after that," Brule barked.

"That's right," Braddock replied. "Around eleven. Lash left the bar around one. Your pickup truck was left at Mannion's on the Lake, but *not* your van here. Can you verify where you were between one and, say, seven in the morning on July 5?"

"I was at home sleeping."

Tori laughed. "Well, isn't that a familiar alibi. Can anyone verify that?"

Brule didn't respond.

"Look at it from my perspective, Gunther," Braddock replied reasonably. "You like guns and have experience. You work at an explosives plant, where I bet you could get ahold of some mercury, *and* you have this van over here."

"Why are you so interested in my van?"

"Maybe you ought to ask yourself that question," Tori replied.

"I've got nothing against you guys."

"So you say," Tori answered, but then she held up her bandaged hand and pointed to the slightly covered but still visible scratch on her left cheek. "You better hope you didn't have anything to do with this."

"What's that supposed to mean? Is that a threat?" he asked directly.

"No," Braddock replied evenly with his hands in his pants pockets and his posture relaxed, countering the heat and hostility of his partner, until he cocked his left eyebrow and dropped his voice. "But, if you did, we'll figure it out, and then you'll have a lot of questions to answer, and not just for taking a shot at us." He looked over to Tori. "Let's go."

Braddock and Tori turned to leave, and while starting to walk away, Braddock took out a pair of rubber gloves. He handed them to Tori, along with an evidence bag, and they stopped at the cigarette that Brule had flicked away.

Tori leaned down while Braddock took three quick photos with his cell phone. She picked up the cigarette butt and dropped it into the evidence bag before looking back at Brule with an evil grin on her face.

Brule just glared back at them.

Braddock and Tori walked farther down the street and got into an unmarked sheriff's department Ford Explorer.

Once inside the truck, Braddock smiled over to her. "You know what, I think we've earned a beer of our own."

"Lead the way. I'll buy."

*

Brule checked his rearview and side mirrors constantly as he drove west out of town. Having had three beers, he was careful to follow the posted limit along the way, coming to a complete stop at all stop signs and lights while continuing to look back for a tail. The mirrors remained mostly clear all the way home, including his last glance before turning slowly left and taking the narrow, tunnel-like, tree-lined gravel driveway that led to the open clearing where his one-story house and sizable detached garage were located. With all his tools and equipment, an old fishing boat that he was restoring, and his Dodge Ram pickup truck taking up all the room in the garage, he pulled his van to the right of the structure and parked it on the exposed cement slab.

As he angrily stalked to the house, he peered warily back down the driveway, but it remained dark. Inside, he put the keys on the hook by the back door and went to his refrigerator and pulled out a bottle of Budweiser. He twisted off the top and took a long, gulping drink with narrow streams of liquid trickling down his cheeks, downing at least half the bottle before pulling it from his lips and wiping his mouth with the back of his hand. He was pacing manically around his kitchen, agitated. He started working from window to window, peering around the edges of curtains or tweezering open blinds, looking out, trying to see if anyone was coming for him. Not satisfied, he went outside and walked down the driveway, walking tight to the thick treeline. When he reached the end, he was careful to hang back just inside the edge of the treeline and crouched down as he peered west and then east back toward Manchester Bay. The road was quiet. He didn't see anyone parked and observing his property.

He walked back to the house and called Eddie Mannion.

Eddie answered on the second ring. "Hey, Gunth—"

"Did you drive me home last night?" he asked, suspicious.

"Uhhhh, yeah, don't you remember? You were like *way* too hammered to drive."

He sighed and exhaled. "That's what I thought, or at least that's what I thought I remembered."

"Why do you ask?"

"You drove my van back here?"

"Yeah, why wouldn't I have?"

"Who drove *you* home?"

"Jeff. He followed us there and helped me get you in the house because, my friend, you needed help getting in the house. I got you into bed, left a glass of water on the nightstand— because I'm that kind of friend—and then left you to sleep it off. Jeff dropped me back off at home. Now again, why?"

"Because someone tried to shoot Tori Hunter this morning."

"I know, I've heard. Everybody's heard. It's all over town."

"And someone tried to blow up Will Braddock," Gunther replied anxiously. "You know him, right?"

"Sure. I've heard that too, his truck exploded. But again, so?"

"I think they think I tried to do it."

"They?"

"Tori and Will Braddock," Gunther answered and then related the confrontation with the two of them at the VFW. "I'm telling you, Eddie, they think I did it."

"What did you say to them?"

"I tried not to say much, although you know me, I got a little pissed," Gunther answered, sighing. "Man, this is…"

"What did they ask you?"

"Umm… they kept asking about my van and then they asked what guns I own."

"Tell me you didn't say anything."

"On the guns, no. I said nothing, that it was none of their business, and maybe something about them needing a warrant."

"You suggested a warrant? Dude, there's some red meat for them," Eddie replied, exasperated.

"They put me on the spot, man. I mean, they asked about the guns, but they asked more about the damn van. Then they picked up the cigarette butt I tossed on the sidewalk and put it in a plastic bag," he finished as he took another beer out of the fridge, twisted off the top, and then took a long drink.

"Gunther? Gunther?" Eddie asked.

"Sorry, I was slamming a beer," Gunther replied as he wiped drops of beer off the front of his shirt. "I don't get why they're so fixated on the van. They kept asking me if I was out driving on County Road 96 this morning around seven, or maybe seven thirty."

"Were you?"

"No! God, you sound like them, Eddie."

"I'm just asking questions, buddy," Eddie replied. "I'm just trying to help."

"I was sleeping. I was fuckin' passed out drunk sleeping. I didn't wake up until like noon. What the hell did I have to drink last night?"

"I don't think anything out of the ordinary," Eddie answered. "Now, did they tell you why they think you had anything to do with it?"

Gunther shook his head. "No, they just kept asking questions about the van and what I was doing this morning. Like I said, they asked again and again if I was out driving on County Road 96, stuff like that."

"Huh."

"Huh what?" Gunther asked, hearing the questioning tone from Eddie. "Huh what, Eddie?"

"I wonder."

"You wonder *what*?"

"I wonder if they're asking about County 96 because what I'm hearing is that the shots at Tori Hunter came from high on the bluff on the west side of the H-4, a couple miles north out of town. The shots happened around seven, maybe a little earlier. The shooter had to get away from there so I'm guessing that someone thinks they saw you, or maybe your van, or a van like your van in that area this morning."

That has to be it, Gunther thought as he took another long pull of his beer before setting the empty bottle down on the counter. "Man, Eddie. The way Tori and Will looked at me, talked to me, and *challenged* me, I think I might need a lawyer. The guy I used years ago when I had that thing with my ex, he's retired now. How about Jeff? He'd scare the hell out of them. Would he help me?"

"I don't think he could represent you. Criminal law isn't his area, nor his law firm's. At least, I don't think it is. But I'm sure he knows somebody that we could hook you up with. I'll give him a call. Are you okay with money, for one?"

"I have some money in the bank," Gunther replied, pacing nervously around his house. "But I'm not like you, Eddie, there isn't a bottomless well of cash."

"What are you going to do?"

"I'm going to go up to my cabin and think. Knowing this town, a thousand people already know the police were talking to me. I need some space."

*

Braddock drove them to JJ's Saloon, a small, out-of-the-way bar ten miles west of Manchester Bay on the outskirts of the small town of Pillager. They grabbed a snug booth in a dark corner and ordered beers and a pizza.

"So, you bring me all the way out here. You're either embarrassed to be seen with me or perhaps you have ulterior motives, Will. Which is it?" Tori teased good-naturedly.

Braddock snorted a laugh. He wasn't sure what his motives were at this point. "Well, first, no man in his right mind would be embarrassed to be seen with you, Tori. As for ulterior motives, there is another way of looking at that."

"Which is?"

"As you've discovered, Manchester Bay is a lot bigger now, but it still behaves like a small town. We go have a beer somewhere in town, just you and me, and it'll go viral. Well, at least as viral as something in Manchester Bay can go."

"Really?"

"How long did it take for word of your arrival to get out?"

"Not long."

"How long did it take me to find out you'd appeared at the Steamboat Bay Tap Room?"

"Even less time."

"I rest my case," Braddock replied and then steered into safer territory. "So, were you standing in front of your sister's killer when we were talking to Gunther?"

"Maybe," Tori answered mutedly after taking a drink of her beer and giving it a moment's thought. "The way he looked at me when I walked up to him inside, the way he looked at me out on the sidewalk, it was like he…"

"*Lusts*," Braddock finished the thought. "I mean, he was looking at you like he wanted to…"

"Do me?"

"Oh yeah, for sure."

"I got that vibe, too. His look *was* predatory."

"He has the off-center look, manner, and oddness to him that he looks like…"

"A killer," Tori supplied. "He looks like it. Is he?"

"One way to find out is to take that cigarette butt we just retrieved and get a DNA comparison to the ones we found this morning. That would answer the question. I was wondering if maybe you could Rapid DNA it through the Bureau."

"Consider it done."

"Good," Braddock replied, taking a long pull from his beer and sitting back into his side of the booth. "You know, we ran a good little game there on him."

"I was thinking the same thing," Tori said with a smile and then turned serious, moving to take care of something she'd been waiting all day to address. "I need to apologize to you for yesterday."

"Tori, it's okay…"

"No," Tori insisted, shaking her head, reaching across for Braddock's free hand and taking it in both of hers, pausing for a moment. "No, it's not. It's not. I was *so* out of line yesterday. So out of line. I was wrong to say those things and I'm just really, *really* sorry I did."

"Tori, look…" Braddock paused, glancing away for a moment, collecting his thoughts. "One of the things I sometimes forget is that… you're not just a cop here. You're a victim. I lost sight of that yesterday."

"That doesn't give me the right to behave the way I did, to say the things I said."

"You were tired," Braddock demurred. "We both were. Fuses were short. Going like we were both going, a blowup was inevitable."

"Still…"

Braddock softly patted Tori's bandaged hand. "I'm just glad you're okay. I'm glad we both are."

"Me too," Tori replied, looking up to Braddock, "me too."

CHAPTER TWENTY-ONE

"The simplest answer is usually the right one."

Tori woke up and went for a run on the treadmill in the hotel's gym. Once she'd finished and showered, with a Starbucks coffee in hand, she coordinated with the BCA crime lab in Bemidji, arranging for Brule's cigarette butt she'd collected last night and a sample from one recovered yesterday morning to be shipped to the FBI lab at Quantico for Rapid DNA testing. Then, relaxing in the lobby and enjoying her coffee, she placed a call to her friend at the lab, Kelly Wong, who promised to get the test run as soon as possible. "You know us, Tori, open 24-7, 365 days a year and still behind. I'll squeeze it in somewhere, maybe this weekend when nobody is looking."

"You're the best. How can I take care of you for this?"

"I accept wine as payment."

"Done," Tori said and made a note to send Kelly just such a good bottle of wine.

At 10 a.m. she drove over to the sheriff's office and found Braddock in his office working. "I meant to ask you last night, how is your son doing?"

"Quinn's in Michigan having the time of his life."

"I assume you haven't told him about the truck bomb?"

"I might have neglected to mention it, although his grandfather cross-examined me pretty thoroughly on it. He strongly suggested I join them in Michigan."

"Bet you were tempted."

"You have no idea."

"What about your house? What about the windows? All that glass."

"I'm lucky, let me tell you. My next-door neighbor is a home builder and a total mensch. His guys came in within a few hours of the blast and hoovered up the glass and inserted plywood in the windows. Then he measured everything up and called his windows supplier and placed the order himself. The new windows will be here tomorrow, and they'll install them. My insurance guy, another good dude, lives just down the road. He's getting the claim processed. Those two together are looking after it. It'll look like new in a few days, other than the scorch marks, of course. I'll deal with those later."

"The house isn't a complete mess then."

"No," Braddock answered, "although I went around again this morning with the vacuum. There's still a few glass shards around."

Steak and Eggleston stepped into Braddock's office. Braddock sent them out to once again chase down Lash's friends to press them about Brule and to follow up with Fran Larson with the pictures of the van.

"What are we doing?" Tori asked.

"Going to see Gail Anderson. I bet you thought I'd forgotten about Katy."

Tori shook her head. "No, I know better now. It's just that no matter how much I think about her and what happened, I can't figure out her role in all of this."

"Me neither," Braddock answered. "And I've been a skeptic, but the timing is what it is. It's hooked into this somehow."

Gail Anderson was relieved to see the two of them. "I heard about yesterday," she said warily with her arm wrapped around Tori. "Who is doing these things?"

The three of them sat out on the front porch, sipping iced tea in the shade while Braddock explained the reason for their visit. Gail knew who Gunther Brule was since he'd gone to high school with Katy, but she had no recollection of having seen him recently. "I'm sure Katy hadn't seen him in years. She hadn't seen *anyone*. Honest to God, Tori, you were the first friend she'd really talked to in years. So as for Gunther Brule, he certainly never showed up around here, and I can't think of any reason he'd have an issue with Katy."

Their next step was to confirm Gunther's whereabouts on Tuesday night, stopping first at Jeff Warner's law firm where they were informed he was working from home. "He's the boss, it's going to be a beautiful day, so…".

Tori and Braddock drove to Jeff Warner's home on the lake. "This place must be worth a couple of million," Tori remarked, looking around in wonder as they walked up the flagstone sidewalk around the house.

"Easily," Braddock affirmed. "I can't believe he didn't lose it in one of his divorces."

They eventually found Warner out on his large dock, sitting at a table under an umbrella, a laptop open and a legal brief in his hands. There was a beer already open and two more in a small ice bucket. "I don't suppose I could offer you two a refreshment?"

They waved off the beer.

"I heard about yesterday." He looked to Tori. "How's the hand?"

"Stitched but usable."

"Who the hell is doing this to us? To you?" Warner asked.

"That's why we're here," Tori replied.

"How can I help?"

"We have some questions about Gunther Brule."

"He's a friend, you know."

"Are you his lawyer?" Braddock asked, looking up from his notepad.

"No," Warner replied with a headshake. "Just friends. What do you want to know?"

"Tell us about this past Tuesday night at Eddie Mannion's."

Warner confirmed he was at Eddie Mannion's on Tuesday night and had drinks with Brule. He defended his friend in a backhanded sort of way. "Look, Gunther's a pretty good guy but certainly not the brightest. In fact, he does some flat-out stupid-ass shit."

"Such as?"

"He rides his four-wheeler around without a helmet and waterskies sans life jacket because he finds it too restricting. And, of course, in front of dozens of witnesses he pinches a woman on the ass."

"Do you think he thought Genevieve Lash would actually be interested in him?"

"No, even he isn't *that* dumb," Warner replied whimsically, shaking his head. "Again, he does some stupid shit. But he's basically a decent guy."

"He knocked his ex-wife around," Braddock noted. "That doesn't sound so decent."

"No," Warner replied, nodding before taking a small sip of his beer, "it doesn't. Stupid shit again. Are you detecting the theme here?"

"You're suggesting there's a correlation between his drinking and his judgment," Tori surmised.

"Exactly. Now, look, I didn't get along with either of my ex-wives, but I never ever thought once of striking them no matter how much we argued. You just can't go there."

"So, why did he?"

"If I had to guess, I'd say it's because he has some issues. Gunther…" Warner shook his head sympathetically. "The guy came home from Iraq and he was not the same."

"PTSD?" Tori asked.

Warner nodded. "Probably. I've said to him more than once that he should go down to the VA and get some help, but he's just a stubborn redneck, ya know."

"Does it make him violent?"

"Not that I've ever seen personally," Warner answered and then looked over to Tori. "But as you said, I'm aware of the issues with his ex-wife, so it's there. I would simply note that it tends to spring from drinking. Sobriety is better for him."

"So you and Gunther were at Eddie's Tuesday night. Do you guys drink every night?" Tori asked, good naturedly.

"In the summer, yeah," Warner said with a grin. "I'm single, Eddie is perpetually single, and Gunther is single so, not too odd for us to gather at one of our houses and have a drink or two on a weeknight."

"And how was Gunther at Eddie Mannion's?"

"I gotta say, Gunther must have been hitting it pretty hard because he ended up smashed. I was surprised he went at it that hard being a Tuesday and all, but he said something about having the week off from work, so I figured he decided to tie one on."

"Could he drive?"

"No, no, no," Warner answered, shaking his head. "Eddie drove Gunther and his van back to his house. I followed to give Eddie, someone who *is* my client, a ride back home. I helped Eddie get Gunther in the house and then we left."

"And Gunther was asleep?"

"As far as I know. Eddie got him into the bedroom, so you'd have to ask him to be sure."

"And would we find Eddie like you, on his dock working on a lovely Thursday afternoon?"

Warner chuckled, "A beautiful day like today, I would indeed look for him there before I did at his office."

Eddie Mannion's house was the next stop. If Warner's place was spectacular, Eddie's was another level or two beyond.

"Cripes, would you look at this place?" Tori said, looking around Eddie's massive stone and brick one-story walkout in wonder, stopping in front of the detached five-car garage. The doors were all open. Eddie had himself quite a collection of vehicles: a shiny new Cadillac Escalade, a black Land Rover, a red Porsche 911, a BMW Z4 convertible, and a Tesla. "It appears the mid-life crisis has hit."

"When you have money to burn," Braddock replied, "you burn it."

Eddie was reluctant to talk at first when Tori said the subject was Gunther. "Look, he's my friend."

"Mine too," Tori answered.

"I'm not so sure about that. I know about you two getting up in his grill last night at the VFW."

"Do you now?" Tori asked.

"You two are accusing him of some pretty serious shit," Eddie replied hotly. "I'm not exactly in the mood to help you make things worse for him."

"Look, Eddie, we're here as a courtesy. But I'm fine with making a point of bringing you in to the government center in front of plenty of people. You decide."

"Do I need a lawyer or something?" Eddie asked suspiciously.

"I don't know, Eddie. Do you?" Braddock asked. "Is there something we should know?"

"I'm not saying I do, Will," Eddie retorted. "But you two seem to be on the warpath around here all of a sudden."

Tori held up her bandaged left hand. "Getting shot at tends to do that."

"Lots of missing women to account for," Braddock added. "Not to mention my burned-up Tahoe and house, so I'm pretty much out of patience."

"Look, we're asking about Gunther, not you, Eddie," Tori interjected calmly. "Come on. We're just trying to confirm some information we've gotten elsewhere."

Eddie eyed Tori and then Braddock, who held his hands out as if to say, *What's it gonna be?*

Eddie's body language relaxed as if the air had leaked out of him.

Tori thought much of it was all an act anyway so that he could say to Gunther later that he put up a good fight. She started with an easy question. "Tuesday night, he was here with you, right?"

"Yeah," Eddie Mannion confirmed, having decided to converse. "And I guess Gunther had a lot to drink. I didn't really think he'd had any more than he normally does—he generally can put it away pretty good. But when it came time to leave, he couldn't really stand, let alone drive, so I drove him home."

"Were *you* okay to drive?" Tori asked.

Eddie shrugged. "Good enough. I drove Gunther back, parked the van in the driveway, and Jeff and I helped Gunther inside his house. We got him to bed and Jeff drove me back home and that was it. I was home by midnight, I think, give or take."

"But Gunther was passed out?" Braddock asked.

Eddie nodded. "Yeah. I mean he was dead weight as I hoisted him onto his bed. He was pretty wrecked."

"What was he drinking, beer?" Tori asked.

"No, at my place we usually drink whiskey, or when Jeff is here, he usually brings along bourbon, good bourbon, so we had that."

"Who was mixing drinks?"

"We all were. We were on the pontoon for a bit early on and then sitting out on the deck looking out at the lake, so whoever went inside usually brought refills back."

Eddie, as had Warner, professed that Gunther had his issues. "But, Tori, he's a good guy. You know him. He's a little off-putting but basically a good shit. He wouldn't kill anybody."

"Good grief, Eddie, look who you're talking to. Do you have any idea how many people have said that to me over the years about monsters living in their midst? You've seen it, the next-door neighbor looking shocked. 'Oh, he was so nice,' and it turns out the guy killed ten young boys or ran off with the neighbor's twelve-year-old daughter. And as I understand it—and I hate even saying something like this, and I respect that he and you both served, I really do, Eddie, I really do," she said sincerely, "but from what I hear, Gunther came back from Iraq a changed person, and not necessarily in a good way. He smacked his ex-wife around too, so don't tell me there isn't a tendency to violence lurking in him."

"He went to war and came back damaged. Lots of guys did, Tori. The war, it was bad. But let me tell you something. Before he left, he was harmless, and he sure as hell wouldn't have killed Jessie. None of our friends would have."

"I sure hope you're right," Tori replied bitingly as she and Braddock turned to leave.

"Boy, you laid that on pretty thick," Braddock remarked when they reached the Explorer.

Tori nodded. "Warner talked earlier about Gunther not being too bright. I don't care how nice Eddie's house is or that there are three cherry sports cars in his five garages. I think Eddie's a few cards short of a full deck, too."

"Perhaps."

"At the same time, he basically confirmed what Warner said and, heck, what Gunther said to us last night."

"You believe Eddie and Jeff?"

"Yeah, I do. You?"

"Neither of them strikes me as being willing to fall on the sword for Gunther. Too much at risk."

Tori climbed into the Explorer. "What do we do now?"

"I'm hungry, let's go get a bite to eat. How about Mannion's?"

"A working lunch, then."

"Lunch?" Braddock replied with a light laugh. "It's nearly four thirty, I think we're at early dinnertime."

Mannion's on the Lake was the original bar and restaurant in the family restaurant empire, one with restaurants in many states, as reflected on the map on the wall behind the hostess stand. There was a decent crowd around the bar and out on the patio that overlooked Northern Pine Lake, typical on a warm summer day, but there were still a few tables available.

"Thursday is a good night to go out to eat if you're a local. By tomorrow night, all the restaurants are packed with the weekenders."

They were working, both carrying a sidearm, so there was no alcohol. However, Tori quickly realized there was another reason that Braddock had wanted to come out to Mannion's. The bartender and waitress working the night of Lash's disappearance were there tonight.

"Did you know they'd be working?" Tori asked.

Braddock shrugged knowingly as he perused the menu. "Educated guess. Dinner is fairly quiet right now, but this place will be packed later with the early arrivers for the weekend. Thursday, Friday and Saturday nights are the nights to work at the bars and restaurants on the lake if you want to make some money. So I figured…"

"There was a chance they'd be on," Tori finished. "Otherwise, we would have been chasing them down."

"Correct."

Braddock made a point of asking the waitress and bartender to come over.

"It was over in like a second," the waitress stated.

"What happened?" Tori asked.

The bartender snorted a laugh. "Brule was drinking and was being a little obnoxious but nothing out of the ordinary. He was seated at the corner of the bar with Eddie Mannion. That's why I remembered it because he was sitting with the boss, ya know. They had a few other friends with them earlier, but when this all went down it was just Brule and Eddie. Genevieve and her friends were on the other side of the corner. They were partying like they usually do, and Genevieve was dressed like she always was."

"Which was suggestive," Braddock provided, looking to the bartender. "Am I wrong?"

"No. She was in here all the time. She liked low-cut shirts and skimpy shorts and she was in both that night. That Brule guy was leering at her, as were probably twenty or thirty other guys at a minimum. However, this guy, this Brule guy, was two feet away from her." She looked to the waitress. "Do you remember?"

"Yeah. I was at the side station getting my order filled. I was looking over there and Brule just plain as day reached over and grabbed Genevieve on the ass and pinched her. She turned around, looked him over once, and said something to the effect of, 'Know your place.'"

"And *that* set him off," the bartender added. "He started off his stool, but before it got out of hand, Eddie, and then a few seconds later Kyle, stepped in and separated them."

"The whole thing lasted less than a minute," the waitress added. "But when Genevieve gave him the 'know your place,' I thought we might have a blowup. She practically spit on him."

"She did, at least verbally," Braddock replied, taking some notes.

"Kyle wouldn't happen to be around, would he?" Tori asked.

"Yeah, actually he is," the bartender replied. "He's sitting out on the patio with some people. I'll go get him."

A few minutes later, Kyle made his way over to the table and joined them, taking a seat next to Tori. He confirmed his employees' version of the events. "Gunther is a friend of Eddie's. Unfortunately, as I'm sure you're now aware, he drinks too much. But he's a pretty good worker."

"How do you know?" Tori inquired.

"He works for me out at the explosives plant."

"You own that?"

"I own a majority piece of it," Kyle answered. "I own a piece of a lot of businesses around here."

"Let me ask you," Braddock jumped in, "do you guys have mercury out at that plant?"

"I'm not an explosives expert, but I'd venture we do. Why do you ask?"

"Just curious."

Kyle looked over to Tori. "I've been remiss not to reach out to you since you've come back. I know why you're back. I'm sure it's dredged up a lot of memories and not all of them good. But as someone who loves this lake, this town, and this area, I really appreciate you coming back. I really do."

"Thanks, Kyle," Tori replied softly. "That's very kind of you. It's not a view universally held."

Kyle glanced over to Braddock, who looked away while mumbling, "I didn't say anything."

"Hah!" Kyle laughed and then looked back to Tori. "Well, I mean it. So, welcome home. Dinner is on me."

"That's okay, Kyle," Braddock replied, holding up his hand. "We can't do—"

Kyle smiled. "Will, the server is going to deliver you a bill. You'll put a credit card in the folder. She'll take it and then she'll come back and you're going to sign a bill for zero and it's my treat in *my* place. And by the way, I recommend the ribeye tonight. It is particularly good."

Braddock took Kyle Mannion's advice, while for the first time in twenty years Tori had walleye. "Oh my gosh, I've forgotten how delicious a great piece of walleye could taste."

"You have to have had all kinds of great fish and seafood living on the East Coast."

"Oh, I have," Tori answered with a satisfied smile. "But people there don't have any idea how good a fillet of walleye can be. The sheriff, my dad, he loved walleye. We'd catch it out of the lake. We'd cut up the fillets in the garage and then he'd cook them up. He would have so loved this."

"Careful, Tori," Braddock warned with a smile, "or you might start sounding like you like it here."

"Like Kyle said, there's lots of memories here, not all of them good," she replied and then after a moment, with a small smile added, "but not all of them bad, either."

As the waitress cleared their plates and left the faux bill behind, Tori asked, "Where are we at?"

Braddock signed and pocketed his credit card, leaving a twenty-dollar bill on the table. "Let's go see Cal."

Cal owned a house on Norway Lake. It was a smaller, quieter lake, reachable from Northern Pine via a long, winding channel on the northwest corner of the lake. In Cal's kitchen, sipping decaf coffee, they discussed the case.

There was a clear connection between Brule and Lash, brief as it might have been. A van with a description matching Brule's was spotted in the area from where Tori was shot at. He had no alibi for the morning, or at least no one to corroborate it, nor one for when Lash went missing. He liked guns, was skilled in their use, worked at the explosives factory, and, given his professional and educational background, possessed the knowledge of how to use mercury. There was all of that, along with some history of violence against women.

Braddock checked in with Steak. He reported that Fran Larson was certain that the van she'd seen on Wednesday morning was

Gunther's van. "She said it was *that* van, no question. I mixed in some different white panel vans to a photo array, but she picked it right out."

That was what they had thus far.

"So, you guys tell me he was in an inebriated state on Tuesday night?" Cal asked. "How does that square with him shooting at you Wednesday morning?"

"He faked it," Tori answered. "Jeff and Eddie both said he didn't seem to be drinking any more than normal, yet he was blotto and couldn't drive, had to be helped into the house, and passed out on the bed."

"Because he knew he wouldn't have an alibi," Cal surmised.

"Exactly," Tori answered. "The next best thing is to get two impeccable local witnesses beyond reproach to essentially say he was in no condition to be out taking shots at me and trying to blow up Will's truck."

"That's how it could have happened," Braddock replied. "But there are still a lot of holes in that theory. And I don't know…" His voice trailed off.

Tori recognized his reticence. "You're thinking about all of the other women, right?"

Braddock nodded.

"Me too."

"And does Genevieve Lash get in his panel van on County Road 163?" Braddock asked. "After what happened at the bar?"

"Fair point," Tori replied. "But then there was the weather—"

"And maybe he apologizes and says let me make it up to you."

"Hold on," Cal interrupted, shaking his head. "Just hold on a second."

"What?" Braddock asked.

"You two are suffering from a case of paralysis by analysis," Cal stated.

"Meaning what?" Tori asked.

"You're making this harder than it needs to be," Cal replied. He frowned at his coffee cup, tossed it into the sink, and went to the fridge. He grabbed three Buds out of the refrigerator and passed them out.

A beer was a good idea, with Braddock and Tori both taking long sips from their bottles. "Listen," Cal started, "might you both accept an alternative theory from yours truly?"

"Which is?" Tori asked, taking another drink of her Budweiser.

"This old man thinks two very smart people are overthinking this. Forget about the other women for a minute," the sheriff counseled. "I know you two have a lot of time invested in that, but they're in twelve states, it's over many years, and there is no physical evidence in those cases. They might be connected, but it's probably more likely they're not or someone would have gotten onto it by now. Women go missing, people go missing, all the time. They're taken when other people aren't looking. It's a fact of life. In this case, just because you have twenty-three seemingly similar women who've disappeared over twenty years doesn't mean they *are* all connected."

"I don't know…" Tori started, skeptical.

"Victoria, let me finish. Gunther Brule, on the other hand, he fits what's happened here. Doesn't he?"

Tori slowly nodded and looked over to Braddock. "Cal's right, he does."

"That's right," Cal asserted. "Let's sit down with the county attorney and get ourselves a search warrant. I think our probable cause is a little weak, but I bet we can coax ourselves a warrant out of a judge."

"If we had that…" Braddock started.

"Right," Cal continued. "I want to search his van and run the tires on it. With the warrant, we can evaluate his guns and run them against the shell casings and bullets we have. Let's go deep on this guy. Call his ex-wife and ask her about the domestic assault.

Get his work records. And most of all, after we do all of that, let's get his ass in one of our interrogation rooms and really go to work on him and get answers. If we eliminate him, we eliminate him. Fine, and we keep going, but it's time to force the issue."

Tori looked to Braddock. "What could it hurt?"

"It's either Gunther or it isn't. There's only one way to find out."

"Exactly," Cal affirmed. "The simplest answer is usually the right one. You guys have a break here. I say run with it. But then again, I'm just a simple county sheriff here in the north country, and you two are elite investigative minds, so what do I know?"

Tori thought it over. Gunther Brule checked some important boxes. He'd been around the night Jessie went missing. There was a connection to Genevieve Lash. He was a soldier and liked guns. His van had been seen in the area of the shooting, and he worked at an explosives plant and likely had access to mercury.

"And Gunther is in the database," Braddock noted.

"You know, any one of these facts in isolation can be explained away," Tori said, looking to Braddock. "But you start adding all that up and it tells a story."

"The evidence says Gunther Brule is your guy," Cal counseled. "Let's go get him."

"Do you think we'll get the search warrant?" Tori asked as Braddock drove into the Radisson parking lot.

"I think so," Braddock answered as he pulled to a stop under the canopy. "If we get pushback, I have a couple of cards to play."

"Such as?"

"I've got someone I can call who has influence around here with people who run for election."

"Might that be the guy who comped our meal?"

"Could be," Braddock answered, "could be."

Tori smiled. "Thank you."

"For what?"

"For working this like you have."

"It's my job."

"No. You've been going above and beyond here. I know that."

Braddock nodded, looking away for a moment. "The town needs answers." He turned back to Tori, locking his eyes on hers. "And I want to nail this guy and even more, you need closure. If I can bring that about, well, it's worth all I can give."

Tori nodded lightly before quickly leaning in, turning and then cupping his cheek with her hand, and kissing him, a soft peck on the lips. "I'll see you in the morning," she whispered before pulling away.

"Yeah… uh… okay," Braddock replied, taken totally by surprise. "I'll… yeah, see you in the morning for sure."

Tori opened her door, looking back with a quick smile and nod before descending from the Explorer.

Braddock watched her walk inside the hotel, lightly touching his lips, thinking to himself, *I didn't see that coming.*

CHAPTER TWENTY-TWO

"Not the dramatic confrontation you expected."

Shepard County Attorney George Backstrom thought their probable cause was thin but said, "The Honorable Elmer Henderson is the judge available today. He's a former prosecutor who has been known to view the Fourth Amendment as imbued with a certain useful elasticity."

Braddock, Tori, and Steak completed sworn affidavits in support of the request. At 1 p.m. they went before Judge Henderson, who issued the warrant with just minimal inquiry. Unsaid was that if it was about the Genevieve Lash and Jessie Hunter cases, everyone wanted to see something happen, including the court.

But they couldn't find Brule.

When Braddock and Tori went to serve the search warrant at Brule's home, he wasn't there. The white van was gone. Steak went to the explosives plant, but Brule wasn't at work, nor was he answering calls on his cell phone

Braddock looked to Tori. "Did he skip town?"

"If he did, he can't get far," she answered. "I wouldn't have bet on him running on Wednesday night. He was pretty combative."

"Maybe that was for show. If he was acting all drunk when he wasn't, he could have been acting all combative when he knew the jig was up," Braddock reasoned. "I should have put someone on him. *Shit*."

"Don't beat yourself up," Tori reassured him. "I was right there with you. I didn't think it was necessary."

A full-on search was commenced. Deputies checked in with known friends and associates. Eggleston tried the VFW to no avail. Tori called on Jeff Warner. "I have no idea where he could be. I can try and call him."

"If you would."

Warner called back fifteen minutes later. "Sorry, Tori. No answer. But I'll keep trying. If I get him, I'll call you."

Tori tried Eddie Mannion.

"I have no idea where he could be."

"Would you tell me even if you did?"

"I don't know where he is," Eddie answered curtly and hung up.

Jeff Warner called Tori back. "He has a cabin up on Benedict Lake."

Tori looked to Braddock. "Do you feel like taking a drive?"

Benedict Lake was due west of the small lakeside town of Walker. Walker itself rested on the far west end of Leech Lake, a behemoth of a lake, a little under an hour's drive north up the H-4. Braddock called ahead, and Cass County Sheriff Corbin Hansen was waiting for them.

"Hello, Will," Hansen greeted with a warm handshake.

Braddock introduced Tori.

"I knew Big Jim Hunter," Hansen bellowed, taking Tori's small hand in his huge bear paw of one. "I had great respect for him. He was good people, real good people."

"Thank you, Sheriff."

"Call me Corbin. Now, tell me what's all this hubbub about?"

Braddock handed Hansen the search warrant, explaining its import.

"Well, then, we best get out there to see if this Brule character is about."

Hansen had one of his deputies join him, and Braddock and Tori followed them both out of Walker.

"Sheriff Hansen seems like an amiable guy."

"Corbin is about as folksy as they come," Braddock replied. "He's been sheriff up here forever. He has a little house on Walker Bay, does the sheriff gig, and fishes all year long."

"A good life."

"I've sure come to think so."

"You love it here, don't you?" Tori asked, smiling.

"I do."

"You must have had some doubts when you made the move."

Braddock nodded. "I'll admit I was worried that I might get bored pretty quickly. I feared Manchester Bay was a great place to visit for a week in the summer, but not to live here year-round."

"You thought you were moving to Siberia."

"Exactly. But it's been great. Instead of a cramped, two-bedroom Brooklyn condo, we live in a nice house with a yard on a gorgeous lake with boats, wave runners, and fishing. Quinn is beyond happy around all his cousins and friends, playing baseball and hockey. And last winter he played travel hockey; he was a first-year squirt. I was introduced to a new concept—the safety meeting."

"What's a safety meeting?"

"A meeting where the hockey dads go to the bar before their kids' games and discuss all things safety over beer and chicken wings."

"Ahh, pre-gaming."

"Exactly. It was fun. Don't get me wrong, Quinn misses his mom, as do I. I think of her every day. But my boy is having a wonderful childhood and gets to do so many things he'd *never* get to do in New York City. I have a good job, I've made some nice friends, and I have family close by, something I never had as a kid. Between life insurance, selling Meghan's piece of the design business, and our condo in Brooklyn, I'm comfortable financially. So it's all good here."

"I get it."

"You do?"

"There's nothing like living on the lake."

"Really?" Braddock replied, surprised. "I pegged you as all citified now."

"I may be, but I lived on Northern Pine growing up too, Jessie and me. We spent our summers doing all the stuff Quinn's doing now. And just like Quinn, I lost my mom when I was young, but I still had a great childhood. I should remember that more often than I do."

It was a ten-minute drive northwest out of Walker on County 38. Turning left off the county road, they motored west along a tight, winding, gravel lane through a tunnel of thick woods. At the end of it they found an even narrower driveway through more woods that led to the smallish, boxy, one-story cabin.

"He's here," Tori reported, seeing the white van parked in front of the detached garage to the cabin's right side.

The cabin was set close to the lake on what appeared to be a wide, isolated stretch of property with a plentiful collection of mature pines, spruces, elms, white birches, cedars, and oaks. It was a quintessential old-school working man's Minnesota lake cabin.

With the search warrant in his hands, Braddock led the four of them to the front door, with Braddock and Tori taking the steps while Hansen and the deputy positioned themselves on the sidewalk. Braddock knocked repeatedly but there was no answer. He looked back to Tori, putting his right hand on the butt of his Glock. Tori stepped back from the front door and down the steps, drawing her weapon. Sheriff Hansen and his deputy did the same. Hansen gestured they would take the left side of the house, leaving Tori to monitor the front, and Braddock fanned out and took the right.

Braddock moved his way around the side of the house to the back. It was eerily quiet and the lake was calm, with just a few distant boats out enjoying the sun. As he peered out along Brule's long dock, he could see the fishing boat on the lift, sitting up and out of the water.

He looked left. There was a small square cedar deck fronting the cabin. Braddock took the three steps up onto the deck and approached the sliding glass door, peering around the edge to the room inside.

"Ahhhhhh, shit!"

"What is it?" Hansen asked, approaching.

Gunther Brule was slumped in a chair, his arms hanging over the chair's rounded arms, a gun lying on the floor below his right hand.

Hansen grabbed a blanket from his vehicle and wrapped it around his right fist. He punched the small windowpane just left of the deadbolt of the front door, breaking the glass, and then he carefully reached inside and flipped the lock open.

Once inside, Braddock crept to the chair and saw that the gun lying on the floor below Brule's hand was a Smith & Wesson .38 Special Revolver. Brule had a dried bloody hole in his right upper forehead with an exit wound out the lower back left.

Tori simply stood staring at Brule. Was this her sister's killer? Had he killed himself because they were going to finally, *finally* catch him? "He was defiant and now he's dead," she muttered quietly.

Braddock crouched down, examining the gun's location and the entry wound high above Brule's right temple, almost on top of his head. "It ties up all nice and neat, doesn't it?" he said under his breath before looking over to Tori. "Not the dramatic confrontation you expected."

Tori simply shook her head as she took one last look at Brule and then walked out the sliding glass door. Braddock watched as she slowly walked down to the lake and out onto the long dock. She sat down on the bench and gazed out to the water.

Braddock looked back to the dead body of Brule and couldn't help but think about what Tori had just said: *He was defiant and now he's dead.*

CHAPTER TWENTY-THREE

"There is acceptance and there is belief—they're two different things."

Tori had long thought that if her sister's case was ever solved, if that moment ever came, she would feel a sense of relief. She would know what had happened to Jessie. There would be a sense of finality. She could move on.

Yet as Braddock drove her back to Manchester Bay, she didn't feel that sense of relief. Nor later, as she lay in bed, did she feel any sort of finality. Instead, her mind whirred.

Sleep was fitful at best. She stirred at the slightest sound, whether it be the air conditioner activating, a random noise from the hallway, the ambient street noise, or the distant siren at 4:30 a.m. Only from pure exhaustion did she eventually drop off. At an unusually late 7:45 a.m. she got up. As she stood in the shower, letting the water wash over her, she concluded that her restless night was indicative of the fact that she wasn't yet comfortable accepting Brule as their killer. She had too many unanswered questions.

Did she have doubts because of what Braddock had said, that there wasn't that dramatic confrontation she'd envisioned?

Was there doubt because there wasn't an admission from Gunther that he'd done it?

Or was it that Gunther, after twenty years, would go out so meekly without leaving behind any answers? And if he'd done that, what was the point of sending the newspaper article in the first place?

What she needed to do was go back up to that cabin where the investigation was ongoing and see if she could find enough answers to put her mind at ease.

As she toweled off she thought about calling Braddock, but he beat her to the punch with a text. He must have been thinking like she was as he suggested she should go back up to Brule's. Braddock also said he was busy working on a project and he'd check in with her later. She texted back asking what project, but he replied cryptically that they would talk later. She'd come to learn Will Braddock was a man who kept things close to the vest until he was ready to discuss them, so for once she didn't push and simply replied with an okay.

With a bottle of water and a Starbucks coffee, Tori made the drive back up north to Brule's cabin. With the Power Loon classic rock station filling the car with Aerosmith, Def Leppard, Bon Jovi, Journey, Kansas, Springsteen, and then some Rolling Stones, she slowly found herself relaxing on the winding drive up through lakes country.

It was approaching eleven when she arrived. She flashed her identification to a Cass County sheriff's deputy and then stepped under the crime scene tape and walked up the driveway to find an energetic hum of activity around Brule's cabin. She found Steak, dressed in a brown suit with his tie already loose from his collar, standing on the front steps. "This is a different look," he said, looking down admiringly.

"I'll take that as a compliment." Tired of her pantsuits, she'd let her hair flow down to her shoulders and dressed more casually in tight black jeans and an aqua-blue, open-front, linen blazer with a soft cream top.

"Good, it was intended as one."

"What's going on around here? I see lots of activity."

"I figured you'd have come up with Braddock earlier."

"He was here?"

"Yeah, early. Five thirty this morning. He walked through the place for about an hour and then took off."

"Huh," Tori answered, surprised. "He texted me that he was working on a project of some kind."

"About this case?"

Tori shrugged. "I assume so. I'm sure you'll be surprised to learn he doesn't tell *me*, the person who has perhaps been the bane of his existence as of late, everything."

"Bane of his existence?" Steak chuckled, shaking his head with a wry smile on his face. "I don't think it's been that bad, Tor. I think he kind of likes you."

"Oh, I don't know," Tori started in reply.

Steak waved her off. "You got the invite out to his house for that night we barbecued and waterskied. Only friends get those."

"I must have been the exception, then."

"Nah, he's a good judge of character. And he knew you needed a break like the rest of us. Admit it, you had fun that night."

"I did." Tori smiled, nodding. "So, what's all the activity around here?"

"You don't know, do you?"

"Know what?"

"Oh, there's lots. Follow me," Steak replied, waving for Tori to follow him to the detached garage. He led her inside and to the workbench. "What do you see?"

"Liquid mercury." The mercury was in a small glass bottle from Sidwell Explosives, where Brule had worked. "And the glass and wiring?"

"The forensic team says those are the kinds of pieces you'd need for a mercury tilt switch. I sent a couple of cell phone photos to the bomb squad guys, and they confirmed that the electrodes and wiring were like those found under Will's Tahoe. And there's more."

"More?"

"Oh, yeah, let's go in the cabin for the clincher," Steak suggested.

Tori followed him inside to a spare bedroom at the back of the cabin. Deep inside the closet was a compartment with the wood panel cover removed. Inside were two vertical gun racks.

"There were three different Ruger rifles with scopes that were discovered in here after you guys left last night. They were all sent to the lab in Bemidji, and the ballistics tech was called in at midnight to go to work."

"Do we have a match?"

Steak nodded. "Yeah, heard an hour ago."

"And Braddock knows."

"Yes. And one other thing."

"What's that?"

"The tire treads on the van match those we found in the woods not far from where he shot at you."

"The loose ends are being tied up."

"Indeed, they are," Steak replied as his phone started buzzing. "If you'll excuse me."

They had the gun that was used to attempt to kill her. There was mercury and mercury switch materials in the garage. He shot himself with a .38 right by his hand. The tire treads for the van were a match.

The physical evidence said it was him, which explained why she received a text from Braddock about a meeting in Cal's office in ninety minutes with the county attorney, among others.

As she drove back south to Manchester Bay with the Power Loon rocking away once again, she ran the case through her mind, including everything they knew and then everything they didn't.

The evidence, physical and otherwise, said Brule was the shooter and the bomber. If he was the shooter and the bomber, the only reason he would be those things was because he was the killer of Jessie and of Lash.

It wasn't an uncompelling case. Nevertheless, as all of that marinated in her mind, something seemed amiss. It didn't seem completely right. She couldn't put her finger on why she still felt that way, but she did.

That was the last thought running through her mind as she entered Cal's office. Shepard County Attorney George Backstrom and Assistant County Attorney Anne Wilson were sitting on the couch. Leaning against the wall opposite was Braddock, holding a manila folder in his hands.

"What's in the folder?" she asked with a whisper before taking one of the chairs in front of Cal's desk.

"We'll talk about it later."

"So, before you came in, Victoria," Cal started, "we were talking about congratulations being in order."

"That's a bit premature, don't you think?" Tori replied guardedly.

"Perhaps," Backstrom answered. "But the momentum here is undeniable."

The evidence that Brule was their man *was* undeniable, and the Shepard County attorney said there was more than enough to build the case. "As we keep digging, I suspect we'll find even more tying Brule to Lash beyond their little incident at Mannion's."

"Perhaps," Tori replied with continued reticence, glancing to Braddock, whose face betrayed nothing.

"Special Agent Hunter, you surprise me," Backstrom replied, almost amused. "At long last we have your sister's killer, yet you don't seem so happy."

"I won't deny what the evidence we do have seems to show," Tori answered.

"Seems?"

"It's circumstantial. We don't have any direct evidence he killed Lash or my sister."

"We've convicted with less," Backstrom argued, "and what about all the evidence we do have?"

"What about what we don't have?" Tori retorted.

"Such as?" Assistant County Attorney Wilson asked.

"Where is my sister's body?" Tori asked. "Where is Genevieve Lash's body? If Brule did all of this, where are the bodies? We've seen no sign of those yet."

"No," Cal answered. "The best guess is he either dumped them somewhere, or they're somewhere on that cabin property, all that land in the woods outside of town where his house sits. That house in the woods was his parents' property and they've both been dead for twelve or thirteen years. That property is isolated, expansive, and has several open clearings we need to explore. The same is true for his cabin property. I've already placed a call to the BCA. Tomorrow we'll have dogs and the BCA's ground-penetrating radar, and we're going to set a grid and search every inch of both pieces of land. But Victoria, you must realize we may never find the bodies. That won't mean he didn't do it."

"Then we may never know if it was Brule," Tori protested. "He didn't leave a note. He committed suicide."

"Same thing as a note if you ask me," Wilson answered quickly.

"That's right," Backstrom joined. "You two sweat him a little outside the VFW and that night he goes up to his cabin in the woods, gets into a bottle of Maker's Mark, and then offs himself. I think that's a pretty solid admission."

"I agree," Cal added. "He saw the writing on the wall." He took the measure of Tori. "You seem less than convinced. I thought you would look at this as closure. I mean, you want closure, don't you?"

"More than you can imagine," Tori replied. "But I want to know for *certain* that it was Brule." She shook her head, looking away. "I don't know, something seems… not quite right," she remarked as her gaze drifted over to Braddock. He'd remained silent during the entire conversation.

"What seems off?" Cal asked.

"The article," Tori replied, turning back to Cal, Backstrom, and Wilson. "That's what got me here in the first place. Gunther tracks me down, sends me that article, draws me here, and then he… commits suicide?"

"It didn't work out how he thought it would," Wilson theorized. "He missed the shot at you. He failed to take out Will here, thank God. His grand plan failed."

"He was going to lose, couldn't face it, so he took the easy way out," Backstrom added.

"I don't know," Tori said, shaking her head. "I just don't know. And what about Katy Anderson? How does she fit in all of this? Everyone in here talks about my sister and Lash, but what about Katy? What ties Gunther to her, beyond being in the same high school class? What was he doing the night she went missing?"

"Maybe we don't talk about Katy because Katy isn't part of this," Wilson answered. "Something happened to her, but that doesn't mean it has anything to do with Brule, your sister, or Genevieve Lash."

"Awfully coincidental, don't you think?" Tori replied, unconvinced.

"Or he saw you go over to Katy Anderson's house, saw you meet with her, and then with Katy leaving the house, maybe he killed her, too."

"Why?" Tori asked. "For what reason? If she knew something about Jessie's case, her best friend's case, you don't think she would have said something twenty years ago?"

"Maybe she knew something she didn't realize she knew, but Brule knew," Backstrom replied. "Before she figured it out, before she realized it, and especially with you here for the first time in twenty years, Brule had to act. Think about it. With you here she might finally put two and two together."

"And when you went to see her, especially the second time… he knew he'd have to act," Wilson posited. "He'd planned on that, and Katy made it easy for him when she left the house later that night—a crime of opportunity."

"I show up and my old best friend ends up dead, is what you're saying," Tori retorted.

"I'm not blaming you."

"No, I'm sure," Tori said bitterly, now struggling to rein it in. She was about to blurt something else when Braddock lightly grasped her shoulder.

"It's alright. It's okay," he said quietly while giving the stink eye to Wilson, who realized she'd veered down the wrong alley.

"Perhaps tomorrow's search can give you more of the answers you need," Cal suggested. "Maybe the BCA will find the evidence you're looking for. As for me, and this is not a criticism, Victoria, but I'm probably a little more objective here, and I'm feeling pretty good."

"Just don't get ahead of yourself and schedule a press conference yet," Braddock stated tersely, finally speaking to the group.

"No, not yet," Backstrom agreed, but his tone said he was close to being ready to do so.

After the meeting broke up, Tori followed Braddock to his office. "You were awfully quiet, other than that little warning at the end. What gives?"

He exhaled a deep breath through his nose and rubbed his face hard. He sat back in his desk chair and with his eyes closed said, "Can we talk in the morning? I'm totally fried. It's been an exhausting week. I just want to go home, take a long, hot shower, and go to bed. The case isn't going anywhere."

"No, I don't suppose it is tonight."

"Thanks," Braddock replied as he stood up. "I'll buy you breakfast in the morning."

"Okay."

Tori watched as Braddock slipped on his sport coat and exited his office. She noticed that the manila folder didn't stay behind.

*

With a sudden free Saturday night, Tori didn't want to sit in her hotel room. She changed into some summer clothes—tan shorts and a pink tank top—and called Corinne to see if she could meet for a drink. Corinne immediately said yes, but then did better than that. Way better.

An hour later Tori met her, along with Mickey and Lizzy, at DePesto's. For three hours Tori let the case go and just enjoyed a girls' night out with her old friends. Tori ordered a nice bottle of red wine while her friends ordered three pasta dishes to be shared family-style. The four of them just talked as if twenty years hadn't passed since they'd been together. Tori laughed in bewilderment as her three friends, all married and parents to preteen and teenage children, told endless stories about their kids and husbands.

"My gosh, those kids have you running everywhere," Tori remarked in amazement. "School, baseball, soccer, basketball, hockey, dance, plays, and concerts… how do you guys do it?"

Her three friends looked to one another and then Corinne shrugged and answered, "We just do. One day I'm going to wake up and wonder where my thirties went, that's for sure."

"Do you get any time with your husbands?"

All three of them laughed. "Not much," Mickey remarked. "Jobs, kids, kids' activities, collapse—day after day. It's a vicious cycle."

"Lizzy did get away with her husband for a vacation, just the two of them, last winter. A week in Cabo," Corinne reported.

Lizzy smiled. "We made up for a lot of lost time that week."

"You two went on a fuckcation is what you did," Corinne replied jealously.

"Corinne!" Lizzy protested.

"Oh, whatever, you came home glowing from that thing."

"I did not," Lizzy replied and looked to Mickey. "Tell her I did not."

"You totally did."

"Oh my God," Lizzy replied, shaking her head but smiling. "What can I say, we got about a year's worth in that week." She looked over to Tori, hoping to change the subject. "How about you, single girl looking all in shape and sexy? Who's your guy?"

"There is no guy."

"That's not what I hear," Mickey teased, shaking her head. "I heard you were all nice and cozy with Will Braddock the other night."

"What in the world are you talking about?" Tori replied.

"You weren't at JJ's in Pillager? The two of you in a little out-of-the-way corner booth."

"How do you know that?"

"Oh, please," Lizzy replied with a wave, "Mickey has sources *everywhere*. The oracle knows all."

"Well, yeah, we were there, having a beer and pizza after working all day. But I was not… all cozy with him. We sat on opposite sides of the table."

"I received a report of hand-holding."

"From who?"

"I don't reveal my sources," Mickey replied with a big grin. "Never."

"Well, we were not *holding hands*," Tori protested. "I was… Oh, never mind. It was not what you think."

"It's okay, Tori. This is us you're talking to. I mean, you have to admit," Lizzy took a quick look around the restaurant before saying in a low voice, "he is kind of hot."

"Oh, yeah," Corinne agreed. "Come on, Tori, I know you're all New York City and all now, but tell me you haven't at least thought about it."

"I…" Tori started to deny it before letting a little smile slip. "It has not escaped my attention that he's a good-looking guy."

"I told you guys!" Mickey exclaimed. "I told you."

They all laughed out loud.

"All I know is he was right when he said it's still like a small town around here," Tori mused, shaking her head ruefully. "Everyone knows everything. *Everything*. There are no secrets."

"And all I know," Corinne remarked, "is we'd all be sitting around probably doing nothing tonight but for—"

"You, girlfriend," Mickey finished, toasting Tori with her wine glass. "This was such a treat."

"It's *my* treat," Tori replied, holding up her credit card.

A little after nine Tori returned to her hotel, sat down on the bed, crossed her legs, and opened her case file. She went through the evidence again, wanting—almost willing herself—to trust and believe that Brule was the killer. When they boiled it down, all the actual evidence, physical and circumstantial—it pointed to Brule.

Her phone rang. It was Kelly Wong from the FBI Crime Lab. *This should confirm it.*

*

Braddock wasn't in a celebratory mood when he arrived home and was reminded of his last several days by the massive, misshapen, black charred spot on his cement driveway and the visible scorching of the siding of his house.

Inside he took that long warm shower, letting the water stream over and steam his body. For an hour he relaxed on his deck, silently sipping a beer and gazing out to the lake, trying to empty his mind and failing miserably.

The case was heading inexorably in a direction that he was now certain was the wrong one. But Backstrom and Cal were calling the shots. It was out of his control and he feared he wouldn't be able to stop them.

That was the biggest reason he'd told Tori he wanted to be alone. She'd been through so much, was so consumed with the case and filled with guilt and fury, that he dreaded having to be the one to disappoint her. He wasn't ready to break that news to her and needed a night to steel himself for it.

Eventually he went back inside, opened another beer, and climbed the steps to his office. He sipped from the bottle while once again reading the contents of the manila file folder in front of him.

He had a large United States map pinned up on the wall opposite the desk. The colored dots on the map identified all the women missing and unaccounted for over the past twenty years. The first one was Jessie Hunter, followed by more than a four-year break. Then for the past sixteen years it seemed as if one to two women went missing per year. The four women whose bodies were found were marked by red dots, the missing women by green.

Were they all abducted by the same man? He thought they were.

So, as he reviewed the contents of the manila folder, the records contained therein, and compared them to the dots, the facts, the circumstances, and the locations of the missing women, the growing pit in his stomach ached more and more. The circumstances of the missing women and the facts as he knew them on Gunther Brule were in complete conflict. All of that was percolating through his mind when there was a sudden urgent pounding at the back door. He hustled down the steps and then turned into the kitchen, racing to the urgent knocking. He opened the back door.

"He didn't do it!" Tori exclaimed, barging inside before turning around, distraught. "It wasn't Brule. He didn't try to shoot me. I don't think he tried to blow you up. He didn't kill Jessie or Genevieve or even Katy." She looked to Braddock, expecting him to ask her why.

Instead he simply nodded.

"You know this? How?"

"You first."

"The FBI crime lab. The DNA on the cigarette butts is not a match to Gunther."

"*Hmpf.* That wasn't necessarily the fact I was expecting, but it figures." Braddock sighed, leaning back against the kitchen counter.

"Why? Why does that figure?"

He nodded his head toward the steps. "You better come upstairs." He led Tori up the steps and into his home office.

Tori froze, seeing the massive map up on the wall to the right and the manila folder opened on his desk to the left.

"I thought you left work at the office," she remarked quietly.

"Not this case," he replied, adding in a whisper, "Not this case."

She'd seen the map on his computer back at the office and had a copy of it on her laptop. But seeing it up on the wall like this with handwritten sticky notes detailing the facts of each disappearance was startling. She looked back to Braddock. The compartmentalizer was every bit as obsessed as she was. He handed the manila folder to Tori.

"What's this?"

"Time clock records for Gunther Brule at the explosives factory. They go back ten years—that's all they keep, although he's been there for nearly sixteen years. I've eliminated him from ten of these women completely with those records. On four more I think it's virtually impossible for him to have been the man who abducted them. The rest might be possible but only because I don't have records going back far enough."

Tori flipped through the attendance records and timecards for Brule at Sidwell Explosives. "How'd you get all of this?"

"Kyle Mannion," Braddock answered. "I picked them up this morning. I don't care what Cal said about forgetting about the other women, I never really bought that. I still believe they're all connected. That's why I was here much of the day going through the records. And that's how I eliminated Brule from many of these abductions. He *couldn't* have been there. So, *if* all of these disappearances, including your sister and Genevieve Lash, are all connected, Brule didn't do it. Does that mean he didn't take your sister? Does it mean he didn't abduct Lash? Does it mean he didn't try to pop you and me? I suppose it's still possible but…" He shook his head in frustration. "I just don't think he did."

Tori dropped her face into her hands. "I knew it was too good to be true." She looked up. "How long have you had doubts?"

"Since last night at the cabin."

"Last night? What did you see last night?"

"It was more something you said that got me thinking, about how he was defiant and now he was dead. That just didn't add up to me. He does all these things, goes to the lengths he did to get you here, and then kills himself at his cabin without any explanation?" He shook his head. "I didn't buy it. These records tell me I'm right."

Tori nodded her understanding then gazed back at the map.

"Tori, I wanted it to be Brule. I stood in Cal's kitchen and I desperately wanted it to be Brule. I wanted to have that answer, but something about him just doesn't sit right with me. He doesn't fit as the killer. And I could tell in Cal's office today you had your doubts."

"What are you thinking?" Tori asked. "What's triggering that?"

"All these women and no answers. All these *pretty* women and no answers. I've looked at the pictures, many pictures, of these victims. They are attractive, educated, and talented women. Every one of them."

"It would take someone pretty cunning yet somehow also safe and trustworthy to abduct them," Tori observed.

"Right. Does Gunther Brule strike you as that kind of a mastermind? As someone able to evoke that level of trust in all these women?"

"No. I could possibly see Gunther killing someone. I'm sure he did in Iraq, and there was always something off about him. But you look at these women—they're all attractive but all of them might also treat Brule the way…"

"Genevieve Lash treated Brule at Mannion's," Braddock finished. "They might not be as condescending as Lash, but they would likely reject him. Then I thought, maybe that's what triggered him. The rejection. These women rejected him and, in vengeance, he took them. So, that's why I asked Kyle for Gunther's employment records. Was it possible he was in all those places? Those records prove he wasn't."

Tori shook her head in frustration and then her jaw dropped. "Will, did we jack Gunther up the other night, accuse him of all this shit such that he went up to his cabin and killed himself? Did we do that?"

"I don't know," Braddock replied softly. "I've been wondering about that, too."

"The killer is still out there somewhere, jerking us around."

"Yeah, he is."

"But we're the only ones who think that. We need to keep working this. We have to."

Braddock shook his head in resignation. "Tori, we can hold off Cal and Backstrom for only so long. I told them not to schedule a press conference, but you know they're itching to—and if that happens," he gestured to everything up on the wall, "I'm going to have to drop the case."

"Hold on a second, you can't just do that."

"I will be forced to," Braddock answered, his voice almost hoarse. "The sheriff is my boss, a boss I like very much and who has been really good to me. I have a son to care for and I can't do that without a job."

"But what about the truth?"

"Sometimes the truth is a luxury."

"I know you don't believe that."

"No… I don't. I am going to fight for this, Tori. I am. And I'm trying to think of how to do that. But I may get backed into a corner that I won't be able to get out of."

"I don't operate that way," Tori replied bitterly.

"You sure about that? You mean to tell me you haven't been told a case is over when you don't think it is? A child who's been missing for months, and no evidence or signs of hope? You haven't been ordered to stand down? To go home? Heck, last week you left this case, *this case*, to go to Des Moines because you were ordered to."

"But on this case, we have evidence that—"

"That what? If you take this map out of it, if you take these twenty-three other women out of the equation, even with the negative DNA results there is a very plausible, well-supported by evidence, and *convenient* conclusion that Gunther Brule did it. Even though you and I both know he didn't."

"I don't have to accept it."

"There is acceptance and there is belief—they're two different things. I don't believe it, you know I don't, but I may have to accept it."

"I don't believe it or accept it," she replied and then picked up a small framed picture of Will and Quinn off the top of the small narrow bookshelf in the corner. It showed the two of them sitting arm-in-arm on the backseat of their speedboat, a happy father and son living an idyllic life. Who was she to imperil that?

Tori nodded and turned to face him. "But… I understand, Will. I do."

The two of them stood in silence for a minute, taking the measure of each other. The tension long-existent between them now melted away. It was replaced with a common belief but the improbability of acting on it together.

Braddock wearily looked back to the map. "All of these women. No evidence, no witnesses, and nobody sees a thing," he muttered dejectedly. "The families don't know what happened to their daughters. You don't know what happened to your sister. I don't even want to think about what I'd be feeling if Quinn went missing and nobody had any answers." He looked to her. "Tori,

I can't imagine what the last twenty years have been like for you, not knowing. And then last night…" His voice trailed off as he looked to the floor. "I hoped last night would've been your answer. I wanted it to be your answer in the worst way."

Tori felt immense guilt for ever having questioned Will Braddock's commitment to the case and to her cause. She wanted someone to be as invested as she was, and standing across the room was an exhausted and totally spent man who was in it all the way.

Their eyes locked and they stood in silence, gazing upon each other.

Slowly Tori walked to Braddock. She stopped and stood in front of him before looking up into his weary, deep blue eyes. Gently reaching up with her right hand, Tori cupped his cheek tenderly, brushing her thumb along his stubbled skin.

Braddock looked down into her moistened green eyes, and for the first time he saw a softness in her, a vulnerability. "You have to be the most defiant and uncompromising woman I've ever met."

Tori nodded gently in reply as she kissed him with a light, soft, and lingering kiss. "You did say that fire can be a good thing."

"When channeled properly."

"That's what I'm doing now," was her hushed reply as she moved her arms down to first untuck his shirt then push it up before he took over, lifted it over his head, and dropped it to the floor. She took a long moment to admire his long and toned torso before slowly reaching up to touch him. Lightly and ever so slowly, she brushed her fingers up and down, slowing working her way down his chest, savoring the feel of him. Her hands found their way down to his waist, moving her fingers to unbutton his shorts, and letting them just sit open. While looking up to him, she moved her hands teasingly along the top edge of his boxers. She let her fingers slide just between the waistband and his skin, feeling his toned stomach quiver to her touch, relishing the feel of his reaction and the murmur of his voice. She slid her hands back up to his muscled chest. The fingers of her left hand lingered over the two oblong scars just above his right nipple, the wounds from Times Square. She softly kissed them while sliding her arms around him, pulling him closer and softly running her fingertips up his smooth back.

Tori looked up to see him gazing down at her, looking upon her eagerly, yet with a gentle approach. He reached with his hands to caress the backs of her toned arms before easing his hands lower. Searching for the bottom of her tank top, he started to gently lift it when she moved her hands down. Leaning back, she deliberately pulled it over her head, allowing him to admire her taut stomach and soft breasts. He exhaled a breath and his eyes locked onto hers. He gently undid the button and then the zipper on her shorts before sliding them down and letting them fall to the floor, letting Tori step out of them. He took a half-step back, peering down admiringly.

Tori reached up on her tiptoes to softly kiss him again and again, each one lingering a little longer before opening her mouth, kissing him deeply, hungrily, wrapping her arms around his neck, easing him down to her, his long arms slowly enveloping her into him.

"Let's just forget about all of this tonight," she murmured, her lips a centimeter from his. "I just want to let it all go. I want to let go."

Braddock lifted her up, letting her wrap her legs around his waist as he carried her out of the office and down the hallway into his bedroom.

CHAPTER TWENTY-FOUR

"Is that the foundation upon which you want
to build your house?"

Tori awoke to the hum of the house's air conditioning kicking in. She glanced at her watch: it was ten minutes after six.

Waking up in bed with a man was usually cause for Tori to make a quick and stealthy departure to avoid the potentially awkward emotional repercussions of the night. She immediately realized a hasty escape would prove exceedingly difficult.

Braddock's long left arm was gently wrapped around her waist but tightly holding her. A bit to her surprise, she was okay with that, content to let her body comfortably and securely lie enveloped in his massive body. She found herself wanting to stay in the moment, to hang onto that feeling just a little longer.

Last night had been a needed respite, not only for her but for Braddock, too. And it felt good, *both times*, which made her snort a little while her thoughts drifted back to it. Braddock was equal parts tender, energetic, caring, and exuberant. And she'd responded in kind, with a fevered passion and a desire to be there for him.

Yet, as good as it felt to just lie there in a comfortable bed in a house along a tranquil northern Minnesota lake, she knew she needed to let the night go.

She carefully lifted Braddock's arm just enough to allow her to squirm loose and roll her naked body to the edge of the bed to sit up. She stifled a small laugh when she saw her little white thong hanging on the doorknob to the walk-in closet, recalling Braddock tossing it away after he'd laid her down on the bed and slipped it off.

Tori slowly stepped off the bed and tiptoed over to the closet door, grabbed her underwear, and then looked left. Lying on the floor between the bed and wall was her white lace bra, but her plan to slink away was already foiled.

Braddock was awake with his eyes focused on her as she brought up her underwear and bra to cover her chest. With everything gathered in her arms, she turned to start for the bathroom, in search of a bit of privacy, when Braddock laughed.

She looked back. "What's so funny?"

He had a wry smile on his face, sitting up in bed now. "You look like you might have done this once or twice before."

"What?"

"The quick getaway."

Tori stopped, her bra and underwear barely covering her naked chest as she clutched them closely to it. "I've never been good at this part."

"What part is that?"

"The aftermath."

Will laughed out loud and grinned broadly. "Oh my God."

"What?"

"Well, maybe that's because you call it the aftermath, Tori. It makes it sound like something tragic, and from firsthand experience, I can assure you last night was not tragic."

"It's just that I've never been very good at this, Will," she replied, looking at the floor. "I don't have a real solid track record of success with men, other than... you know, the part we did last night. Remember? Pain in the ass, uncompromising... all of that ringing a bell there, big guy?"

"I see," Will said quietly as he threw off the blankets. At some point in the night he'd managed to slide his boxers back on. He stood up and slowly approached Tori and reached for her hand, interlocking his fingers with hers. "Well, first, you can keep calling me big guy if you want."

Tori shyly giggled.

"Now I can't speak for other men, but I thought last night was pretty great. I thought *you* were pretty great."

"Yeah?" Tori asked nervously, looking up at him.

"Oh, yeah," Will replied, leaning down, kissing her softly on the lips and then wrapping her in his arms.

She dropped her things to the floor and accepted the embrace, burying her head in his chest. The two of them held onto each other for a quiet minute.

"Now at the risk of freaking you out, I have a really important and maybe sensitive question to ask."

"Which is?" Tori asked warily, looking up.

"Would you like some breakfast? I'm really good at making breakfast."

Tori smiled. "Yeah, okay."

"Good. Get dressed; shower if you want. The extra towels are under the sink. I'll start cooking."

Tori took a quick shower, and when she came down to the kitchen there awaited scrambled eggs, toast, sliced fruit, orange juice, and coffee along with Braddock, who was hanging up a call.

"What's up?"

"The BCA will be at Brule's with the ground-penetrating radar within the hour," Braddock answered as he poured a cup of coffee for Tori.

They ate in relative silence before Tori finally said, "You're right, though."

"About what?"

"We really don't know what to say."

"About how we handle this going forward?"

Tori nodded. "It is, after all, the elephant in the room."

Braddock shrugged. "How do you want to handle it? Other than, I'm sure, keeping it quiet."

"I don't know," she replied, shaking her head, a bit flustered. Talking about her own emotions and feelings, especially when it came to men, was not her strong suit. "I haven't slept with someone I've been working a case with before."

"Neither have I," he replied, smiling. "This is a bit of quandary, isn't it?"

"Don't joke. Not about this."

"I'm not. I'm searching for the right words and failing."

"What do we do?" she asked, suddenly panicked.

"Does there have to be an answer?"

"Don't we have to figure out how we're going to deal with this? We're working together," Tori stated. Their relationship was complicated and intense enough as it was, she thought, and now they'd added sex to the equation.

"Do you think we need ground rules?"

"I don't know," Tori blurted out, looking down at her plate. "Last night was great. I mean… really great."

"It was."

"But now I'm… confused with how to handle the…"

"Aftermath."

"Yeah." But now she smiled.

"Me too." Braddock thought for a moment. "Why don't we just see how it goes and not put any big expectations in play? This case could be done today. It could be done next week. Three months from now. Maybe never. Or three hours from now you could be leaving because a child has gone missing somewhere and you're needed there."

"So play it by ear, then?"

"It's all we can do for now," he replied calmly. "Are you okay with that?"

Maybe it was Braddock's confident, laid-back manner in not pressuring her, not expecting anything, that made her relax. He was proposing to live in the here and now. She was good with that. "Yeah, I think so," she replied, smiling as she finished the last of her toast and juice and then looked at her watch. If they were going to be spending the day at Brule's property, she needed to get back to the hotel to change into something far more appropriate than her little pink tank top and tan shorts.

She got up from her stool at the center island, walked over, and leaned into Braddock and kissed him. Then she slid her right arm around his neck and kissed him again, this time holding the kiss for an extra moment. "Thanks for making breakfast."

"My pleasure."

Ninety minutes later, Tori was all business, dressed in a dark olive pantsuit. She walked under the crime scene tape and up the driveway to find Braddock chatting with Cal. BCA agents were onsite with two ground-penetrating radar units. A property grid had been laid out and the teams had split the property in half.

"It'll probably take two days to scan the properties," Cal reported. "Even with all the wooded areas, there is plenty of open space to work. If we don't find anything here, we'll go up to that cabin of his, and as I'm sure you've heard, we have dogs here as well. If there is something here, we'll find it."

"Do we really think he'd bury the bodies on his own property?" Tori asked, not hiding her disbelief. Braddock had to play politics; she didn't.

"Well, *Victoria*," Cal admonished, "you asked the other day, where are the bodies? He has two pieces of property, so we need to search them. I too have doubts that the bodies are here, but we'll know soon enough." He folded his arms. "Now, young lady, if you have other ideas where to look, I'm all ears. Or you and Will here could spend some more time investigating Brule and figuring out where else he might have buried the bodies," Cal added acerbically before strolling away.

"Great. Now I'm pissing him off," Tori remarked.

"Look on the bright side. You're no longer pissing *me* off," Braddock replied lightly.

"Do I get more leeway with you now that we've slept together?" Tori asked impishly.

"Don't push it," Braddock cracked in reply as he turned and looked back down the driveway to the road and the media trucks arriving. "That's not going to help."

"No," Tori agreed as a cameraman was already out of the van, putting his camera on his shoulder, walking up to the edge of the crime scene tape. "We kept this quiet enough for a few days but now the circus has arrived."

"You and I have reservations, big ones," Will murmured quietly. "Cal knows we do, but instead of antagonizing him and the county attorney, we need to keep our powder dry for now and let this play out."

"That's fine. But they're not going to find anything. Yet, they're still going to be thinking it's Gunther. What do we do then?"

"Let's play it by ear."

"I can only handle so much playing it by ear," Tori teased.

"Okay, let's cross that bridge when we get to it."

"Any other clichés you want to throw out?"

"No, but I can't help but sit here and think that we might be trying to sabotage this thing. I don't like that," Will remarked under his breath.

"I don't think we're trying to sabotage anything," Tori replied. "If my sister's body is here or if Lash's body is here, then despite our reservations, we were wrong. I'll be the first one to admit it, and I'll be glad to do so. Do you think we are wrong?"

Will shook his head lightly. "No, but you're right. Even if they don't find a body, they're going to proceed as if Gunther was the killer unless we can show it wasn't Gunther."

"Any idea on how to do that?"

"Not yet," Will answered, but then he saw Steak walking past and had a thought, waving him over. He explained to Steak that he wanted him to dig through everything on Gunther, *everything*. "Financials, travel, phone, land ownership, talk to his ex-wife, his lawyer, anyone you can think of. Have Eggleston help you."

"To nail it down that it was Gunther?" Steak asked, then sensing there was an ulterior motive he followed with, "Or am I supposed to find something else?"

"We can't be wrong about him; we can't miss anything," Will lied to his detective, feeling guilty as he did so. "We need everything we can put together on Gunther. If you find something of interest, let me know. But Tori and I have been working this, and I want a fresh set of eyes on it."

"How does that help us?" Tori asked as Steak strolled away, pulling out his cell phone and no doubt calling his partner.

"I have to be true to myself. We play it straight. You and I are assuming we aren't going to find a body here or up at the cabin."

"Yes."

"Then as I think this through, if we don't find the bodies, I can't turn around and argue it's not Gunther if I haven't done everything in my power to prove it *is*. So, I put my two best investigators on the case to dig up everything they can on him."

"No games."

"No games," Braddock echoed, "other than maybe sending my two best detectives on a little bit of a wild goose chase."

"And there is one other thing we have in our back pocket."

"The negative DNA on the cigarette butts," Braddock replied, reading her mind. "I think we continue to keep that under our hats for the time being."

"Agreed, but while that might help, there is one other thing we really need to do," Tori replied.

"What's that?"

"Well, if it's not Gunther, then who is it? Because *that* will be the question Cal and the county attorney will have. We can have all the suspicions, but if we don't have someone else to plausibly point to and create doubt about Gunther, we're toast."

"You're right about that," he agreed. The two of them stood quietly, watching the proceedings. "By the way, you look and smell very nice."

Tori smiled inwardly. "Thanks for noticing."

"I'm a detective. It's my job to notice."

The day dragged on as the BCA techs worked their way through two-thirds of Brule's property. By the time the sun started setting in the west, there were no signs of a body. Cal, Backstrom, and a senior agent for the Minnesota BCA addressed the media gathering out on the road. Cal went to great pains to say that no conclusion had been made, but the story cake was already being baked. Gunther Brule was a person of interest. The fact that he was dead of an apparent suicide was raw meat for the newsies, who were running with him as the potential killer of Genevieve Lash and that he could also be tied to the twenty-year-old Jessie Hunter disappearance.

Cal and Backstrom came back up the driveway to find Tori and Braddock waiting for them, displeased.

"We had to say something," Backstrom stated.

"We can agree to disagree on that," Braddock replied brusquely.

"You don't have to run for office," the county attorney retorted.

"And what if you're wrong? How does that play at the ballot box?"

Tori explained, "You do realize, don't you, that the only real proof you have of anything on Gunther is that he might have taken a shot at me or tried to blow up Will. I mean, your only tie to Genevieve Lash is that he pinched her on the ass. Is that the foundation upon which you want to build your house?"

"You do realize, don't you, Victoria, that he committed suicide," Cal noted, not pleased with her tone. "Shot himself after you two confronted him. And by the way, since when have we *not* closed cases on good circumstantial evidence?"

"Why won't you two just take the win?" Backstrom asked dismissively.

"Nobody wants to solve this more than Tori or me," Braddock snapped back. "Nobody!"

"Easy, Will," Cal cautioned.

Braddock took a breath. "All I'm saying is please be careful about getting ahead of yourself, Mr. Backstrom."

"I'm not."

"Oh, but you're getting ready, sir. I can tell how anxious you are to declare victory here, so you can get Kyle Mannion and Skip Sauer and the rest of the business community off your back."

"Don't you want them off yours? I seem to recall Sauer coming after you pretty hard in Cal's office."

"So what?" Braddock answered, once again feisty. "I'm not going to rush my case and miss something just to satisfy him or anyone else. Especially this case. On this case we can't be wrong. We just can't. With what all the town has been through with this, we have to be as sure as we can be. This case has been going for twenty years—what's a few more days to lock it down?"

"Well, tell you what, Detective," Backstrom replied, not pleased with being so tenaciously advised by someone he deemed his subordinate. "We'll make it easy for you: it won't be *your* call.

It'll be Cal's and it'll be *mine*, and once it's made—and it will be made—you better get in line and smile for the cameras, son."

"And if I don't?"

Backstrom took a breath and gave Braddock a good, long look. "Will, I like you. I always have. Don't put me in a position where I have to re-evaluate that view of things," he warned before looking over to Cal. "I'll call you later," he said, shaking the sheriff's hand then walking away.

"Well, that was fun," Cal remarked lightly once Backstrom was out of earshot. Then he turned and stepped up to Braddock. "I think you've been hanging around Victoria a little too much lately."

"Hey!" Tori protested.

"Will, be careful, and don't you get too far ahead of yourself," Cal counseled. "I'm not running again in a few years, but Backstrom is and he'll win. He's more political than legal, but he's smart, popular, and connected. He has Jeff Warner's and Kyle Mannion's support and money backing him. As I've counseled, you want and need to be friends with them."

"Like you?" Tori asked.

Cal pivoted, paused, and gave her a severe look. "Victoria, I've certainly been smart enough to not make any of those gentlemen my enemy." He looked back to Braddock. "When I'm gone there will be a new sheriff, and you're going to want to have friends who have your back. Backstrom can be one, and he'll bring others along with him, but not if you talk to him like that. I'd suggest you chew on *that* a little tonight." With that Cal walked away.

"He's probably right, you know," Tori stated once Cal was out of earshot.

"Yeah, he is," Braddock answered, shaking his head. "I'll need to go see Backstrom and clear the air."

"What happened to letting things play out? Keeping our powder dry?"

"Those two went and basically hung everything on Brule to the press. It was dumb, an unforced error that will… it's just going to cause problems in the coming days," he replied, shaking his head. "So, I went off, more than I should have. Doesn't happen often."

"I absolutely loved it," Tori added.

Braddock chuckled. "I imagine you did."

"So…" Tori turned to him. "Detective Braddock, now that we're off the clock, do you have any plans?"

"What do you have in mind?"

"What I have in mind is your place. Right now."

CHAPTER TWENTY-FIVE

"I see, so someone else was shooting
from the grassy knoll."

By the end of the next day, events had transpired just as Tori and Braddock had anticipated and feared.

The search at Brule's Manchester Bay property had ended by mid-afternoon. In fact, one team had finished the search of its half of the property by 10 a.m. and was dispatched to the Benedict Lake property. The second team had left the Manchester Bay property and joined them in the early afternoon. By 7 p.m. both parcels were fully searched and no bodies were found.

Cal and Backstrom gathered Assistant County Attorney Wilson, Tori, and Braddock in Brule's cabin garage for some privacy. "I don't care that we didn't find any bodies, it's time to call it," Backstrom declared.

"I think that is a really bad idea," Tori posited and then dropped something she and Braddock had been holding back. "There isn't a DNA match on the cigarette butts found next to the shell casings."

"How long have you been sitting on that?" Cal asked, annoyed.

"Two days," Tori replied. "I wanted to see how the search played out, and it played out how I thought it would—no bodies."

To Tori's dismay, Backstrom and Wilson were nonplussed by the disclosure and unbothered by the result.

"Were I actually prosecuting a case, that might give me a little discomfort," Backstrom stated while looking over to Wilson, who nodded her agreement. "But I'm not, so I'm not worried about that, again particularly because of how Mr. Brule was found three nights ago—dead, a gun below his hand."

"That's an admission in my book," Wilson added. "What could be clearer?"

"No note," Tori offered.

"He didn't exactly seem like the writing type," Cal quipped.

"What if it's not him?" Braddock asked reasonably. "What if what Tori and I did was get an innocent and wounded man, a veteran with PTSD so panicked about what was about to happen to him, that he couldn't handle it and he killed himself?"

"You and Tori did nothing wrong in questioning him, even if it was aggressive, even if you did run a game on him," Cal replied. "That was just good police work."

"Still, what if we're wrong?" Tori pressed.

"Who else would it be?" Backstrom inquired.

Tori looked to Braddock, with a *what do you think* look.

Braddock gave her a nod.

"This will take a few minutes to explain. Will and I think it's someone who's killed or abducted up to twenty-three women in twelve states here in the Upper Midwest, and out in Wyoming, Colorado, and Montana as well," Tori answered.

"It started with Jessie Hunter," Braddock explained. "There was a gap in time, maybe four years, and then the killer has taken one to two women per year since, with the most recent victim not being Genevieve Lash but a woman named Joanie Wells in Brookings, South Dakota. The week before last!"

Tori explained that most of the women had disappeared, although there were four women who were found bound, strangled, and stuffed in the trunks of their cars. "Those four could probably be eliminated."

Then she started ticking items off with her fingers. "The killer, whoever he actually is, is very good and very skilled. He gets to these women and nobody ever sees him do it. Nobody ever hears anything. No forensic evidence is left behind. He takes them in places where there is no surveillance, no security, and where nobody is watching. In most cases the woman's vehicle is involved in some way. In many cases it's damaged."

"All of that requires advanced scouting and planning," Braddock added. "A lot of scouting and planning by someone who—if not regularly in that area—has at least spent enough time there to know it well and to know the gaps in security and surveillance."

"Which means, at least based on my experience, it requires a level of intelligence and even some charm to get this close to these women, traits that Gunther Brule did not possess," Tori opined. "He's an ass-pincher. He is not that smart. If that's not enough, the work records Braddock has prove Brule couldn't have been in some of those places at those times. Gunther Brule didn't kill all these women. He didn't kill Genevieve Lash and he didn't kill my sister," Tori argued. "It's not him."

The garage was silent for a minute.

Backstrom and Wilson were incredulous. Cal's expression was one of dismayed annoyance, having thought he'd convinced the two of them to shelve the other women and just focus on Jessie Hunter and Genevieve Lash.

"So, you think *we're* getting ahead of ourselves?" Backstrom asked in disbelief. "You think *we're* wildly speculating on this case? Did you two just listen to yourselves? My gosh, you both act like the last thing you want is for this case to be over."

"I want to know who killed my sister," Tori growled. "I want the person who did it."

"I do too, Agent Hunter," Backstrom barked back. "And I know who it is. It's Gunther Brule."

"It can't be," Braddock answered, holding up Brule's work records. "These exculpate him."

"Assuming all of those cases *are* connected, then you *might* be right," Backstrom conceded. "But that assumes all of those cases are connected, and that assumes that Jessie Hunter and Genevieve Lash are part of all of that. I can make a far more compelling argument that they're not."

"Let me hear it then," Braddock retorted.

Backstrom looked over to Wilson.

"For starters, answer me this," the assistant county attorney began, transitioning to cross-examination mode. "For Hunter and Lash—when their vehicles were found, there was no evidence of a struggle, correct?"

"That's true," Braddock and Tori replied in unison.

"So, there was no evidence of a fight of any kind. Their purses were gone, Lash's phone was gone, and their cars were locked. The trunks and spare tires were not accessed. What's that tell you?"

"They knew who picked them up," Tori answered.

"Exactly," Wilson answered. "And they *both* knew Brule. He was familiar to both of them."

"Except Brule was drunk and driven home from Mannion's the night Lash disappeared," Tori replied.

"Can anyone verify he was still at home later that night?" Wilson asked.

"No," Braddock answered honestly.

"He owns two vehicles, right?"

"He does."

"Fine, he gets dropped off. Nobody is at home, nobody suspects he's up to anything. He gets in his *other* vehicle. He goes back to Mannion's, angry at Lash. He sticks a big knife in her tire," Wilson argued and then gestured to Tori. "Just like he did to your sister twenty years ago. He knows cars, right? I've seen his garage, it looks like a NAPA auto parts store. This is a method that worked once, twenty years ago, correct?"

Tori and Braddock both reluctantly nodded.

Wilson kept going, painting her picture. "So, he follows Lash and pulls up to her a minute or two after she pulls over with a flat tire. Maybe he says he was sorry when he pulls up. Maybe she gets apologetic because Genevieve Lash isn't exactly the tire-changing type, and she wants a ride home late at night with a violent thunderstorm hanging overhead. She's a woman in distress, out on that backwoods road. He says he'll drive her home to make amends. Genevieve may not like him, but she can suffer through a three-mile ride with him, given the circumstances. It doesn't take much imagination to figure out the rest. Case closed."

Wilson's case was straightforward and simple. It made sense with the added feature she'd never have to make it to a jury.

"Anne, put yourself in that spot on that road," Braddock suggested. "Yes, there is a storm, but you're three miles from home. You have a cell phone, and your father—as would any father—would come and pick you up. So, do you call your dad or do you jump into a white panel van with a guy who was escorted drunk from the bar after pinching you on the ass three hours ago?"

Wilson shrugged. "It doesn't matter what I would do. What matters is what she did. She got in the van. Maybe he was holding that .38 on her that he killed himself with."

Tori wasn't buying it. "And then what? He goes home and mails me a copy of a newspaper article from when my sister disappeared? Why do that? How does that fit in?"

"To make a point. To play a game. To rub it in since he just killed again on the twentieth anniversary. To celebrate and to cover what he did to Lash. There could be any number of reasons to do that."

"That is so weak," Braddock replied dismissively.

"Who knows why he did it?" Wilson answered.

"And we'll never know now, will we?" Braddock lamented.

"I don't have to know," Wilson retorted.

"No, I think you do," Braddock asserted.

"We *do* know," Backstrom argued emphatically. "He killed himself because he knew the two of you had figured it out. Come on, it's like I said yesterday, you two have done a great job. *A great job*. Take. The. Win."

Wilson continued, "And the more I think about it, the less I'm worried about the lack of a DNA match on those cigarette butts, especially because of all of the other evidence that says Brule's the killer. He has a history with Lash."

"History? He pinched her ass," Tori rebutted. "That's a history? That makes him the killer? Gimme a break."

"He had a history with her," Wilson insisted. "Genevieve Lash told him to know his place. On top of that, he lived in the town when your sister went missing. He has a record of domestic abuse. Convicted? No. But we'd get that evidence admitted if we had a trial. There's a ballistics match for the gun that he used to take those shots at you, Agent Hunter. He works at Sidwell so he's familiar with and has experience with explosives. We found mercury switch materials at his house, along with mercury from Sidwell. His van was positively identified leaving the area by a credible witness."

"Fran Larson saw a van speeding away that looked like Brule's," Tori countered.

"She identified *that* van," Wilson answered, undeterred. "I saw Steak's report. She didn't equivocate."

"And the cigarette butts? You really don't think that's an issue?" Braddock inquired.

"Those cigarette butts could've been from some guy out hunting for all we know," Backstrom lamely replied.

"Really?" Tori asked, jumping on the response. "You know, I haven't been back for twenty years, so did the laws change? Is there a hunting season right now in mid-July?"

"It's not hunting season," Braddock noted. "And even if it was, nobody would be hunting there."

"They're not from any hunting season," Tori argued. "Those butts aren't from last year. They were fresh and they were found by the spent shell casings. Brule's a smoker, but he didn't smoke those."

"So, what are you saying, Agent Hunter? You think they were planted? What evidence is there of that?" Backstrom posited. "As a prosecutor, I think I could pretty easily explain that away."

"I think someone else was the shooter," Tori explained.

"And then what? They fail to get you and Will, so they set up Gunther Brule?" Wilson asked.

"He's a patsy," Tori blurted.

"I see, so someone else was shooting from the grassy knoll," Backstrom quipped derisively. "No way."

"Success or failure, Gunther Brule was going to be set up either way," Braddock replied calmly, having seen the question coming for ten minutes. "If the person we're after had succeeded and killed me and Tori, you would have investigated the case the way the two of us have—and you'd have what? Gunther Brule. That's what the killer wants, and Gunther isn't alive to proclaim his innocence. That makes it awfully easy for you to just pin everything on him and call it case closed."

"Nice theory," Backstrom replied, "but the simplest answer is almost always the right one. I know whose version of events makes more sense and which version I could win a case with, and it isn't yours."

"The operative term there was *almost always*," Braddock countered as his cell phone rang. He read the screen on his phone. "Excuse me… I should take this." He stepped outside of the garage.

"And by the way, we're not going to court," Tori continued, pushing the argument. "Brule is dead."

"But we can put to rest at least the recent disappearance of Lash, the shots at you, and the attempt on Will's life… and I honestly think you could consider your sister's case closed," Cal offered in a measured tone that nonetheless indicated which version of events he agreed with. "The evidence is strong on all of that," he added.

"Heck, we just need the autopsy and some forensic reports completed so we have everything. That's the direction this thing is going," Backstrom said reasonably.

"But what if that's the wrong direction?" Tori persisted. "And what about Katy Anderson? How does she fit into all of this?"

"Why does that even have to be connected?" Wilson asked. "It could just as easily be a coincidence, and in fact it is more likely unrelated. Hell, I'm sorry, Tori, but she was crazy. She could have jumped on a bus to Seattle and simply be gone."

"Really? Really?" Tori replied in angry exasperation. "You guys can just wipe away evidence and disappearances with the wave of a hand, as if they're irrelevant because they don't fit your neat little narrative. Aren't you the least bit curious as to how she fits into all of this?"

"Look, I'm sorry, Agent Hunter. I know she was your friend," Wilson said apologetically.

"Genevieve Lash disappears. I show up and then visit Katy and now Katy is gone, and you don't think that's related? What are you smoking?"

"Given what I've just listened to the last half-hour, I could ask you the same thing," Backstrom snapped back.

*

Braddock's call was from Dr. Galen Renfrow, the medical examiner.

"Is the autopsy complete?"

"Yes, I suppose," Renfrow answered after a moment. "I've had it done for twenty-four hours but… well, I've been sitting on it." Renfrow was leading somewhere.

"What's the delay, Doc?"

The coroner exhaled. "Because I have a finding that is… well, curious. I was hoping the searches at Brule's properties would clear it up."

"A curious finding? Curious how?"

"Based on preliminary blood tests, Brule's blood alcohol content upon death was point two-six."

"No shock there. He was getting up his courage to pull the trigger, Doc."

"And that, I suppose, is one *possible* explanation for the angle of entry on the wound."

Braddock caught the tone. "What bothers you about that angle, Doc?"

"Let me ask you a question. Do you *want* me to be bothered?" Renfrow asked, picking up on Braddock's inquiring tone. "Tell me, do you question whether Brule is your man?"

"Are we off the record?"

"For now, sure."

"I have to be honest. There's plenty, *plenty* that says its him," Braddock replied truthfully, describing the case he'd just heard Wilson and Backstrom lay out. If he was being honest, it was a convincing case. "So, there is the obvious case that says yeah, Brule's our guy. But there is an alternate theory that says he's not." He provided Renfrow with the abbreviated version of that line of thought as well. "Right now, the first theory is the prevailing one shared by Backstrom, Wilson, and Cal, the decision-makers. And while it has a few holes, it's a persuasive case, especially since Brule is lying dead on the slab in front of you. The alternative theory is one posited by me and Tori Hunter, and it's not currently finding a receptive audience."

"I see."

"So, since we're off the record, what do *you* have?"

"The angle of entry and exit of the bullet is oddly steep."

"Meaning what, exactly?"

"From what I can tell, he was holding that revolver at a *really* high angle over his head, almost vertical, not at all horizontal. And the exit wound confirms that steep angle: it's out of the left lower base of his skull."

"Is it possible to do that?" Braddock asked, sitting down and trying to mimic the shooting angle with his right hand. "Pronating his wrist like that seems really awkward… and unnecessary."

"Yes. And I know we're talking about someone who supposedly died of suicide, so if he did, he wasn't necessarily rational in his thinking. But no matter his state of mind, I'm not sure why you would hold the gun at such an angle to shoot yourself. Put the barrel in your mouth, up to the temple, or stick it under the chin. That's what we usually see in suicide cases."

"You said supposedly. Are you saying it's *possible* he didn't shoot himself?"

"I don't know, Will. That angle really bothers me."

"Are the angles of entry and exit more consistent with someone else shooting him?" Braddock inquired.

Dr. Renfrow was quiet on the other end for a long moment. "He was in that chair, right?"

"Yes," Braddock answered. "And if the blood tests are accurate, very intoxicated."

"Go on."

With Renfrow's insight, the scene at Brule's suddenly played differently to Braddock. "Doc, he's drunk and passed out in that chair. His head is tilted down, drooping to the left, like how someone often sleeps in a chair."

"And if I follow, Detective, someone walks up and shoots him in the head from a higher angle because they're standing."

"Right," Braddock agreed. "Did you test Brule for gunshot residue?"

"I did. There was a small trace on his right hand."

"The gun used on him was the .38, correct?"

"Yes. That's confirmed. We extracted that bullet out of the back of the chair."

"We found five in the cylinder; obviously the one that went through his head was extracted from the chair. But if there was someone there and they did shoot him, it's not hard to put the gun in Gunther's hand, pull the trigger on a second bullet and then replace a bullet in the cylinder."

"Shoot it where?"

"Outdoors. From that chair you could open the sliding glass door fifteen feet away and shoot it out toward the lake. With Brule dead, our second man could come up with some sort of way to silence the sound of the gun." After a moment's thought, Braddock thought that could have happened. "But of course, we're off the record here."

"We are."

"Anything else bothering you?" Braddock asked.

"Isn't that enough?" Dr. Renfrow replied with a rueful chuckle. "But look, other than that angle, I don't know that I have anything medically or forensically I can point to that says it's *not* a suicide."

"In other words, your report could go in a couple of directions."

"Yes."

"What are you going to do?"

"I'm going to continue to take my time and… ponder my analysis. I need to think it through, but I'm glad I called. My delay might give *you* more time to prove your theory. I can tell you have serious doubts about Brule."

"Tori and I don't think he killed Jessie Hunter or Genevieve Lash. The longer you take the better."

"Then the question is, and this isn't my department, mind you… but if it isn't Brule, who the hell is it?"

"We're working on it, Doc."

*

Cal wanted everyone to reconvene tomorrow, after a night off. "We all have a lot to think about," he stated while casting an aggravated look in Tori and Braddock's direction. "I think we need to get to the point where *everyone* is singing from the same hymnal."

As they dispersed from the garage, Tori mumbled, "What are we going to do?"

"Go back to my place and strategize while we still have some time before we have to sing "Ave Maria" in five-part harmony."

Braddock stopped at Mannion's on the Lake and picked up a pizza to go, then met Tori back at his house. They retired to his office with the pizza and a six-pack of beer and stared at the map up on the wall. Braddock related his call with Renfrow. "He's sitting on it, but he can only do that for so long."

"He called you. He has doubts. That helps," Tori said with a hopeful tone.

Braddock was more sanguine. "He has some doubts, sure, but the far more compelling case is that Brule pulled that trigger and killed himself. Renfrow might not ultimately like it, but he'll swallow it and sign off that Brule did himself in, and the reality is, that would withstand any sort of scrutiny."

"And," Tori replied, "Cal, Backstrom, and Wilson are ready to call it. For all intents and purposes, they have."

"When they do, we're dead in the water," Braddock stated. "I mean, the sheriff is my boss."

"But…" Tori protested.

"They're convinced that Brule did all this, and if they decide to go all in on it? It gets harder and harder for me to keep this open and keep investigating. You heard Cal's none too subtle warning about getting on the team. My hands will be tied."

"Yours might be. Mine aren't."

"You have a boss, too, who will be calling you back home soon enough. In fact, I wouldn't put it past Cal to pay your boss a friendly call and see if he has a crying need for you to return. And if that happens, then what? Are you going to defy them?"

"I don't know."

"Let's face it. We might have to do what Backstrom says. Take the win. I don't like it, but right now I don't see a way around it. Especially since we don't have an answer to the question of if not Brule, then who?"

Tori stood up and paced around the room, quiet in thought, before giving the map on the wall one last, long look. She knew he was right, at least for tonight. Tori looked back to Braddock, who was sitting in his desk chair, studying her with eyes that said he was done working.

She slowly began walking toward him. With her eyes locked on his, she deliberately unbuttoned and then unzipped her slacks and let them fall to the floor. With both of her hands, she slowly lifted her sleeveless blouse over her head to reveal her toned body, wearing only a white lace bra and underwear.

Braddock quietly admired her body for a moment before he sat back in his chair, welcoming her to him. Tori climbed on and straddled him in the chair, reaching her arms around his neck and drawing him in for a soft, lingering kiss.

"You're right, I might have to leave soon," she whispered before pecking him softly on the lips, resting her forehead against his.

"You might," Braddock answered in a murmur, lightly running his fingers up and down the soft skin of her back. "But you're here now."

She looked into his eyes. "I am, and after the last two nights, I know this much: if I do have to leave soon, I want to do as much of this as possible before I go."

CHAPTER TWENTY-SIX

"Nobody will be surprised that I went rogue."

Tori stepped out of the shower to find a thick, soft towel, a toothbrush, and a fresh red rose waiting for her.

It stopped her in her tracks.

She couldn't remember the last time someone had made such a romantic gesture. Of course, you needed to provide someone a reason to want to be adoring, and on that score, Tori failed most of the time. Often willingly.

It wasn't that there were never men in her life. Attracting men was never really an issue for her. She had attractive features, kept herself in fantastic shape, was professionally successful, and—despite her occasional prickly demeanor—was approachable and welcoming of the attention of men.

What she wasn't was emotionally available. That part of her was closed off. The men she let into her life from time to time served a singular purpose. They tended to the occasional need for sex and companionship, perhaps a needed date for a wedding or formal party, but that was it. Before she ever let it get any further, and before there was ever a conversation about where something might be going, she found a way to nuke it. Usually, the convenient excuse was another case to go chase. She'd leave on a plane, cut off contact, and immerse herself in the investigation, and then when the case was over, she'd return home to find the man had moved on by then—a result that rarely, if ever, bothered her.

Because of those life choices, there were seldom romantic gestures like flowers. Yet there was one this morning, and as she dressed, she found herself constantly glancing at the rose, twisting it in her fingers, and putting it to her nose. As she was wont to do, she analyzed her infatuation with the flower. Was it the gesture itself or who had made it that had her feeling some lightness?

Careful, Tori, she silently admonished herself.

"Breakfast will be ready in five minutes," Braddock bellowed from the kitchen.

"Okay," she called back.

She finished by putting her hair up in a damp ponytail. She picked up her rose and glanced at her watch: 6:32 a.m. As she strolled out of the bedroom, down the hall, and past the office, she saw that the beer bottles, used paper plates, and pizza box from last night remained on the desk. *I should clean that up.*

Tori went into the office and glanced to the ever-present map on the wall with all the victims and their locations before she started depositing the empty beer bottles into the small office garbage can, along with the plates and balled-up napkins. Next, she looked to the Mannion's pizza box. She flipped the top over and saw there were three slices left inside before securing it again. On the cover of the pizza box was *Mannion's*, written in red cursive, and a map of all the Mannion's restaurants throughout the Upper Midwest and Mountain States. As she picked up the box, she looked at the cover again and froze.

"Wait a… minute."

Tori looked from the map on the pizza box to the map on the wall, with all the dots of the missing women, then back to the pizza box. Then she looked back to the wall and then back to the box again.

"No way."

She took the box over to the map on the wall, her eyes darting back and forth. "Holy shit!" Tori ran out of the office to the landing. "Will! Will!"

"Yeah, what is it?" Braddock asked, coming into the family room, a set of tongs still in his hand. He looked up to her. "What?" he asked, catching the alarmed look on her face. "What is it?"

"You have to come up here and see this!" she exclaimed, holding up the top of the pizza box.

"See what?"

"Just come up. Just come up right now."

Braddock quickly climbed the steps three at a time to meet an ashen Tori on the landing. She reached for his hand and pulled him into the office.

"What's wrong?"

"Just look at this," Tori commanded, holding the cover of the pizza box up next to the map.

She watched as Braddock's eyes first slowly and then with more rapidity moved back and forth, the slow recognition followed by the stunned disbelief.

"What? *Whoa!*" Braddock blurted as he grabbed the pizza box from Tori and held it up in front of the map, his eyes still darting back and forth between the two. Finally, he looked at her. "Is this really possible?"

"You tell me."

Braddock stepped over to his desk, sat down, and powered up his computer. He clicked his way to the Mannion Restaurant website.

"I know exactly what you're thinking," Tori stated. "Go get the breakfast and bring it up. I'll do the research."

For fifteen minutes they devoured pancakes and sausages while they put black Xs on the map to mark the Mannion's locations. They were, in all cases, remarkably close if not directly on top of the green and red dots for the victims.

"It's frickin' uncanny," Braddock mused with a muted laugh, slowly shaking his head. All twenty-three disappearances were within fifteen miles of a Mannion's.

"What we need to do is get more data points to either prove or disprove it," Tori said, analyzing, with her arms folded. "If we go in right now and tell the sheriff and county attorney about this, they'll…"

"Have us committed. They're practically ready to do that to us now," Braddock finished, still looking back and forth between the two maps, still questioning what he was seeing. "We created that database. Gunther was in it. I wonder how many Mannion's employees are in it," he wondered as he sat down at the desk and remoted in to his office computer and the database. With several keystrokes, he refined his search. "Man, a lot of people work for a Mannion-related company in this area."

"It's a company town now. How many?"

"That fit the age and residency criteria? Seven hundred and twenty-six." Braddock shook his head in despair.

"Would it have to be a Mannion's employee?" Tori asked.

"Don't you think so with this kind of correlation?"

"I bet you that number gets significantly smaller if we limit it to the restaurant operation side of the business," Tori noted. "That would be a data point to help sift."

"We could try and see if we could drill that down, but… Hmm, I wonder…" Braddock turned back to his laptop and the web page for Mannion's on the Lake. He clicked on locations, which listed all the Mannion's restaurants.

The first Mannion's expansion was to Bismarck, North Dakota. He clicked on the restaurant, which pulled up its vital information: address, phone number, hours of operation, and then there was a history link. He clicked on it, which popped up a picture of the restaurant on its opening day along with the date. He called to Tori, "What date did Carrie Blaine go missing from Bismarck?"

Tori looked to the map on the wall. "May 24, 2004."

"Mannion's opened there on May 23, 2004," Will replied, turning his computer around. "That's a picture of the opening. All the local dignitaries along with Kyle and Eddie Mannion are holding the big scissors to cut the ribbon."

Will went back to the locations page and clicked on the link for Oshkosh, Wisconsin. "Oshkosh opened September 15, 2009."

"Ginger Zeller went missing… September 14, 2009," Tori replied. "Leanne Benson, Cedar Falls, Iowa, she disappeared on November 1, 2011."

Braddock clicked back to the locations page and then clicked on Cedar Falls. "Opened November 3, 2011. Joannie Wells disappeared from Brookings on July 12, 2019." He clicked back to the locations page for Brookings, South Dakota. "Mannion's opened in Brookings… two days earlier on July 10, 2019." He exhaled a long, anxious breath. "Oh, boy."

"We better start from the beginning," Tori murmured quietly.

For the next half-hour they worked through each restaurant opening in order. In each instance, their victim disappeared within three days before or four days after the opening of a Mannion's restaurant. While Will confirmed all the openings and disappearance dates, Tori got online with her laptop. Using her FBI access to every publication available, she found five newspaper articles tied to the early expansion openings of the restaurants with pictures of Eddie and Kyle at the ceremonies.

"Is this really happening?" Tori asked in shock before locking eyes with Braddock. "Will, if this is Mannion Companies, how many people from the company are *always* going to be at the openings?"

"I know where you're going."

"Yeah, I mean over nearly twenty years, it's going to have to be one of the two guys in the pictures."

Braddock closed his eyes and shook his head. "Man, I've really enjoyed living here. If I go down this route, I can kiss my ass goodbye."

"That's why… this one's on me," Tori answered.

He started to protest. "Hold on a second."

"No. If need be, I made this connection all on my own—me and my friends at the FBI—because I was so frustrated dealing with Backstrom, Wilson, and even Cal, who just wanted to bury the case with a dead man," Tori replied with a wink. "Nobody will be surprised that I went rogue. Nobody."

"Well," Braddock let out a wry chuckle, "that's true."

"I'll take this part of it from here," Tori added while placing a call. Special Agent Tracy Sheets answered right away. "Trace, I need your help. Are you available like… today, maybe?"

Braddock watched as Tori listened and then mouthed a *yes* with a fist pump, then held up one finger and mouthed *an hour*.

"You rock, girlfriend, you know that?" Tori exclaimed, smiling. "I'm going to owe you massively, and I will pay. Have you seen *Hamilton* yet? Well, you and your husband are going to. Now, when you get free, we can discuss this more. In the meantime, I'm going to send you an electronic file that will be helpful."

A minute later Tori was off the phone. "She can talk in an hour. She obviously has more access and resources available to her to dive into this, but in the meantime, we need to throttle back Cal and Backstrom. We need to buy some time."

"I'm on that," Braddock replied, reaching for his cell phone and placing a call to Dr. Renfrow for another conversation. "Doc, how do we stretch this out a little more? Even just a day."

"I'm waiting on some additional bloodwork, but it's really not *that* consequential. But you know, until either Cal or Backstrom starts pressing me, I feel no real need to be in a big hurry," Dr. Renfrow answered. "Although, Will, it's only a matter of time before I do get the call."

"Understood, Doc. I'll be in touch."

With Renfrow still slow-walking his report, the sheriff and county attorney couldn't call the case closed.

"I think you and I should both make ourselves scarce today," Braddock suggested.

"That's easy for me. I plan on burying myself at the hotel on my computer," Tori answered. "But what are you going to do? You can't hide."

"But I can take a road trip," Will replied with a wink.

The road trip was back up to Brule's cabin outside of Walker. The crime scene tape was still up. Braddock checked in with a deputy standing post at the end of the driveway and then he drove up to the cabin.

If Dr. Renfrow had his doubts, Brule's cabin demanded another look. This time as a murder scene. Once inside the front door, Braddock set his backpack down and deliberately walked around the family room and kitchen area, once again familiarizing himself with the scene and visualizing Brule slumped in the chair, the gun beneath his right hand. He stood in the middle of the family room with Brule's chair to his left, the coffee table in front of him, and another chair to the right with an old rust, beige, and green plaid couch on the other side of the coffee table. He wondered, *If Brule didn't shoot himself, how did it happen?*

He went to his backpack, took out a manila folder, and walked back to the middle of the room. In the folder were pictures of the crime scene. One by one he sifted through the photos, many of which were of Brule slumped dead in the chair, but some were of the space around the seating area. He spread the photos on the floor in front of him and crouched down to view them all. He organized them left to right based on what the photo captured, whether it was Brule and the chair, or the coffee table in front of Brule showing a coaster and glass, and finally two photos where the photographer had stepped back to get more of a panoramic view of the room.

He paced gradually left to right, glancing down at the photos, often pausing to look between the photos and the chair or the coffee table. At the second to last photo he stopped and picked it up. It was one of the panoramic shots. There were two coasters out on the coffee table. One was in front of where Brule was sitting, which the photos showed had Brule's drink glass on it when he was found, and one was resting on the other end of the table, in front of the chair at the opposite end.

"If someone was here, perhaps they were sitting in the other chair," Braddock mumbled as he walked around the chair in question. He looked to another photo, which was of the 750-milliliter bottle of Maker's Mark, which was found nearly empty. The bottle had been purchased on Wednesday night, not long after they'd paid him a visit at the VFW. He'd bought it with a credit card at five minutes to ten, just before closing time for the liquor store. The expenditure was for $25.99, which included the bottle of Maker's Mark and a bottle of Diet Coke, based on the receipt that Eggleston had chased down.

They'd confronted him at the VFW around 8 p.m., and that had lasted perhaps fifteen to twenty minutes. He took out his cell phone and called Steak.

"Cal's looking for you."

"You haven't seen or heard from me, got it?"

"Uh, okay."

"I need you to access Brule's phone records from the night Tori and I went to confront him until we found him dead. I want to see if he made any phone calls. But, Steak, be discreet and keep your head down."

"I presume this relates to why Cal's looking for you and why you're unavoidably detained?"

"You should be a detective."

Braddock took another look at the photo of the bottle of Maker's Mark, which had been photographed sitting on the counter in the kitchen. He walked into the kitchen and shook his head in wonder. He often thought that for a single parent with an active eleven-year-old boy, he kept a respectably clean house, but Brule, the ex-soldier, had taken it to another level. That part of his training and discipline had not left him. Aside from the bottle of liquor, there was nothing else on that stretch of counter that ran along the south wall of the house from the sliding door to the kitchen sink in the corner. In the sink, oddly or maybe not oddly, was a single glass. He started to reach with his gloved hand and then stopped.

He walked to the front of the house, picked up his backpack, and brought it back to the sink. From the backpack, he took out a camera and snapped several photos of the glass in the sink, along with photos of the entirety of the kitchen. He also took out his notepad and jotted down that he'd found the glass in the sink.

With the documentation taken care of, he reached down with his gloved hand into the left side of the sink and carefully, with as light a touch as possible, picked up the glass and inspected it. It was clean, not a spot on it. *A glass in the sink, perfectly clean, but not put away in an orderly and organized kitchen where nothing is out.* He examined the glass again, holding it under the bright light of a lamp, only to confirm that the glass was perfectly clean. "Hmpf."

He walked out of the kitchen and back into the living room, over to the chair opposite the one Brule was found in. The one with the coaster in front of it. Braddock snapped two photos of the coaster, noting the coaster holder on the table to the right of Brule's chair. He also noted that there was a glass on the table in front of Brule. *Two glasses. One for Brule. Who was the one in the sink for?*

He started thinking out loud. "Okay, so let's just say someone *was* here, drinking with Gunther. He waits until Gunther is trashed, his head bobbing, maybe he's passed out. Then, he takes out the .38, walks over and… shoots him."

Braddock crouched down to the left of the chair where Brule's arm had been hanging down, the gun underneath it. "Now, you know you need Gunther to have fired the gun." He walked over to the sliding door, unlocked it, and slid it open. He then walked back to the chair.

"You just fire another bullet out the sliding glass door out to the water. That gets you gunshot residue on Gunther." The cabin was somewhat isolated. To the west were dense woods. To the east, the next cabin was a good hundred yards away. But what if he wanted to avoid the loud pop of the gun? Particularly with the window open?

He walked back into the kitchen and found the garbage can under the sink. It was empty other than a few crumpled-up paper towels. The other garbage cans in the bathroom and the two bedrooms were empty as well. He even went to the garbage can on the side of the garage, which was also empty. He took another look through all the crime scene photos and didn't see what he was looking for: the two-liter bottle of Diet Coke. "And if you were mixing the Maker's Mark with Diet Coke, you could empty out the bottle, hold it on the end of the gun, that would be a little clunky with a .38, a bit dangerous but Gunther isn't fighting you to aim the gun, you could be deliberate, get it just right and… that could be your silencer."

That could work, he thought. *That could really work.*

He went back over, closed the sliding door, locked it, and then stopped.

The cabin had been locked when they'd arrived.

So how would a killer have been able to lock the cabin when he left?

Braddock stepped outside and began searching around for a key, looking under the mat at the front door, under all the windowsills, beneath the metal hose holder and water meter, and all along and under the cedar deck. Next, he worked his way around the detached garage, checking the three windowsills, the top of the side door, and under the one empty flower pot on the concrete apron to the left of the garage door. He spent the better part of an hour looking in all the obvious—and what he thought would be less obvious—places around the entirety of the cabin grounds. He did not find a key.

He could have simply taken the spare key with him. But then thought it through some more. *If there was a key, the killer would have left it behind because you wouldn't want anything to be amiss or create any reason for someone to question whether it was a suicide.* There were people he could ask to see if Gunther kept a spare key outside. *But let's assume he didn't, then what?*

Braddock stepped back inside the house and pondered. Brule probably had a spare key somewhere inside the house, but would the killer know that? That depended on who it would be. If they knew him well, they might know, but what if they didn't? *Again, say you can't find a spare key, what would you have done?*

Will pulled out his phone and called Dr. Renfrow. "I assume you inventoried everything on his body."

"Yes."

"What did he have?"

Braddock could hear Renfrow shuffling through papers on the other end. "Wallet, his cell phone, and a set of keys."

"How many keys?"

"Hang on, let me get that stuff." Renfrow was back on the phone two minutes later. "There is a truck key, a key fob, and six others that look like door keys, plus another one, two… no, three that are small keys. They look like filing cabinet keys."

Renfrow was back down in Manchester Bay. "Doc, I'm on my way to you."

*

"What are we working on?" Tracy Sheets asked.

Tori explained what she and Braddock had stumbled onto earlier, the status of their case, and the fact their backs were against the wall. "I emailed you this database and a list of Mannion's employees. We need to start sifting through these people and seeing if we can tie them to these towns or victims somehow. But I will say this up front, I think it'll come down to just a couple of possible people."

"And how quickly do you need to do this?"

"Like yesterday," Tori replied emphatically. "And I'm working it on this end as well. We have to move fast."

*

Dr. Renfrow handed him the evidence bag with the keys in it, and a clipboard with a release form.

Braddock signed it and handed the clipboard back. "I'll be back in a couple of hours."

His first stop was Brule's house outside of Manchester Bay. A sheriff's deputy was parked out front. "Deputy, I'm wondering if you wouldn't mind following me up to the house. I need another set of eyes."

At the house Braddock took the keys out of the evidence bag. There was a key for the van, a fob with a Dodge Ram logo on it, and six other door keys. He went to the back door of the house and started trying keys. The third key—a copper one and the oldest-looking of the six—opened the deadbolt on the door. He and the deputy walked to the front of the house and confirmed that key was also good for the front door deadbolt. Braddock took notes and then a picture, noting that the key's usage was witnessed by himself and the deputy.

Next, Braddock walked them over to the detached garage, which was now closed, but there was a side door. An older silver key, the second in the key rotation, opened that deadbolt, so two of the six keys were accounted for. They again did the paperwork on it.

An hour later, Braddock rolled back up to Brule's cabin. This time he asked the Cass County deputy to join him. There were four keys in play. Braddock first went to the small detached garage. The first key worked on the deadbolt for the side door. Pictures and documentation were completed.

"That leaves three for the cabin," he mumbled. Yet, none of the three keys worked on the deadbolt or the knob for the front door of the cabin, the only door with a keyed lock. Pictures, notes and signatures were collected. "Thank you, Deputy."

Another hour later he was back dropping off the keys with Renfrow. "Will, Cal just called, asking for an ETA on my report," Renfrow explained. "I told them it's nearly complete and that it would be ready tomorrow. I'm sorry."

"Did Cal ask you about your conclusions?"

"No, he just asked if I was done yet. I don't think he expects anything other than Brule died by suicide. As you know, I have some questions in mind as to what happened there."

"Your call, but I say play it straight," Braddock counseled. "If that's your thought, if you're concerned about that, then we need to put it out there and let the chips fall where they may."

*

A little past 5 p.m. Tori sat forward with her elbows on her thighs, looking down to the floor. Quiet. Contemplative. Wrathful.

"Tori, you're not surprised by all of this, are you?" Tracy's voice called from the speaker on the phone. "You said if you and Braddock were right, it could come down to a couple of people."

"No, I'm not, but…" Her voice trailed off at the thought of it. "Tracy, above and beyond—thanks for everything today."

"Hey, anytime, and we're not done here. I'll forward you everything I've put together on this by the end of the day. Tomorrow we keep digging for more. In the meantime, what are you going to do?"

Tori sat up and straightened her back. "Fight for this on my end," she answered as she looked to the picture on her computer screen.

*

After he finished up with Renfrow, Braddock made his way to the government center, where, to his relief, all was quiet at 5.30 p.m. Cal and most of the others were gone for the day.

He went to his desk and found a note from Steak on top of a folder. Inside he found Brule's phone records from last Wednesday night. Brule had made one phone call after he and Tori had left him at the VFW.

His phone vibrated in his pocket. It was Tori. "Hey, I think I need to buy you dinner. I have an out-of-the-way spot."

"I accept," Tori replied. "We have a lot to talk about."

CHAPTER TWENTY-SEVEN

"I hate water metaphors."

Braddock pulled under the canopy for the Radisson at seven thirty on the dot. Tori came striding purposefully out of the entryway in a faded jean jacket, tight jeans, and a silver top with her hair hanging loosely.

He smiled when she jumped in. "Uhh, Special Agent Hunter, did you do some shopping? You look really nice."

"I ran over to a couple of the boutiques since I had a spare hour," she replied while closely inspecting Braddock. She liked his loosely styled hair and the look of his untucked, off-white, long-sleeved, button-down shirt, faded blue jeans, and casual, gray, canvas slip-on loafers. Plus, she caught the scent of cologne. "You know, you clean up nice yourself. How long is the drive up?"

"Forty to forty-five minutes."

"Good," Tori said. "Because I have a name for you."

"Eddie Mannion, I bet."

"Yup. Buckle up, this could be the start of a bumpy ride."

"This would be different how?"

As they pulled away from the hotel, Tori asked, "So how did you conclude it was Eddie? Other than we thought it could be him or Kyle this morning. You must have learned something else."

"Brule called Eddie after we confronted him at the VFW. I'm guessing he told Eddie where he was going." Braddock explained what he found at the cabin, his testing with the keys, and his discovery of how Brule could have ended up with residue on his hands. "Someone killed Brule, I'm pretty certain of it."

"Eddie?"

"That can't be proven based on what I found today. All I found were a couple of pieces that might go toward establishing Brule didn't commit suicide. They say nothing about *who* killed him. What did you find? You *clearly* learned something else."

"A lot."

There was a Mannion's restaurant in or very near the towns in which each victim was last seen. However, the Mannion's restaurants weren't always named Mannion's. "There are Victory's and Ansel's, four of each." Tori added that a review of recent corporate reports indicated there were more Victory's and Ansel's openings on the horizon, set in college towns. "But all of them fall under the umbrella of the Mannion Restaurant Corporation."

Braddock speculated, "I talked to a couple of other investigative agencies about these disappearances, and there was never a common tie anyone could find. If it is tied to Mannion's, perhaps that's why nobody picked up on it earlier. Because not all the restaurants are *named* Mannion's. Maybe that's why they started getting away from the Mannion's name for some of the locations."

"Regardless of the name, who is at every Mannion Companies restaurant opening?" Tori asked.

"Eddie Mannion."

"Eddie Mannion," Tori echoed. "There are pictures of Kyle and Eddie Mannion together at a lot of these restaurant openings, especially in the early years, but now it's strictly Eddie. He's the president and CEO of Mannion Restaurant Corp. Eddie is quoted in these articles talking about the restaurants and the towns, and how happy they are to be there and adding the town to the Mannion family of restaurants. I mean, I had twenty-three missing or dead women, and in a day's research, between what you and I unearthed this morning and what Tracy and I found during the day, we found—"

"Twenty-three connections with the Mannions, with Eddie Mannion," Braddock finished and then whistled as he opened his Explorer door. "And we know Eddie was in those towns when the women went missing?"

"For a number of them, yes," Tori replied. "Based on photographs and FAA records. Eddie always takes the Mannion jet to those openings, and we can put that plane in those towns for every disappearance since 2009, which was the year they purchased the plane. From then to now, that is fifteen of the women. Before that, it appears Eddie flew commercial on occasion, with arrivals and departures of his commercial flights putting him in those towns on the dates of the disappearances."

"And what about Kyle?"

"In the early years he was at those openings, but best as we could tell, he hasn't been to one of those in eight years. Ever since the rest of the Mannion Companies profile took off, that's been his focus. I don't see how it could be him."

"Oh, boy."

"Like I said, the water is about to get choppy."

Braddock snorted. "I hate water metaphors."

"I'm just saying. You're going to need a bigger boat."

"Yeah, because now we're going after the local great white shark," Will replied.

Braddock's friend Bert, owner of the supper club, greeted them at the front and immediately walked them to a secluded corner booth. Tori quickly ordered a bottle of wine and then they ordered their entrees. Bert checked on them again and even made a point of taking a photo of them on his phone. The two of them moved close and smiled. "You two look good together," he remarked, turning the phone around for them to see. He forwarded the picture to Braddock, who then sent it to Tori.

The two of them examined the photo. "You'll have something to remember me by," Braddock stated, smiling.

Tori nodded, smiled back, and then flipped her phone face down, getting back to business. "Now," she said, leaning in, "here is what might be the kicker. Tracy dug into Eddie's background, particularly in the military. Turns out Eddie had some legal issues when he was in the Marines. He was brought up on charges for sexually assaulting a woman when he was stationed at Camp Lejeune."

"Sexual assault?" Braddock asked, intrigued.

"Yes," Tori replied. "His JAG lawyer pulled some clever Daniel Kaffee maneuvers and got him off with some fairly light discipline, but the record is there. Tracy made some calls, and in his military record, as part of his case, there was a psych evaluation."

Tori paused while their server opened the wine bottle and then poured them each a glass.

After the server departed, Braddock asked, "And the psych evaluation said what?"

"Eddie claimed he was severely abused by his old man. Now, I'm not that surprised to hear it," Tori stated. "I often wonder how Kyle turned out to be such a successful guy because Irv Mannion was an absolute asshole."

"Kyle is six years older than me and Eddie. He went away to Ohio State for college, and Eddie, after he graduated high school, went into the service. I think to get away from the old man. Not long after, Irv died of a heart attack. Kyle took over the restaurant and the few other small manufacturing businesses his father owned, and went to work building the Mannion business empire. Once Eddie was honorably discharged from the Marines, he came home and went to work for his older brother."

"I've always perceived Kyle as the alpha and then his little brother as kind of the tag-along type," Braddock remarked.

"That's probably true from a business standpoint. One guy graduated with a business degree from Ohio State plus an MBA from the University of Minnesota, and the other was in the Marines. But one thing occurred to me about Eddie and the service. That period of time could explain the gap between Jessie and the next victim, Carrie Blaine from Bismarck."

Braddock nodded. "Yeah, he's gone four years, starts working for the restaurant business, and Kyle has it ready to expand. Eddie gets to Bismarck and…"

"Kills again," Tori finished the thought. "The sexual assault allegation in the Marines suggests he was on the verge of being active in those four years. Now that he was out of the Marines and out of town, he was free to satisfy his urges."

"I'll tell you what else is true about Eddie Mannion: he and Gunther Brule were friends," Braddock noted. "And who is it that Gunther calls after we jack him up?"

"Eddie," Tori answered. "Does that make Gunther a patsy or…"

"A helper. Was the call, maybe, I'm not going down for this?"

"We've not seen any evidence of that."

"Other than maybe taking a shot at you and trying to blow me up," Braddock answered. "And since he failed, he was a liability Eddie had to eliminate."

"It could be that Eddie was using Gunther. He's a killer—what's someone like Gunther to him?"

"That'll all come out in the wash," Braddock answered. "If we can ever get Eddie in the box and go to work on him."

Tori shook her head. "Eddie had the major hots for Jessie. And Eddie wasn't at all awkward like Gunther. We both thought Eddie was good-looking. He's still a sharp, handsome guy."

"Money helps," Braddock replied. "It makes him look good."

"Are you implying that all women apply a sliding scale based on money and looks in their choices of men, Braddock?" Tori said in a mildly scolding tone. "Are you suggesting character is not something we women take into consideration?"

Braddock winced. "Let me rephrase."

"Good idea."

"Braddock analysis take two. What I'm trying to say is that it could be that Eddie hunts for women he thinks will be… welcoming of his particular collection of charms. What are his charms? Good looks, money, cars, flashy clothes, you know, the whole ensemble he brings to the table. Some, not all, but *some* women see all that, they might not see a killer lurking behind that flashy facade."

"That assessment makes sense," Tori agreed. "I can tell you that the night Jessie's tire blew and she had to pull over, if Eddie had pulled up, she wouldn't have thought twice about jumping in his car. She would have trusted him implicitly. I would have trusted him without question. Eddie was a friend, a good friend—a *safe* friend."

Braddock nodded, took a sip of wine, and then slowly swirled his glass, deep in thought.

"What are you thinking?" Tori asked. "That it will be a nightmare to pursue this?"

"That and," Braddock replied before turning to her, eyeing her wide, soft gaze, "I'm wondering how you feel about all of this."

Tori sighed. "You're wondering if I feel betrayed?"

"Don't you?"

"For twenty years, I never even contemplated a friend of mine did this. I would have never believed it, as close as our friend group was. But no matter how hard I find it to believe, I can't ignore what we've found. I can't ignore the evidence. If Eddie killed Jessie, I don't care if he was a friend. He can burn in hell, and I won't stop until I deliver him there."

"You really think it was him?"

"Do you have doubts?"

"I'm asking, do you think it was him? Do you *really* think it was him? Could he do it? Take all of the other women out, including Lash and Katy; take all of them except Jessie out of it. Back then, could Eddie have done it? Could he have killed Jessie as a seventeen-year-old?"

Tori sat back in the booth and took a drink of her wine. Braddock had asked an important question. She gave herself a long moment to think it through, taking another generous sip before nodding her head. "Knowing what I know now about Eddie, especially the beatings he took from Irv and the impact it had on him… Also, now knowing about the sexual assault, or at least alleged sexual assault, when he was in the Marines… Guilty or not, something pretty rough happened with that, so… yeah, I think… he could have done it."

"Is he smart enough, though?"

"He might be smarter than we think. He is running the restaurant business, and it's thriving. He might be pulling a rope-a-dope on us and beneath the party-boy exterior is a ruthless son of a bitch. After all, Irv was. And violence against women? Maybe the apple didn't fall far from the tree. Irv knocked his wife around, after all. As we've discussed, Eddie had the sexual assault charge against him. Maybe if we dig a little more, we'll find that wasn't an isolated incident."

Their entrees arrived, Tori's filet and Braddock's prime rib. He poured each of them another glass of wine, his a little shorter than hers. "I'm driving."

"Or you're trying to get me drunk so you can take advantage of me."

"Two birds, one stone. Besides, I hate to let a fine bottle of wine like this go to waste," he replied and then returned to the topic at hand. "I don't have to tell you we need to tread carefully."

"The Mannions?"

Braddock nodded. "Our gut is not enough on this. The evidentiary connections you and your colleagues found, provocative as they are, aren't enough, at least not in this case. We need more than what we have. Particularly since the sheriff and the county attorney are pointing the finger at Gunther Brule. If you are someone who runs for election, what sounds better? Gunther Brule as the killer or Eddie Mannion?"

"We do have a good circumstantial case on Gunther and he's dead, so there's nobody to really challenge it," Tori agreed. "With the evidence we do have, we almost have to point the finger at him. We won't find Jessie's or Genevieve's bodies, but so what? Gunther buried them somewhere and we'll never find them, or so the story can plausibly go."

"That's what Cal and especially Backstrom are thinking. It's nice and clean. No fuss, no muss, lots of evidence to support it, no need for anything messy… like, for instance, taking on the Mannion family."

"I don't blame them, but—" Tori held up a small copy of the map "—this map tells us, along with Gunther's employment records, that he's *not* the guy. This map, those records, and what we found today say Eddie is."

CHAPTER TWENTY-EIGHT

"I am aware of the imperative of discretion."

Dr. Renfrow called everyone over to the medical examiner's office for the results of the autopsy. At nine, Renfrow was ready to go along with Braddock, Tori, Backstrom, and Wilson. They were all waiting on Cal, who was out in the hallway on a phone call.

The atmosphere in the room was, in a word, awkward. Backstrom and Wilson had gone toe to toe with Braddock and Tori two days ago, and there was still some residual enmity, at least on the part of Tori and Braddock.

Typical of a lawyer, Backstrom acted as if the other day hadn't happened at all, making small talk with Braddock as if the two of them were the best of buddies. Braddock saw right through it, but mindful of Cal's warnings about the future, he engaged Backstrom pleasantly in return. Though, he was laughing inside as he threw a wink at his partner.

Tori, whose future was not at all tied to warm and friendly relations with the powers that be in Manchester Bay and Shepard County, stayed true to herself. She was wholly uninterested in playing the game as Wilson tried the same friendly, let bygones be bygones tactic. Instead she was giving Wilson her crossed arms, pursed lips look with one-word answers.

"Sorry," Cal apologized as he came into the autopsy room. "We had a missing person call over in Aitkin County that they requested assistance on. I needed Steak to get on it."

"Let's get to it then," Renfrow started. The medical examiner noted that the gun found beneath Brule's hand *was* used to kill him. There was, in fact, trace amounts of gunshot residue on his hand. His blood alcohol content was point two-six.

"He did himself in, then," Backstrom quickly surmised. "Why did this take four days?"

"I'm not done yet," Renfrow replied with just a hint of annoyance. Then he stirred the pot. "The angle of the bullet entry into Brule's head is troubling—*very* troubling."

The doctor stepped to Brule's body, unzipped the body bag, and pulled it open. He inserted a thin red rod into the messy bullet wound on the high right side of Brule's forehead and pushed it through so that it came out on the low left backside of Brule's skull. "That is a very steep angle."

Tori and Braddock shared a knowing glance but stayed quiet. After a moment, Cal looked over to them with a raised eyebrow. As a long-time detective in his own right, he quickly realized where Renfrow was going.

"I'm not following, Doc," Backstrom admitted.

"Let me demonstrate then," Renfrow replied as he pulled an office armchair over to the group. "Mr. Backstrom, please sit down in this chair."

Backstrom did as he was instructed. "Now, Brule is at a point two-six blood alcohol level. That could mean he's steeling himself up to do the deed—"

"Which is what I'm thinking," Backstrom interjected.

"Or it could mean something else," Renfrow continued as he pulled the gun out of the evidence bag and showed that the cylinder and chamber were both empty. He put the gun barrel up to Backstrom's head, high on his forehead, at the angle the bullet had entered, and then reached for Backstrom's right hand. "Try and reach up with your right hand and hold the gun at this angle."

Backstrom found it extremely difficult to pronate his wrist to keep the gun at the proper angle while pulling the trigger. "That's hard to do. Why would he do that?"

"He wouldn't," Braddock answered. "Nobody would."

"If someone else pulled the trigger, that might explain it," Tori suggested, going through the door Renfrow had opened.

"He didn't say that," Backstrom retorted.

"Are you sure about that?"

"Let's say it wasn't suicide," Braddock proposed. "At point two-six, he was clearly intoxicated and maybe even passed out in that chair."

"He would be more slumped in the chair, wouldn't he?" Cal noted, tracking along with where the doctor and his people were going.

"Likely," Braddock replied as he took the gun from Renfrow. "Mr. Backstrom, slump in the chair as if you were intoxicated. Your head would be tilted down, drooping."

"And based on where he was shot in the head, probably listing to the left," Renfrow noted.

Backstrom reluctantly did as he was instructed. Braddock, standing at a forty-five-degree angle, put the gun barrel to Backstrom's head at the angle of entry for the bullet. He could hold the gun naturally.

"You think he was murdered, don't you?" Cal asked Renfrow before looking to Braddock and Tori, who both nodded.

"Hold on…" Backstrom started.

"That more logically explains the entry angle for the bullet," Renfrow stated.

"And I presume," Cal said while looking to Braddock and Tori, "that you guys have some other evidence or theories to buttress this? I mean, clearly you two *anticipated* this might be the finding."

"I have a few things from the scene," Braddock replied, opening his backpack and pulling out the file. He mentioned the ordered nature of the house, the glass in the sink, and the coaster on the table. "Now, I'll admit that all of that isn't terribly convincing. But the one thing that occurred to me while I was going through that cabin again yesterday was, if Brule was murdered, how did the killer get out of the house? We found it locked up tight."

"This is nuts," Backstrom muttered.

"He locked the cabin with a key," Wilson offered with a sideways glance, trying to figure out where Braddock was going while wary of irritating her boss.

"Right. *What* key?" Braddock asked.

Backstrom and Wilson shared a quizzical look. "Was there one outside?" Wilson inquired.

"Not that I found," Braddock answered. "And I looked for over an hour. And if there was an outside key, a killer would have certainly left it behind since he set it up to look like a suicide to begin with. However, I took the keys on his key ring and tested them."

"And none of them worked on the cabin deadbolts, right?" Cal asked, following where Braddock and Tori were going.

"Correct. How does Brule get in without a key? There was no key on the key ring. I think what happened is the killer took the cabin key from Brule, locked the cabin, and left but made the mistake of not leaving the key behind."

"Or he could have concluded that leaving the key behind would be a mistake, if it turned out you interviewed friends who said Gunther never left a key outside," Wilson replied. She was slowly buying in. "You know, the smarter play would have been to leave the cabin unlocked."

"Agreed," Braddock answered. "He overthought it."

"Have we dusted the inside of the cabin for prints?" Cal asked.

"No," Braddock answered. "We should have the crime scene team go back. I suspect if the killer was this careful, he won't have left anything behind, but who knows. I used gloves on the keys."

"Me too," Renfrow answered. "We can get these dusted, too."

Backstrom looked around the room, perturbed. "It appears I'm the only skeptic, and everyone else around here now apparently thinks Brule did not commit suicide and was murdered instead. Is that what I'm hearing?"

There were nods all around the room.

"Sometimes we have to take the hard way," Braddock stated flatly. "That's the job."

"I think at this point, there is certainly reason to question the idea that he committed suicide," Renfrow replied, hedging just slightly. "That angle *really* bothers me."

"Gunther was murdered," Tori commented, not hedging, "and set up."

"Set up?" Backstrom asked.

Braddock winced and then sighed for dramatic effect. "Tori has a possible name that we need to investigate more. A lot more."

"Who?" Backstrom asked.

"Well, Tori brought it to me based on some work she and some of her fellow FBI agents did. I didn't know they were doing it so I'm a little… leery and not ready to disclose it. I'd like to have more time to dig into it myself, before I even mention the name—"

"Eddie Mannion," Tori blurted on cue.

"Dammit, Tori!" Braddock barked. "I told you—"

"Come again?" Cal asked in disbelief.

"Oh God," Backstrom moaned.

Braddock gave Tori a severe look, just as they had planned. It was all part of the Will Braddock protection plan.

"I don't have time to consider the political niceties of it," Tori replied. "Let's just get it out there."

"Will?" Cal asked. "Do you have something to say to the class?"

Braddock shook his head in anger at Tori, still play-acting. "It's *your* theory, *you* tell them."

Tori, cutting Braddock out of the explanation, went through what she had learned about the connection between the abductions of the women and the opening of Mannion's restaurants, and the fact that Eddie was always there.

When she finished, the room remained silent for a moment.

"And you knew nothing of this?" Cal asked Braddock skeptically.

"Of Mannion? Not until last night," Braddock answered and then gestured angrily to Tori. "She went off on her own on this. I told her to lock it up for now, but she didn't listen. Go figure."

Backstrom looked to Tori. "Are you out of your mind?"

"No, I'm of quite sound mind, thank you very much," Tori replied sharply, standing her ground.

He looked to Braddock. "Will?"

"I don't like the way she got there, and I don't like that she blurted it out now, but… George, I did warn you to not get out too far in front of this."

"I know you said that, and you were perhaps right… as it pertains to Brule. But do you have any idea what the Mannions could do to you? To me? To all of us if we're wrong?"

"And what if I'm right?" Tori asked feistily. "What then?"

Braddock glared at Tori again, shaking his head. She was still the bad cop, so he assumed good cop status. "George, I do know what they could do to me, to you, to all of us, and what it could do to the town. But flip it: what if Tori's right and we did *nothing*? What if it turns out that Eddie Mannion was a serial murderer living in our midst, yet we didn't even investigate out of fear of losing our jobs because big brother Kyle would be upset? How does *that* play?"

A worried Backstrom looked over to Cal, who simply shrugged and said, "He's right."

"Let me investigate it with Tori," Braddock reasoned, "that way, *we* retain some control. Otherwise, I can pretty much guarantee Tori goes to the Bureau with it and… well, who knows where it goes from there? Why don't we investigate this carefully—very carefully—and see what we find?"

After a moment, Backstrom nodded, but like any smart lawyer and politician, he kept his options open. He started by looking over to Renfrow. "Don't file your report yet and keep quiet. Not a word to anyone, especially the press."

"I understand."

"You send all that shit my way."

Renfrow nodded.

"We're going to do this, but I'm going to take Braddock's advice and not get out in front of it, so for now Brule is still the guy as far as anyone knows."

"I follow you," Braddock replied and then glanced to Tori. "We *both* do, *don't* we?"

After a moment of faux contemplation, Tori nodded in agreement.

"And for crying out loud, you two, be discreet," Cal counseled sternly. "Detective Braddock, you need to proceed *very* carefully. You too, *Victoria*. Perhaps you could be considerate of the ramifications for those of us who *still* live here."

"I am aware of the imperative of discretion," Tori answered earnestly. "We can't be wrong, not on this."

"And you two are coming to me before going after documents and dragging anyone in for interviews. Heck, before you start surveillance on him, watching his every move, we're going to have a long talk about what you have," Backstrom stated emphatically. "Fair?"

Braddock looked over to Tori. Backstrom was trying to shackle them, at least to a degree. It wasn't so much to protect the Mannions as it was to protect George Backstrom. However, they had what they wanted—the green light to investigate Eddie Mannion—even if they were to tread very carefully.

"Fair?" Backstrom pressed.

"Fair," they both replied in unison.

As they left Renfrow's office, Braddock leaned over to Tori and whispered, "And I just thought of the first person I should call. He can do some of our dirty work for us."

Tori rubbed her eyes and yawned as she leaned back in the chair, stretching her arms before glancing at her watch: 11:25 p.m. She looked over to Braddock, behind his desk, his hair disheveled, a weariness apparent as he tried focusing on a document. Sitting on the couch with his head tilted back and eyes closed was Cal.

They'd worked through the day nonstop and now deep into the night. Over the course of the day they'd been able to further firm up the information on the dates of the Mannion's restaurant openings and then the disappearances. In the process, Braddock had made discreet contact with law enforcement in the towns where the women had disappeared. He asked local investigators to subtly go back and interview friends and family of the victims to see if anyone remembered the opening of a Mannion's, Victory's, or Ansel's restaurant, and Eddie Mannion in particular. If so, did they remember him having any contact with the victim or missing woman? Braddock requested discretion, providing the other jurisdictions with a photo array of six men, one of whom was Eddie Mannion.

He was particularly hopeful of what Detective Bruening in Brookings, South Dakota, might be able to do. That was Braddock's first call. The Joanie Wells disappearance was still fresh, and now Bruening had a potential suspect to question witnesses about. Unfortunately, Bruening hadn't called yet with an update.

Later in the evening they'd heard from the police in Macomb, Illinois. A student at Western Illinois University named Justine

Colander had disappeared in October three years ago. She was last seen leaving her apartment on a Sunday night on her way over to the university to study and then had plans to go to her friend's after. She never made it to her friend's, and her car was found in an alley downtown. Victory's opened its third location in Illinois, with a grand opening in Macomb, four days prior to her disappearance. Justine had been to Victory's twice, once on Saturday to watch college football with some friends and then on Sunday to watch the Bears game. She also had a job across the street at a coffee shop.

Sam Knight, the Macomb police chief who investigated the case at the time, went back and tracked down Colander's friends. Two people independently picked Eddie Mannion out of the photo array and remembered him being around the restaurant.

"One of her friends remembered him, this Mannion fella," Knight reported. "She recalled he was at the restaurant, going from table to table, making sure people were having a good time. He came back to the table a few times, handing out coupons, promoting drink specials, and making sure they understood that they loved having college kids at the bar. He was nice, but he was having fun too, even having a shot with people at the next table over."

Knight had a similar conversation with another friend who'd been at the restaurant on Sunday for the Bears game. "This friend I talked to said Mannion was at the restaurant on Sunday and had remembered Justine, as she'd been there on Saturday. Mannion stopped by the table a few times, bought them all a round of drinks, asked people's names, and, again, wanted everyone to know how much he appreciated they were there. But," Knight noted, "the reality is while he stopped at their table three or four times, in all they thought they probably talked to him for less than ten minutes."

"Did he show any particular interest in Colander?" Tori asked Knight.

"I asked that question," Knight replied. "This friend of hers said the guy, Mannion, was friendly and was high-fiving people, posing for pictures, handing out T-shirts, can coolers, and hats, and was loud and boisterous. That's why, even after these few years, she remembers him. As to whether he showed Justine any special attention, this friend said Mannion seemed to remember Justine because she was there the day before, made a point of thanking her for coming back, but beyond that she didn't think much of it."

Braddock and Tori wondered if they'd get more calls of a similar nature over the coming days.

"You know, the one thing these friends seem to suggest is that Eddie is friendly. The gracious and gregarious host. In other words, he might not be perceived—"

"As a threat if you saw him on the street or in a parking lot, or wherever," Tori finished Braddock's thought. "Genevieve Lash wouldn't have perceived him as a threat, nor, for that matter, would Katy."

"Still trying to tie that in to all of this?" Cal asked, his eyes closed.

"Just making the point."

Cal opened his eyes now. "I admire your tenacity, Victoria. I always have." The sheriff stood up. "I'm going home to bed. You two should go to bed as well."

"Excuse me?" Tori replied, feigning indignation.

Braddock chortled, yet with a little flicker in his eye.

"I didn't mean… Cripes," Cal replied, flustered, shaking his head and waving his hands. "Victoria, you should go to your hotel, and Will, you should go home."

"Oh, okay," Tori replied, shaking her head in mock disapproval.

"I didn't mean to suggest…"

"Don't worry about it, Cal," Tori answered, now laughing.

Braddock chuckled as he glanced at his watch. "I do need some sleep." He looked over to Tori. "What do you say I drop you off at the Radisson?"

"Thanks."

*

Ten minutes later, Braddock and Tori had long since driven past the Radisson and were turning onto the winding road that led back to his lake house. The two of them laughed about Cal.

"You don't think he suspects, do you?" Tori asked.

"I don't know," Braddock replied with a weary smile. "I think he was tired and didn't think about what he was saying. But even if he does, so what? We're consenting adults."

"We're working together."

"That's temporary, though," Braddock replied. "Right?"

"Right."

"Alright then, so he knows or if he finds out, so be it. We'll deal with it," Braddock answered. "You know what I really need before I go to bed?"

"What?"

"A shower. Care to join?"

Ring! Ring! Ring!

Braddock's eyes fluttered open and he turned his head to the nightstand, where his phone was ringing *loudly* like an old-fashioned telephone. It was 4:20 a.m. "Nothing good ever happens at this time of night," he muttered as he turned on the nightstand lamp and reached for his phone. "Braddock," he answered.

"It's Steak."

"Yeah, man," Braddock replied with a yawn. "What's up?"

"You know that case Cal has me working?"

"Yeah, uhh, missing person. Woman from over in Aitkin County or something, right?"

Tori stirred awake. "What's…?"

Braddock put his finger to his lips and mouthed, *It's Steak*.

"Yeah, that one," Steak replied. "I found her, and I just sent you a photo. You need to see it."

"Okay, hang on," Will answered, rubbing his eyes to get them going before he tapped his screen, clicked on the text from Steak, and opened the picture.

It jolted him awake.

He instantly showed the picture to Tori.

Tori's jaw dropped wide open in shock before looking to Braddock.

The picture was of a woman stuffed in the trunk of her car, bound and strangled. She looked exactly like their four victims. The ones they'd been discounting.

"Steak, where are you?"

"In Holmestrand, we just found the car. And one other thing."

"What's that?"

"She was last seen leaving the Serpent Bar in Deerwood two nights ago at closing time," Steak reported, "with Eddie Mannion."

CHAPTER TWENTY-NINE

"A pattern of hunting."

The victim's name was Sarah Craig.

It was just before 5 a.m. when Braddock pulled to a stop behind a Holmestrand police cruiser, its light bar still flashing. A small, early-morning crowd had gathered across the street, taking in the scene.

He held up the crime scene tape and Tori dipped underneath. The two of them walked hurriedly a half-block up the alley to find Steak and Eggleston standing with notebooks in hand, observing two crime scene techs beginning to conduct their analysis of the vehicle. Braddock and Tori both approached and peered into the trunk of the car to see the body, bound, with red ligature marks and bruises visible around her neck. Tori took four photos out of the case file and held each of them up for the two of them to compare to the body in the trunk.

"Look familiar?"

Braddock nodded.

"That's why I called," Steak added. "I saw those photos the other day, and the similarity is… unmistakable."

Braddock led Steak by the elbow away from the car, deeper into the darkness of the alley, and Tori and Eggleston followed. "Tell me about Mannion."

Steak paused for a moment before speaking. "I just can't believe we're going there."

"*What* do you have on him?" Braddock pressed.

"He left the Serpent Bar with her at closing time Tuesday, I guess two nights ago now," Eggleston reported. "And she hasn't been seen by anyone since."

"And Mannion?"

"We haven't spoken to him yet; we were going to do that first thing," Steak replied. "A bartender at the Serpent said he was working and remembered Eddie and Sarah Craig being all friendly and flirty-like, and at closing time they left the bar together."

"Left at the same time or left to be together?"

"To be together," Eggleston clarified. "That was the bartender's impression of how they left, given their body language."

"As the bartender said," Steak added, "he's seen two people leave like that a thousand times before. It always means one thing and one thing only."

"Except that night," Tori answered. "That night it meant something else."

"Detectives?" a crime scene investigator hailed from Craig's car.

They all looked back to see that the investigator waving to them had set up two portable lights and had the rear, driver-side, passenger door open.

"What do you have?" Braddock asked, leading the group back around the car to the open door.

The investigator was crouched down with a flashlight, pointing to a dark-reddish smudge on the leather seats of the car.

"Blood?" Tori asked.

"Likely," the investigator replied with a nod, but then reached for a different light, a black light. "Now look at this." The investigator leaned into the door, hovering the light over the backseat, to reveal a tight collection of uneven spots on the seat, glowing brightly under the black light.

"Semen?" Tori blurted before looking to the investigator, who nodded. She turned to the rest of them. "Let's go wake Eddie's ass up and start asking questions," she demanded. "Right now—roust him out of bed."

Braddock slowly shook his head. "No, we need to talk to Cal, Backstrom, and Wilson first."

"Why?"

"One, because we said we would," Braddock replied. "Remember? Two, nothing has changed just because of Sarah Craig, or what we just found here. Now, if that semen can be matched to Eddie?"

"Wait a minute," Steak said, "you two aren't surprised by this, are you?"

Tori shook her head. "Sorry, Steak, but no. We suspect Eddie of… all of this."

"*Aw shit*," Steak replied, crestfallen. "When were you going to tell me *that*?"

"Sorry, man, we were under orders not to," Braddock answered apologetically. "But now, well, you know."

"With semen," Tori suggested, "we might be able to…"

"Get a DNA sample," Braddock said, nodding. "I'll call Backstrom."

"Detective?" the investigator called to Braddock from the trunk. "There's one other thing I've just noticed."

"What's that?"

The investigator pulled up the back of the victim's blouse. On her lower back were two sets of reddish, dot-like lesions. The lesions were about an inch, maybe an inch and a half, apart on each set.

"What do you think?" Tori queried, looking to Braddock.

"Could those be the markings from a stun gun?" Braddock asked the investigator.

"Maybe. I'll have that checked."

Braddock and Tori shared a knowing look and walked away.

"That's how he does it, you know," Tori stated. "That's how he gets these women."

Braddock nodded in agreement. "He approaches them. They know him and don't sense danger. He distracts them or gets them in his car and slyly hits them with the stun gun. Then they're all his."

"By the time they come to…"

"It's too late."

First thing in the morning, Braddock and Tori briefed Cal. The three of them then made their way over to the county attorney's office to meet with Backstrom and Wilson. Braddock explained that Sarah Craig had been found murdered: strangled, bound with rope, and stuffed in the trunk of her car. She was last seen leaving the Serpent Bar in Deerwood with Eddie Mannion. Then Tori laid out the photos they already had of the previous four women, and then crime scene photos of Sarah Craig. She recited the details of each of the four cases and how they compared to how Craig was found.

"What do you think?" Braddock asked.

Backstrom sourly shook his head. "I thought you two were crazy."

"How about now?" Tori asked.

"Not so much. What do you need?"

"A search warrant for Eddie's property, his phone and financial records, and I want a DNA sample from him," Braddock added. "If we have enough for those."

Backstrom and Wilson took a moment to answer, flipping through the documents in front of them. They shared a look and then Backstrom shook his head.

"We're with you on this, but you're not there yet," Wilson stated.

"If this were your run-of-the-mill case, yeah, we could get them. No sweat," Backstrom added. "But we're talking a Mannion here. The judges will be understandably cautious. They run for re-election, too."

"Hey, now wait a—" Tori started.

"No, George is right," Braddock stepped in, cutting her off. "We have to leave the judge no choice but to sign."

"Right," Backstrom agreed, nodding. "I'm with you, Agent Hunter. But lock this shit down. Get with the bartender. Confirm and be certain that Eddie Mannion left that bar with Sarah Craig. And if you can lock down more than that, so much the better."

"We're on it," Braddock replied and then turned to Cal. "Until we can get all of this taken care of, I want twenty-four-hour surveillance on Eddie. With that Mannion jet sitting over at the airfield, he has the means to flee. If he gets a whiff that we're onto him…"

"Consider it done," Cal answered.

Braddock and Tori, along with Steak and Eggleston, retraced Sarah Craig's steps before her disappearance.

Sarah Craig was a thirty-two-year-old insurance agency customer service representative. She was vacationing up at her parents' cabin on Mille Lacs Lake, just north of Garrison twenty miles to the east. Her credit card activity for the night of her disappearance showed she started at Antlers Grill in Crosby, a town five miles northwest of Deerwood, before coming back east to the Serpent Bar in Deerwood.

Braddock assigned Steak and Eggleston to work Antlers Grill. He and Tori took the Serpent Bar. They were met by the owner, who showed them in and introduced them to his staff.

The bar itself had a rudimentary surveillance system that focused on the long bar running along the length of the back wall. In the owner's office, they sat down at his desk and reviewed the footage.

"I've been through that night ever since I got a call from your Detective Williams. On the night Sarah was in here, I've got her on tape a few times." The owner had jotted down the times and played them through. It was on the fourth snippet that Eddie appeared. There was a five-minute stretch from the 11:47 p.m. to 11:52 p.m. mark where the two of them were close and talking at the bar. Each whispered in the other's ear with a little close touching—a mating ritual taking place. There was another two-minute stretch from 12:40 a.m. to 12:42 a.m. where they appeared on the footage talking. The footage showed Sarah's face but only Eddie's back. It appeared Eddie was talking and Sarah was nodding before he leaned in close and whispered in her left ear, causing her to smile and then nod.

"He closed the deal right there," Braddock stated.

"Like a pro," Tori noted.

The owner made a copy of the footage for them to take.

The bartender had been interviewed a day ago by Steak. On his second interview, he again related his impressions of Mannion and Sarah Craig leaving together. "He's a good-looking guy. He has the Mannion name and touch."

"Meaning?" Tori asked.

"You know—the money, the sports car, and the name. He seems nice enough, gets a little loose with his cash, and is generous as long as he gets his way."

"What do you mean by 'gets his way'?"

"You serve him what he wants, when he wants it, and you don't stop serving him."

"Clearly, he's been in before," Braddock commented.

"Oh, sure," the bartender answered as he rearranged liquor bottles along the rail. "He's been in here a few times. Back in the day, I worked at the White Hawk down on Bay Lake and he'd roll in there often and have a good time, especially in the summer. He doesn't know my name, but he recognizes me when he comes in and says, 'Hey, dude, good to see you again, how ya doing,' and whatnot. So that move with Sarah Craig at the end of the night? I've seen him pull that off a few times over the years."

Sarah Craig had been with two friends that night, Pam and Trish, who were staying at another cabin on Mille Lacs. Tori and Braddock traveled to see them. The two of them had been crying, their eyes red and puffy, their cheeks flushed.

"What happened to Sarah?" Trish asked. "What happened to her?"

Tori provided them with some more detail about how Sarah was found.

"My God," Pam croaked.

"We're sorry for your loss," Braddock said solemnly. "We're hoping you can help out with the details of her last night."

The immediate interesting detail they added to the story was that it wasn't the first time that Eddie and Sarah had met.

"We ran into him a night earlier in Holmestrand at the Bay Water. Eddie was there with a bunch of his friends. His posse, so to speak."

"Do you remember their names?"

Pam shook her head. "I was introduced but I can't remember any of them, except one guy. He was sharply dressed with a tie, had just come from work and said he was a lawyer."

"Jeff Warner?" Tori asked.

"That sounds right," Pam answered. "He was a guy very impressed with himself, that I remember."

"Oh, that's probably him then," Tori replied with a knowing nod. "He's brilliant, just ask him."

"You met up with Eddie Mannion at the Bay Water the first night and then it was Antlers the next night?" Will asked.

"Yes," Pam answered.

"And were his friends with him?"

"No. Eddie came by himself to see Sarah. Anyway, around ten thirty we told Sarah we wanted to go back to Deerwood to get closer to our place, so we wouldn't have to drive so far at closing. We left Antlers, and she and Eddie followed us to the Serpent," Pam described. "We hung out until closing, but while Trish and I were heading home, those two were making plans."

"Do you know where they went?" Braddock asked while taking notes.

Both women shook their heads. "Sarah just said they were going to meet up. I suppose it could have been at her cabin. I know her parents were back down in the Cities."

"Would it be possible they met up in… the backseat of her car?" Tori said cautiously. "Would Sarah do something like that?"

Pam and Trish shared a look and then after a moment they both nodded. Pam sighed and shook her head, and then dabbed at her eyes. "Sarah did that two summers ago up here. In the parking lot at the Blue Goose over in Garrison with the guy who was her boyfriend at the time, so…" Pam's voice trailed away. "Oh Sarah…"

"She was a little bit of a…" Trish sniffled and wiped her nose. "She was a throw-caution-to-the-wind type of person."

"Sarah lived in the moment," Pam said, patting Trish on the thigh. "It's what made her so fun to… be with."

I'm just so shocked it was Eddie Mannion who could have done that to her," Trish charged. "I just can't believe it. I just can't."

"We don't know that it is," Tori replied.

"He was *so* nice to us, Pam and I, and Sarah too," Trish asserted.

"He's Eddie Mannion, local millionaire, a well-known guy, not someone nobody had ever seen before," Pam said. "I still find it hard to believe that he would do that to her." She shook her head, "I just… can't…"

"Again, we don't know that to be the case," Tori said. "But you're telling me she left with him, correct?" she gently pressed.

"Yes," they both answered, nodding.

"She *told* me she was leaving with him," Pam added. "She told me."

"But after you two left the bar, you never heard another word from her?"

Pam and Trish both shook their heads.

On the way back to Manchester Bay, Braddock called Renfrow. "Doc, I know it's early, but do you have any idea of time of death for Sarah Craig?"

"I'm running some tests, but preliminarily rigor mortis and liver temp suggest she was killed between three and six on Wednesday morning."

After the doctor hung up, Braddock looked to Tori. "She was last seen around one in the morning, leaving the Serpent. Preliminarily, she's dead two to five hours later."

"Yet the car doesn't show up until three in the morning, twenty-four hours later. Weird."

They made their way back to Braddock's office and kept digging. Sarah Craig's phone showed no activity after she left the Serpent. In fact, her phone hadn't been found with her, and they'd been unable to locate it.

"If he killed her that quickly, maybe he dumped her phone immediately," Tori concluded. "First thing he would do. At a minimum, he'd power it down, and around there it would take two minutes to find a body of water to toss it into."

Braddock set out crime scene pictures on the table, along with his notes. He picked up a photo of the car. "Odd to park it there," he mused. "Something about that seems... strange."

"Is it?" Tori asked. "He parked four other cars with women's bodies in the trunk within ten to fifteen miles of where the women had last been seen. I'd argue it's entirely consistent. What I don't get is why most of the other women disappeared but Sarah and the other four were left to be found?"

Braddock's phone rang. It was a call he'd been waiting for. "Detective Bruening. We've had some developments here on our end." Braddock told him what had happened.

"Well, Detective Braddock, I think I can help you then. Two nights before her disappearance, Joanie Wells was at the grand opening of Mannion's here in Brookings. And at closing time, she told a friend she was meeting up with—"

"Eddie Mannion."

"Correct. She identified him right away. He was putting the moves on her all night and she left the restaurant with him. That was two nights before she disappeared. She went to his hotel, the My Place. I have surveillance footage of them entering the hotel and then of her leaving around six the following morning. So, he knew Joanie Wells."

"How about the night she disappeared? Anyone see Mannion that night?"

"No, not with her, at least yet," Bruening replied. "But I was able to confirm that he was here in Brookings that night."

"Was he at the restaurant?"

"He was there during the day, but not that night."

"What about the hotel?"

"He is seen on footage entering the front at six-thirty in the evening, and we don't see him leave again until late the following morning. However, he had a main floor room with windows looking out the back. He could have easily removed the window screens and gone out the back, and nobody would really have known. There is a small wooded area behind the hotel."

"And he left Brookings when?" Tori asked.

"His plane didn't leave Brookings until midday following the night Joanie Wells disappeared."

Braddock and Bruening spoke for a few more minutes before agreeing to stay in touch.

"We've got a pattern of behavior developing here," Braddock said, looking to Tori. "A pattern of hunting."

"It's adding up," Tori said, shaking her head. "It really is. I can't believe it, but it really is."

They went to Backstrom.

"Now we should have enough," Braddock said after summarizing what they had, finishing with, "Eddie was the last one to be seen with her. The doctor is running tests to confirm, but he puts time of death between three and six in the morning. That doesn't really leave time for anyone other than Eddie. Then in Brookings, we have it basically confirmed that Eddie slept with the victim two nights before she disappeared. Then you look at Sarah Craig and what happened. It paints a compelling picture," Braddock finished.

"One woman was found; one wasn't," Wilson noted.

"Two methods, one man," Tori answered. "Why? I would love to ask him."

Backstrom sighed. "What are you thinking for warrants, Will?"

"His house, Mannion Companies, any other property he has, his financials and phone records. Hell, let's see if he ever purchased a stun gun. I want anything and everything I can get."

Backstrom nodded. "Let's get typing."

Braddock, Tori, Steak, and Eggleston all completed affidavits to support the warrants, and Renfrow called and confirmed time of death. Backstrom and Wilson went to court with the judge hearing the request in chambers with only himself and a court reporter.

"You're good to go," Backstrom reported.

They quickly accessed Eddie Mannion's credit card records. His American Express card showed over $200 of activity the night he met up with Sarah Craig. There was no other activity on any of his other credit cards that night. His cell phone showed calls were made early in the evening but none after 9:53 p.m. until the following day, with a call made at 11:04 a.m. to his brother, Kyle.

Later in the evening, Backstrom had search warrants for Eddie's home, a piece of lake property on Lake Vermilion another two hours northeast, and hunting property in Cass County an hour away.

Everyone was concerned about serving the warrants on the company. "It's a massive company," Cal noted hesitantly. "Lots of people around. We're not going to be popular. It's going to get people talking."

"You're just afraid of Kyle Mannion," Tori needled.

"We are a company town, Victoria," Cal admonished. "You go after the company, and people worry you're jacking with their futures, their jobs, and their lives. Some of those people could be your friends."

"I… understand," Tori replied quietly, chastened.

"Right now, the search warrant is for just the restaurant component of the business," Backstrom explained. "That's Eddie's business and not Kyle's. Now, depending on what we find, we may have to go to court to expand it. We'll need to be clear about that. The warrant is for all records, computer files, hard copies—all of it for the restaurant business."

"In other words, it's isolated to Eddie Mannion," Wilson added. "And *his* business."

"Still," Backstrom sighed, looking to Cal and Braddock, "I can only imagine the look you're going to get when you show up with this."

"Let's get the BCA to serve it," Braddock suggested in a sudden brainstorm, helping everyone chicken out. "We handle Eddie, the state serves Mannion Companies. I clued them in earlier about where we were at and that we might be calling on them. The BCA superintendent offered any assistance we needed, as he has all along. This would be assistance we need. Let *them* take the hit."

"I kind of like that," Backstrom replied with relief. "Do it."

CHAPTER THIRTY

"What do you care what you do to us now?"

Braddock and Tori strategized that they wanted to question Eddie first before serving the search warrants for the properties and the company.

"I don't want to give him time to prepare," Tori said. "I want him to react and talk."

"If he'll talk," Braddock answered skeptically.

"He'll talk," Tori replied confidently. "We've already seen it. He loves to talk about himself, about his ability with the ladies. His vanity is his weakness. Lead him where he wants to go."

Braddock nodded along. "And we might get something as we interview him that helps expand the warrants. Most importantly, I want to lock down the probable cause for the DNA sample."

"And besides, we're just *questioning* him at this point, getting his story," Tori added. "Unless, of course, if he admits it…"

"And unless he actually admits it, or comes damn close, you're not arresting him," Backstrom answered. "We need to keep amassing evidence. But this is obviously a big step."

"And just to play devil's advocate, maybe he tells us something and we have to call off the dogs," Braddock noted, seeing another angle. "Better safe than sorry."

*

Steak and Eggleston were at Eddie's house at 8 a.m. to ask him to come into the government center. Eddie warily agreed, although he asked to call his lawyer first, which wasn't unexpected. What was unexpected was who he brought. Braddock had half-expected the lawyer would be Warner, but instead it was a well-known local attorney named Ben Westlund.

That was a mistake.

Westlund, in his mid-sixties, was a good ol' boy, jack-of-all-trades practitioner with a small firm that handled a wide array of legal matters, including some criminal work. Braddock had worked an occasional case against him and always found him to be amiable and competent on straightforward matters, but this case was a whole other animal.

You're in way over your head, Ben, Braddock thought.

"Eddie didn't want Kyle to know," Tori speculated.

"Maybe," Braddock replied.

"You're thinking something else?"

"Possibly."

Tori gave him a perturbed look.

"I, unlike you, do not always feel the need to share every single thought that I have. Sometimes I just like things to marinate in my mind."

"Just afraid your thoughts might be wrong?"

"If I never tell you, you'll never know. I'm going in." Braddock stepped into the interrogation room.

"I didn't think you were involved with this, Will," Westlund commented as Braddock sat down. "It was Steak who asked Eddie to come in."

"Being the lead investigator for the county, and given your client's standing locally, I thought it best if I handle this."

"Handle what? Why am I here?" Eddie asked testily.

"Sarah Craig," Braddock answered.

"Sarah? What about her?"

"Were you aware that she's been missing for two days?"

Eddie was taken aback. "No, I wasn't."

"Well, she has been. We've been looking for her, and in retracing her steps we have witnesses, many, who say they saw you leaving the Serpent Bar in Deerwood with her two nights ago. Is that true?"

"Yeah," Eddie replied easily.

"Where is this going, Will?" Westlund asked warily, already sensing danger.

"I just have some questions, Ben," Braddock answered lightly. "So, you left the Serpent Bar with her at closing time two nights ago?"

"Yeah, I did."

"And then what did you two do?"

"Eddie," Westlund interrupted. "I really think—"

"Relax, Ben, Will knows I left with her and that's why he's asking these questions," Eddie said, waving off his lawyer before explaining that he and Sarah Craig each drove their own cars—her Mazda M6 and his little BMW convertible—over to Cuyuna Golf Club. They parked in the southwest corner of the long, narrow parking lot. Then they moved to the backseat of her car and they had sex. "It was nothing unusual."

"Classy, Eddie."

"What can I say?"

"Why *that* parking lot?"

"Her place was fifteen miles away and my place was twenty miles the other direction, and there isn't a hotel in Deerwood worth a damn. So, I suggested how about we act like kids and use the backseat. She laughed and smiled at the suggestion. There was more room in her car than in mine."

"And then what happened?"

"Like I said, she was game. We did the deed."

"Was it conventional sex or was it rough?" Braddock asked, pen at the ready.

"What? Do you want the dirty breakdown?" Eddie replied with a gregarious laugh. "You want positions? The *Kama Sutra*? What?"

"I simply asked if it was rough."

"Eddie, don't—" Westlund started.

"No!" Eddie exclaimed indignantly, blowing past his lawyer. "Not at all. It was casual, nice, and fun. She was *totally* into it, Will. Since you're asking, she spent most of the time on top because it was a little easier in the car."

"And this all lasted until when?"

"I suppose it was two, maybe a little after, something like that. After we finished, we laughed a little, touched a little, kissed a little more, and talked about maybe getting together again and using a bed."

"And then what happened?"

Eddie shrugged. "We got dressed. I said goodnight. I got out of her car and into mine. I saw her start her car and turn her lights on, and then I drove away. She followed. I turned right out of the parking lot and she turned left. And that was the end of it."

"And you've had no contact with her since?"

"No."

"You two finished, said your goodnights, and left the parking lot, and that was the end of it?" Braddock asked, seeking confirmation.

"Yeah."

"That's it?"

"That's it."

"You're sure?" he pressed.

"Yes."

There was a light knock on the one-way mirror behind Braddock.

"If you'll excuse me for a moment." Braddock stepped out of the interrogation room and into the observation room to find Tori, Steak, Eggs, Cal, and Backstrom and said, "We've got him on the DNA."

"I agree," Backstrom replied.

"Is there more to be had?" Tori asked in a tone that said she thought there was.

Eddie's tongue was loose. He was cocky, confident, and talking, and he didn't seem to see his vulnerability. His lawyer was wary of where this was going but he was also out of his depth and clearly didn't have the clout to control his client.

It was a situation ripe to be taken advantage of.

"I've taken my shot at him. Let's change it up."

Braddock stepped back into the interrogation room.

"Anything else, Will?" Eddie asked, checking his wristwatch.

"Just a few more questions."

On cue, Tori opened the door and stepped into the interrogation room carrying a folder.

"Counselor, this is Special Agent Tori Hunter with the FBI."

"I know who Agent Hunter is."

"What's she doing in here?" Eddie asked, suddenly guarded. He knew Tori was only interested in one case.

Tori sat down next to Braddock and peered to Eddie, leaning forward; her posture was aggressive and her demeanor austere. Her eyes narrowed and bored in on him. They might have been friends, but that wasn't what she saw now. Now she saw a killer. There would be no preamble. "Eddie, I've been watching. You're not telling us everything."

"Excuse me?"

"You haven't been totally forthcoming," Tori declared as she opened the plain manila folder, took out a photo, and slammed it down on the table. The picture was of Sarah Craig, dead in the trunk of her car. Her arms were bound behind her back and her ankles were tied together with a green nylon rope. "You left something out."

Eddie recoiled from the picture. "Whoa!"

"Eddie, don't say a word," Westlund ordered, reaching for his client's right arm, a panicked look on his face.

"I didn't have anything to do with that!" Eddie declared dismissively, ignoring Westlund, shoving the photo away.

"You were the last person to see her, Eddie," Braddock stated. "We found semen in the backseat of that car. Given what you've told me, the court will grant me an order for a sample of your DNA—that will match up to *you*. I have blood in the backseat of that car; it's *her* blood. And there's blood in the trunk of the car. Her blood."

"I didn't hit her. I had sex with her and that's it."

"Really?" Tori replied in disbelief. "That's what you're going with, Eddie?"

"Come on, Tori. You know me. You know I couldn't do something like that."

"Do I?" Tori replied coldly.

She stood up and made a point of deliberately laying out four photos on the table. The pictures were of the four women who'd been found dead in the trunks of their cars. In all four photos, their hands were bound behind their backs and their ankles tied together with green nylon rope. The victims were lying on their stomachs, their heads turned toward the camera, the bruising visible on their necks from the strangling, and their faces bruised and beaten with blood smears. Their names and the dates the photos had been taken were detailed on the stickers. Next to the photos of the dead women, Tori placed an individual headshot of each victim. Then she added a fifth victim, photos of Sarah Craig, to the array.

"Do they all look familiar, Eddie?" Tori asked in a cool, monotone voice as she slowly moved her finger between Sarah Craig and each of the victims, watching Eddie's eyes focus on the pictures. She saw the recognition in his face and then the shock. What she was having a hard time determining was whether it was the shock of seeing his handiwork, of being found out, or something else, like the genuine disbelief at seeing such photos.

She glanced to her right to Braddock, and she could tell he saw it and was questioning it, too. It was time to dig into that.

"You know them, don't you, Eddie?"

Eddie shook his head. "No, I… don't."

"So, you want to play that game, okay. Let me remind you of their names," Tori declared, working left to right. "The first one here is Kristin Quales in Vermillion, South Dakota. This one here is Sierra Brooks, Manhattan, Kansas. This one here is Barbara Korn, East Lansing, Michigan, and then last year, Kelsey Zimmer, Green Bay, Wisconsin," Tori explained. "And then Sarah Craig two nights ago."

"You know what all the locations of those murders have in common, Eddie?" Braddock asked.

Eddie didn't respond verbally, but he nodded almost imperceptibly.

"That's right, Mannion's restaurants. In Green Bay and Vermillion, those were Mannion's locations. In East Lansing, it was an Ansel's. In Kansas, it was a Victory's. All of them are part of the Mannion family of restaurants."

Eddie's mouth opened. "Uh…"

"Eddie!" Westlund growled. "Stay quiet. Don't respond." Then to Braddock, Westlund declared, "Will, just because these women were murdered in towns where a Mannion's restaurant is located doesn't mean anything."

"I'm pretty sure if Eddie thinks on it real hard, looking at the dates on each photo, he'll understand the significance," Tori replied with her arms folded. "Because he was there—for each and every one of them."

Eddie Mannion rubbed his face hard with both of his hands, as if he was trying to wake himself up from the nightmare he was now in.

Tori piled on. "Counselor, all four murders occurred within just a few days of the opening of each restaurant."

Braddock, taking his partner's cue, took out a set of newspaper clippings and photos. In each, Eddie Mannion was front and center, cutting the ribbon at the grand openings of the restaurants with various dignitaries behind him clapping and smiling. The dates all corresponded with the four murdered women.

"The. Man. Of. The. Hour," Tori taunted, slowly waving her hand across the photos. "Quite the array, Edward."

Westlund spoke up. "I see what you're trying to do, Agent Hunter. But good luck trying to tie these four women to him just because their deaths occurred coincidentally with the restaurant openings."

"Oh, these four women *aren't* enough for you, Counselor?" Tori asked. "I see. Well then, why don't we just add more?"

"More?" the lawyer asked, stunned.

Tori leaned in to both Eddie and Westlund. "Yeah. *Nineteen more*, in fact."

Braddock rolled out the map. It had a total of twenty-three dots on it, numbered one through twenty-three. "There are another nineteen women who have gone missing and the dates they went missing." He then rolled a transparent map over the one on the table. It had the Mannion restaurants listed and the dates they'd opened. "And guess what?"

Tori glared at Eddie. "You were at every one of them."

"Including this one here in Brookings." Braddock pointed on the map. "And who is missing from Brookings?" He placed a picture of Joanie Wells on the table. "Remember her, Eddie?"

"Joanie," he murmured.

"That's right, Joanie. I've got a witness who says you slept with her two nights before she went missing from Brookings." Braddock laid another photo on the table. "This photo is from the hotel lobby, of you walking her in that night for your little rendezvous."

"At least you used a bed that time," Tori tweaked.

"Two nights later, she goes missing—hasn't been seen since."

"And you were still in town," Tori noted. "That private jet of yours didn't leave until the day after she disappeared."

"And, of course, there are two more to add to this," Braddock noted flatly, "because they occurred right here in Manchester Bay. One is Genevieve Lash," he pointed out, tossing a photo of her in front of Eddie. "You were in town... Heck, you were at your own family bar the night she went missing."

"And then we have the one that started it all," Tori stated icily. "Jessie."

Tori placed a picture of Jessie in front of Eddie Mannion, slowly and repeatedly tapping it with her right index finger.

"Don't say anything," Westlund counseled, trying to get Eddie's attention.

Tori moved around to the side of the table, leaning toward Eddie with the photo of Jessie in front of him.

"Look at her, Eddie, just look at her," she demanded in a low, calm tone. Tori gestured to the whole table. "Look at *all* of them. We know you were in each one of these towns when the women disappeared." Tori declared. "All twenty-five of them. *You. Were. There*. Twenty-five for twenty-five. I mean, what are the odds?"

"Twenty-six now when you include Sarah Craig," Braddock added. "And while we're at it, Katy Anderson disappeared two weeks ago. Are there any others, Eddie?"

"He's not answering that or any other questions," Westlund announced and turned to his client. "Let's go!"

Eddie looked up from the photos, clippings, and maps, first turning to Westlund with a blank, stunned look on his face and then, after a moment, shifting in Tori's direction.

"Eddie, I'm telling you as your lawyer, don't say a word."

"How could you think I would do that?" Eddie said softly to Tori, a look of betrayal on his face. "How could you think I'd do that to... anyone? To Sarah, to Joanie, to any of these poor women… but especially to Jessie, to *you*. We were friends, Tori. You and Jessie were my friends."

"Eddie, stop!" Westlund warned.

"I look at Sarah Craig. Katy is missing. Jessie. I've seen what you do to friends, Eddie," Tori replied coldly.

"That's what you think of me?" Eddie asked with a heartbroken look on his face. "How could you… think I'd do this? I spent days helping to search for Jessie."

"Lots of killers do that, Eddie. They do it to cover their tracks," Tori replied, standing up and then pacing behind Braddock on the other side of the table. "You know, Eddie, it's not all your fault. Your father, what he did to you, how he beat you, how my dad had to come out and beat him back to protect you and your mom. Irv was an awful man who left a trail of destruction behind at the end of his pitiful life. He did this to you."

"Eddie, come on," Westlund pleaded, pulling at his client's arm, trying to get him to stand up and leave.

"Trauma like that damages people," Tori continued. "It can trigger them to do things, terrible things. It can make them lash out and harm others. It can turn them into monsters." She stopped and looked back to Eddie. "For example, it can turn them into a sexual assaulter when they were a United States Marine."

Eddie looked at Tori in horror, shocked she knew about that. "That was… that was a mistake."

"Enough, Agent Hunter!" Westlund exclaimed, trying to take control of things but getting steamrolled as Tori wouldn't relent.

"Where's Jessie? Where's her body, Eddie? Where?" She pounded the table, yelling, "*Dammit, where?*"

"You're going to ruin me. Ruin my family. Ruin Kyle."

"No," Tori answered. "You did that yourself."

Eddie Mannion didn't respond; he simply looked down and slowly shook his head, finally disengaging.

"Unless you're arresting my client, we're done here," Westlund declared, standing up and then prodding Eddie to follow. "Let's go, Eddie. Let's get out of here—*now*!"

Tori looked to Braddock, who lightly shook his head.

They'd hammered Eddie, showed him what he was in for, but despite all the theatrics, at this point Eddie had only admitted to having sex with Sarah Craig. In and of itself that was vital, but there was more work to be done. This was merely round one. There was more to come before they arrested him.

Eddie finally stood up, with Westlund leading him by the arm to the door.

Tori pivoted to watch them leave. Braddock stepped forward and handed three documents to Westlund, who quickly scanned them and then looked up to Braddock.

"Now, Mr. Mannion, your attorney is holding search warrants for your home, your cabin, and your hunting property. Those searches will be commencing now. A search warrant will also be served on the restaurant division of Mannion Companies by the Minnesota Bureau of Criminal Apprehension."

Eddie looked at the warrants and then over to Tori. "I'm not a perfect man. In fact, I'm a pretty careless one with much of my life."

"Eddie, come on." Westlund tugged on his arm.

"How do you think I could do something like that? I didn't kill those women and I didn't kill my friend Jessie, and you ought to know that. Go think on that. Think about what you're doing to me, to this town, to your home, or…" Eddie snorted and took his turn to throw a dagger. "Then again, I guess you left all of us behind a long time ago, didn't you, Tori? What do you care what you do to us now? After all, you don't live here. What do *you* care? You're just going back to New York anyway."

Eddie let that hang in the air for a long moment, staring Tori down, before he finally turned and left the interrogation room, the door closing behind.

Braddock glanced back to Tori. She simply looked straight ahead, a tear slowly trickling down her cheek.

"Are you two going to go take a look at the parking lot at Cuyuna?" Cal asked.

"After we run by Mannion's house," Braddock answered. "Steak is already there, and the rest of the warrants are being executed. Corbin Hansen is handling the hunting property. The St. Louis County sheriff is up at Eddie's place on Lake Vermilion. Eggleston is up there, too."

"That was quite the show in there," Backstrom remarked. "You went a little further than I thought you would."

"He was talking," Braddock answered. "It was worth a shot, putting everything in front of him. But look, my sense is that this is a case that'll fall based on the circumstantial evidence and what we found in the backseat of Sarah Craig's car. We have a good case on Craig." He looked to Backstrom. "If we get a first-degree murder conviction with a life sentence, maybe he opens up and we get answers on all the others, including Jessie."

"We still have to prove it," Tori blurted quietly while staring out the window.

Everyone in the room turned to her.

"What's on your mind, Victoria?" Cal asked quietly.

"There are a couple of questions that we're going to need to confront," Tori replied, still looking out the window. "First, twenty-five women and never a sliver of evidence is left behind?" she asked, turning and looking to Braddock, who nodded, thinking back to their earlier conversation on the topic. "Except for now. Why? Why so careless so close to home? I can't figure that out."

"You mentioned a couple; what's else?" Cal asked.

"Other than Craig, Jessie, Lash, and maybe even Katy, all of the other disappearances tie to one of the restaurant openings."

"Right, that's how we tie Mannion to them," Backstrom replied. "He uses those trips as cover for his killing. I point to Joanie Wells in Brookings as a potential Exhibit A."

"Yeah, so how does Sarah Craig fit? I know what the physical evidence shows and what the witnesses have said, but how does she fit in? She's a woman he picked up and had sex with in a car. There's almost always a several-month gap between a disappearance or murder, usually because that's the gap between openings. Yet here, three weeks after Lash, two weeks after Joanie Wells in Brookings, he strikes again, *near home*." She looked to Backstrom. "You're going to have to answer those questions, right?"

"Yes, Agent Hunter, we'll have to deal with that, and I've already been thinking about it," Backstrom replied. "As you noted, Genevieve Lash wasn't tied to a restaurant opening. Nor was Katy Anderson, nor was your sister. So, there are at least three other times where he deviated from his established pattern. As for Joanie Wells, she seems to fit the pattern perfectly."

"And," Cal added, "as for him being sloppy, that's how we usually catch killers. They make a mistake somewhere along the line. Sarah Craig is five foot nine, one hundred and forty-five pounds. She's bigger and stronger than the other victims. He might have underestimated her. Possibly she fought back? Or maybe he didn't intend to kill her, but then she presented him the opportunity to do so and then things went awry. Or maybe he's just so hungry to kill now, the thirst is so strong, that he couldn't fight back the impulse. Genevieve Lash, a week later Joanie Wells, and then Sarah Craig and maybe Katy Anderson, too. The urge to kill is overtaking him. He's out of control."

"Who knows why? Motive—the why to kill—perhaps is weak at the moment, but as you noted, Tori, the physical evidence is not." Backstrom stated, nonplussed. "I tend to agree with Will. The case against Eddie Mannion on Sarah Craig is solid, and what happened in that interrogation room did not hurt that, it only strengthened it. And Wilson is already working on a warrant for a DNA sample. We'll have that soon enough. If we match that, this case can fall."

The county attorney took a moment, peering over to Tori, his posture and expression softening. In almost a murmur he asked, "Agent Hunter? Tori, if I might," he sighed, "it has to be… devastating to know your sister was killed by someone you thought was a friend."

Tori nodded, looking to the floor.

"Yeah, I bet it is," Backstrom replied quietly. "And you know what? Eddie Mannion knows it, too. You've asked a couple of different times, back a few days ago when I didn't believe you and Will, why did the killer send you the article? Right? You remember asking that?"

Tori nodded.

"Now I think I know why. Because he's a cold-blooded killer. Eddie Mannion sent you that article to first taunt you and then draw you here. Once you were here, he let you hunt for him before he tried to kill you. That didn't work. So now he's doing the next best thing. He's killing you by driving a stake into your heart. He wants you to die a little each day knowing the truth. He knows that every time you think of Jessie, you'll think of him."

"He's been dying to do it for twenty years and he just got to do it, and he's going to want to continue doing it," Cal noted quietly. "I just thank God he did it in that interrogation room and not someplace else, know what I mean?"

Tori nodded again.

"In that interrogation room he was playing, fronting all kinds of surprise, but then at the end he showed his true colors. At the end, that was him twisting that knife," Backstrom stated, softly putting his hand on Tori's shoulder. "Tori. Don't let him do it. Instead, help me finish proving he did it."

"Let's finish this, Victoria," Cal said. "Let's nail him."

CHAPTER THIRTY-ONE

"Trust the evidence."

After ducking the media that had been tipped off, Westlund had immediately called his former associate, Jeff Warner, on the way out of the government center. Warner, who'd been returning from the Mannion Companies Restaurant Division building after reviewing the search warrant, had them go immediately up to his offices. The next call had been to Kyle Mannion, who now glared aghast at his brother as the family name and company he'd worked tirelessly to build was tied to a murder—perhaps multiple murders.

"Tell me what happened," Kyle demanded through gritted teeth. "All of it."

Westlund took them through the interrogation. "Braddock and Hunter started with what happened to Sarah Craig."

"And what *did* happen?" Kyle asked, looking to Eddie.

"I had sex with her," Eddie answered before looking away in embarrassment, mumbling, "in the backseat of her car."

"Are you fucking kidding me?"

"But that was it," Eddie pleaded in reply. "I didn't kill her. I got out of her car and drove away. I'm telling you, just like I told them, she was alive in her car."

"How old are you?" Kyle barked.

Eddie just looked away, muttering, "Oh, whatever, Mr. Perfect."

"Last time I checked, I'm not the one looking at life in prison, dumbass," Kyle shot back.

"Tell me what happened next," Warner inquired, getting back on task.

Westlund took over. "Well, after they covered the Sarah Craig murder, they launched into Eddie about all of these other dead or missing women. Four who were murdered just like Sarah Craig, and then nineteen more that are missing from towns where you have your sports bars and restaurants. They all went missing or were murdered around the times you opened the places. They had pictures and records of Eddie being at those locations when they opened. They also had a map which showed where each woman went missing and the location of each restaurant, including one from a few weeks ago in Brookings."

"And what did you think when you saw it?" Warner asked Westlund.

The attorney hesitated.

"Don't hold back, Ben."

Westlund grimaced, making a point of avoiding eye contact with Eddie. "It was damning. That, and I realized I was in over my head in there."

"Ben, I'm not Monday-morning quarterbacking, but why didn't you end it?" Warner asked. "And get him the hell out of there?"

"I kept trying," Westlund replied, "repeatedly." Then he gestured to Eddie. "I said don't answer, don't respond, don't say a word, this is over, let's go. I said all of that again and again and again but Eddie just kept talking and talking and talking."

"You what?" Warner exclaimed, looking over to Eddie angrily. "Will you ever fucking learn? How many times have I told you that when your lawyer tells you to shut up, you need to shut the hell up?"

"I didn't do anything!" Eddie railed back. "Tori is standing there thundering away at me, accusing me of killing all of these women. Begging me to tell her where Jessie is buried. I don't know what happened to Jessie Hunter."

"Clearly, she thinks you do," Kyle asserted.

"No! I don't!" Eddie yelled back at Kyle and then looked to Warner. "And *that's* what I told her. That's *all* I told her. I didn't admit jack shit."

"Other than having sex in the backseat of a dead woman's car," Kyle griped.

"Move on, big brother."

Warner leaned back in his desk chair with his arms folded. "I'm a little surprised they didn't arrest you. Shocked, really. But since they're serving search warrants everywhere, I assume it's only a matter of time."

"There is one thing," Westlund said after a moment.

"What's that?" Kyle asked.

"When we were leaving. When I finally had Eddie moving out of the room, he said something to the effect that he didn't kill anyone. He said he didn't kill Jessie Hunter, and then he kind of… took a shot at her, at Agent Hunter."

"I'm not following you, Ben," Kyle said, perplexed.

"He said she abandoned everyone around here… What did she care what she did to Eddie, to you, to the town. I think that last part actually got to her a little bit."

"To who, Tori Hunter?" Kyle asked.

"Yeah," Westlund replied somberly, nodding. "She was all fire and brimstone and then at the end she couldn't look Eddie in the eye."

"Huh," Warner snorted, "maybe she has some doubts, then? Is that what you think, Ben?"

"I don't know," Westlund replied tiredly, slumping back in his chair, exhausted from his unexpectedly intense day. He looked over to Eddie. "You and Agent Hunter were friends. That seemed to hit her when you said that."

"I wasn't feeling a whole lot of warmth from her, I'll tell ya," Eddie bitched.

"But Ben, you think she had some reservations?" Warner asked, turning his gaze from Kyle back to Westlund. "That could prove helpful for Eddie's defense if we can get an admission of that uncertainty."

"I don't know, Jeff. I don't know if it was doubt, angst, betrayal, or sadness. Who knows, maybe it was shock. Shock that twenty years ago her sister went missing and she thinks it was Eddie who did it."

"Would you quit fucking saying that?" Eddie demanded, screaming at Westlund. "*Jesus Christ*, Ben, I didn't kill anyone!"

"Well, they might not have arrested you just now, but you can bet it's coming. And we're dealing with search warrants, demands for company records, all kinds of issues," Kyle replied.

"Oh, you're all heart, big brother," Eddie remarked.

"No, I'm not," Kyle retorted. "I'm all about the business of protecting you and *my* business. Right now, you're in deep shit again, little brother, and the company *will* follow. From now on, I'm making the calls here. The first call is you're going to go home—after the police have left, of course—and stay in the house and start shutting the hell up and listening to your lawyers." He looked over to Warner. "Jeff, we need some options for his defense, and we need them fast."

"I agree with you on that," Warner affirmed. "We need to protect the company, too."

"Gee, thanks, Jeff," Eddie gripped.

"You aren't the only one exposed here. I've got over fifteen years of my life invested in the company. Your cavalier behavior has my balls in a vise here too, so damn right I'm looking out for my backside." Warner turned to Kyle. "I can make some calls within the firm and get us some defense counsel referrals. And

I'll probably need to use the Mannion name to get interest from the right people."

"Do that," Kyle replied. "But keep in mind, we need a defense lawyer that will play around here. Do you understand?"

"I hear you."

"I want someone that will make George Backstrom and Anne Wilson quake in their shoes. That is, if they are the ones to try the case."

"On it. I'll start making some calls to Minneapolis and Chicago and get moving on this."

Kyle glanced over to Westlund. "Ben, no offense, but we're going to get ourselves lawyers who specialize in this kind of case."

"No offense taken," Westlund answered as he stood up from his chair. "And since I'm not going to be Eddie's lawyer, the less I know at this point, the better."

"Agreed. Come on, I'll show you out," Kyle said, putting his arm on Westlund's shoulder as the two of them walked out of Warner's office toward the elevator in the lobby. "Now, send me a bill for your time today. Just send one for the whole day and I'll take care of it. If you get sucked into this thing further for some reason, bill your time and charge it to me."

"Sure thing," Westlund answered.

The two of them stood quietly waiting for the elevator.

"Do you really think Tori Hunter has doubts?" Kyle asked.

Westlund shrugged. "Maybe." After a moment, he turned to Kyle. "Look, I'm just a little country lawyer, so take this for what it's worth."

"I need all the insight I can get at this point."

"That map, the newspaper clippings, the details on how those women disappeared or were murdered around the time of the restaurant openings, and that Eddie was there *every* time…"

"Every time?"

"He was there every time, Kyle." Westlund grimaced and slowly shook his head. "I don't think a jury of his peers will believe it's just a coincidence. The disappearances and murders are all tied to those openings, and they have photos from newspapers with Eddie there cutting the ribbon, giving speeches. I mean, he was there, and I'm sure that warrant they're serving on your company will reveal records that verify all of that.

"And then there's the woman in Brookings. Eddie was with her, had sex with her two nights before her disappearance, and now she's missing. Eddie admits to having sex with Sarah Craig and now she's dead. It's… not good."

The elevator doors opened and Westlund stepped inside. Before the doors closed, he added, "Kyle, I'd be very worried about your brother if I were you."

*

Braddock and Tori drove to Eddie Mannion's house, where Steak was overseeing the search. "We're going through room by room," Steak reported. "The forensic team is hunting for fiber evidence, particularly for Sarah Craig, although I'm dubious."

"Why?" Tori asked.

"Even he wouldn't be dumb enough to kill her here. There isn't much information in his home office relating to business records; I expect that he does most of that work at the company office. How's that going?"

"The BCA is there now, as is Cal," Braddock answered. "The warrant was served. Kyle sent Warner over there. Warner read it and said they had to comply. The restaurant business is in its own building on that corporate campus. The BCA is inventorying the records and securing the computer system. I suspect there will be more to come on that."

"From Warner?"

"Him and whoever they hire to represent Eddie. I'm sure Kyle will hire a high-powered, flesh-eating criminal defense lawyer," Braddock replied. "And whoever that is will put Backstrom and Wilson through their paces."

"Kyle won't hesitate to spend," Steak said in agreement.

"Right," Will replied, "I don't need to tell you that we could use more evidence."

Well, on that point," Steak stated, handing Braddock a folder. "That's his first divorce file."

"And?" Tori asked.

"There are pictures of his first ex-wife in there with a couple of black eyes and a swollen lip."

"Really?" Braddock flipped open the folder, thumbing through the pictures, shaking his head.

"He turned out like Irv," Steak noted angrily. "I remember his first wife. I remember them getting a divorce and her moving away. But I don't remember anything about this. Eddie kept it quiet."

"More likely Kyle," Braddock muttered, closing the folder. "Good work."

"Yeah, I guess," Steak replied with a drained sigh. "There are days this job sucks. I've known him since I was eight."

"Me too," Tori said quietly.

"It's a kick in the balls, I know," Braddock stated. "Keep searching," he encouraged, handing the folder back, clasping Steak on the shoulder. "Do the job. Take your time. Be thorough."

"On it," Steak answered, turning to head back inside the house.

By mid-afternoon Tori and Braddock made their way over to the parking lot at Cuyuna Golf Club, the parking lot that Mannion claimed he and Sarah Craig drove to after leaving the Serpent Bar. There were perhaps twenty cars sprinkled around the long, narrow parking lot, with people out on the golf links for the overcast and humid afternoon.

Braddock inspected the lot, taking a long look and walk around the area where Eddie said they'd parked, which was in the southwest corner. The location was far from the clubhouse and tucked back between the two maintenance sheds for the course.

"*If* they parked here, nobody could see them from the highway, that's for sure. Not that anyone would be looking at that time of night. For anyone else to have seen anything that Eddie and Craig were doing, they'd have needed to drive back here, don't you think?" Braddock asked.

When he didn't hear a response from her, he turned around to see Tori at the far edge of the parking lot, staring off in the distance out over the lush, deep green hues of the golf course. He slowly walked over to her. "Are you thinking you want to go out and play a quick nine?" he asked.

"I'm sorry, what?" Tori replied, snapping out of her trance.

Since they'd finished with Eddie, she'd been quiet and distant, deep in thought, and had hardly spoken on the half-hour drive over from Manchester Bay. "What's on your mind?"

Tori shrugged her shoulders. "I understand what Cal and Backstrom said. It's hard to argue, but I can't stop thinking about Eddie, about what *he* said."

"I see. Is it the 'I didn't do it' part or the 'what do you care what you do to us?' part?"

"More the former than the latter. I mean, I keep running it around in my head. Why kill Sarah Craig? Why? Why here and then leave the body in her car in Holmestrand? I think about it and it doesn't make sense."

"Sometimes a murder doesn't have to make sense."

"No, not for these killings, Will. Not for these. Twenty-five women and not a clue, a forensic speck, nothing. And now he has sex with her in the backseat and leaves semen and DNA behind.

Then he kills her, stuffs her in the trunk, and then parks the car in a place for it to be found. Tell me you're not asking yourself this question. I mean, at least a little, right? I go from he did it to he didn't, to he did and then back again."

Braddock nodded. "I figured that was what was on your mind. But I think there's another way to interpret this morning."

"Which is?"

"Serial killers almost always get caught. BTK, the Boston Strangler, Son of Sam, the list goes on. Sooner or later, unless you're the Zodiac, the police or the FBI catch them because they make a mistake. In some cases, they get caught almost because they *want* to get caught, because they want to talk about it. Talk about the game, how they played it, how they were so good at it."

"You think Eddie wanted to get caught?"

"I think there was some truth in what Cal and Backstrom said. About twisting the knife. He wanted you to catch him so he could stab you with that knife."

"Me?"

"Yeah, maybe you're the why, Tori. Tori Hunter, the sister of his first victim. A renowned, brilliant, relentless FBI special agent obsessed by her career and her sister's case. He sent you the article on the twentieth anniversary of when he took Lash to draw you here, and it worked. He took Katy after you saw her to torment you, to show that he *could* torment you, and it worked. He set up Gunther Brule, supposedly his good friend, to have you get the wrong man—again to torment and maybe even embarrass you. That almost worked."

"What about the shots at me?"

"Did he hit you? Or did he miss just to scare the hell out of you?"

"What about trying to blow you up?"

"I got lucky, but how would you have felt had he succeeded?"

"I don't want to answer that," Tori replied quietly, looking away. "I don't even want to think about that."

"What impact has Katy's disappearance had? Nothing but guilt, right?"

Tori nodded lightly.

"You know what I believe?"

"What?" Tori asked, looking back to him.

"The evidence."

Tori picked at the tar with her shoe, slowly nodding, understanding where Braddock was going, which was always to the basics.

"Let me tell you something else. I've been trying to understand the psychology of this too, but I come at it from a different perspective."

"What's that?"

"I've observed Eddie Mannion from afar for five years. He's a Mannion, a man about town. He seems like a good guy, but also kind of a wannabe if you ask me. I'm torturing *The Godfather* analogy a bit here, but to me he's the Fredo Corleone to Kyle's Michael. Kyle is the older brother. He took over the family business and became the mogul. He runs the family empire. He's beloved locally, has a nice family, a pretty wife with a bunch of cute kids, and is a generous giver to his community and church. He's the all-American hero."

"And then there's Eddie."

"Eddie is the antithesis of Kyle. Twice divorced, out partying and carousing all the time, and generally comes off as irresponsible. Kyle props Eddie up. He sends him off to do the light lifting of opening new bars and restaurants and being the life of the party. That's the public image and Eddie seems okay with it."

"But what if he's not?" Tori asked.

"Yeah, what if the arrangement where Kyle is the boss, the brains of the operation who gets all the glory, doesn't sit well with Eddie? Kyle probably gets a lot more of the money, and that cuts at Eddie. Eddie thinks he's smart. He wants respect. He doesn't get it from his brother. He doesn't get it from people around town, who see him riding big brother's coattails. Nobody understands he's smart, that he's… brilliant, really. He's done this thing, killed these women without getting caught, and nobody even knows it because he's been so good at it."

"But to get the respect he wants, to have his brilliance acknowledged…"

"He *had* to get caught," Braddock finished. "If you don't get caught, nobody will ever know it was you. And he had to get caught by the best—by you. It had to be in a confrontation with you. *That's* what I see. And as he gets to demonstrate his brilliance to us, who does he get to hurt in the process?"

"Kyle."

"Right. He's going to make us work for it, no doubt, and we might have to prove it at a trial. I mean, what would be the ultimate for Eddie?"

"To go to trial and…"

"Walk. That would be the ultimate, to pull off the murders then skate away because *we* can't prove it, because *you* can't prove it. We need to keep grinding on this thing and lock it down, lock down the Sarah Craig case. We do that and…"

"The rest can fall."

"Yeah."

Tori looked away, thinking about what Braddock had to say. It made sense, especially if you believed the evidence.

"I can't walk in your shoes on this," Braddock noted, reaching for Tori's hand, holding it lightly in his. "I know he was your friend, and right now you're trying to figure out if you should feel betrayed or ashamed, right?"

Tori nodded.

"Trust the evidence."

Braddock's phone rang. "Braddock."

"Will, it's Corbin Hansen. Son, you better get up here—and you better bring Tori along."

*

Braddock sped north with his siren blaring as he approached Mannion's hunting property, the concealed entrance marked by a Cass County sheriff's Explorer parked at the end of a dirt road. The deputy pulled forward and Braddock drove ahead, following the winding road to a grouping of three other Cass County vehicles parked at a small doublewide trailer.

Sheriff Corbin Hansen was waiting for them.

He had them get into his truck then drove them along a different tight, winding road deep into thick woods, passing two deer stands mounted up high in the trees along the way. Hanson eventually turned right, along an even tighter path, with tree branches brushing along both sides of the truck. As he slowly turned to the left, two of his men were visible ahead, standing next to an old, aqua-colored Toyota Camry and a green tarp lying to the side.

"That, my friends, is Gail Anderson's car," Sheriff Hansen declared. "The car Katy Anderson took the night she went missing."

"And Katy?" Tori asked.

Hansen exhaled a deep breath then led them to the trunk of the car and opened it. Katy's dead body was inside. "I'm sorry."

"Oh my God," Tori croaked, her hand going to her mouth.

Braddock wrapped her in his arms. "I'm sorry, Tori. I'm so sorry," he whispered, holding her tightly. "I'm so, so sorry."

*

Gail Anderson was surrounded by friends when Tori and Braddock stepped inside the house. Gail took one look at Tori and knew.

"Gail, I'm… I'm…"

Gail embraced Tori, holding her in her arms. "It's okay."

"It's my fault. If I hadn't come back out here… If I hadn't talked about that trip. If…"

"Shhh, no, sweetie, no," Gail replied, hugging Tori. "No. Don't say that. It's not your fault. It's not your fault."

*

Tori stared silently out the passenger window as Braddock spoke with Cal all the way back to Manchester Bay.

"The noose is getting tighter," Cal stated. "Backstrom was in court this afternoon getting an order for us to get a DNA sample from Eddie. We'll have it tomorrow, and we can get a sample and test it against the evidence from Sarah Craig's car. If we have that and match it, the case gets tighter. Now that we've found Katy Anderson's body, Tori is proven right. Katy's disappearance was all part of this. With these two cases, we can go to work on closing Jessie Hunter and Genevieve Lash. Backstrom and I were discussing getting the FBI along with the United States Attorney involved and letting them run wild on these other twenty-three cases."

"Agreed," Braddock replied as he glanced to his right to Tori, who simply watched the countryside pass by.

Braddock dropped her off at her hotel just before 7 p.m. Tori wanted some time alone.

"Are you sure? You can grab some things quick and come out."

Tori shook her head. "I'll come out in a few hours, okay? I'll even stop and buy a bottle or two of wine. Maybe we can sit around the fire or something? Just you and me."

"Sure."

Tori turned to get out of the Explorer when he reached for her hand. "Are you okay?"

"Yeah," she replied softly with a nod. "Or at least… I will be." She leaned back into the truck and kissed him softly before moving in to let him embrace her, letting herself be held, needing to be comforted.

Braddock wrapped her in his arms again, quiet, just holding her.

Tori let out a sigh and broke gently from the embrace before looking up and pecking him on the lips one more time. "I'll see you in a little while."

"Okay."

Tori took the two hours to decompress. She drew herself a long, hot, soapy bath, closed her eyes, played soft music in her earbuds, and let the warm water work therapeutically over her body. She wanted this time for herself, to wrap her mind around... Eddie.

For two hours she thought back to the time before Jessie disappeared. Was there something she should have seen? Were there signs? Was there a reason that she and Jessie should have been wary of Eddie? She drew a blank. There was nothing that said she should have seen it coming.

She finally lifted herself out of the tub and dried off before slowly getting dressed in blue shorts, a sleeveless white linen blouse, and sandals. She pulled her hair back in a ponytail and quickly applied a little makeup.

Tori walked out the front of the hotel and texted Braddock that she was on her way. First, though, she needed to buy wine. She turned right out of the hotel parking lot onto Lake Drive and made her way to Knorr's Liquor and Wine, which Mickey had informed her had the best selection in town.

Mickey was right, Tori thought as she patiently perused the many shelves. For some reason the Billy Joel song "Scenes from an Italian Restaurant" was playing in her head as she picked her way through her options— *white, red or perhaps a bottle of rosé instead.*

Eventually she settled on a Chardonnay and a Cabernet.

She paid at the register and walked out the back of the store to her car, typed a text to Braddock as to what she'd bought, and then hit send.

The pavement scraped behind her.

She spun left.

Her body started spasming.

Tori's eyes fluttered open. She grunted as the left side of her body bounced hard against the unforgiving and uneven surface she was lying on. She couldn't groan, at least out loud, not with the duct tape over her mouth. And she could barely move. Her wrists were bound so tightly behind her back that it felt like the restraints were knifing into the skin. It was the same with her ankles, bound tight, leaving her only with the ability to bend her knees and nothing more. Then there was the burning sensation on her left lower back, where her skin felt like it was on fire.

With her senses coming back online and her heart beating rapidly in the pitch-black darkness, she tried focusing her eyes to look around. She discerned that she was in the trunk of a car and it was driving along a smooth, paved road, although she was jostled every time the rear tires hit a seam or imperfection in the pavement. Her left side kept bumping against a spare tire and jack underneath the thin fabric of the trunk cover beneath her.

She tried to get a sense of the trunk and see or feel if there was anything she could use to free herself. She contorted her restrained body to reach, mostly with her feet, but felt nothing. The trunk seemed empty, other than her own presence.

The car veered sharp left and began to slow, and then she heard the rhythmic clicking sound of the turn signal. Tori strained to turn her body to look back to her left, where she could see a small, vertical sliver of yellow flashing light. A left turn was about to be made. To where? And how long had she been in this position?

She hadn't blacked out, but there was some time when she was out of it and disoriented, as if she was paralyzed. The last thing she clearly remembered was coming out of the liquor store, texting Braddock, getting to the car, hitting the fob to unlock it, and then sensing movement behind her. As she'd started to turn, she was stabbed in the lower left back, like electricity had shot through her. She seemed to faintly remember being picked up and then tossed into the trunk and being jostled around, but it was all a fuzzy blur.

This is how it all went down, she thought, understanding her predicament. Joanie Wells, Genevieve Lash, Sarah Craig, Jessie, and all of the others. Immobilized, trapped, unable to escape or scream for help. Lying in the trunk of a car with nothing but time to imagine what horror and fate awaited before the brutal end came.

The car began to decelerate and then stopped for a moment before slowly moving forward and then accelerating up a steep incline, causing her to take a half-roll back, crunching her right hip into the trunk latch. After a few seconds, the car leveled out and she tipped a half-roll forward. The road was uneven now; the car was jostling left and right, and the tires were crunching on a rough gravel road.

She felt the car veer slightly left. Tightly bound, she had little body control, tipping forward as the car started down a gentle incline before again leveling out and then finally coming to a stop.

The engine was turned off.

Tori peered around again, listening for any sound, trying to get some sense of where she was. But there was no movement or sound for her to get such a sense. Instead, there was just an ominous, eerie quiet.

Then there was a click and the trunk latch released, letting in some light. Tori strained to roll her body to look back to her right but could only see the trunk hood lightly bobbing.

A car door opened. After a moment, she heard footsteps behind her on the driver's side, a slow deliberate walk to the back of the car. There was a long pause before the trunk was lifted fully open.

"Hiya, Tori," Jeff Warner greeted with a wicked grin.

CHAPTER THIRTY-TWO

"What was this internal investigation about?"

Braddock showered, shaved, and dressed in khaki shorts and a light-blue, soft cotton, button-down shirt that he left untucked. He even dabbed on a small dollop of cologne. *You sure do seem to work hard at cleaning up for her, buddy*, he thought as he evaluated himself in the long mirror on the back of his bathroom door.

His phone pinged. It was a text from Tori saying she'd picked up the wine, a red and a white. He slipped the phone into his pocket and ran his hand through his hair one more time. He walked out of his bedroom and into his home office. His laptop was still open to his email and he saw two more messages from Sheila. The first contained Eddie Mannion's full cell phone history. Sheila had listed the names of the people Eddie had called or received calls from in the margins. He scanned back several days to the night Gunther had called him, confirming the call was made. Then Eddie had made a call ten minutes later. "Hmpf. That's interesting."

He clicked out of the phone records and opened the second email from Sheila. It explained that attached was a record of stun gun sales in the six-county area from four of the top manufacturers. Sheila had noted that Eddie's name hadn't shown up. He quickly scanned the names on the spreadsheet and recognized many as police officers and sheriff's deputies who had to buy their own equipment, although they were often reimbursed for the expense. There was a business name on the list that was intriguing. "Another way to cover his tracks, I suppose."

There was a knock on his back door. "That was quick," he muttered as he went to the office window and looked down, but it wasn't Tori. Kyle Mannion was standing at his back door, peering in the window.

Interesting timing, he thought. *What does he want?* He went back to his bedroom nightstand, took his Glock 17 out of the drawer, chambered a round, and held it low to his side as he walked down the steps. He peered around the corner to see Kyle Mannion looking in through the curtains framing the back-door window. Kyle saw him and waved.

Braddock cautiously approached and peeked out the window to see where Kyle's hands were before he undid the deadbolt and stepped back to open the door, making sure Kyle saw the gun in his right hand.

"Do you want to frisk me?" Kyle asked, holding his arms out with a thick manila folder in his left hand.

"Walk in the door and place your hands on the island."

Kyle complied while Will patted him down with his left hand, keeping the gun in his right. He pulled out car keys, a cell phone, and a thick money clip and tossed them onto the center island. He stepped back and let Kyle put all of it back in his pockets.

"Why are you here, Kyle? You sure as hell shouldn't be."

"I'm not trying to burn you."

"I'm already feeling singed."

"This is off the record," Kyle offered. "This conversation never happened if what I have here doesn't... sway you."

"Come on, Kyle, you know that doesn't work. You need to leave—now."

"This conversation never happened," he insisted. "I'll still use what I have here for Eddie's defense. Worst-case scenario for you is you're getting an advance look at defense strategy."

"Kyle…"

"I'm putting my neck on the line coming here, too. I could really be screwing Eddie far more than I'm compromising you."

"I don't know."

"Just hear me out," Kyle pleaded. "The reason I came out is Ben Westlund said Tori… might have had some doubts. That was his read."

Braddock shook his head. "She doesn't, Kyle. At least not anymore—not after we found Katy Anderson's car on your brother's hunting property."

"What if she was right, though?"

"I'm not following you."

"Listen, I *know* it looks bad for my little brother. We were at Warner's office today. Ben told me about the evidence that you and Tori put on the table in front of him and Eddie this morning, and hell—" Kyle shook his head disgustedly "—I can get there. Eddie has had his issues over the years."

"It sure looks like it."

"He was beaten by my old man, that worthless SOB. I know that you know Eddie has some history of abusing women. It wasn't just in the Marines down at Camp Lejeune, either. He smacked his first wife around pretty good."

Braddock nodded. "I know. We found the photos at his house today."

"Typical," was Kyle's annoyed response. "He was so stupid to keep those there. We kept that all quiet. We even hid it from the court. We used money to do it. I'm not proud of it, but that's what I did to protect him and my business. And like I said, you know about what happened when he was in the Marines."

"Where are you going with this?"

"Right," Kyle replied. "When I learned that there is the map of our restaurants and these women are all missing, I could see how you got there, how it looks like Eddie killed those women. I looked at our business records myself today for all those restaurant openings, and no doubt, my brother was there for all of them. With his history and all those links, I can see it. I really can."

"I sense a *but* coming."

"Eddie tries to project the image of being a big part of the success of our business. We do put him out front on all the restaurant openings. He's technically the head of that part of our operation. He's at the ribbon cuttings, gets quoted in the papers, signs the documents on behalf of the corporation, and so forth. Eddie is good at that, too. He comes off as the outgoing, fun-loving, life of the party guy. But the reality is, Eddie is pretty… weak. He's kind of broken. I think he chases all the women and drinks the way he drinks to project something other than what he really is. But here's something else I know: he couldn't kill anyone. He doesn't have the stomach for it."

"Kyle, we shouldn't be talking about this…"

"Just give me a few more minutes. I'm not trying to compromise you. *I'm not.* Actually, I think I'm helping you and me," Kyle added before he handed the manila folder over.

"What's this?"

"It's a file that has records of all of those restaurant openings. I know Eddie was at all the grand openings, and you have all of that. But there's a lot of other work that goes into opening those restaurants that Eddie plays very little role in—the licensing, the contracts, the hiring of employees, and negotiations with the local governmental authorities. Eddie doesn't do that; he doesn't possess the skill set, the education, or the intellect. He's listed as the owner, and he signs off on stuff and does some marketing and promotional work, but really, Eddie's biggest role is to fly in for a week or two when we open the joints. Someone who works for us does all that other work, travels to those towns repeatedly in the build-out and licensing phases, and is also often there when the restaurants are opening."

"Are you going to tell me that person is Jeff Warner?" Braddock asked.

Kyle did a double take. "How did you... know that?"

"You first."

"Jeff started working for me back when he was in law school. He was clerking for Ben Westlund's firm, which I used when we were a small business. Eddie liked the restaurant business, and Jeff showed a real aptitude for what it took to get a new restaurant off the ground. In those early years, he was working with me and Eddie when we opened our first places in Bismarck, La Crosse, and Sioux Falls. Then when he graduated law school, he came back and joined Ben's firm for a couple of years and continued to do the work. When he went out on his own, we stuck with him even though he was really a baby lawyer."

"Why?"

"Because Jeff could do the work, and I could tell he was going to be a damn good lawyer. He graduated at the top of his high school, college, and law school classes. He's fucking wicked smart."

"Why'd he come back here then?"

"His mom. She was ailing. Otherwise, he'd have probably gone to some big city firm and killed it. But he was here, and I realized he was the real deal. I kept giving him work and he kept knocking it out of the park. As we grew, he grew with us. But the point is, he's always been in the background, doing all the groundwork for when we open the restaurants. He still does. I mean, he's involved in all of the other intricate technical work and businesses we operate, but he still does the restaurant work, too."

"I see," Braddock replied as he flipped open the file, turning over the loose pages resting on top of a binder-clipped set of documents.

"But that's not all that's in this file. The clipped set of documents there are for an internal investigation we conducted on Jeff."

"Internal investigation?"

"A significant percentage, as much as eighty percent, of all the business that Jeff has is from my company. Historically, while he has his office in town, he was embedded in our offices so he could be right there when we needed him. He had a corner office out at our campus. It was just easier that way, or at least it used to be."

"What was this internal investigation about?"

"He got divorced for a second time a few years ago and it was a little messy. I thought at the time that it sent him into a bit of a tailspin. One night after the divorce he got a little too handsy with a secretary in our office."

"Handsy?"

"She reported that she was in a car with him one night after an impromptu happy hour." Kyle shook his head angrily. "He demanded that she give him a blow job. She refused and he didn't force it, but she felt harassed."

"I see."

"Now Jeff was in the middle of preparing us for going public with our drone business. He'd just gotten divorced. I figured he'd had too much to drink and made a bad mistake. But then another woman from my company came forward and said she had the same experience with him. And then there was another."

"You had a problem."

"A sensitive one. I couldn't just fire him, not at that time, anyway."

"It would have damaged going public. It would have been a financial problem for you."

"Yes," Kyle replied. "So, we…"

"Swept it under the rug."

"We settled with the three women very discreetly, very expensively, and with ironclad confidentiality agreements. Jeff apologized and said he'd get some help. We had him stop working out of our offices altogether and he started working strictly out of his own law firm's offices."

"You kept him?"

"We finished the public offering, but we made a few changes. Jeff had done a lot of work, and he was supposed to receive a significant offer of stock as part of it. I'd been willing to waive that legal conflict of the lawyer getting a piece of the action. But given what I'd had to deal with, what I'd paid out in settlements, and, to be honest, what I'd compromised of my own beliefs to get it all done…" Kyle paused for a moment. "Well, in the end he didn't get that."

"What did that cost him?"

"Right now, I'd estimate as much as five million dollars, based on the stock options he'd have received. If the business continues to prosper as it has, the value of those options would only have grown over time. But his transgressions were also expensive. I felt they changed our relationship."

"How so?"

"It was my intent over time to reduce his… involvement. He'd get enough work from me to stay comfortable, to save face, but I was going to find some other law firms to work with."

"And he found out about this when?"

"Six months ago. But there's one other thing I need to tell you."

"What's that?"

"The third woman who made a complaint. She wasn't an employee of mine. She was an employee of one of my contractors, Jerry Lash."

"Oh, shit."

"Will, why did you blurt Jeff's name when I handed you the folder?"

"Gunther Brule didn't commit suicide. He was murdered."

"Murdered?" Kyle asked, his jaw dropping.

"Yes. Tori and I confronted him at the VFW. After that he went up to his cabin and he was murdered."

"And you think by Eddie?"

"Well, Gunther only placed one call that night, and it was to your brother."

"I see."

"But then your brother called…"

"Jeff."

Braddock nodded. "Here's the other thing. Sarah Craig was found to have two small dots on her lower back, two inches apart. One theory is that those dots are the markings from a stun gun. We ran a search for stun gun purchases, checking if Eddie had purchased one."

"Did he?"

"Not that I've seen," Braddock answered. "But there was one purchased and delivered seven years ago to the law offices of Jeff Warner, before he merged his firm with Wilson Day."

"Look," Kyle started, "you're developing your theory on Eddie based upon that map and that he was at those restaurant launches. I know Jeff Warner has this image as the great lawyer with the national law firm and all, but he was at or around all of those openings, too. His behavior toward women, including Jerry Lash's employee, is… alarming. He was in those places Eddie was, and in high school, Eddie and Jeff ran in the crowd with Jessie and Tori Hunter and Katy Anderson. And there is one other thing."

"What?"

"He doesn't like small planes. He almost never uses our corporate jet. He often drives instead or flies on a larger commercial plane."

"Meaning… you don't have track of him all of the time when he's on the road for you."

"Right. He could have stayed longer or gone back after we thought he'd left the town, and nobody would know."

Braddock was thinking Tori needed to hear all of this and checked his watch, having lost track of time. "Where the heck is she?" he muttered.

"Where's who?"

"Tori," Braddock answered. "She should be here by now."

"She was coming out here? Now?" Kyle asked, surprised, checking his watch. "Are you two…?"

"Kind of, sort of while she's been here," Braddock replied as he held his cell up to his ear. After a moment, he frowned. "Huh. She's not answering. That's unusual." He tried calling her again, and then one more time. No answer.

Given what Kyle had just showed him and his own discoveries on Warner, Braddock suddenly felt his chest tightening. He sensed it. Something wasn't right.

It was at most a ten-minute drive from Manchester Bay. She'd last texted fifty minutes ago that she was on her way. She should have been here easily by now.

"I just tried Warner," Kyle reported worriedly, gesturing to his phone. "He's not answering, either."

Braddock tried Tori at the hotel but there was no answer. His next call was to Steak, who lived in Manchester Bay. He quickly explained his sudden concern and what he'd just seen. "I need you to get over to her hotel. She's not answering. I'll explain it later, but from what I've just seen, it may not be Eddie Mannion. It might be Warner, and we can't get him on the phone either."

"Warner? Jeff?"

"Yeah, Steak, he might have been playing all of us."

"You're worried, boss?"

"I have a bad feeling."

"Then I do, too," Steak replied. Braddock could tell his deputy detective was already on the move, hearing a door slam in the background. "I'm leaving now."

"You said she was buying wine?" Kyle asked.

"Yes," Braddock answered, and realized Kyle was making a point with the question. He quickly checked his watch: 9:50 p.m. The liquor stores all closed in ten minutes. He reached for his phone again, calling in to the sheriff's department dispatcher. "Coordinate with Manchester Bay PD. We need a check of all liquor stores in town to see if Tori Hunter was in tonight. Get a picture out. We need to canvass them all before they close!"

Ten minutes later, Steak called back. "Her hotel room was locked with the lights off. The front desk receptionist recalls her leaving earlier, more than an hour ago."

"Get over to Warner's house."

Braddock was thinking he needed to get out and start searching, but where?

Five minutes later, Steak called back. "I'm at Warner's. It's all quiet here. Nobody is home."

"Okay, I need you to join in the search at all the liquor stores. Go! Go now!"

Braddock kept calling Tori's cell.

*

Steak sped away from Warner's house, located on the southeast shore of Northern Pine Lake, and back into Manchester Bay on the H-4, taking the Lake Drive exit. He reached for his radio, calling into dispatch. "Where have we checked?"

Dispatch reported back.

"Has anyone checked Knorr's?"

"Not yet."

"I'm going right now," Steak informed them, turning a hard left onto Interlachen Avenue and driving two blocks south before taking another hard left into the parking lot. The lights inside the liquor store were still on. He pounded on the locked door and saw a clerk look down the hallway toward him.

Steak held up his badge and identification. "Sheriff's department."

The clerk came to the door and scanned the identification before undoing the lock.

"Thank you." Steak pulled up a photo on his iPhone. "Did you see her in here tonight? She probably bought wine. Her name is Tori Hunter."

The clerk examined the photo. "I think so, yes. Yes! She was in about an hour ago, maybe a little more. She bought a couple of bottles of wine and then she walked out the back down the hallway."

Steak went out the back door and stepped into the parking lot. There were only two cars parked in the lot, neither of which was Tori's dark blue Nissan Maxima rental car. Then he heard a ringing sound for what he thought was a cell phone. He started searching around, homing in on the rhythmic ringing before seeing a cell phone lying at the edge of the parking lot.

"Ah, shit!"

The screen had a name on it: Braddock.

Steak carefully picked up the phone and answered, "Will?"

"Steak? What the hell…?"

"Will, her phone was lying on the ground at the edge of the parking lot behind Knorr's. There's no sign of her."

CHAPTER THIRTY-THREE

"I bet you say that to all the girls."

Warner lifted Tori up out of the trunk, slung her over his shoulder, and took her inside a small house that looked to be used more as a shed, with shovels, rakes, hoes, and other gardening equipment visible. He dropped her to the floor and then reached down and pulled back a throw rug to reveal a wood door embedded in the floor, which he opened. He picked her up and threw her over his shoulder again, carrying her down a narrow and steep set of steps into the cellar underneath. Once they were in the cellar, he sat her down onto an aged, round-top, wooden barstool.

Tori took immediate inventory of her surroundings. The cellar was all cinder block. Behind her was an old, sturdy, thick, metal office desk. Above her there was a single light bulb hanging from the ceiling. Warner was on the opposite side of the cellar, standing to the right of the steps, crouched over a small workbench. She could tell he was using a honing rod to sharpen a long knife. To the left of the steps in the other corner was a gun case. Through the glass door front she was able to see several rifles, including one that looked like an AR-15 assault rifle.

"I'll be with you shortly, Tori," Warner commented casually while he held up and examined the long, jagged knife under the light of the swinging bulb. Tori read Warner's playacting for what it was: a ploy to heighten her anxiety. He needn't have bothered; she had plenty of it.

Her wrists and ankles both remained tightly bound with nylon handcuffs. She noticed the small clock mounted over the workbench, the red second hand clicking around the face—the time was 9:40 p.m. There was also a small television turned on. It was for a surveillance camera that looked like it was focused on an iron driveway gate.

If the time was right, and it felt right to her, she should've been at Braddock's at least a half-hour ago. That she wasn't there by now might be raising an alarm with him, or it would soon enough. He'd be calling, looking for her, and start wondering where she was. But he needed time, lots of it, and she needed to buy it for him in the hope he'd somehow figure out Warner was the one responsible.

She turned her gaze back to Warner.

He was scary smart, but she also knew that ever since they were kids, he was imbued with an almost pathological need to have his intellect acknowledged. People like that wanted to show how exceptional they were. She needed to engage him, get him talking and reveling in his brilliance.

Warner made his way over, picked up another barstool, dropped it down five feet in front of her, and sat down. He had the knife in his right hand, which rested on his thigh.

Tori averted her eyes, keeping her breathing regulated and staring straight ahead, preparing for what was to come. Warner stood up, took a step forward, reached for the duct tape, picked at a corner to loosen it, and then yanked it off. She flinched but did not make a sound other than an exhale.

Warner peered down at her with a satisfied smirk on his face. "Well, my friend, here we are."

Tori shook her head, looking him in the eye. "Why?"

"Ahh." His eyes brightened. "You want answers?"

"I want *all* the answers. I think I've already figured some of them out, but I want them all."

"Where do you want to start?"

"Where do you think?"

"You're sure you can handle it?"

"Let's find out."

Warner sat back down and relaxed, crossing his right leg over his left. "You know, honestly, I didn't intend to kill Jessie that night. I wanted Jessie—hell, I wanted Jessie *and* you. You were both hot, and you were both ready to give it up. I mean, you were off that night with Jason Rushton for that very reason, right?"

"I had the good sense to pick someone decent."

"Tell me, being off with Mr. Decent, isn't that why you felt *so* guilty about that night? That you weren't with Jessie? You have to have thought for these last twenty years, if only *you* were there, if only *you* hadn't been so selfish off popping that cherry, Jessie would be alive."

Tori stared angrily, seething.

"Oh, you have felt that, haven't you?" Jeff hissed with a self-satisfied smirk. "The guilt has eaten at you for years, hasn't it? I bet that guilt is the fuel that drove you, isn't it? *Isn't it?*"

Tori didn't respond. Her expression answered the question.

"I figured," Warner continued. "You know, the Internet is such a beautiful thing, especially if you're an expert researcher, which, of course, I am. It let me follow you, your career, your ascension in the FBI. You know, Tori, you've really had a remarkable career. I applaud you for it."

Tori snorted. "Right."

"No, now there's where you're *wrong*, Tori. I do, I honestly do," Warner replied without any hint of condescension. "I respect it. I respect excellence because I exude it in everything I do, and you do, too. Saving and returning all those children to their families. You're a legend."

"Whatever."

"It's admirable, it really is. You've made an impact. You've made a big difference in people's lives. You will leave an impressive legacy behind when your name goes up on the FBI Wall of Honor. But that impact also allowed me to keep tabs on you, to watch you. Not that you knew, of course."

"Watch me?"

"Sure. Business took me to New York every so often. I tracked you down; it wasn't hard. I watched you exit the FBI field office and followed you to your condo. I've watched you take your long runs along the Hudson, all sleek and sexy in your designer running clothes and shoes. Hell, I was sitting on a park bench two different days last summer, in sunglasses reading the *Times*. You went running right on by, so focused and intense and pushing yourself to the extreme, oblivious that I, your old friend, was sitting right there. I could have literally reached out and touched you, we were *that* close."

Warner stood up from his stool and eyed her up before taking a step forward. She steadied herself as he raised the knife, brushing it lightly along her face then slowly tracing her neckline and down her sternum, sliding the tip of the knife underneath her breasts.

Tori just stared straight ahead, holding her breath, rigid.

"You're in such amazing shape," he remarked as he walked behind her. "That night we were walking to the Steamboat Bay Tap Room, do you remember that? The whole time we were walking down the street, I hung a step or two behind just so I could check out your tight little ass and those toned legs. I thought you were absolutely phenomenal for thirty-seven. I've been envious of Braddock, getting to repeatedly tap all that. He just doesn't deserve it."

That drew a glare from her.

Warner just snickered. "I even watched you compete in a triathlon once, out on Long Island. You're really quite intense and determined in everything you do."

"Glad I was able to provide you such entertainment."

"Oh, I don't think it was entertainment per se. It was more just keeping track, anticipating that a day might come when we would confront one another. And now… here it is."

"Is this a confrontation?" Tori asked, looking up, her eyes piercing. "Doesn't a confrontation connote a reciprocal opportunity?"

"It's not my fault that you didn't see me coming."

"Is that what happened to Jessie? She didn't see it coming, did she?"

Warner sat back down on the stool. "Well, it started when I drove up and stopped beside her. She had that flat tire and she looked at me like I was her hero."

"A tire that *you* made go flat."

Warner blew past the comment. "I knew you weren't with Jessie. I knew that she'd be alone. I punched that hole in it when we were at the party that you skipped because you were where again?"

Tori didn't respond.

"It worked perfectly, of course," Warner continued cockily, basking in the glory of his victory. "I told Eddie I needed to leave early but after he dropped me off, I made my way back to Peterson's. I followed Jessie as she drove out to Katy's and dropped her off. I could see the tire was riding low when she left Katy's house. The question was, would it give out before she got home?"

It was all Tori could do to not jump off the chair after him.

"Of course, it gave way, and just four or five miles from home. Oh so close, yet oh so far away."

Tori could do nothing but glare at him, breathing through her nose.

"I drove up after she pulled over to the side of the road on 48. She got right in the car, thanking me for coming along, glad that it was me. She didn't even ask me what I was doing there. Jessie wasn't the least bit suspicious. Heck, she didn't even ask me to take her home. She just *assumed* I would. She always just assumed boys would do whatever she wanted, whenever she wanted it."

He looked Tori in the eye. "You know it's true about her. Toying with people, playing with them."

"She wasn't a mean girl, Jeff," Tori growled in reply.

"You sure about that? She played head games all the damned time," Warner railed. "Well, I had her in the car, and I had a fucking game for her."

"She didn't want to play."

"She *should* have wanted to."

"Couldn't handle rejection, could you?" Tori snorted. "Not the great Jeff Warner, not the smartest guy in school, the class president, football quarterback, Mr. Perfect. Nobody could *ever* say no to you. You were just entitled to whatever you wanted."

"I'd be very careful if I were you," he replied darkly, gripping the knife hard in his right hand. "I can skip the answers and get right to it, you know. I owe you nothing."

Tori shook her head, looking away. It was an idle threat. He was too self-satisfied. He was just getting rolling.

"I drove for a while and then pulled over off the road to make my move. I kissed her, but… the little whore, she resisted."

"Oh, I bet she did."

"She was just playing hard to get, like she always did. Jessie the fucking tease, playing her fucking games. Well, I was *done* with games. I wanted it, I wanted her, and deep down despite what she was fronting, she wanted it, too."

"She didn't want you. She wanted nothing to do with you. *You* weren't good enough for her. She thought you were so arrogant and full of yourself."

"That bitch!" Warner screamed as he leapt up and slapped her with the back of his hand, knocking her off the stool and sending her careening face-first into the cinder block wall.

"*Ooh*," she groaned. Her cheek seared in pain and her head ached as she looked up through blurred vision to see Warner standing over her, enraged, his body quaking, and the tip of the knife shuddering mere inches away from her face. With the rage seething out of him, Tori thought this was the end and steeled herself for what was next. But he just stood over her, and slowly his breathing eased, though the viciousness of his expression lingered. He pushed her hard onto her stomach and then yanked her up off the floor by her bound wrists before shoving her back down on the stool.

With the side of her face throbbing, Tori closed her eyes and tried to get her own breathing under control. Warner sat back down on his stool, still a ball of wrath. She needed to keep him talking. "My sister fought back, didn't she?" she asked through gritted teeth, feeling the metallic taste of blood in her mouth.

Warner burped out a sadistic laugh. "She slapped me then punched me. Can you believe that shit? Little Jessie punched me."

"She fought," Tori replied after spitting out blood to the floor. "I'd love to have the same chance. I dare you to give me the same chance."

"Oh, she fought alright. She reached for the car door handle to try and get out, to get away. That was her big mistake. I couldn't let her go then."

"You hit her."

"I had to subdue her, and you know what?"

"Oh, I know. You liked it, Jeff. I've seen your handiwork."

Warner nodded. "Oh yeah—I got off on it," he added, the savagery returning to his eyes and the deep wrath to his voice. "It was the *power* of it. I *owned* her. I could do whatever I wanted. Jessie wasn't dictating the terms anymore—I was. I hit her again and then I got on top of her and ripped her blouse open and yanked off her shorts and undies." Warner was suddenly euphoric, reliving it, back in the moment. "Your sister was so hot—just like you are now. Her body was perfect, her little round firm B-cup tits, the flat stomach, and that tiny, tight little athletic ass."

"No!" Tori howled. "How could you?"

"And Jessie fought back, which made it all the better. The fury of it all. I hit her again, and then again, and then I flipped her over on her stomach, and then…" He leaned forward, getting in Tori's face. "I fucked your sister. I fucked her so hard."

"You sick fucking piece of shit," Tori growled before spitting in his face.

Warner burst off the stool and punched Tori in the face, just below her left eye, knocking her backward onto the old desk. Her momentum carried her over the top of it and she tumbled hard to the floor on the other side, scraping her face along the wall on the way down.

As she lay on the floor with her face aching and head throbbing, she could hear his unhurried footsteps. He slowly came around the desk and once again stood towering over her.

"That's how I hit her, Tori. You're just like your sister; you never learned to submit."

Tori spit out blood, looking back up from the cold cement floor through blurred vision, breathing hard yet grimacing out a bloody smile. "I bet you say that to all the girls."

Warner croaked out a sick laugh as he reached down, hoisted her up again, and dragged her back around the front of the desk. He picked up the stool and pushed her back down on it before going back to his own. Tori closed her eyes and tried calming her breathing while her face and forehead ached, the stinging pain pulsating through her head.

"Hurts, don't it?"

Tori just kept inhaling long breaths through her nose, her eyes closed, re-steeling herself. There was more pain to come.

"Come on now, Tori," he teased, snapping his fingers in her face. "Pay attention."

She slowly opened her eyes and bored in on Warner. She spit more blood out of her mouth as if to say, *Bring it.*

*

Braddock and Kyle moved up into the home office, where the map of all the women was still taped up on the wall. Kyle was transfixed by it, shaking his head at the detail and the dead women tied to his business. "What have I allowed to happen?" he murmured in dismay.

"Kyle, think. Come on. You know Warner—where would he take her?"

"Uh, I… don't know, Will. I-I-I just don't know," Mannion stammered. "God, if anything happens to her…"

"We just have to find them," Braddock replied as he looked at the map up on the wall, focusing on the dots for Jessie and Lash around Manchester Bay. "If he has her, he'll need privacy. And he couldn't be on the road long with her. It's too risky. He'd have a place to take her."

"What's he going to do with her?" Kyle asked.

Braddock turned and shook his head.

"Oh God," Kyle croaked out.

"So, where would he go?" Braddock muttered. "Where would he go? Does he own any other property?"

"Umm…" Kyle's eyes brightened. "Well, there's his mother's old house. Out on County Road 48."

"County Road 48?"

"Yeah. Jeff's parents divorced when we were kids. His dad lived here in town. His mom had an old family place out on 48. The property has a family cemetery on it, so Jeff kept it."

Braddock spun around.

On the wall behind his desk was another map. It was a framed map of Manchester Bay and Northern Pine Lake and the sur-rounding area, a touristy map he liked. He'd had it matted and framed for the office. The map included all of the roads and the smaller nearby lakes on the Northern Pine chain. The eastern shore of Northern Pine ran at a rough angle to the northeast. The new H-4 bypass ran at roughly the same northeast angle a mile east of the lake until it reached the northeastern corner, where the bypass bowed out further east at least another mile before eventually looping back northwest another two miles before straightening out north on its way up to Holmestrand. County Road 48 hewed tight to the east side of the lake for three miles out of town before snaking its way east-northeast from the lake through the area of the bow until it reached the H-4.

"Where is Warner's place?"

"Right here." Kyle pointed to land on the north side of the road, a mile short of the H-4.

"Is that why Katy Anderson went missing?" Braddock asked, tapping the place on the map.

"Katy Anderson?" Kyle asked. "What…?"

"That bulge in the bypass." Braddock pointed to it. "That was all because you and Jeff Warner led a group that raised holy hell about the bypass, so it would go by your land for your corporate campus."

"Well… that wasn't the only reason…"

"I don't care about that now, but the original H-4 bypass path was a more direct northern route that would have gone right through—"

"Warner's property," Kyle finished for him, getting what Braddock was driving at. "But what's the significance of Katy?"

"Katy was last seen there by two witnesses who drove by her. She was there a few nights after Genevieve Lash went missing. She went there after Tori and I went out to see her, and Warner's property is there and…" He looked over to Kyle Mannion. "Let's go."

CHAPTER THIRTY-FOUR

"You're fighting, you're defiant. *I love it.*"

Warner was so satisfied with himself he was rolling now. It was like with Eddie—he wanted to talk; she just had to lead him. While listening to him and prodding him along, Tori was at the same time starting to strategically evaluate her surroundings. Despite his size and strength, straight up, she could fight Warner, she could hurt him enough to get away. So while Warner droned along, her main thought was: *how could she get loose?*

"After I did Jessie, I realized how much I liked it. And it wasn't the sex, Tori, it was the…"

"Power."

"Oh yeah, you understand, I knew you would. You get it, Tori, you get it. I always knew you would."

"I understand the mind. I've spent years chasing child predators. You're not much different."

"Then you'll understand that after a while I realized sex was… boring compared to this. I mean sex was something to get, to pursue, to have, but I didn't need it. It didn't satisfy me, not like *this* does. This? What I have right now, right here, I *need*."

"I know."

"After Jessie, I eventually needed to do it again, and then again, and then again. I mean, not weekly or monthly, but every so often

I needed that fix, and those out-of-town trips to open those god-awful sports bars in all those college towns were perfect. I could get out of town, find a girl at the bar or at a nearby business, bring her back here, and have my way with her for as long as I wanted, to do *whatever* I wanted."

"Let me ask, were there girls when you were in college? Did you kill then? After Jessie."

Warner grinned. "You're smart, Tori. To answer your question, you can't possibly think I could have stopped when I was in Arizona."

Tori shook her head in disgust.

"There were two in Mesa, right by school, and then one down in Tucson. I buried them all way out in the desert. Then I came back home and, well, I had this," Warner stated, waving to the room. "Grandma was dead. Mom eventually died of cancer. I had a… playroom."

"What about the five you killed and left in the trunks of cars? Why treat them so different? Why deny them this room?"

"So I could use someone like Sarah Craig to fuck over the Mannions."

Tori shook her head in amazement. "You just want to destroy everybody here, don't you?"

"Yes, but I wanted to use *you* to do that for me. I wanted you to tear down Kyle and Eddie and their town. I mean, who better to do it than you? The person whose life was forever changed, damaged by the tragedy of Manchester Bay? And you've done it for me."

Tori shook her head in anger. She'd been lured and then played.

"Eddie is going to be arrested, and from there it's just a matter of time before Kyle goes down, too."

"You're going to go down for all of this. Maybe not now but you will."

Warner was unfazed. "No, Tori, I'm not. I'm playing chess and the rest of the world is playing checkers," he replied with a demented grin, twirling the knife in his hand, all impressed with himself. "I'm winning and I'm about to achieve the ultimate victory."

"Which is what, exactly?"

"Two things. I've really wanted to fuck over Kyle, Eddie, and this whole damn town that worships at the Mannion altar. Thanks to you and Braddock, I'm getting it. But I've also long wondered what it might be like to have *you* in this room. I've thought time and again about what it would be like to get the great Tori Hunter down here. And you know what? It's better than I could have ever imagined. You're fighting, you're defiant. *I love it.* You're so different from the others."

"Different? How am I different, Jeff? How am I any less of a victim?"

"Because you're not pleading and whimpering for your life—at least not yet."

"In your dreams, asshole."

"We'll see," Warner snickered. "We'll see. It's amazing what a woman will say when she's sitting there on that stool, just like you are now. After she's suffered how you're going to suffer."

"Here? You sat here and talked to them just like this?"

"Sure, although you and I are old friends and we have so much to discuss. As for all of those other women, they're sitting there desperately thinking that if they can say just the right thing, in just the right tone, I'll spare them." Warner laughed, shaking his head. "It's such a waste of time. I can't let them go, and *you*, more than anyone else who has ever been in this room, understand that. I learned that with Jessie. After I finished with her, after I'd had my way with her, I couldn't very well let her go home to her father, to the *sheriff*. I mean, what would have happened to me?"

"Where is she?"

"Jessie?" Warner glanced to his right. "Oh, she's probably about seventy-five feet to your left from here. She's been there since about two weeks after I killed her. Until things calmed down, I hid her body up on the Mannion hunting property, not far from where you found Katy's car. Then, when it was safe, I brought her body out here to bury it."

Tori glanced to the left.

"That's right, Tori," Warner replied, getting off his stool, moving into her line of vision. "Jessie is right out there. They're *all* out there. All those missing women you and Braddock identified. They're out there in that cemetery."

Tori just looked to the wall, envisioning Jessie out there. Now she knew what had happened to her, what had happened to them all. Now she knew the fate that awaited.

Warner shook his head. "I must say, I kind of underestimated you and Braddock."

Tori turned her eyes back to him. "How so?"

"I thought this would take a lot longer to all play out. *A lot longer*. I figured I'd have to leave out this long trail of breadcrumbs. But then to my great surprise, I learned you and Braddock were onto all of these other women. I thought that would take a lot longer, and then I realized in watching the two of you that you'd tied it all to the restaurants. I was surprised. That was impressive."

Tori shook her head. "Whatever, Jeff."

"No, it was extraordinary. How'd you do that?"

Tori didn't respond.

"Seriously, how did you do that?"

"Whatever."

"I'm serious. How did you do that?"

"Wouldn't you like to know?" Tori sneered.

Warner took a step forward and slapped her with the back of his hand. It was a hard smack, not so hard as to knock her off the chair but enough that it stung. "I won't be so gentle again, Tori. Answer my question, please."

Tori glared back at Warner and then snorted a bloody laugh. "Would you believe the Mannion's pizza box covers?"

Warner looked at her, perplexed. "Really?"

"We matched the map on the front of the pizza box to the map we had of all of the killings. It matched up almost perfectly. Once we put it all together, the restaurants and the women, we did it all in about an hour."

"The pizza box covers. Huh." Warner shook his head, still stunned. "I never even thought of that. Doesn't happen often."

"You set up Gunther, didn't you?"

"And you found everything I wanted you to find, including the cigarette butts, right?" Warner answered. "And you ran those through a DNA database, figuring you'd match it up to Gunther, and then… they didn't, right?"

Tori nodded. "How do you know all of this?"

"A little from Cal Lund, but Backstrom for most of it. He is very good at staying informed himself. He likes to be the big shot, to talk, to sound important, to keep in Kyle's and my good graces. I'd just go to lunch with him and get everything I needed."

"Politicians," Tori said bitterly. "They're such inveterate asskissers for money."

"That's what makes them useful. I'd get information from him, and I was watching you and Braddock, so I knew where you two were going with the investigation. All it needed was a little nudge here and there."

"Such as killing me and Will?"

Warner nodded. "I missed you, intentionally so, but I wanted him dead to turn up the heat. That fucker should be dead. Using his remote starter in the middle of summer—who'd have thunk that?"

"You missed me? Intentionally?"

"Come on, Tori, you were standing still. It was an easy shot to hit the water bottle. That I nicked your hand was a nice touch, I thought. And for the record, I could have had you on any of the other shots I took as you ran through that field and then dove into the trees. Bet I scared the shit out of you, didn't I?"

Tori closed her eyes and shook her head.

"Of course, then it only took you guys a few hours to get onto Gunther. His van, reputation, and the fact he pinched Lash on the ass all made him useful. If the case was about all those missing women, I expected anyone who investigated it to have doubts about Gunther in time. That dumbass slyly picking up those women without a trace? Come on, it doesn't stand up to logic when you really work through it. I mean, that's what you and Braddock thought, right?"

Tori slowly nodded her head.

"Which is why Braddock got Gunther's attendance records from Kyle, and they showed he couldn't have done those women."

"It was you who was driving the van."

"I spiked Gunther's bourbon when we were at Eddie's. God, he was a puddle at the end of the night. Eddie carried him back to the bedroom, and while he did, I made a clay impression of the van key. Came out later that night and took the van. I knew Gunther wouldn't be up until noon at least. Plenty of time to get the van back, and it worked perfectly, of course."

"And then you killed him, didn't you?"

"You could always count on Gunther to drink his sorrows away," he replied flatly. "Eddie called me and said you two were all over Gunther such that he thought he needed a lawyer and asked if I could help him find one. He also said that Gunther was going up to his cabin. From there it was easy. I knew what the dumbass redneck was doing. Sure enough, I get to the cabin and he's drunk. He made it so easy. I just had to wait for him to pass out, pop him, and then leave. It was all part of the plan."

"To lead us to Eddie."

"Well, if it wasn't Gunther, he clearly was set up by someone. Who set him up and why? The setup had to be just a tiny bit sloppy, so it looked like Eddie did it. So, I laid out just a few crumbs to Eddie, and you and Braddock brilliantly yet dutifully followed them."

"This is all just a game to you, you narcissistic piece of shit."

Warner just shrugged. "You two did a good job of playing it. I had plenty more little clues or threads I could have put out there, but I didn't need to. You two were on Eddie just like that, and if things had broken right, you might have even swept up Kyle in the process. I mean, think about it. Who'd ever think of a *double* setup? It's fucking brilliant."

"I thought Eddie was your friend. He's been your friend since we were kids, Jeff. We were all friends—you, me, Jessie, Eddie, Steak, Corinne, Mickey, Lizzy."

"Friends," Warner huffed. "There's a quaint thought."

"You don't believe in friendship, Jeff? Are you *that* broken?"

"People are either useful or they're not. When they're no longer useful, you no longer need them, and you get rid of them."

"And Gunther was no longer useful? Eddie is no longer useful, then?"

"Eddie is what he always was—a tool. Kyle's been carrying his ass forever, burying this fuckup or that one. I carried his dumb ass too, getting all those restaurants open. You think Eddie was capable of any of that shit? Irv beat him into a mental mess. And Kyle? You think Kyle would get to where he's gotten to without me and all the shit I did for him and for the company? All the work I did to launch business after business for that ungrateful prick, and Kyle thought he could screw me out of my piece of it!" Warner screamed. "I don't think so!"

"What did you do, Jeff?" Tori asked, spitting away some more blood. "How is it Kyle screwed you?"

"I did all that work for Kyle. I set his ass up and negotiated all these deals for him, made him all his money. He's a billionaire because of me."

"*Right*," Tori replied through a bloody smile. "Kyle had *nothing* to do with any of it. No brains. No smarts. No guile."

Warner's eyes narrowed, his muscles tensing. Tori readied herself for the strike.

It didn't come.

"That's bullshit, Tori!" he yelled, gesturing with the knife before walking in a slow circle around the cellar, his muscles tensed again, the anger in him rising. He stopped and looked her in the eye. "Tell me you don't get sick of special agents in charge taking credit for all of your work. You rescued that girl in Iowa, and did you get any credit? Were you on the news? Did the press ask you any questions?"

"My reward was the girl being safe."

"Give me a fucking break, Tori," he replied bitterly. "You wanted the credit. You crave it."

"No, I don't," Tori answered. "I'm not motivated by credit; I'm motivated by what happened to me, by what you did to Jessie. I just want families to have their kids come back."

"Oh, you're *sooooo* selfless," Warner mocked. "What a life it's left you. Nothing but work. No husband, no children, no family, nothing but… loneliness."

"I don't regret my sacrifices. As a matter of fact, sitting here right now, knowing what fate awaits, I'm proud of my life. You're going to take what you're going to take, but you won't take that."

"You keep telling yourself that for what little time you have left here. But Kyle? He'd be nothing without me. He'd never be remotely close to where he is today without *me*."

"You didn't get anything out of the deal, Jeff? He didn't make you any money?" Tori asked incredulously. "You're a partner with a national law firm. You don't seem to be living check to check from what I can tell. I've been to your house on the lake."

"He paid the bills that I sent him, but his company and the millions—fuck, billions—he was going to make? I set all that up for him, *all of it*. And I'm finally supposed to get a piece of it, but he takes it away because I got fresh with a secretary or two. Because I put my hands on Jerry Lash's employee's ass? That means I lose my stock, my money, my payday? Fuck no! *Fuck no.*"

"That explains Genevieve Lash. There *was* a reason you chose her." Tori realized Braddock had been right to focus on her all along. "So that's what this all is? An elaborate setup of the Mannions?"

"It's part of it. I want to ruin them. I want to fuck them and then fuck you. Win-win. It's a clean sweep."

"Is it, though?"

"What?"

"Have you ruined them? Now that you've taken me, that whole setup falls apart, doesn't it?" Tori asked.

"That's not an issue," Warner replied confidently. "You found Katy's car on Eddie's hunting property, didn't you?"

Tori didn't respond. She wanted him to keep talking.

"And what's funny is, I bet before you did, you had some doubts as to whether it was Eddie, didn't you? At least, that's what Westlund told us. He thought Eddie might have gotten you to have doubts. You couldn't believe your childhood friend could have done that to your sister."

"Turns out I was right."

"And look what it got you. I mean, had you gone all in on Eddie today and arrested him, I might have let this little thing between you and me pass, at least for now. I could have come after you later but there was just enough doubt that I had to take you now and finish this off."

Tori coughed and spit out more blood before turning her eyes to Warner, shaking her head in pity at him. "You always thought you were the smartest. You had that arrogance, the cockiness that you were superior, and you always wanted people to acknowledge it—to kiss the ring. But other people are smart, too. Kyle Mannion will figure this out. He'll realize it wasn't *just* Eddie at all those places; the records will show you were there, too. It isn't Eddie or Kyle Mannion who has me here—*you do*. They'll both have alibis for tonight, you can count on it. Hell, we have twenty-four-hour surveillance on Eddie right now. You'll get me tonight, sure, but your burning desire to beat me, to get your clean sweep, is going to cost you the whole game. It's only a matter of time before the Mannions and Will figure this all out."

Tori kept her eyes on Warner, his expression twitching ever so slightly, a hint of doubt in his mind. He paced around the room again, for once quiet and deep in thought, running the scenario through his head. After a moment, he spoke again.

"Tori, you really, *really* disappointed me just now."

"How so?"

"You haven't lost your Minnesota DNA. That was such a wonderfully passive-aggressive way of pleading for your life."

Tori coughed up a laugh. "I wouldn't give you the satisfaction of that. I'm not going to beg."

"Oh, I bet you will. Before I'm done, you'll beg me to end it. They *all* do," Warner replied, gesturing at her with the large knife. "And let me tell you why you're wrong. Sure, there will be some records of me in those towns, too—I did all that work. But for only half of the women will the records show me being in those towns *when* they disappeared. However, as you already know, and as I have made certain, for Eddie they show him *always* there. Eddie is my insurance policy.

"See, I don't like to fly on that small corporate jet. For some reason it freaks me out. My solution was to drive to most of these places. Then I'd make a point of leaving to come back here, but I'd drive back to those towns and I'd take those women *after* the records show that I'd left town. Then I'd bring those women back here."

Tori shook her head in dismay at the sick wickedness of it all.

"So, Tori, you're wrong. *Everyone* is going to look at Kyle and Eddie when you're gone, disappeared, vanished. Tomorrow, when you're under six feet of soil, it'll be obvious who is to blame. The Mannions will be the prime suspects, especially after I take out Braddock in the next day or two—and this time I won't miss him. Heck, to make it look truly awful, I'll take out Braddock and his kid. Who would have more motive than the Mannions? The danger that such an investigation poses to the company and the fortune… They'd do *anything* to protect it."

"Nobody will believe that."

"Yes, they will. I've seen to it."

"You're insane."

"No, just insanely intelligent. I still have access to everything at the company. You know what else I have?"

"What?"

"I have two million in a Cayman Islands bank account that I've siphoned from the company, and nobody knows about it. Nobody will detect it. The auditors go through the books year after year, and nada. I've laundered that money with some other folks down there who know people who will kill if you ask the right way and pay them. You think I haven't already created the documentation and a money trail to a numbered account in Zurich? That money went to the account when? A week ago—two weeks after who came back to town for the first time in twenty years to investigate her sister's disappearance? That money is now gone. Collected by who? The person who will have killed Braddock, or so it will appear.

"Now there is a little transaction I added back in, traceable in the company's corporate records, for those dollars—and who'll be at the company, overseeing discovery responses to the criminal investigation as corporate counsel? That's right, me. I won't make it easy. I'll put up a big fight, but I will make sure that record is discovered. Kyle is worth over a billion. With so much to risk, they'll see this record and *know* it was him. With all of that, *nobody* will ever look to me, Tori, nobody. As good as you are, as good as I've discovered Braddock to be, you still are *so* far behind."

Tori shook her head in disbelief at him.

"You see, Kyle isn't that smart. And as for Braddock…" Warner laughed and gave a dismissive wave. "Honestly, Tori, I think all that sex you've been having with him has caused you to overestimate what he's really capable of."

"How long have you been following me, Jeff?"

"Pretty much since you got here, even the other night, all the way back to Braddock's house. Oh… I could hear it the other night, Tori. I stood right below that bedroom window just feet away, listening to you two up there, you and Braddock carrying on with each other. Was it really *that* good? Tell me, Tori, is it the best you've ever had?"

"Like I'd give you the satisfaction. He's a man, which is more than I can say for you."

Warner leapt forward, slapping her across the face again, leaving her teetering on the edge of her stool before she tipped off. She plummeted to the floor, contorting her body in the air to land on her right shoulder, letting it take the brunt of the fall.

Damn my smart mouth, Tori thought as she saw stars from the slap. *Don't fire back. Don't push him that way.* She needed to keep Warner going, keep him basking in the brilliance of his plans. There was plenty to ask him about, and he was in love with his own genius. She had to keep using that.

"Why Katy?" Tori asked after a moment, looking up from the floor. "What happened to Katy?"

"Katy." Warner shook his head as he lifted her back up by her restraints and sat her down, this time more gently, on the stool. "That was not a contingency I planned for, I can tell you that."

"Why kill her? What did she do? She's not your type."

"You're definitely right about that."

"So why?"

"She left me no choice," he pleaded and then gestured to his right, to outside the cellar. "I'm out there burying Genevieve Lash and Katy comes waddling up the hill from down on County 48. Surprised the hell out of me."

"And you killed her, just like you're going to kill me?"

"No. No, no, no." Warner shook his head. "Not just like you. Not just like the others. Are you kidding me? Katy had no business being in this room. No, I just hit her on the head with a shovel and stuffed her in the trunk of her car."

*

"The gate is up on the right," Kyle directed.

"Gate?"

"Yeah, he has a big iron gate for the road up to the house," Kyle replied. "I asked him about it once. He said it keeps people from driving up the road. Apparently, there was an issue with that once, someone breaking into the house, which I guess is in the same state it was in when his mother died. He keeps it as some sort of shrine to her."

"If I had a nickel for every serial killer who had mommy issues." Braddock sighed as he pulled to a stop where the edge of the driveway met the road. He peered up to his right and saw the iron gate ten yards up the driveway. "What else do you know about the property?"

"There is the main two-story house at the top of the driveway, and then behind the house to the left down a narrow path that's, I don't know, fifty or sixty yards, is where the little family cemetery is located," Kyle answered. "There is a light pole out there and another small house."

"Okay. Anything else?"

"He likes guns. He shoots competitively and likes to hit gun shows. I know he owns an arsenal. He keeps a gun case down in the cellar of that little house by the cemetery. If he's here with her, that's where he'd have her, and if that's where he has her, he'll have guns at his disposal."

"Wonderful."

Braddock turned off the Explorer's headlights and pulled into the driveway and up to the iron gate. He got out and checked the sturdiness of the gate. It was closed and locked but there was a narrow gap between the two swinging halves that provided some give. He ran to the back of his department replacement Explorer and opened the rear tailgate. Kyle joined him, and Braddock handed him the shotgun. "You know how to use one of these?"

Kyle took the shotgun and chambered two shells. "I hunt, too. What do you need me to do?"

"Work your way west around to that little house, but maintain your cover in the woods," Braddock answered while he released, checked, and then slid the magazine back in his Glock. He grabbed two more magazines and stuffed them in his back pocket. "It might get a little sporty around here."

"What are you doing?"

"Giving you a minute and then I'm ramming this gate with the lights and siren on. I'm going right up that driveway. If he's down at the little house, I'm going to draw him away."

"What am I doing?" Kyle asked.

"Finding Tori."

*

Warner was starting to tire of the questions. The answers were shorter. His face was less animated.

She could see the mounting hunger in his eyes, the craving for her, and then there was the aggressive, almost animal-like posture he was starting to assume. He'd been pacing around, stalking around her slowly, lightly brushing her face with the knife, teasing her, making her wonder and anticipate when the assault would start. Then when he was done, after he was good and satisfied and the domination complete, the knife would be coming. She could feel the jagged edge of it now as Warner lightly grazed it down her cheek.

Tori just sat still, staring forward, but one thing that had happened in the times he'd hit her and knocked her off the stool was that her restraints had loosened ever so slightly, especially around her ankles. If she was going to use that somehow, she needed to keep him in front of her.

Warner stood there now, leering hungrily.

Tori avoided eye contact, staring straight ahead, but then she darted her eyes slightly right and her heart skipped a beat. On the monitor on the workbench she could see an Explorer at the iron gate. A man got out.

It was Braddock.

She could tell by his height and his gait. He was testing the iron gate.

Tori flashed her eyes left, back to Warner, meeting his eyes for a moment. *Keep him focused on you*, she thought.

Warner moved in and she steadied herself, watching the knife, which he left hanging at his right side. Instead, with his left hand, Warner grabbed the collar of her blouse and ripped it down, popping the buttons off, exposing her chest.

"So nice," he murmured sickly, staring at her breasts. "Oh, so nice."

Tori kept her face tilted down but her eyes slyly glanced back right again, looking at the monitor.

The Explorer with lights flashing was coming fast, turning right into the driveway, and charging the gate.

"I'm going to enjoy—"

There was a faint sound of a siren. Then the truck hit the gate and there was a loud distant crash.

Warner wheeled around at the sound, looking to the monitor.

Tori leapt off the stool and jumped forward, throwing her shoulder into Warner's back, knocking him off balance. Her shove sent him staggering forward, crashing into the steps.

She managed to keep her balance. Still on her feet, crouching with her knees bent, she angled her body with her left foot slightly forward.

Warner leapt up and charged her, leading with the knife.

Tori was ready for him with her knees bent, her legs coiled, and up on her toes.

When he was two steps away, she jumped back and kicked out and up with her legs, catching him with her feet, her heels landing square in his sternum. The force of the kick sent him careening backward again. The knife went flying out of his hand as he landed awkwardly against the left edge of the steps before crumpling down to the floor.

Tori rolled over on her right side.

Dazed yet raging, Warner pushed himself up to his feet and quickly searched for the knife, but he couldn't find it. He gave up the search and went for the gun case, opening the door.

Tori struggled to push herself up onto her knees and with a grunt rocked up to her feet, keeping her eyes on Warner.

He'd pulled out an AR-15 and was slamming in a magazine.

Tori turned to the right, hopped once, and dove forward for the top of the desk. She landed on the slick top, slid over, and then crashed down the other side to the floor as the shots from Warner whizzed overhead, hitting the cinder block wall just above her and then into the metal desk.

"Will! Will! Will!"

*

The house was dark, but as he glanced to the left, Braddock saw Tori's rental car parked down at the little house that Kyle had described. He sped forward and came to a screeching stop thirty feet short of her car, with his driver's side door open before he'd even stopped. He jumped out and heard her voice.

"Will! Will! Will!"

"Tori! Tori!"

He took two quick running steps forward before he saw movement at the door of the shed. "Oh, shit!"

Warner had appeared in the doorway. He had an assault rifle.

Braddock dove back and away as the hail of shots pelted the Explorer. He scrambled on all fours to the back of the vehicle as shattered glass rained down on him. Braddock worked his way around the back and over to the rear passenger side and peeked around the corner.

Warner saw him and fired. Braddock ducked back; more glass shards showered down.

"I know it's you, Warner!" Braddock yelled, peering around the back corner.

Another hail of shots fired at him from the shed.

As the Explorer was pelted, Braddock looked back to the treeline, which was fifteen yards away. *I can make that*, he thought. He stayed low as he set his feet to fire, preparing to run. "I know you've killed all those women, Warner, you sick fuck. It's not Eddie Mannion, it's you, Warner! It's you!" Braddock yelled as the shots kept coming. And then the shots stopped.

The magazine was empty.

Warner would have another.

Braddock peered around once more and saw Warner pulling out the expended magazine. He rose up and fired at the open door; Warner ducked back inside.

He took off and sprinted for the woods, reaching the edge and diving forward just as Warner fired again.

*

Tori could hear the mass of gunfire and then she heard Braddock's voice. After another long moment there was more firing, but she sensed it was moving away and she squirmed forward to look around the corner of the desk. She peered up the steps but couldn't see anything. There were ten steps up. They were steep. The door was open. *I can make it*, she thought.

She strained to push herself back up off the floor, fighting against the restraints, when she glanced back to the stairway. Kyle

Mannion, with a shotgun in hand, was coming down the steps, alternately looking back up and then over to Tori.

"Get me out of here!" she exclaimed.

Kyle saw the nylon cuffs and went to the workbench, frantically looking for something to cut them with.

Tori pushed herself up and hopped toward the workbench to join him when she saw the knife. "Kyle, on the floor, under the steps!"

Kyle turned around, reached down, and grabbed the knife. He started slicing through the cuffs, first freeing her hands then cutting her legs loose.

"We gotta help Will. Is that thing loaded?"

"Locked and cocked."

Tori took it from him, and ignoring the tingling and numbness in her legs, feet, and hands, she ran up the steps.

*

The blind dive into the woods was a bad move.

Braddock tumbled down the steep hill, head over heels, until he crashed against the base of a tree. He was deeper into the woods, but he was now in a narrow crevice that looked back uphill, ceding the high ground to Warner. He was lamenting his attire, especially his light-colored shirt and shorts. He got to his feet and peered back up the steep hill with his gun up, scanning. He sensed movement to his left.

Warner had flanked him.

The first shot jerked Braddock to the right, his upper right arm grazed. He spun away, stumbling, but staying on his feet, he ran and jumped through the woods, deeper into the crevice, trying to evade fire.

"Ahh!"

He'd been hit on his lower left side, knocking him off his feet. He somersaulted uncontrollably twice before his back landed hard against the massive trunk of a downed tree.

"Aw, man," he groaned. Breathing hard, he looked up to see Warner approaching him, carefully working his way down the hill with the steep grade and gravity bringing him rapidly closer. His own gun was lying on the ground ten feet to his right. Braddock tried to move and crawl over to it, but his body wasn't responding.

"I have to admit, Will," Warner said breezily from ten feet away, raising his rifle and setting his feet, getting ready to finish him off, "I didn't think you were smart enough to truly figure it all out. Well done, really, well done. But I'm afraid you still lose the game."

Braddock snorted a laugh. He looked down to his bloodstained lower left abdomen before looking back up at Warner, then leaned his head against the tree trunk. "You know what helped me, Warner? You know what *really* helped?"

"No, what?"

Braddock smiled, a bloody grimace. "A really… good…" And then his pupils rolled left. "Partner."

Warner spun to his right.

The first shot from Tori hit Warner in the left shoulder, twisting his body toward her. Then it was on. Tori *and* Kyle, who'd grabbed another shotgun from the gun case in Warner's basement, both unloaded. The impact of the shots strafed Warner as he tumbled backward into a pile of brush and cut branches, his assault rifle falling out of his hands to the ground.

"Will! Will!" Tori exclaimed as she and Kyle quickly worked their way down the rest of the steep pitch of the hill. Tori stepped over Warner, still coming to Braddock, while Kyle stopped. He kicked at Warner's leg before shooting him twice in the chest at close range—finishing him off.

Tori kneeled to Braddock's left.

"Took you two—" Braddock coughed out with a wan smile, spurting blood "—long enough."

"Stay still. Try not to move," Tori ordered worriedly, carefully lifting away his shirt and inspecting the wound.

"Man, that Explorer, did you see it? It's like me, all shot up," Braddock said before coughing. "Two vehicles in a week. Cal will never give me… he'll never give me another one."

"Is that really your biggest problem at the moment?"

Braddock coughed out a laugh. "Tell me, Special Agent Hunter. Do you always shoot people in nothing but a lace bra?"

"Would you shut up?" Tori replied but with a little smile. "Just lie there, would you?"

Kyle Mannion was already on his cell phone, calling for an ambulance. "Warner place, off of East Gull Road," he relayed. "We have a sheriff's detective shot out here! Get moving now!"

"We got him, Tori," Braddock said, laboring to breathe. "We got him…" His eyes closed.

"No! *No, no, no*," Tori wailed, reaching for his neck, checking for a pulse. "Come on. Come on! Will! Will!"

Braddock's eyes fluttered open and he grinned. "Hey, Tori, you got plans later?" he asked hoarsely before coughing again.

"Oh, sweet Jesus, would you just stop talking?" Tori admonished, her eyes locked on Braddock's. "Kyle, come on, we gotta apply pressure. Where is that ambulance?"

"It's coming," Kyle replied as he pulled his dress shirt over his head and pressed it to the wound. "It's coming," he said again as a siren became faintly audible in the distance.

CHAPTER THIRTY-FIVE

"It'll define us only if we let it."

It took the paramedics another five minutes to arrive. Then another two minutes for them to traverse their way down to Braddock with their equipment and yet another five to stabilize him and get him loaded on a stretcher. In the meantime, the fire department arrived. The firefighters, along with the paramedics, Tori, Steak, Cal, and Kyle, were able to climb their way back up the scraggly incline of the crevice, lifting the stretcher over downed trees and around debris piles to get him to the ambulance. By the time the ambulance doors closed, Braddock had lost a lot of blood, having suffered two wounds to his lower abdomen in addition to a flesh wound on his upper right arm.

Cal and Steak led the ambulance back to Manchester Bay and the Shepard County Medical Center. Braddock made it to the hospital alive—barely. He was rushed into the emergency room and shortly thereafter into surgery.

Tori, upon her arrival at the hospital, was taken into a treatment room; her face was streaked with dried blood and bulging with swelling from Warner's blows. The doctor got the 10,000-foot summary of the physical beating. He examined her eyes in addition to the cuts and bruises from being struck repeatedly. She also had a CT scan. "Agent Hunter, you are going to have a rough next couple of days."

"What's the damage?"

"Your pupils are quite large and you're slurring your speech a bit. Now, some of that slurring could be due to being punched in the face several times, but those blows to the head have left you with a concussion to go with all these bruises and cuts. That pretty face is going to swell up like a great big pumpkin, but I don't think there is any long-term damage. Ibuprofen, ice, and lots of rest are going to be your friends for the next several days. If you need a stronger painkiller, we can get you one."

After receiving treatment, she joined Kyle, Eddie, Steak, Cal, and Backstrom in the waiting room while Braddock was still in surgery. An hour into the waiting, she pulled Eddie and Kyle into a separate room. Ten seconds in, Tori started tearing up. She apologized to them both, and especially to Eddie. Then she just lost it. The last three weeks and the last twenty years flowed out of her in a guttural cry.

"Just let it go, Tori," Kyle murmured. "Get it all out."

"I'm so sorry, Eddie. Oh my God, I'm so, so sorry. I accused you of all those awful things. God, I…"

"Jeff played all of us, Tori," Kyle said quietly. "You, me, Eddie, everyone. For twenty years, he got us all."

"But he isn't going to get anyone else now," Eddie consoled with a soft voice, sitting down next to her, wrapping an arm around her, and drawing her in. "We have the answers and now we know what happened to Jessie, Katy, Genevieve, so many others."

"My gosh," Tori said after sobbing herself out, wiping away the tears, and getting her breathing back together. "The damage this is going to do to all of you, to the town…"

"We'll just have to put everything back together," Kyle answered, undaunted, already looking ahead to life's next challenge. "It'll define us only if we let it."

*

"If what Warner said to me is true, there are a lot of bodies buried on that property, just outside that little house," Tori explained to Cal and Steak.

"I think we're going to need help," Cal surmised.

"Yeah, a lot of it," Steak agreed.

At 7:50 a.m. the surgeon found them all still congregated in the waiting room.

"He's alive," the doctor reported, taking off his surgical cap and slipping off his glasses to rub his tired eyes. "Detective Braddock was hit twice in his lower left side, in his back, but those bullets found their way into his abdomen. He lost a lot of blood because those bullets got into his intestines, exploded, and rattled around in there, making a bunch of little holes, but I think we plugged them all."

"Is he going to make it, Doc?" Kyle asked.

The doctor nodded. "I'm very encouraged, Kyle. He made it through the surgery. We got him closed and the vitals are holding, so right now I'm not seeing any signs of trouble. But we'll be monitoring him *very* closely, especially the next twenty-four hours. If we get through that without any issues, I think we'll be good."

"Can we see him?" Tori asked.

"From the viewing room. We're going to keep him sedated and in the ICU for now."

"And recovery?" Cal asked.

"In time, I'm optimistic that he'll make a full recovery, but he's got some downtime ahead of him, that's for sure, Sheriff. It was a little hairy when he got here with all that blood loss. It's fortunate, I guess, that there were a couple of you there to apply pressure to those wounds. Otherwise…" The doctor's voice trailed away. "But that's not what happened so let's all think good thoughts and get him through this."

*

Tori made her way back to the hotel. She collapsed fully clothed onto her bed, with two ice packs on her face. She slept hard for five hours, waking a little after 3 p.m. with a pounding headache. Her jaw, chin, and cheeks throbbed. She went to the bathroom and took in the damage. She looked like she'd just gone fifteen rounds with Ronda Rousey. She had two nasty black eyes. Her right cheek was varying shades of yellow, red, and purple, with multiple cuts to her lips and two runs of stiches on her left upper forehead.

She called the hospital. Braddock was stable but remained unconscious. He was now being watched over by Roger and Mary Hayes and his son, Quinn, who'd flown back from Michigan on Kyle Mannion's private jet early in the morning.

Next, she checked in with Cal, who was back at the Warner place in the woods. "If you're up to it, you might want to come out here."

Cal's call was followed up by one from Special Agent in Charge Richard Graff, her boss in New York. After talking about the case for a bit and checking on her physical and emotional wellbeing, Graff stated, "I do need you back here at some point."

"You should see me right now. It's not pretty, sir."

"Bruises and cuts heal. I'm more worried about you… mentally. Do you need to talk to somebody? Whatever you need, I'll see to it."

"I'm fine. I'll be back," Tori answered. "I just have to take care of a few things here before I leave."

An hour later, Steak picked her up outside the hotel. As she climbed up into his truck, he couldn't hide his concern for the cuts and bruises that were visible even though she was wearing large sunglasses. "Hey, we don't need to do this."

"I'm okay."

"You sure?" Steak reached for his friend's hand. "We can do this later."

"No, let's go."

Steak nodded and pulled away, exiting the parking lot and making his way north on the H-4.

Tori asked, "What's going on up there?"

Steak sighed. "I just think... You just need to see it for yourself."

The two old friends drove quietly together back to the Warner place. As they approached the driveway, a sheriff's deputy backed up his patrol Explorer. Steak drove through the mangled iron entrance gate and up the steep hill to the main house and parked among the sea of multicolored police vehicles.

The two of them slowly walked down the narrow driveway to the small house and the clearing, teeming with investigators now led by the Minnesota BCA, although Cal was present along with agents from the FBI. There was a rectangular area with two lines of four gravestones each: the burial ground for the Warner family. To the south of the rectangle was another long and wide rectangular stretch designated by small orange flags stuck in the ground in two parallel rows.

"The flags signify what?" Tori asked.

"Bodies," Steak replied calmly. "Warner didn't lie to you. The BCA has that ground radar going. There are a lot of bodies buried out here in neat rows, as you can see. All very orderly."

*

Later in the evening, the crew exhumed the body buried closest to the shed and cemetery. Twenty-four hours later, the skeletal remains were identified with dental records.

After twenty years, Jessie Hunter had been found.

In a small private ceremony two days later attended by Tori, Cal and his wife Lucy, Steak, Eddie and Kyle Mannion, Mickey, Corinne, Lizzy, and select other high school friends, Jessie Hunter's remains were properly laid to rest next to those of her mother and father.

*

One other thing Warner had told Tori was about the women he'd taken while in college.

Cal placed calls to police in Mesa and Tucson, Arizona. There were three unsolved disappearances of college co-eds in the years Warner was in college in Arizona.

The three disappearances bore many of the signature elements of Warner's abductions.

*

Tori had one more thing to do, and she'd needed to wait two more days until Braddock was fully conscious. She was able to come in early in the morning, when he was alone in his room. He was gaunt and weak, but he was in the clear and would be released from the hospital in a few days.

"Hey," she greeted him softly as she came to the side of the bed. She gently cupped his face for a moment before she sat down in a chair. She reached for his right hand with both of hers.

"You're starting to heal up," he observed.

Tori simply nodded and sighed a big breath.

"You're coming to say goodbye," he said with a raspy voice and a wan smile. "I'm a detective, I know things."

Tori nodded her head while looking down to the floor, unable to meet his eyes. "Duty calls."

"Does the job always come first?"

"For me, it has."

"Maybe that's because you never had a reason to put something in front of it."

Tori finally looked up and met his eyes, giving him a little smile.

"I was kind of hoping I could get you to think about staying," Braddock said, his eyes locked on hers. "You know, try something new."

Tori smiled. "I thought I drove you crazy."

"Oh, without question."

They both laughed lightly.

"But I think I've come to like it a little bit. You have a certain charm."

Tori tried to stay stoic, but her eyes betrayed her and the tears were forming. She'd done a lot of crying lately. "I just… can't."

"Can't or won't?"

She kept her head down but held his hand in hers.

"Why?" He wasn't going to let her off easy.

She respected the fact he wasn't afraid of difficult questions or hard truths. Tori shook her head, looking away. "I don't think I'm wired right. I'm kind of broken, I think."

"Anything that's broken can be fixed."

"But this place, all of the…"

"Pain," Braddock offered, nodding his understanding. "It's too much to overcome, I guess?"

She brushed her hand along the side of his face. "*You* have such a good life here with Quinn. You deserve someone who will be good for *both* of you. Me? Here? I just… I don't think I could do it. I'd screw it up eventually. I don't think I could take that."

"I think you're selling yourself short."

"No, Will," Tori replied as she stood up and kissed Braddock on the forehead and then his lips. "I'm doing the right thing," she said before kissing him one more time. "Goodbye."

Tori turned and left the hospital room. Dabbing away tears, she walked briskly through the hallway and down the stairs and then burst out the front doors of the hospital, only to run into Cal, who was climbing the steps on his way inside.

"Leaving?"

Tori nodded as she tried to look away.

Cal, understanding, hooked his left arm out. "Come on. I'll walk you to your car."

After a moment's hesitation, Tori slipped her arm through his, and the two of them slowly and silently walked out to the parking lot. When they reached her car, Cal asked, "Will I ever get to see you again?"

"I don't know, Cal. This place…"

"Is home," he replied in his best fatherly voice. "You only truly have one place in your life that is home. Warts and all, life and death, Manchester Bay is it for you. Remember that."

CHAPTER THIRTY-SIX

"I need your help."

Two weeks later

"Which room is it?" Tori asked, examining the two-story motor lodge through binoculars.

"The manager says it's number nineteen, so third one in from the left on the second level."

Tori and her team were on the search for Siena Monroe, the fifteen-year-old daughter of New York State Senate Majority Leader Daphne Monroe. Siena had been missing for three days. Tori and her team had been called into the case in Mamaroneck, north of New York City. The local police's initial concern was that Siena had been abducted. Siena told her mother she was going over to a coffee shop to meet up with a friend named Jamie. Daphne asked her daughter about Jamie, as she'd never met or even heard of a friend by that name. Siena said Jamie was a new friend from school. Since her daughter had a limited social life, a new friend to hang out with from school was deemed a promising development, and she inquired no further.

Daphne was running for re-election. Her own district was secure, but she was traveling around New York state campaigning on behalf of other candidates, collecting chits for when she made her move to run for the United States Senate in two years. When she returned home late in the evening, she was alarmed to find that Siena was not home and was not answering her phone. When Daphne attempted to find her phone using the cell phone app, it appeared to be in White Plains, a half-hour away. Siena's phone was later found in the bottom of a garbage can. That's when the alert went out and a call was made to the FBI, and Tori and her team were immediately brought in.

Siena's mother described her daughter to Tori as not having a lot of self-confidence. "She's an extremely self-conscious teenager, gangly and maybe a little awkward."

While the police tracked down Siena's movements from the time she left home, Tori and her team interviewed two girls named Anna and Madi, Siena's two close friends. "The only Jamie I remember is one I saw on ChitChat—a chat room," Anna said.

"Yeah, I think I chatted with…" Madi paused for a second. "You know, I guess I'm not sure if Jamie was a girl or a guy. I kind of thought maybe a guy."

"Definitely a guy," Anna stated. "Jamie asked for a picture. *Definitely* a guy."

"Did you send a photo?"

"No. I never respond to those requests, at least not from people I don't know."

"How about you?" Tori asked Madi.

"No, it never got that far with me."

"What about Siena?"

"I know she was on the chat thread. Whether they went one-on-one and discussed that, I don't know," Anna stated.

Tori and her team dug into Siena's computer and cell phone records. Focusing in on her ChitChat activity, and finding the discussion threads with Jamie, Tori agreed with Anna. Jamie was a man. As Tori dug into Siena's discussions over the past few weeks, she started to discern a pattern.

"Do you see it?" Tori asked Geno Harlow.

"Oh yeah, he's totally grooming her."

They both sat down with Daphne Monroe.

"This Jamie was bunny hunting her," Tori explained, showing what they'd found to Daphne Monroe.

"What's bunny hunting?"

"It's the process whereby an online predator, which is what we think this Jamie is, picks a potential victim and then grooms them. Your daughter is online a great deal, correct?"

"I think so," Daphne replied sheepishly. "She's in her room alone a lot. I assume she's on her computer. What you're telling me is that she was talking online to this Jamie."

"Yes. What happens is the predator goes through social media posts and public chat rooms and so forth to learn about a potential target. Your daughter profiles as being somewhat lonely or certainly wishes she had more of a social life."

Daphne nodded. "That's probably accurate."

Harlow opened his laptop and turned it around so Daphne could see it.

"Once the predator selects their target, they start grooming, first by reaching out to the target's other friends and contacts. See here, Jamie starts by conversing with Anna and Madi, and then Siena gets in on it a little bit later."

Tori maneuvered the mouse. "See this chat thread here, the conversations with Jamie start with Anna, then Madi and Siena join in. Four days later, Anna and Madi start dropping off from the conversation chain, and it's just Jamie and Siena, so then they move into a private chat room. Then I see it right here." Tori pointed to the screen. "On this brief conversation chain, there is a conversation that moves to text, as Siena sends Jamie her number, but you'll notice he says, 'I'll text you.' He didn't type his number in the chat room."

Tori reached for her own laptop, flipped it open, and clicked a file that had copies of Siena's texts. "On your daughter's phone, her text history shows a series of messages with someone named J, who we think is this Jamie. The number your daughter is texting to? It's a burner phone with texting capability. Then what happens yesterday morning? They talk on the phone for a few minutes and then that's it. She leaves the house and I think she goes to meet Jamie and now it's all quiet."

"Can you trace his phone?" Daphne asked, now frantic.

"We're working on it," Tori answered.

Unsaid to Daphne Monroe was that the pattern reminded them of two other missing girls in the last year. In both instances, the girls had not been found.

Jamie had dumped the burner phone, but he'd made the mistake of leaving it turned on, which allowed them to trace it to a different area of White Plains. With the actual phone, they were able to backtrack to its purchase from a convenience store in Hamilton, New York. The sale was made on June 14, at 9:47 a.m. At the store, two FBI agents were able to access the surveillance history of the camera covering the cash register. A man in his mid-twenties had purchased the phone with cash. Using the two exterior surveillance cameras for the convenience store, the agents were able to track the man to a white 2007 Nissan Pathfinder with the spare tire in a rack on the back. The spare tire was covered in a tarp that looked like a target, and they were able to get the plate. The vehicle was registered to James Ernley of Erie, Pennsylvania.

With a bulletin out for the Pathfinder, it took twenty-four hours for the call to come in from the police in Sarasota Springs, New York. A convenience store clerk had seen the Pathfinder, remembering the target cover on the spare tire. "Agent Hunter, there was nobody else in the truck, but the clerk says the man bought multiple sandwiches and sodas. He could be holed up somewhere around here."

Following the call, Tori and her team made a beeline up to Sarasota Springs, a town a half-hour north of Albany and three hours north of Mamaroneck. As they pulled into town, the Pathfinder was spotted in a local motel parking lot. The FBI, Sarasota Springs police, and county sheriff's department moved into position.

Tori raised the radio to her mouth. "Sheriff, are you ready to move in?"

"I've got three units ready," the radio burped. "Just say the word."

"Go," Tori ordered.

The sheriff and two more units pulled into the parking lot, followed by Tori and her team in two black Suburbans. Two deputies ran up the steps to the second floor, two steps at a time. A third followed with a battering ram. The officer swung the ram back and then through, blasting the door open. The deputies poured inside. Delaying two seconds, Tori and two of her agents came into the room with weapons drawn. The deputies already had Ernley on the floor, securing him. A deputy caught Tori's eyes and nodded toward the bathroom.

Tori stepped over Ernley and gently opened the door for the bathroom. Holstering her gun, she walked inside to find a very scared Siena Monroe cowering in the bathtub, her hands and feet bound, with a handkerchief gag stuffed in her mouth and tied around her head.

"It's okay. It's okay," Tori said as she knelt and loosened the gag, letting it fall around the girl's neck. "Are you Siena Monroe?"

The girl nodded.

"I'm an FBI agent, you're safe now," Tori said, holding up her identification for Siena to see. "Let's get you home."

The return home of Siena Monroe was big news in New York. James Ernley immediately became the primary suspect in two other disappearances. That investigation was being led by the New

York Bureau of Criminal Investigation. Perhaps Ernley's capture would lead to closure for two more families.

Back in her office, Tori fielded a congratulatory phone call from the governor of New York. At home that night, she received calls from the two United States senators for New York as well as the Director of the FBI.

It was the biggest case of her career. She should have been celebrating with the open bottle of fine Chardonnay that sat on the weathered trunk in front of her. Yet, she could barely convince herself to even lean forward to reach for the half-full glass next to it.

She gazed around her condo, a unit she'd lived in for five years and a place she'd not bothered to make look like a home. Long-neglected, unpacked, but deteriorating cardboard boxes were still lying about. For years she'd had Jessie's disappearance as an excuse in moments like this. She would tell herself the reason she wasn't married, didn't have a relationship, a family, or even a semblance of an active social life was because of the job. It was her job to make sure nobody experienced what she had when she was seventeen years old, and that always seemed to be enough to get her through until the next new case came along.

She didn't have that anymore.

Jessie's case was solved. She knew what had happened. All the questions had been answered. She had closure.

Now, all she had was work.

Tori pushed herself up from the couch, picked up her wine glass, and took a long sip as she walked to the kitchen. On the counter she found her phone plugged in and charging. She picked it up and swiped left on the screen to the photo icon, which she tapped. With her left thumb she clicked on the small picture to open it up. It was a familiar picture, the one of her and Braddock at the supper club in Crosslake with his arm around her and the two of them smiling like a happy couple.

Tori shook her head. Her friends all had numerous photos on their phones that they would show her of their husbands, boyfriends, girlfriends, and kids at parties or on vacation. Tori had no such photos, other than the one of her and Braddock. If she bothered to open the boxes in the condo, she wouldn't find any other photos like that. The one with Braddock was the only one she had, and she found herself frequently cherishing it.

She closed the photo app and then pressed the green phone icon. She scrolled quickly into the Bs for Braddock's name and let her thumb hover over his number, so tempted to tap it and call him to just hear his voice. She'd conducted this exercise more than once in the two weeks since she'd returned to New York. She'd look at the photo, click to the phone number, and then stop, telling herself it could never possibly work. Living in Manchester Bay would be impossible. How could she live there with all that had happened? How could she ignore all that?

Sure, she was thinking about him a lot, but what if things didn't work out? What did they really know about each other? And Braddock had a son—how would that work? She found missing kids for a living and understood children and teen behavior in the context of her job, but what did she know about relating on a day-to-day basis with kids? She'd never done it. No nieces, no nephews. Heck, she'd never even babysat in her life.

And what happened between them… what made that so special? Was it Braddock? Or was it the idea of someone like him? They were working under intense circumstances and ended up in bed with each other. It helped them both get through a difficult time, but they couldn't make anything out of that which would last.

Or could they?

Or the question really was: could she? That was the question she kept coming back to. Could she do it?

"Not if you're such a basket case, Tori," she muttered out loud, taking another drink of wine, shaking her head as she thought about something else Braddock had said to her once: "Come on, Tori, live a little."

She looked around her undecorated, empty, lifeless, and emotionless condo. She thought about the fact that on the night that was the pinnacle of her career with the FBI, she was alone with nothing but an expensive bottle of Chardonnay and a cell phone photo she wistfully kept coming back to.

There was nothing else.

Tori closed her eyes, exhaled, and out loud told herself a hard truth. "This isn't enough anymore." But if she wanted more, she had to make some changes. It was time to test something else Braddock had said: "Anything that's broken can be fixed."

Tori looked back down to her phone and tapped into the directory. She scrolled to the Rs and found the number she was looking for. Chelsea, now Dr. Chelsea Reid, psychologist, her college roommate. She clicked on her number and Chelsea picked up on the third ring.

"I need your help."

CHAPTER THIRTY-SEVEN

"To live."

October 18

Manchester Bay, Minnesota

It was a gorgeous Minnesota Indian summer day for mid-October. The temperature was a balmy sixty-eight degrees with the fall colors in full bloom. Tori smiled as she pulled up to Braddock's house to find a new and shiny, black dual cab Chevy Silverado parked in the newly paved driveway. The repainted back of the house no longer showed any remnants of the burn marks. All evidence of the explosion was gone. She parked her own Audi Q5 behind the new truck.

As she got out of the car, Quinn came bounding out the back door of the house and stopped. He'd seemingly grown another two or three inches since she'd seen him back in the summer. He was going to be tall and angular, just like his father. She slid her sunglasses up on top of her head and smiled. "Hi, Quinn. Do you remember me?"

"You're Tori, right? Tori Hunter."

"That's right," she replied, walking over to him. "How are you?"

"I'm good." Quinn's face was painted in navy- and sky-blue stripes, the Manchester Bay Lakers colors. He also had a navy-blue football jersey on over a sky-blue hoodie.

"Nice face paint. Where are you off to all done up like that?"

"I'm going over to my cousins'. We're going to the football game tonight. It's the big game."

"Ah, would that still be Alexandria? The mighty Cardinals?"

"That's right. How do you know that?"

"Hey, I'm a proud Laker grad. I went to that game every year when I was growing up," Tori replied. "Is Alex good this year?"

"Yeah, but the Lakers are unbeaten so we're going to roll. The crowd is going to be massive. We're going to get there early and tailgate in the parking lot."

"That sounds fun," Tori answered with a smile and then looked to the cabin. "Is your dad around?"

"Yeah, but he's out on the boat. He said he wanted to take a trip around the lake before he and Steak take it out for storage tomorrow. You can wait for him inside if you want."

"Thanks, I think I will. You have fun tonight."

"Thanks, I will."

She watched as Quinn jumped excitedly onto his bike and pedaled speedily down the road without a care in the world.

Tori stepped inside the house and walked through the kitchen to the front, peering out the large picture window to the crystal waters of the lake. *On a day like today, why wouldn't you take the boat out?*

She looked back to the kitchen and saw a beer bottle cap and opener sitting on the island. *That's a fine idea*, she thought as she opened the refrigerator and grabbed a beer of her own. She stepped out the sliding glass door, slid on her sunglasses, and leisurely made her way down to the end of the dock.

Tori sat down and relaxed on the bench, sipping from her beer, bathing in the warmth of the sun as light waves lapped gently by the dock and into the shore. The view couldn't have been more picturesque. The brilliant orange, red, yellow, brown, and rust hues of the fall leaves were transposed against the cloudless, light blue sky and the cool dark blue water of the lake. The air was fresh and crisp. The tranquility was interrupted only by the occasional rumbling of a distant boat or the melodic call of a loon. As she raised her beer to her lips, she thought that, yes, she could get used to this again.

Tori glanced left when the red Malibu speedboat came around the point to the northeast.

*

Braddock, resting comfortably in the driver's seat, gently turned his speedboat. His left hand was casually draped over the steering wheel while his right held a bottle of cold beer—his first one since he'd been shot. His doctor probably wouldn't yet approve, but the day was just too damn nice not to have a real beverage or two before heading to the football game.

Following the contours of the shoreline, he turned gradually to the east, enjoying one last ride around the lake for the season. He came around the point to turn into Murphy Bay and that's when he saw her, sitting on the bench at the end of the dock.

*

Tori sat casually on the bench and watched as he slowed, pulled back on the throttle, and approached the lift. She smiled, happy that she was finally able to see him.

She'd been planning her return for over a month, having sold her condo in New York and arranging to rent a small house in Manchester Bay. On a weekly basis, she'd checked in with Cal about how Braddock was progressing, and reminding Cal, "Make sure he doesn't find another girl before I get back there."

"I'll see to it that he doesn't," Cal responded. "But Victoria, don't wait too much longer. There are plenty of single ladies around here just dying to help him get back on his feet."

Braddock looked really good, she thought, albeit a little thinner. He was rocking a ruggedly handsome look with his unbuttoned red flannel shirt and black T-shirt, his windswept flowing black hair, and his eyes hidden behind a classic pair of Ray-Bans. He gazed upon her as he slowly pulled straight ahead and into the boatlift, taking a last sip of his beer, a little smirky smile creasing his face.

He was happy to see her, she could tell.

He killed the motor, and once the boat had stopped, he used the remote for the lift to elevate the boat out of the water.

Tori stood up. She was casually dressed in a white North Face down vest, a white, tight-fitting, long-sleeve T-shirt, faded blue jeans, and gray, suede, knee-high boots. Her hair was longer and a slightly lighter shade of auburn now, and flowing well off her shoulders.

Braddock stepped from the boat onto the dock and took off his sunglasses but didn't say anything.

The first move was hers to make.

Tori slipped off her own sunglasses and looked out to the lake, closing her eyes and taking in a deep breath of the fresh air. "I'd forgotten just how beautiful it can be on the lake at this time of year." She turned back to him, opening her eyes. "I guess I'd forgotten a lot of things about this place."

"You look good, Tori," Braddock said, and after a moment he observed, "You look different, though."

"I know. The clothes, the hair, I've kind of given myself a makeover and—"

"That's not what I mean," he cut in with a light shake of his head. "Although you look… absolutely gorgeous."

She smiled.

"But more than that, you just seem so relaxed. The way you're smiling and standing, you look so… at ease."

"I am. I feel really good," Tori answered, nodding, smiling. "I quit my job."

Braddock was surprised. "Really? Why?"

"A lot of reasons, I suppose. I'd done all I could do. I'd sacrificed enough. I decided that I just didn't want that life anymore. I took the advice of a *very* wise man and decided I needed to live a little."

Braddock smiled at that. "Is that what has you looking so happy?"

"*That* and some long hours of work with a very good doctor friend of mine."

"It takes courage to do that."

She nodded. "It was long overdue. We spent a lot of time talking about everything. My sister, my father, my mother, the investigation, Katy, being in that room with Warner, and finding Jessie. We talked about all of that, got it all out there and dealt with it. And—" she shook her head "—it was… freeing. It's like I'm not carrying it all anymore, you know?"

"I think I can understand that."

She exhaled and looked him in the eye. "It also made me realize how much of life I'd been missing out on. So much so that I decided I wanted to come back here."

"To visit?"

Tori shook her head. "To live."

"To live?"

"Yeah. I rented myself a little house right in town. I'm going to look after Gail Anderson. I'll eventually take a job, but mostly, I want to continue to get better and make up for lost time. And then, of course, there was this guy I met back here."

"I see."

"So, I came out here to tell you that I'm going to be around from now on. In fact, I know this is very last-minute and all, but I was kind of wondering what you were doing tonight. I hear there's a big football game."

"There is," he replied with a grin. "And you know, funny that you mention it… I was going solo, to the tailgate even, where a bunch of your old friends might be. So, you know, if you were maybe interested in going…"

"I am," Tori replied eagerly, stepping to him and reaching for his hand, interlocking her fingers with his. She took a deep breath. "I walked away three months ago, and I hope you can understand why I did. Back then I wouldn't have been good for you or Quinn. I wasn't ready."

"No, I understand."

"Yeah?"

"You needed to heal, Tori. I knew that and I hoped you would."

Tori looked up to him, gazing into his deep blue eyes, smiling. "I'm ready now."

Braddock smiled, nodded, and stepped toward Tori, wrapping her in his arms, leaning down to kiss her. "I'm ready, too."

Tori wrapped her arms around his neck and gave him a beaming and relaxed smile. She was home.

A LETTER FROM ROGER

Thank you so much for reading *Silenced Girls*. The support and positive response from readers for this book has been overwhelming and very humbling. If you want to keep up to date with all my latest releases, just sign up at the following link. Your email address will never be shared and you can unsubscribe at any time.

www.bookouture.com/roger-stelljes

Starting a new series with all new characters is always an adventure. My goal in every book I write is to have the readers be so engrossed in the story, so drawn in, that they cannot put the book down. They must read one more chapter, then another, and then another such that they keep reading late into the night to see what happens next. I love that experience as a reader, and I want my audience's experience to be the same.

I hope you loved *Silenced Girls*, and if you did, I would be grateful if you could write a review. I'd love to hear what you think, and it makes such a difference helping new readers to discover one of my books for the first time.

I enjoy hearing from my readers—you can get in touch on my Facebook page, through Twitter, Goodreads, or my website.

Thank you for reading.

All the best,
Roger Stelljes

 @rogerstelljesbooks
 @RogerStelljes
 www.RogerStelljes.com

ACKNOWLEDGMENTS

I wish to extend a heartfelt thanks to Ellen Gleeson and the team at Bookouture for all their work on *Silenced Girls*. And as always, my thanks to my family for supporting me every step of the way on this journey.

Made in the USA
Las Vegas, NV
29 July 2024